ASSASSIN

OF

CURSES

Book 3

Jessie D. Eaker

Jessie D. Eaker
jessieeaker.com

Cover art by Daniel Eaker
Book Layout © 2017 BookDesignTemplates.com

Assassin of Curses/ Jessie D. Eaker — First edition
ISBN 978-1-7341293-4-2

To Becki and Daniel...
For keeping me sane.

Contents

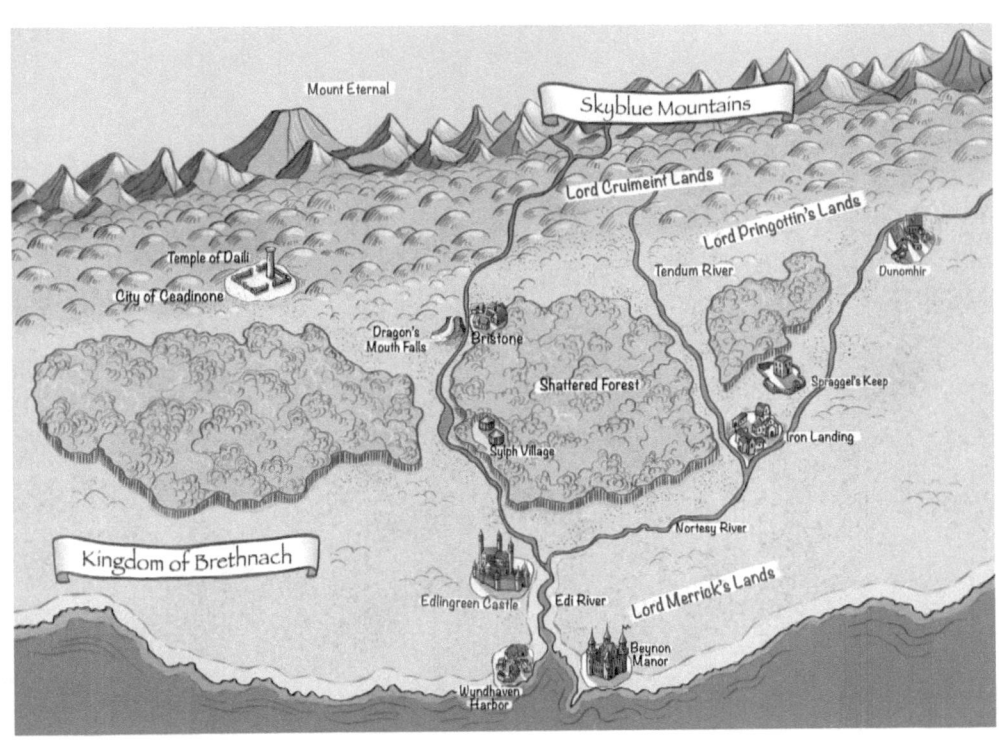

CHAPTER ONE

An Unexpected Guest

Edlingreen Castle was quite the change from my old home. Looking up from my journal to stare at the rafters over my head, I couldn't help but marvel at the wood's beautiful stain and highly polished finish. Not to mention being entirely devoid of cobwebs and dust. The brightly lit room smelled pleasantly of spice, and the gently glowing fire provided ample warmth against the frigid morning.

I looked down at the paper in front of me. Despite the improvement in my surroundings, it was unfortunately blank.

The nearby window was open, yet through some trick of myst, only allowed in the light and none of the cold outside air. Very different from what I was used to, where the spiders living in the rafters would frequently drop down and offer to correct my spelling.

Could that be the reason the words were coming so slowly this morning? Could it be I missed the dust, the cobwebs, and even the old musty smell of my previous home, Revenhill Keep?

I brushed the end of the quill against my lips. My spelling had indeed been a little off lately.

I sighed. *No.* It was just that I was distracted. Too many thoughts— too much had happened in too short a time. I shook my head. A world-renowned knight and explorer had to be better than this. Knights were focused. Their arms were as strong as trees—their minds as sharp as their blades. And of course, their thoughts were so highly organized, and their observations so revealing any reader would gasp in awe.

I looked back down at the blank page. Well, maybe crafting a complete tomb of all my wisdom was a bit too optimistic. At this point, I would settle for getting my thoughts down accurately without too much embellishment.

The minstrels certainly didn't mind stretching the truth. While I had established contact with the mysterious keepers, uncovered the Mirror of Bygone Tears, and saved the princess from an evil myst user—not to mention helped restore her to the throne—it wasn't like it was this huge thing. I had only done what needed to be done—and of course, I had lots of help from some very good friends. But to hear the minstrels tell it, I, Coren Hart, had saved the world or something. I shuddered. A new ballad, 'The Cursed Knight,' was gaining popularity, and I was tempted to have the princess execute whoever had written it.

Unfortunately, the historians weren't any better. They had already proclaimed me one of the great explorers of this generation and were busily scribbling their scholarly essays arguing over my motivation for this or that. *Why had I not forced Wynn's hand earlier? Why did I allow the princess to be captured? Why did I wait until the last moment to save her life?* I sighed. Believe me, if I'd been half the hero they made me out to be, I wouldn't have done it that way either!

If I had any hope of having an accurate account, I was left with no other option but to write it myself. Which was why my notes were scattered over the table around me. I looked them over, the undisputed king of my jumbled mess. I had to somehow bring all of it into a coherent whole. I shook my head. But all that was for another time.

Today, I was trying to come up with some tiny pearl of wisdom to include in my journal. Or at least a few striking observations that would help the kingdom—and prove to someone very important to me—that I was a little bit useful.

A slumbering sigh made me glance over to the room's other occupant, Princess Zophia Olwenna Xernow. While actually the kingdom's queen, she had decided against giving up her princess title until her coronation, which was still a couple months away—if even then.

She rested, fast asleep, slumped over her desk—her head cradled on her left arm—while her right hand still loosely held her writing quill. She had finally succumbed to exhaustion, something I had been predicting for the last few hours. She had worked late into the night writing letters to the kings and queens of the surrounding kingdoms, warning of the Dark Avenyts invasion and asking for their help. Unfortunately, this was the second round of letters. None of them believed her. The Dark Avenyts were the stuff of stories told to frighten children, not something to be taken seriously. They had been banished from the world a thousand years ago. So none of them offered her help. And worse yet, all refused to send supplies.

I wanted to help her so badly. But I was beginning to think only the Creator himself could help her now. Her kingdom was in trouble.

The deep kind.

It was not her fault. Her brother Wynn had murdered their father, blamed it on her, put a curse on her, and then took the kingdom for himself. The irony of it was that it hadn't actually been Wynn, but one of the Dark Avenyts controlling him. Or at least that was our current theory. Unfortunately, Wynn escaped our last battle and was still at large. I was confident we had not seen the last of him.

Wynn wasn't the only casualty of the Dark Avenyts possessions. Zofie's cousin Risten Brightmare, who had been her closest friend, had been captured and turned into one of their puppets. Like Wynn, Risten had also gone missing.

Our intelligence indicated Wynn had dispatched Risten to parts unknown right before we managed to retake the throne. It was apparently some sort of special mission. But whatever it was, we were sure the Dark Avenyts inside Risten would use her deadly sword-master skills to succeed.

That is where I come in. I am this generation's Thief of Curses. Using my Abhulengulus curse, I not only helped Zofie regain her throne, but I was also able to take control of, or steal, the curse Wynn had placed on her. While she still bore it, I was at least able to mitigate the worst of its effects.

Abhulengulus, or Abe as I generally called him, was quite the unique curse. He possessed his own intelligence. A most disagreeable one, I might add. And not only could he steal other curses, he could also influence my luck. Which usually turned out bad.

I couldn't help but glance at the curse anchor on my left wrist—a most unusual placement I had been told. Most people bearing a curse would also have a symbol high on their chest where the curse attached to their body. It generally resembled a round coin-sized tattoo. But mine, being such a unique curse, was located on my wrist and oddly shaped. It took the form of an almost flowing triangle with a single eye in its center. And when the eye opened, Abe would talk to me in my head, so only I could hear him. He would even answer my questions.

If he felt like it.

Zofie groaned in her sleep and frowned. Having an unpleasant dream, no doubt. Not that I was surprised. There hadn't been a lot lately to have a good dream about. Except perhaps our engagement. But any wedding was going to have to wait until after the kingdom had enough food to make it acceptable to have the celebration.

The possessed Wynn had set out to destroy the kingdom so that it posed no threat to the Dark Avenyts's advance. He did a pretty good job of it too. The royal granaries were empty, and all the coin in the treasury had been spent. Not to mention, about half of the kingdom's precious myst users had been spirited away to parts unknown—or killed outright.

As I looked at Zofie's sleeping face, I couldn't help but smile at the line of drool escaping her lips. She seemed so innocent in slumber, but inside that head of hers was a sharp intellect finely tuned to the art of statecraft. She was a born leader. I had assumed she had gotten it from her father, but as we had recently discovered, her mother had also been the leader of a secretive people called the Keepers. And much to Zofie's surprise, she had also inherited the role of their Guardian.

Unfortunately, they had tried to force Zofie to forsake her kingdom and immediately assume the role. But with the help of my curse and a rather large crab, we managed to make them understand Zofie's fate lay in a different direction. They had ultimately agreed to wait until Zofie had dealt with her kingdom first.

I sighed and brought myself back to the present. Looking down at my paper, I stroked my lips in contemplation. *What to write?* What wondrous observation could I make? What pearl of wisdom would be useful to Zofie and the kingdom? I had to move this along. I was under a bit of a deadline.

It was almost time for lunch, and I, for one, had resolved not to miss this meal. Well, actually, I tried not to miss any meal. But for this one, Zofie had invited me to a picnic. When I asked where, she told me I would be surprised, but otherwise, kept her plans secret. It was cold outside today, as one would expect in mid-winter, so I couldn't help but wonder where it would be. I was sure the meal would be nothing special. Zofie had decreed that with the food shortage, we would eat as the people did. But even with all those challenges, I was looking forward to it. We had been so busy lately, a chance for a little recreation would be most welcome.

I looked back down at my paper. I was almost out of time. As they say, it was now or never. I looked up into the rafters one last moment as I constructed the exact wording in my head. Then I carefully dipped my quill in my ink bottle and boldly wrote: "We won't give up."

I nodded in satisfaction. Simple and straight forward, yet from the heart. It was surely my best work.

A knock sounded on the thick door. I started at the unexpected sound and placed a hand over my pounding heart. Zofie jerked upright and looked around in momentary panic. Her eyes locked on mine, and she visibly relaxed. While we both had been expecting the interruption, we were on edge. Things were just too quiet.

True, winter made news travel slowly. But based on past history, Wynn would not be sitting idle. He was likely plotting his next move to dismantle our defenses. This suspicion was supported by our reports from Mount Eternal. There was quite a bit of activity, but none of them left the mountain. They instead stayed close to their otherworldly portal. Indeed, they seemed to be waiting for something. We could only pray they waited long enough for us to get our defenses together.

Zofie rubbed her eyes. "Enter," she called.

The door slowly opened, and a young woman stepped inside, clutching a giant ledger to her chest. I almost laughed every time I saw this. Fumiko was barely larger than the ledger itself.

Fumiko was Zofie's personal secretary. She was of slender build and had black hair just long enough to frame her delicate face. But it was her ethnicity that intrigued people, evident from her eyes and the shape of her face—she came from lands far to the east.

As usual, she wore a simple beige dress with a modest neckline and cut from rough-spun cloth. An earth-colored shawl was draped across her shoulders, likely due to the morning chill. To my utter surprise, she wore plain brown stockings on her feet. She usually went barefoot.

Her manner of dress had earned quite a few whispers from those attending court. Zofie had offered her better clothes, but Fumiko had declined, simply saying she was not worthy and preferred it this way.

Despite her plain clothes and unkempt hair, I could tell she had the potential to be quite the beauty if she so desired. She carried herself with such grace and poise, one would easily think her a dancer. But I knew different.

While traveling to find the Mirror of Bygone Tears, I had been captured by bandits, and Fumiko had single-handedly defeated three armed men. Immediately after, she had sworn me to secrecy, asking I never reveal what she had done. True, she had been under the influence of the curse possessing her at that time. But still—what had been the curse and what had been Fumiko? Even if it was something in the middle, the mysterious lady from the east had at one time received some serious training in personal combat. It was also something she absolutely refused to speak about.

She had also betrayed us.

Or at least, the Dark Avenits possessing her had, using her to steal the mirror. I broke that curse using a charm from the nymph, Lady Autumn, and set her free. It was a debt the young woman took very seriously, and one she fully intended to repay with a life of service.

Fumiko cleared her throat and bowed. "Pardon the intrusion, your highness," she said, her unusually accented voice calm and controlled. Unless you knew her, you might even think it cold.

She continued. "It is time for your picnic. The cook has everything you requested prepared. And watch out, Spraggel...."

But before she could complete the warning, the man himself came barreling through the door behind her. "I know what they're after!" His eyes were bright with excitement, and he wore a smug smile. He moved to the room's center, and in his exuberance, began to bounce up and down on the balls of his feet. Hardly the display of respect one might expect from someone barging in on their ruler.

Spraggel was my elderly master. Or perhaps *had been* was more accurate, although I still considered him such. He was a scribe and a scholar of history, as well as Zofie's senior advisor. He wore his usual gray robe, which was adorned with blotches of ink, and I couldn't be sure, but maybe even some of last night's meal. Although entirely bald, his white beard was starting to get long again. But not nearly as long as it had been before he shaved it off to pretend to be a priest of Dali.

I sighed. "Spraggel, what in the Creator's name are you talking about?"

He smiled brightly. "The Dark Avenyts, of course!"

I shook my head. "But we already know that. They want hosts for their curses."

He paused his bouncing and looked up at me in irritation. "Not that. No, I was talking about why they've been so quiet lately."

We all stayed silent as Spraggel smiled and rocked back and forth on his heels. He was waiting for us to ask the question. *Why have they been so quiet?* All of us had been debating that topic all week—with no answers. None of us wanted to sit through yet another lecture.

His smile began to fade, realizing we were not going to fall for his trap. *"Well,"* he said, disappointed. "It *is* more a guess than anything right now. I need more information to turn it into a working hypothesis." He stepped up to Fumiko and patted her on the shoulder. "Which is why I need to borrow your assistant for a bit. I think the answer lies in the research of Fumiko's old master, Hennion Tormaigh. She knows his work better than anyone. And if I'm right, you'll definitely be interested."

Fumiko hefted her ledger. "I can't. I need to work on the accounts. Zofie needs an accurate count of what the kingdom has and how it's being used."

Zofie put her hands on her hips. "I really do need those completed."

I brightened. "I could do the accounts."

Fumiko grimaced. "Your highness, with all due respect, please don't let Sir Coren near the ledgers. It took me weeks to straighten them out from the last time."

I sprang to my defense. "I didn't do that bad. It was a busy week."

All three of them regarded me in silence.

Zofie took pity and came to my defense. "Dearest," she smiled sweetly. "You were valent to try, but numbers are just not what you're best at."

Fumiko took in a deep breath. "Instead, I could possibly work with Master Spraggel for two hours today. That should not throw me too far behind."

Zofie nodded. "That sounds like a reasonable compromise, but..." She grinned. "After lunch."

Fumiko bowed deeply. "As you command."

Zofie rolled her eyes. "Will you stop with the formality? You're driving me crazy."

Before she could catch herself, Fumiko gave a shallow bow to Zofie and blushed. The Fumiko that was with us right now was not the possessed Fumiko we had come to know at first. The real Fumiko was more formal in her mannerisms and a little more conservative. Zofie thought that part of her timidness was due to the side effects of her possession. Fumiko frequently had nightmares of the curse once again controlling her.

Zofie looked up at Spraggel. "Won't you join us too?"

Spraggel shook his head. "Thank you for the invitation, Princess, but not this afternoon. I've already been sampling the fare in the kitchen." He smiled. "I think Madam Hindenlye likes me." He winked.

I sighed. My master surprised me yet again. Madam Hindenlye vigorously defended the kitchen's food, throwing out any 'poachers' as she called them. Rumors were, she slept in the storeroom. The fact she was allowing Spraggel to sample, spoke volumes.

He continued. "Instead, I'll go await Mistress Fumiko to join after her meal."

Fumiko frowned but said nothing. Although she frequently used them for others, she hated titles applied to herself. Despised, might be a better description. Again something from Fumiko's mysterious past. I sometimes wondered if her fighting skills were not her only secret.

Having accomplished his mission, Spraggel left in a flutter of his long gray robe. Fumiko bowed and said she would catch up to us after returning the ledger to the library. She glanced in my direction, and for just a moment, the corner of her mouth curled up. Then she was out the door. Obviously, Fumiko knew where we were going. *Why were they keeping it from me?*

Arm and arm, Zofie and I strolled out into the corridor.

"Pray tell," I asked. "Exactly where are we headed?"

Zofie smiled mischievously. "To the kitchens."

We started down the stairs. "And then?"

"You'll see."

"So, it's a surprise?"

Zofie chuckled. "Yes, I think you will find it very surprising."

"You're not even going to give me a hint."

She gave me one of her sly smiles. "Nope."

I sighed dramatically. *"And so the doomed knight marched on..."* I quoted. It was from *Betrayal of a Robin* by The Poet. It was a long and boring epic that Zofie liked. She said it was romantic.

She supplied the rest of the quote, *"...Confident his ruler wouldn't betray his trust."* ·

It always amazed me when she did that. She was the only person I'd ever encountered that could complete my quotes.

She frowned. "That's a little weak, Coren. I think I prefer this one instead." She thought for a moment. *"'Twas for love he followed her..."* She glanced at me mischievously.

I puzzled over the quote. "I don't believe I know that one."

She smiled and patted my arm. "That's because I just made it up."

I rolled my eyes as she chuckled softly.

We reached the end of the stairs and proceeded down another hall.

I suddenly sensed that she was troubled.

"Coren," she said. "Are you sure you want to marry me?"

I stopped, facing her. "I think that should be obvious. I'm the one that asked you after all."

Her face held worry. "Sometimes, things change. Do you think you'll be able to stand by me when they do?"

I leaned forward and gave her a brief kiss. "Yes, I considered my decision very carefully before asking. But since you had already stolen my heart, it was a foregone conclusion."

She seemed to relax a little, and I started us moving again. "What brought that on?"

She leaned her head on my shoulder. "Nothing."

I couldn't help but smile. It's funny how a single word could speak so much. I knew she was really saying, '*I have plenty to tell you, but I'm not ready yet.*'

Well, I could be patient.

We shortly arrived at the kitchens where Madam Hindenlye was busy preparing lunch for the others in the castle. It was a simple meal of some kind of soup, but Hindenlye was fussing with it as if it were the most exquisite meal she'd ever prepared.

When she looked up and saw us, she broke out into a huge grin, wiped off her hands, and pulled a surprised Zofie into a tight hug. Hindenlye stepped back, holding her at arm's length. "You've grown up so much." Then she sighed and turned to a nearby counter. She picked up the single basket, with a linen cloth carefully tucked across the top, and gave it to Zofie.

"It's not exactly the same as usual. With everything so short, I had to make some substitutions. I hope you will find them suitable."

Zofie nodded. "I'm sure it will be fine."

Hindenlye smiled regarding her for a moment longer before abruptly turning and going back to her soup. "I had best get this to the table before the poachers start appearing in my kitchen. Then I'd have to kill them, and you'd be angry with me."

Zofie hung the basket from her arm and turned to leave. "Thank you," she said, looping her other arm through mine.

"Oh," Hindenlye called from behind her. "Please give them my regards."

Zofie smiled and nodded. "I will."

I gave Zofie a puzzled look. Were we meeting someone? And Hindenlye knew where? The mystery kept growing.

Zofie led me deeper into the castle, descending to the ground floor. When we kept going down two more flights of stairs, I finally got an inkling of where we were headed.

"We're going to your family crypt, aren't we?" I asked, a little apprehensively. I wasn't afraid of those laid to their final rest, but still, they demanded a certain—reverence. Not somewhere I would expect to have a picnic.

"Yes, we are," she answered, offering nothing more.

We walked on in silence until we came to the crypt entrance, guarded by a single heavy door. It had ornate symbols around the edges, some I recognized and some I didn't. But the one in the center, larger than the others, was easy to make out. It was the crest of the Xernow family. The Griffin.

Zofie laid a hand on the door. "Gatekeeper," she said. "It is time. Will you open for me?"

I noticed movement on the floor, and looking down, I saw the dust move and churn, settling into words.

PASSAGE GRANTED, XERNOW HEIR, they spelled out.

Zofie stepped back, and I reached for a myst lantern hanging on the wall nearby. I couldn't help but wonder if it was the same Gatekeeper that had protected the secret entrance to the castle. Zofie had spoken to it and persuaded it to let us enter. That time, it had used vines to communicate its message. And when Zofie had gone ahead, it had grabbed my arm and given me a private message that I hadn't understood. Something about the first Thief of Curses being a traitor and me having to make a choice. But as to exactly what choice, that was a little vague. I couldn't see myself ever going against Zofie, so I was little worried about it.

As I lit the light and turned back, the words on the floor had once again changed. *GIVE THEM MY GREETINGS.*

I frowned. Even the blasted door knew what Zofie was up to.

With a puff of air that scattered the letters on the floor, the massive door slowly opened. Zofie stepped forward, and I quickly followed, holding the lantern high so we could see.

The passage got narrower as we encountered the first residents of the crypt. Zofie didn't pause, instead moving slowly past them and deeper inside. The darkness stretched along the corridor before us, our passing creating a bubble of light moving deeper into the vast deepness. Large stone blocks had been set into the floor and walls, while along the sides of the wide tunnel, were person-sized sarcophagi. Over each of them were statues of men and women looking stately and wise. The figures were briefly illuminated as we passed, but the darkness behind us quickly swallowed them once more.

She turned and walked backward for a moment talking to me. "I guess I need to explain what we're doing here. You see, after Mother passed away, my father and I started a tradition to visit Mother on her birthday." She turned back around and resumed walking. "It just seemed more appropriate than visiting on the day she died since that was Wynn's birthday. Every year, we would visit, just Risten, Wynn, Father, and I. We would lay out a small meal, setting one extra place for Mother. Then we would take turns telling of important things that had happened to us during the year, like Wynn losing a tooth, or Risten learning a new sword skill, or me, coming into my myst powers."

"But a picnic?" I asked.

She looked over her shoulder and smiled. "If you're going to be my husband, you're going to have to learn some of our traditions."

I shook my head. "I'm all right with family traditions, like how to decorate during the Day of the New or how one exchanges gifts. But Zofie, we're going to have a picnic in a *tomb?*"

She suddenly paused and turned to me, planting a quick kiss on my lips. "It's important to me. This helps me feel... connected. I wanted to share it with you, and hopefully, you'll get to know my parents better."

I took her hand and gave it a squeeze. "I am honored you have included me." I smiled. "Now, let's say hello to your parents."

She grinned, and we resumed walking forward. After a bit, I began to recognize some of the statues. Zofie had brought me here before when we were sneaking into the castle. It was hard to believe that it had only been a few weeks ago. It seemed like forever.

Zofie called over her shoulder. "Mother and Father are just up ahead."

Then two things happened at once: Zofie abruptly stopped, while Abe suddenly shouted into my head.

Coren!

I winced at the loud booming. It felt like he had rattled my brain.

"What is it?" I asked.

There's a Dark Avenyts ahead!

I nearly panicked. A Dark Avenyts? Here? *In the castle?*

Up ahead, I saw a shadow that didn't belong. There was movement and then the gradual illumination from a small lantern. Slowly brightening light revealed a lone woman leaning against the sarcophagi of Zofie's mother. She wore dark pants, a white shirt, and a leather vest topped off with a broad-brimmed hat. The light was too dim to make out her face, but from her posture, I knew in an instant who it was.

"Risten?" exclaimed Zofie in disbelief.

The woman ahead shifted and raised her head, catching enough illumination to reveal Risten's smiling face. Only the expression wasn't from the Risten I knew. It was from something else. Something which twisted her smile into a mocking sneer. It was the final confirmation of the tragedy we had seen through the Mirror of Bygone Tears. Even though it was Risten's body, I knew it best not to even think of her that way. My experience with Fumiko had taught me how disarming they could be.

I also knew we were in deep trouble. If I pulled my sword, she would kill us both before it could clear the scabbard. Risten was that good.

Zofie raised her chin defiantly. "No, you're not Risten. You might wear her body, but you're not her."

The woman nodded. "And she does have an amazing body. Unfortunately, a little short in the myst area—barely enough to sustain me. But, you can't have everything." She smiled. "To make things easier, call me Lilith. It's a name I'm fond of and have used over the years." She adjusted her hat. "I knew you would come today. I have all of Risten's memories and knew it as sure as the sun rising in the morning. She loves you very deeply and is quite frantic at the moment."

"Why did you come?" asked Zofie. "Did Wynn send you?"

The woman gave a short bark of a laugh. "Hardly. He's in a bit of trouble right now. Even we can't find him and fear he may have gone rogue. He was supposed to be in complete control of this kingdom, and you were supposed to be dead. Playing curses with you and running his own agenda had not been in the plan. As for why I am here..." She turned to face us and put her hand on her sword. "I need something. And you're going to give it to me."

"Abe," I whispered while they talked. "Can I steal her curse?"

A Dark Avenyts? You've got to be kidding!

Zofie's eyes briefly glanced in my direction. She could hear Abe too. Using his newfound abilities, I had instructed Abe to bring Zofie into the conversation whenever she was nearby.

He continued, *That's well outside of my size range. When I steal a curse, it becomes an extension of me. Since most curses are dumb, it's not a problem. But the Dark Avenyts are like me. They're intelligent, and they carefully lock themselves into place. I doubt I could steal it, and if by some miracle I succeeded, I would likely be damaged doing it.*

Dammit! I slowly began to inch my hand toward my blade.

But the thing in Risten's body noticed immediately. "Coren," she said flatly. "I wouldn't do that if I were you. You've already got a price on your head." She ran a finger along the hilt of her sword. "A lot of our kind are angry with you." A slow mocking grin spread across her face. "You destroyed one of us. Something that hasn't happened in a thousand years. If they catch you, your death will be quite painful."

Zofie straightened and tried to refocus the conversation away from me. "What do you want?"

Lilith smiled. "I want you to tell me where the *Griffin's Key* is hidden. Only the Xernow heir is supposed to know where it is. And since Wynn doesn't, that leaves you."

Zofie shook her head. "Father never mentioned it. I don't even know what it is."

Lilith opened her mouth to speak but paused. "I think it best for Risten herself to explain this. And how badly we want it. As I said, she is a bit frantic." And then the woman's expression changed. It was very subtle, the tilt of her head, the worry lines on her face, maybe even the tension in her shoulders. But there was a difference.

"Zofie!" exclaimed Risten, tears immediately flowed down her face. "You have to give it to her. They want this thing bad. Real bad. She's going to kill you if you don't. And I won't be able to stop her! You won't be able to stop them! They're too powerful. I've seen it." She wiped tears with the back of her hand. "Kill me if you get the..." Risten abruptly stopped.

Her expression grew harder, and I knew that Lilith was back in control. She grinned evilly and wiped the rest of the drying tears away. "Now, are you going to make your cousin kill you, and increase her misery just a bit more? Another death to add to all the others I've killed while she helplessly watched? Or are you going to tell us where it is? You have to know."

Zofie glared at her. "I'm telling the truth. I don't know. If my father knew, he never passed down the knowledge."

Lilith frowned, and the grip on her sword tightened. "One last time, princess. Where is the Griffin's Key?"

Zofie held her head high. "Do your worst. I don't know. And even if I did, I wouldn't tell you."

Lilith shifted and prepared to draw. "Too bad."

Suddenly, I felt a rush go past me and a pluck at my hip, quickly followed by the clang of two swords meeting. Fumiko, her plain dress fluttering in the breeze, suddenly stood between us and our attacker, blocking the woman's descending sword. Lilith was momentarily surprised. "Where...?" But she didn't finish and instead attacked Fumiko raining down blows fast and furious.

And to my utter shock, Fumiko countered her perfectly. Lilith changed direction and swung crosswise. Fumiko leaned backward, the blade passing barely over her, before she straightened and resumed her attack.

I reached for my own sword and suddenly realized it was gone. Looking closer at the battle before us, I realized Fumiko held it. *Did she just take it as she ran by? Was that even possible?*

I grabbed Zofie's arm and pulled her away from the action. She reluctantly backed away while reaching for the security necklace she wore around her neck. It broke easily as she jerked it off, releasing its special charm: a call to her captain of the guard.

Fumiko matched the sword-master blow for blow, but Lilith had a height and size advantage, which she used to drive the smaller woman back.

"You're quite well trained," commented Lilith. "And your style is not one I've encountered before." She grinned. "But I have your measure now."

Lilith started to rain down blows driving Fumiko back toward one of the sarcophagi, pressing her against it. I pushed Zofie behind me. I didn't see how Fumiko could get out of this one.

And then I felt myst gathering. Time seemed to slow, as I watched Fumiko's knees flex, hands come up, and body bend backward. When her hands touched the sarcophagi, her feet continued upwards, and in one smooth movement, delivered a solid kick to Lilith's chin. The larger woman staggered back. Fumiko continued the flip to a crouch on top of the stone lid with sword held ready.

I stared in shock. That move was definitely impossible. How did she do it?

Behind me, I could hear the running steps of guards approaching. Lilith glared at Fumiko but did not advance. She instead grabbed her hat and threw it on the floor. Immediately, a portal opened on the ground. The hat seemed to float on the portal's shiny black surface but did not fall into it.

Lilith stepped to the portal. "While this has been interesting, I must not get caught just yet."

Fumiko charged, but before she could reach her, Lilith stepped over the portal and instantly dropped through the floor, taking the hat with her. The portal immediately closed.

Zofie turned to the men just reaching her. "Search the castle grounds. That was a short-range portal. She can't be too far away."

Fumiko, breathing hard, collapsed to her knees. "I'm out of practice."

I squatted down in front of her. "If that's out of practice, I can't help but wonder what you were like when you were in practice."

She weakly held out my sword. "I'm sorry I took your weapon."

"Don't apologize. You can definitely use it better than I can." Zofie squatted down beside me and leaned in to give Fumiko a hug. "Thank you for saving us." Fumiko looked down. "Madam Hindenlye had forgotten to include the cups you requested, and I was bringing them to you when I saw her. I…" she looked up with a pleading expression. "I swore to never fight again, but I couldn't let her hurt you."

"Where did you learn to use a sword like that?" Zofie asked. "You used it so well."

Fumiko's expression fell. She looked pleadingly from one of us to the other. "If you command, I will answer. But please don't make me. It's a part of my past. One I'd just as soon forget."

Zofie patted her on the shoulder. "We won't press. Tell us if it ever becomes appropriate."

Fumiko bowed her head. "Thank you, Princess. You have no idea how honored I am to be allowed to be here."

Zofie smiled. "And I to have you as a friend." She pulled Fumiko to her feet and surveyed the group of guards now surrounding her. And in the distance, more were coming. She sighed. "I guess my perfectly planned picnic has been put off."

"I'm sure your mother will understand," I offered.

She nodded sadly. "You're right. It can wait for a bit." She stepped forward and put a hand on her mother's sarcophagus. I couldn't help but feel there was more to what she was saying.

Zofie's movement caused the shadows to shift, and I noticed something out of the corner of my eye. Looking down, I saw a layer of dust had collected on the floor beside the sarcophagus. And the dust had been recently disturbed with a crude message, as if someone had drawn in it with the toe of their boot. Risten had been standing just beside that spot. And it was exactly something Lilith would taunt us with.

I put a hand on Zofie's shoulder and pointed to it.

She looked down and gasped.

It read, *Help me.*

CHAPTER TWO

Interrupted Meal

The attempt on the princess's life prompted a flurry of activity from the guards and staff—the search for the culprit, the investigation of her entry, and discussions on how to prevent its reoccurrence. But one truth was clear—Lilith had gotten away. The guards found evidence of two horses and traces of myst charms in the overgrowth toward the river. How she got in was still a mystery. There had been a fight reported near the castle gates just after dawn. Nothing much had been thought of it since the food shortages made tempers short. But it could have provided someone with intimate knowledge of the castle, just the distraction they needed to slip in.

The flurry of activity didn't die down until early evening, which unfortunately made us late for dinner. (Much to my displeasure, we had missed lunch entirely.) Tonight we would be eating with her senior staff. We had a lot to discuss even outside of the day's events.

So Zofie and I, with Fumiko trailing, entered the dining hall to find Captain Milner and Master Rourke chatting next to the room's one window—now shuttered against the cold. Upon seeing us, they finished their conversation and moved to stand at their places at the long table.

Much to the disappointment of her chamberlain, Eallair, I escorted Zofie to her chair and pulled it out for her. He was well into his midyears and took great pride in having served the Xernows most of his life. He also had an attitude that was just a bit too smug for me. Naturally, he and I had a bit of a competition going on as to who would perform this duty. I couldn't help but gloat. Tonight had been my win.

The princess sat at the head of the table with Fumiko taking her place on Zofie's left. I took the position on the right with Captain Milner next to me where he sat stiffly. He didn't particularly care for these affairs, preferring less formal surroundings.

Captain Milner had been a freebooter when we first met, having been forced into banditry just to survive. When Zofie launched her attempt to win back her throne, the captain and his men threw in their lot with us and were nearly executed. For his loyalty, Zofie had named him captain of her guard.

Master Rourke took his place one down from Fumiko. Rourke was a young man not much older than I and relatively new to his craft—and unfortunately now one of the most experienced myst users in the kingdom. Wynn, during his time as king, had either killed or spirited off all the others. Rourke had been spared only because he had been in a neighboring kingdom for the last year.

Rourke paused at the seat beside Fumiko, noticing she had placed her ledger in the chair. Deliberately, no doubt since Spraggel customarily sat there. Disappointment flashed briefly across his face, and he reluctantly sat to the other side of the empty seat.

It was painfully obvious that he was infatuated with Fumiko and took every opportunity to catch her attention. Yet, she went to great lengths to discourage him. I wondered if it was because he was a myst user. Or perhaps Fumiko had her eye on someone else. In either case, I hoped he got the message soon.

Right after Rourke settled down, two servants started serving our dinners. I was salivating in anticipation.

Even before coming to live in Edlingreen Castle, I loved dinner time. It had been special before my father died, and even after he passed, my mother had tried to follow the pattern. Although my later stepfather always complained about my mother's cooking.

Still, dinner time was special to me. It was the one opportunity for all the people I cared about to be together, eat, and talk pleasantly around the table. The food the castle served was of necessity, simple. Tonight's menu was a meatless stew. I, for one, planned to enjoy it, regardless of the conversation.

Zofie looked at her bowl in sadness. No doubt reminded of the situation her kingdom faced. Food was running out, and we were only halfway through winter. She looked to her secretary. "So, how are the ledgers coming?"

Fumiko looked up from her bowl. "They are nearly done. But it's pretty much as you already suspect. The treasury's been depleted. In fact, several of your family's more valuable heirlooms were sold. It's safe to say, there is nothing left of real value in the castle."

Zofie shook her head. "What did Wynn do with it all? While we weren't exceedingly rich, the treasury was well funded."

Fumiko sighed. "He bought weapons from the neighboring kingdoms. Lots of them and in all shapes and sizes."

Zofie put her spoon down. "But I've not seen any weapons..." Her eyes grew wide. "He sent them to Mount Eternal."

Fumiko nodded. "That's exactly what he did. He used the kingdom's coin to fund the invaders."

"And our supplies?"

Fumiko looked down at her bowl. "The same route. The royal warehouses are nearly empty. What little grain there is, was left over from two years ago. The crops this year were abysmal because Wynn sent soldiers out to harass the farmers. And what was harvested was either sold or sent to Mount Eternal."

Zofie shook her head.

But Fumiko wasn't done. "And the prospects for taxes this year are especially bad. As for tariffs, trade in the port is slow this time of year, so they are at a trickle."

"What about the lords?"

Fumiko sighed. "Wynn pretty much bled the nobility dry. Not much left there. While their situation is improving, you'll likely have a rebellion if you ask any more from them. They do have some stocks which they will be sharing with us, although grudgingly."

Zofie sat up straighter and put both hands palm down on the table. "So how long do we have?"

Fumiko looked at Zofie sadly. "It depends on how you want to do things. We have enough hay to keep our horses for another three weeks, possibly a month, depending on how the rest of the winter goes. The pastures have been overgrazed, but we might be able to get most of our horses through this. Unfortunately, that doesn't leave any for the remaining livestock, and if we reduce their number any further, we won't have enough to rebuild our stock. As for people food, we have enough for two more weeks. A little more if we consume the remaining livestock. We'll also have to continue to support the fiefdoms since Wynn hit them pretty hard."

Zofie paled. "That's not even enough to last until mid-spring." She looked toward Captain Milner. "Any relief possible from the forests?"

Milner shifted uncomfortably in his seat. "Poaching has been rampant, and all the easy game has been taken. Plus, the Sylph have become especially protective of their lands. Anyone caught hunting in the Shattered Forest will never hunt again."

I got to the bottom of my soup bowl and wondered if it would be rude to lick it. I looked up and offered my suggestion. It was a point Zofie and I disagreed on. "Why don't we send an envoy to the far kingdoms again? The neighboring kingdoms snubbed you, but maybe some of the ones farther away would listen."

"Coren!" uncharacteristic anger in her voice. "We cannot send another set of envoys. The far kingdoms won't even acknowledge that I exist, little alone that there are Dark Avenyts loose in the world." Zofie pushed her half-eaten bowl away and leaned back into her chair. I eyed her remaining soup. She had been doing that a lot lately, taking a few bites and then leaving the rest. Was her guilt over not being able to do more making her lose her appetite? Her lack of eating was starting to worry me, and was to the point, I needed to ask her about it.

But not yet.

"What if I led the delegation?"

Fumiko resumed quietly eating her soup. She was wise enough to know that if I was going to brave the fires of hell, that trying to save me would only get her burned too.

Zofie leaned forward. Her mood over the last few weeks had shifted toward the irritable side. "Out of the question. I need my knight beside me, now more than ever. Please don't push me on this."

I looked at her levelly. "Zofie, dearest."

Both Fumiko's and Zofie's eyes went up at the dearest. That was the signal that I too was feeling a little irritable.

"You don't..." I broke off as I caught something out of the corner of my eye. But turning toward it, I didn't see anything. I shook my head and mumbled. "I thought I saw something."

And then I *did* see it—a single tiny flash of pale yellow light. I looked closer and saw a speck bobbing in the air flying gently toward us. It briefly glowed again. A firefly? In the middle of winter?

I snorted and turned back to my companions, preparing to point out the oddity. But Fumiko's expression stopped me cold—her eyes were wide, her spoon paused mid-way to her mouth, and her pale skin seemed even paler. The spoon began to tremble.

Zofie noticed it too and put a hand on her friend's arm. "What's wrong?"

The firefly continued its approach. Suddenly, Fumiko stood, upsetting her chair and knocking her soup bowl to the floor where it shattered. Fumiko looked like she would run if only her feet would allow it.

The firefly paused in its flight at the foot of the table and slowly bobbed up and down. "Your highness," it said. "My humblest apologies for interrupting your meal. This messenger requests an audience." The voice's accent was similar to Fumiko's. It was the gravelly voice of a man, and from its tone, one used to dealing with nobility.

Captain Milner quickly stood and drew his sword while I felt Rourke gathering his myst.

I smiled. They weren't the only ones with weapons now. I had my curse. And he was unlocked. For the longest time, most of Abe's capabilities had been sealed under a passphrase, which I had only recently been able to figure out (with a lot of help from Fumiko).

"Abe," I whispered. "What is that thing?"

Looks like a firefly to me, came his booming voice inside my head.

Zofie glanced in my direction, hearing Abe's side of the conversation.

I hid my mouth behind my hand. "I can see that. There must be a charm or curse on it."

I don't smell a curse, but it might be a charm since fireflies don't usually talk.

I was still getting used to Abe's new abilities. "Can you show me?"

I don't have anything better to do.

My vision changed. Over my normal view of the world, I saw a glowing web stretching across the room—multi-colored lines in varying levels of intensity and complexity. I looked at Zofie and could see her familiar network of blue lines and the bright glow of her curse mark. I also saw similar lines on the other humans in the room. But when I looked to the firefly, it seemed enmeshed in a tiny dark green web with a single line stretching off into the distance.

The view wasn't much help. I was still trying to figure out what the colors and glows meant. And although he would never admit it, Abe was at a loss to assist. I really wished his creator had left some sort of reference to help me.

I sighed. It must be a charm because it didn't have a glow like a curse. Which meant it was not a Dark Avenyts, although that didn't mean it wasn't dangerous.

Zofie stood. She leaned forward and put both hands on the table. I could see the irritation on her face. "This is a grave breach of protocol. Normally, visitors petition for an audience, and then only to appear at court. Not in my dining hall."

"My humblest apologies, Princess Zophia Olwenna Xernow. My name is Tusita Yonge, and I am the Imperial Advisor for his Brightness, Emperor Huang. I am speaking to you through this avatar from his palace in Xiangwei City. I am contacting you this way since time is of the essence. I can provide the necessary validation of my identity should you need it."

Zofie looked puzzled. "The Kuijia Empire? What does the empire want with us?"

The insect flew a little closer. "His Brightness has commanded we contact you. We have heard the Dark Avenyts have once again appeared in our world and are seeking out the ancient artifacts which protected us. A lot of knowledge has been lost since we last fought them, but as you're likely aware, the weapons of that conflict were spread across the world to prevent any one kingdom from gathering too much power. The Kuijia Empire was entrusted with one of them. For a thousand years now, it has been locked safely away in an impenetrable vault. But no vault is perfect. We recently ascertained that they know we possess one of those ancient artifacts. We fear that if they can access the vault, they may be able to open it. And this artifact is a most powerful one that must be protected at all costs. The emperor has decided that the best strategy is to hide it once again."

Zofie looked puzzled. "So, why do you need us? Why not just move it."

"To do that, we need the key to the vault. And your ruler of the time was entrusted with it. We would like for you to give us the Griffin's Key."

Zofie and I exchanged a glance. That was the second time today someone had mentioned that artifact. It was the same one Lilith had been asking about. *What was this thing?*

Zofie shook her head. "That seems risky. Wouldn't it be better to leave it in place?"

"We considered that but felt it safer to move it."

"And what does the artifact in the vault do?"

The firefly continued to bob up and down. "We're not sure what its purpose was. That information has been lost. But we do know it was a most important artifact and is somehow connected to all the others."

Zofie stared at the firefly for a moment. I had a good idea of what she was pondering. It seemed odd that they wouldn't even know what they were protecting. Then again, it had been a thousand years.

She finally shook her head. "I cannot help you. I do not possess this artifact. And even if I were to agree to hand it over, I would have to find it first. And honestly, I have my own set of priorities at the moment. I really can't spare the people."

The firefly paused. "We are prepared to offer compensation."

"Compensation?" asked Zofie.

"We have heard your kingdom is suffering from the neglect of your brother, and proper preparations were not made for winter. We can offer assistance. Even enough food to last your kingdom until Spring."

Zofie's eyes widened, and she slowly stood erect. "That is a very generous offer." She frowned. "What makes you think this Griffin's Key is in my kingdom?"

The firefly bobbed for a moment before answering. "Two things point to it being here. For one, legend has it that the King Xernow of that time gave us this most important item but kept the key."

"And the other?"

"You were approached about it by a Dark Avenyts this morning. This is why the hasty audience."

Zofie's eyes narrowed. "How did you come to find that out? Only my trusted advisors know it was a Dark Avenyts. What is your source of information?"

The voice laughed. "It was quite unintentional, but we have been keeping an eye on someone in your court. We learned through them."

"So, you're admitting you have a spy?"

The voice laughed again. "Not hardly. This person will be most displeased to find this out."

"And who is this person," Zofie asked.

Fumiko slammed her fist into the table. "How dare you!" she yelled.

We all stared in disbelief at Fumiko's outburst.

The firefly calmly bobbed. "Hello, Fumiko—daughter of Yanmei of the Zhangjunen family, who is also the twenty-fourth concubine to his Lightness. Did you actually think we would not keep an eye on you? We were quite surprised to find you had taken refuge in this foreign kingdom—but the fates never cease to amaze. Long before you left us, we snuck a charm on you to notify us whenever you used your myst. It seemed prudent considering your skills. We were just surprised it went this long."

Fumiko's face turned red in anger. She clenched both her fists and almost shook with rage.

The firefly bobbed silently as the two regarded each other. Finally, the firefly spoke. "Your father wishes to see you."

Fumiko raised her chin defiantly. "I have no father."

The firefly bobbed gently up and down. "Do as you will but disobey at your peril. Your father is getting old, and once he is gone, so will be the protections he may have offered."

She shook her head. "But he banished me and put a price on my head. My life is forfeit should I return."

"What you say is true. The banishment is still in force. But for one of your skills, it should be of little consequence."

Fumiko picked up her knife from the table and threw it at the firefly. It landed solidly in the woodwork of the far wall. "I refuse!"

The firefly remained unfazed. "Such a volatile temper. It's what got you in trouble to begin with." The voice behind the firefly paused and then sighed. It turned its attention back to us. "Princess Zophia Xernow, please forgive me speaking with her. In case you haven't discerned it, she was the source of our information, although unwillingly. She is known to us, and we feel it is time to have her back." The firefly paused. "So what say you, Princess? Will you accept our offer?"

Zofie thought for a moment. "How long do I have to consider it?"

"Take as long as you need. But time is short. We fear agents of the

Dark Avenyts are already on their way to the empire. We also fear there will be other attempts to learn the whereabouts of the key." He paused dramatically. "Of which you may not survive."

Zofie considered the insect. "How do I contact you?"

The voice from the firefly laughed. "Have Fumiko use her myst. We will know. And should you accept, please allow her to come with you. She will be a valuable guide. Plus, it will allow her to see her father."

"I won't do it!" Fumiko yelled.

The firefly began to circle toward the floor—its motions becoming erratic. "Such a temper. Don't forget your mother and your sister are still in the emperor's court. Your failure to appear may displease him and put their lives in danger. Don't be a fool."

Fumiko shook with rage.

The firefly landed on the floor. "We will await your answer Princess Zophia Xernow."

It gave one last flicker of glow and then went out.

Fumiko went to where the bug had fallen. She glared down at it for a moment before stomping on it, bringing her foot down again and again. "I... will... not... go...!" punctuating each word with a blow of her foot.

Zofie and I watched our normally calm as ice Fumiko take out her fury on the bug. She looked up at us with tears in her eyes. "I can't."

She ran out of the room, leaving Zofie and I to look at each other in puzzlement.

What the hell just happened?

CHAPTER THREE

Fumiko's Charm

L ate that evening, the door to Zofie's study opened unexpectedly. I jumped to my feet and immediately drew my sword. The princess jerked up from her writing desk, the small knife she kept on its surface, suddenly appearing in her hand.

Spraggel shuffled in the door bleary-eyed, and his hair mussed. Quite the contrast from his morning exuberance. He eyed the blades pointed at him and then looked up at us in surprise. "What?"

"Spraggel!" I scolded. "Knock before entering. One of these days, I'm going to strike before I see it's you."

He gave me a tired eye. "If you ever get that good, *then* I'll knock." He turned to Zofie. "Forgive me for the late hour, Princess, but I have completed looking through my old friend's notes. I thought you might want to hear the results before retiring."

Zofie, ever composed, took a deep breath and returned her knife to her desk. "What did you find?"

"Well, I was able to confirm that the Griffin's Key is indeed some kind of key." Spraggel suddenly yawned. "Sorry, Princess. It's been a busy day."

He moved to a thickly padded chair before the fire and settled comfortably into it. It was Zofie's. He was oblivious that he had just taken the favorite chair of the kingdom's ruling monarch. He leaned back and closed his eyes.

"Spraggel," I scolded. "Don't sit there. That's Zofie's...."

She laid a hand on my shoulder. "It's all right." She gave me a weak smile. "I'm too wound up to sit anyway."

She went over to the fireplace and poked at the embers before throwing another log on the fire. She looked tired. For that matter, we *all* did.

"How's Fumiko?" Zofie asked as she paused a moment to warm her hands.

My old master didn't answer.

She looked over her shoulder at him. "Spraggel?"

The elder's eyes shot open. "I wasn't asleep. I was just resting my eyes." He looked puzzled for a moment. "What were you saying?"

I frowned. "Zofie asked how Fumiko was. She was with you, wasn't she?"

He nodded. "The young miss did join me for a bit but left earlier. She's still upset over our visitor this evening."

Zofie sighed. "I wish she would talk to us? She must be carrying a huge burden." She looked at me sadly. "We might be able to help."

Spraggel laid his head back. "Fumiko will tell us when she's ready."

I nodded. "So what about the Griffin's Key?"

My old master didn't answer. Zofie and I looked to him, and his eyes were once more closed. "Spraggel?" I asked.

He jerked upright. "I was not asleep."

Zofie went to stand beside him and put a hand on his shoulder. "It's all right. Just give us a quick rundown on the artifacts, and then you can go to bed. That's an order."

Spraggel looked at her sheepishly. He reached into his myst pocket and pulled out a book. It never ceased to amaze me when he did that.

His pocket seemed to have an infinite capacity. I'd seen him pull out everything from books, clothes, and half-eaten meals. He claimed his sword was in there somewhere, but he'd never been able to find it.

Spraggel opened the book and took out some hand-written notes. "There is little information on the Griffin's Key and absolutely none on where it might be. Not even a speculation. But what I did discover is consistent with what our visitor from the empire said. Apparently, it is the only way to open this vault he mentioned. It's called the Crystal Vault, by the way."

I nodded. "Sounds like the ancients hiding information again."

Spraggel looked back at his notes. "As our guest alluded to, this key was supposedly held in this kingdom, and its whereabouts entrusted to the Xernow family with the location passed down through the royal line. However, I think there was a break in this chain when the princess's grandparents died unexpectedly." Spraggel rubbed his eyes. "The fastest way to find it would be to use the Wayward's Finder, just like we did for the Mirror of Bygone Tears. I'm sure Lord Dewi Merrick would let us borrow it. Especially since you didn't throw him in prison after regaining your throne."

Zofie moved to stand beside me. She slipped an arm around my waist and laid her head on my shoulder. "What about the artifact inside the vault?"

Spraggel shook his head. "There are references, but none currently at my disposal. The books seem to have disappeared. All I can tell you is that it's called the Forever Nexus Shadow."

She frowned. "My brother likely removed those books." She thought for a moment. "Do you think this Advisor Yonge is telling the truth? That they don't know the purpose of this Nexus thing?"

Spraggel shrugged. "Hard to say. They've been guarding it for a thousand years, and there have been a lot of changes since they got it." He closed his book and tucked his notes away. "You see, at the time the vault was built, the east was a loose collective of twelve kingdoms." He looked up. "But about three hundred years ago, Shun the Great consolidated them into what we know today as the Kuiojia Empire."

Zofie put a finger to her lips in thought. "I'll send Lord Merrick a letter in the morning. I'm confident he will let us use it." She sighed heavily. While she said nothing more about it, I knew what that meant. She would have to deal with Galvyn. He had been her other primary suitor and been infatuated with her for some time now. He very nearly displaced me as her fiancé. However, Zofie saw through to his true nature.

I personally didn't like the bastard. The fact he had punched me on two different occasions had nothing to do with it. (All right, maybe a little.)

"Anything else we should know about it?" I asked.

Spraggel looked down at his notes. "Well, apparently the Griffin's Key can be used to unlock things other than the vault. But for the Crystal Vault, the princess has to be the one to use it."

Zofie nodded. "We best get the key as soon as we can, whether we accept the Emperor's offer or not."

I looked at her. "Do you intend to accept it? His offer, I mean."

The princess gave a heavy sigh. "I don't want to, but I need to feed my people."

I decided there was no time like the present to address the dragon in the room. "Don't you think it's an odd coincidence that the offer came from Fumiko's homeland? And it was through her that the Empire found out about the Dark Avenyts. Can we really trust her? She has that tracking charm on her."

Zofie took her time considering. "I'm not sure. She did save our lives this morning. And before that, she resisted the Dark Avenyts controlling her to pass on a hint about unlocking Abhulengulus." She paused. "Without that, I'd be dead." Zofie looked off into the distance. "It is a strange coincidence though. Then again, where your curse is concerned, coincidences seem to happen a lot."

Zofie was referring to the ability of my curse to affect luck. Maybe even fate itself. The curse did it to protect me, but it could have tragic consequences for those not under its protection. My father had been one of those victims.

She straightened and gave me a weak smile. "For now, I intend to trust her. Fumiko will be a valuable guide should we decide to accept the emperor's offer."

"But what about the tracking curse?"

She sighed. "We'll have Master Rourke examine her in the morning. Hopefully, he can figure out how to take it off."

Suddenly Spraggel's book and papers fell to the floor. We jerked in his direction and saw that he was fast asleep.

And snoring.

I smiled. "I guess I better get Spraggel to his room before he drools all over your chair."

"Here, I'll help."

I shook my head. "No, I've got this. It's late, and you have a letter to finish before bed. You need your sleep too."

She looked at me sheepishly. "I am tired. I'll leave Spraggel to you then."

While Zofie went to her writing desk, I woke my old master and led him to his room. He was asleep before I got him covered with a blanket. I shook my head. We'd all been pushing so hard to get things right in the kingdom.

As I headed back, I happened to see a light under the door to Fumiko's bed-chamber. It was only two rooms down from Zofie's. Fumiko had insisted she be close to the princess should she be needed.

I stopped in front of her door. I couldn't help but wonder what Fumiko knew about this Advisor Yonge, and why hadn't she mentioned it before? Then again, she had also been deeply troubled by the visit.

I thought about knocking. I had considered Fumiko a friend when I first met her. I had found her easy to speak with and marveled at her depth of perception. But she had been under the control of a Dark Avenyts and betrayed us. I knew the woman I had come to know, and the one now, were different. However, I couldn't shake this nagging doubt—had she betrayed us again?

Suddenly Fumiko's door flung open, startling me. She stood on the threshold with a dagger held ready. Seeing it was me, she relaxed and lowered the weapon.

"Coren, what are you doing out so late?" She leaned into the corridor and looked both ways to make sure no one else was there. "Is something wrong?"

I shook my head. "I was walking by and noticed your light was still on."

Fumiko leaned against the doorframe. "There is no way I can sleep now." She looked down at the dagger in her hand. "Too much has happened today."

My eyes were drawn to her dagger, which was of a type I had not seen before, finely made and looking extremely sharp. But its finish was unusual—a dark gray that almost seemed to absorb the light. I wondered where she had gotten it. Since coming into Zofie's service, I couldn't recall a time she had even touched a weapon.

"The dreams again?" I asked.

She nodded, still examining her weapon. She was silent for a moment before speaking. "You'd think I would be used to them by now. Bad dreams visit so frequently." She turned the blade over in her hand and said more softly. "But now my worst nightmare has come for me." She seemed to catch herself and looked up at me in panic. She straightened and bowed her head. "I'm sorry to cause you worry. Our visitor today took me by surprise. And the fact he's been watching me..." She shivered.

Despite my fears of being betrayed again, I couldn't help but feel sorry for her. She was either an excellent actress or had truly been through something terrible.

"Is there anything I can do?"

She gave me a considering look. "I was going to ask you in the morning, but since you're here, would you look at something for me? With Abhulengulus's new abilities, you might be able to help me."

She turned and went deeper into her room. But I stood frozen at the threshold. Stepping into a young woman's room late at night might not be the best thing to do. The staff were forever watching. Rumors could start.

She saw my hesitation and blushed. "I'm sorry. I guess it is improper for one of your station."

I stepped inside. "We'll just leave the door open."

She nodded and turned to face me. She took a deep breath. "Somewhere on me I have a concealed charm. I was hoping you could find it and remove it like you did when the princess was dying from an Abeyance charm."

Removing Zofie's charm had been the first thing I had done after unlocking Abe's hidden abilities. It had been a desperate act to save my beloved princess. I didn't understand what I had done and hadn't had a chance to practice my new skills yet.

"You could just go to Master Rourke in the morning. He's more experienced with this than I am."

Fumiko looked down and blushed. "I'd rather not. He makes me uncomfortable."

"You know he likes you. He probably wouldn't even mind if you went to see him tonight."

Fumiko looked up. "Like I said, he makes me uncomfortable."

We considered each other for a moment and then I sighed. "All right. I'll try." I cleared my throat. "Abe? Can you help me?"

The response was immediate—loud and booming in my head. I winced.

Oh, so he's asking nicely now. He must want something.

I rolled my eyes.

"I want to find out if Fumiko has a charm on her. Can you help me see it?"

She might have more than one.

"All right, can you help me see them?"

So, you want to see her charms? Abe asked, with a touch of amusement.

I nodded. "Yes."

Fumiko looked at me expectantly. "What do you need me to do?"

She couldn't hear Abe's side of the conversation but knew things were progressing.

Abe continued. *The process is simple. Before we can begin, ask her to take off all her clothes.*

"Take off her clothes?" I shook my head. "Why? I didn't have to remove Zofie's clothes when I took off her charm."

Fumiko looked unsure. She grabbed the bottom of her dress to pull it over her head. "I guess I can do that. I'll do anything to get this thing off me."

Abe continued, *Of course, she has to. You want to see ALL her charms, don't you? Especially, her female charms.*

"What?"

Suddenly Zofie skidded to a stop in front of Fumiko's door. "Coren, what in the Creator's hell are you doing?" She was wearing her nightgown, so she must have jumped straight out of bed.

I looked at her in surprise while Fumiko blushed and let her dress drop back in place.

Abe howled with laughter.

Then it hit me. Zofie had been hearing Abe's side of the conversation. Just as the troublemaker had intended.

I looked at Zofie and pointed to Fumiko. "I was going to examine her charms... I mean her hidden charms..." I shook my head. "She wanted me to take them off."

This was not helping.

Zofie held up a halting hand. "I think I understand. Abe's been up to his old tricks again."

I sighed in resignation. "It would appear so."

Zofie shook her head. "Abhulengulus, you shouldn't tease Coren like that."

Sorry, Princess. He's just so... teasable!

Zofie grinned. "He is, isn't he." She sighed and shook her head. "Now, what exactly were you two up to?"

Fumiko seemed to regain her composure. "I asked Coren to look for the tracking charm concealed on my body. I want the thing off."

Zofie grew serious. "Be careful. It's generally best for the person who invoked the charm to remove it. Theoretically, someone stronger than the original caster can do it. However, there can sometimes be complications depending on how the charm was put together."

Fumiko shook her head. "I don't care. I've got to get this thing off me. You won't... no, you *can't* trust me while I still have it. I will be a liability. In fact, it could be listening to this very conversation."

Zofie turned toward me. "Do you know what a charm looks like?"

"Well, I used it on the firefly, and it looked green with a line stretching off into the distance. Also, when I took that Abeyance charm off you, it was a greenish thing."

Zofie shook her head. "Charms aren't green. The colors you're seeing is the color of the person's myst. Everyone's color is unique, like a signature or crest. Most myst users can't see them, only myst seers can."

Zofie looked to Fumiko. "Can you see them?"

Fumiko shook her head. "No, I can't. I was told I was only an average myst user. I can only use it for a few minor charms."

Zofie turned back to me. "Coren, I think it's time you have your first myst lesson. Look at Fumiko and tell me what color her myst is?"

"Abe," I said. "Show me."

He was still chuckling. *Of course. I'll be happy to let you see her charms.*

I sighed and shook my head. "Please, Abe, just show me the myst lines."

As before, my vision changed. I saw a glowing web of multicolored lines running everywhere, moving and churning. I looked in Zofie's direction and saw her familiar blue lines. Hers were a vibrant, almost pure blue. Even the curse mark on her chest was the same shade of blue. Which made sense, considering curses took their myst from the host.

When I turned to examine Fumiko, I saw a web of green lines surrounding her. Not nearly as many as Zofie, nor as complex. And nothing seemed amiss in them. I was hoping I would see a thread leading off somewhere as I had with the firefly, but no such luck.

"Fumiko has a bunch of lines surrounding her. They're a pale green, with a touch of yellow. But I can't see any sign of an irregularity in them." I thought for a moment. "Abe, how about you?"

I don't see anything either. He gave an almost human sigh. *I guess it's time I broke the news to you. Now, stay with me. This is a complex topic which might challenge your monkey brain.* He made a sound like he was clearing his throat. *I can't see what you see. I'm blind to myst. Charms don't even register.*

I looked to Zofie who shared my puzzled look. "But you told me what to do when I removed Zofie's Abeyance charm."

True. But I was going off past experience. Like a blind person knowing a clear sky is blue, even if they've never actually seen the color. If you'll recall, I told you to look for what was different. I have no idea what a charm looks like. You figured that out on your own.

I was kicking myself for not spending more time with Abe since his capabilities had been unlocked. "If you can't see myst, then how do you know what a curse is to steal it?"

I smell them, he said proudly. *And I can only steal them after tasting them.*

My eyes went wide in realization. "Which is why I have to touch the person to steal the curse. You have to taste it."

Exactly. Now, Coren, I'm actually quite impressed. You followed along, so your monkey brain must be getting smarter. I might have to promote you to ape.

Fumiko interrupted. "I'm not exactly sure what is going on between you and Abhulengulus, but do you think you can get it off me? I won't be able to sleep tonight knowing they are watching me."

I sighed. "I would love to, but the problem is I don't see anything different on you. Could you turn around?"

Fumiko turned slowly in front of me, but all I could see was the same pale green lines. I shook my head. "I don't see anything different."

Zofie pursed her lips. "It's probably disguised to blend in with her existing myst lines."

I remembered the Imperial Advisor saying something about it activating when Fumiko used her myst.

I nodded. "Fumiko, try using your myst. Maybe if the charm activates, it will come out of hiding."

The young woman paled. "He'll be able to see me."

I touched her shoulder. "Better now when you're among friends."

She nodded, still a little unsure. She extended her arms out from her side, closing her eyes in concentration. A moment later, I felt myst gathering, and Fumiko rose about two finger's breadth off the floor. She was levitating. It must have been how she had been able to do that strange backward leap when fighting Lilith.

Zofie and I looked at each other in surprise. Fumiko said she was an average myst user. But from what Zofie had told me previously, it took a lot to physically move an object. While likely not near as strong as Zofie, she was not exactly a weakling.

As I watched her myst lines, they vibrated around her like the plucked strings of a harp.

Fumiko settled back down.

I looked to Zofie. "Did you see anything?"

Zofie shook her head. "I'm in the middle of my curse cycle, so I can't tap my myst. I can get some vague images, but not with the detail you're seeing."

I looked back to Fumiko. "I'm sorry. I can't see what I need to remove. Everything looks the same."

Fumiko nodded sadly and looked away.

I felt so bad. I wished there was something I could do. Then a thought occurred to me. If her lines of myst vibrated like strings in a harp, wouldn't she be able to feel them?

"Fumiko, I'd like to try one last thing."

She turned back hopeful. "Please, go ahead."

I reached out and gently stroked one of her lines of myst. I felt it vibrate under my hand.

Fumiko jumped. "What did you do? That felt very strange."

"Am I hurting you?" I asked.

She shook her head. "I wouldn't call it hurting me. More like someone tickling you."

I leaned forward and touched another. She jumped again.

I ran my hand across them, causing them to all vibrate. Fumiko sucked a breath in surprise.

All moved as I expected, except for one on the outside of her thigh. And as I looked closer, I could see it didn't exactly duplicate the pattern on her other leg. I touched it, and Fumiko gave no indication she could feel it. Could this be it?

I pulled on it—

Fumiko collapsed, falling to the floor. She clutched at her throat.

Zofie rushed forward. "What did you do?"

I knelt beside her in panic. "I just touched one of her lines. It seemed different." Her back arched as she writhed in agony. "What have I done?"

And just as suddenly as it started, Fumiko was released. She fell back panting, her face covered in sweat.

"I'm sorry, Fumiko. I didn't mean to hurt you."

She rolled her eyes at me and nodded weakly. "I asked you to." Then she winched in pain. She quickly pulled her dress up enough to expose the thigh where I had seen the odd line of myst.

My eyes went wide, and Zofie gasped. Tiny letters formed there in Fumiko's language. They stayed in place for several heartbeats and then faded.

Fumiko sighed. "I should have known it wouldn't be that easy."

She looked up at us. "It said, *next time... you die.*"

CHAPTER FOUR

Presents from Friends

The next morning we all awoke tired and groggy, none of us having slept well. Fumiko had been so distraught at the threatening message that Zofie had insisted she pass the night in her room. And I slept on the floor in front of the door, fearing another attack from Risten or Lilith or whatever she wanted to call herself.

Naturally, Spraggel awoke refreshed and full of energy. We quickly sent him to the library before we collectively attacked him for his cheerfulness.

But a kingdom waits for no one, and whether you're rested or not, its business must proceed. I helped Zofie as much as I could throughout the morning as she pondered the empire's offer. She wanted to quickly reach a decision.

Mid-morning, Zofie's advisors gathered in her study. She hadn't held court since so much had happened. As they gathered, she stood by the open window deep in thought. She had undone the myst charm that kept the chill out and stood by it, gazing into the distance as she basked in the cold air and sunshine. She wore one of her more formal dresses, and I was struck by her profile as she stared outside. I could almost feel the weight on her shoulders as she considered her decision.

I wanted to take her in my arms and tell her everything would be all right. But now was not the time. Zofie was in her queen role, so the best I could do was offer support.

I went to stand beside her. She glanced up at me with a brief smile before returning her attention to the view outside. After a moment, she started humming. It was a tune I didn't recognize.

She caught herself and gave me a sheepish grin. "I hope my humming doesn't bother you."

I shook my head. "Not at all."

She turned back to the window and touched her shoulder against mine. The contact spoke volumes of how worried she was. "It relaxes me to hear it. It's a lullaby. Father used to sing it to me when I was a young girl." She smiled. "It was the only way he could get me to go to sleep."

"Are there words?" I asked.

She smiled. "I'll sing them for you when things settle down." She patted my arm.

"I look forward to it."

She looked up at me like she wanted to say more, but Rourke, the last to arrive, burst into the room panting—like he had run all the way from his quarters. He was clutching a small wooden box.

With a touch, Zofie re-sealed the window against the chill and turned to Rourke. "Were you able to make it?"

Zofie had sent for Rourke at first light, and together we had come up with a plan to deal with Fumiko's problem.

Rourke smiled. "It was a bit tricky, but I think this should work." He held the box out to Fumiko. "For you, my lady." He grinned like a teen giving his first love a Day of the New present.

Fumiko rose slowly and formally took the offered box with both hands. She bowed deeply. "Thank you for making this. It will greatly ease my mind and let me stay by Zofie's side."

She opened the box and pulled out a strip of leather with a single unpolished crystal tied within it.

Rourke leaned forward. "I'm sorry the necklace is so simple, but it was the best I could do in a hurry. I hope it's not too crude."

Fumiko's expression did not change. She bowed again. "It is a great gift. May I put it on now?"

"Of... of course," Rourke stammered. "Please do."

She took out the necklace and tied it on. As the jewel touched her throat, it immediately gave a flash of white light then faded.

Rourke closed one eye and looked at her, no doubt using his myst sight. "It appears to be working. That should give the bastards something to wonder about. While I couldn't remove the tracking charm, this at least will suppress it so it can't reveal anything."

"Suppress?" Zofie asked. "I didn't think a charm could stop another charm."

Rourke smiled. "Suppress might be too strong of a word. The necklace continuously feeds a harmless image and sound through to the person on the other end."

"And what image is that?" I asked.

"The inside of my toilet closet."

We all chuckled. Rourke shrugged. "It was the most harmless thing I could think of."

Spraggel patted him on the back. "I would *not* call it harmless. You haven't cleaned it since you got here. They'll die in horror."

As we all got another chuckle, Rourke blushed and moved to his seat.

Fumiko then turned to me and bowed. "And thank you Coren, for coming up with the idea."

I shrugged. "I had one that suppressed Abe until he broke it. I just thought it might work for a charm too."

Then she turned to Zofie and gave her a bow too. The deepest one of all. "And you Princess for allowing it to be made. I am once again in your debt."

Zofie smiled. "I'm just glad we were able to figure something out."

The princess then stepped forward, signaling it was time to start. She remained standing and took a moment to look at each of her small group of advisors: Spraggel, Fumiko, Master Rourke, Captain Milner, and of course, myself. Historian, Secretary, Myst Adept, Commander, and Knight. It was such a small group. To complete the traditional council, Zofie needed to fill at least three other positions. But she just hadn't had the time.

She cleared her throat. "As you know, we've received an offer from the Kuiojia Empire to provide us with supplies in exchange for the Griffin's Key. I wanted to get each of your opinions on it before I make my decision."

Rourke perked up. "I think we should accept. The food is too good of an offer to pass up."

Captain Milner frowned. "I disagree. I'm afraid it would make us beholden to the empire. While I agree it would make things easier, we don't know the condition of the supplies or if they will even follow through with their offer."

Zofie turned to Spraggel. "What about you?"

Spraggel nodded. "I don't think we know the value of the Griffin's Key. We could be giving away the kingdom for a pittance. We need more intelligence on exactly what it is and what it does. My advice is to ask for more time."

I chimed in. "I agree with Spraggel. We just don't know enough."

Zofie turned to her secretary. "And you?"

Fumiko shifted uncomfortably. "I will abstain. I might be biased."

Zofie crossed her arms. "There's something you haven't told us, isn't there."

Fumiko looked up in surprise. She gave a fleeting grin. "You read people so well." She looked up at Zofie. "Yes, there is." Fumiko shifted uncomfortably. "I owe you an honest assessment. But it's complicated. I... I am afraid of what you'll think of me."

Zofie gave a gentle grin. "After your outburst last night, I thought there might be something more. And you don't have to tell us every-thing. But you're most familiar with the empire. What do you think of this offer? Can we trust Imperial Advisor Tusita Yonge? I honestly haven't been impressed with the way he's treated you so far."

Fumiko nodded and gave a deep sigh as she collected her thoughts. "I've interacted with Yonge before. And I have no doubt he will do exactly as he said. In the empire, he is known for his honesty and integrity. The common people love him. They even have a festival to celebrate his birthday. He *will* provide you with food and other necessities, and it will likely be quite generous. But..." She paused. The hands resting on her knees curled into fists. I could see the conflict on her face as she fought with her personal demons. "But to me, the man is pure evil." She looked down. "He did something I can never forgive. And he knows it. Which means his confession about the tracking charm and revealing my heritage are all somehow part of his plan. To discredit me in your eyes is only part of it." She shook her head. "There must be another reason he wants the Griffin's Key. Something that he's not telling us. Something important." Fumiko's gaze rose to meet Zofie's. "Princess, whatever you decide, be careful. Be *very* careful. There's only been one time that he didn't get his way." She pushed her hair back from her face. Her hand was trembling.

"And I caused it."

After Fumiko's confession, Zofie let her council go their way. She promised to have a decision before noon.

So I guarded the door while Zofie stood by the windows and contemplated her kingdom's fate. And true to her word, she had me summon Fumiko a little before the appointed time. I didn't ask her what she had decided. She would tell me when she was ready.

And with a knock, Fumiko eased the door open and came to stand before Zofie, her hands rigid at her sides. I think she wished she had brought the giant ledger.

She looked over to Fumiko. "I've decided."

Fumiko reached for the necklace, but Zofie touched her shoulder making her pause.

"I appreciate what you told us earlier. Your words had more impact than you realize. And have no doubt, I trust you. I consider you my friend."

Fumiko nodded. "Thank you." And with that, she took off the necklace. I felt the slight tingle of power as Fumiko activated her myst. "You should be able to deliver your message now."

Zofie then spoke. "Imperial Advisor Tusita Yonge, I hope you're listening. I have reached a decision concerning your offer of supplies in exchange for the Griffin's Key. While we greatly appreciate the emperor's generosity, we feel this is not the time to begin a search for the artifact. Please give my regards to the emperor and let him know we wish to have good relations with the empire. After things settle down, we may be in a position to look for it."

Zofie looked at Fumiko. "How will we know he received the message?"

Fumiko shook her head. "I'm not sure. I..." Then her face screwed up in pain. She hiked up her dress to examine her thigh. It was the same one that received the message from the previous night. Fumiko looked up at us wincing in pain. "It's burning." As we watched, a new series of characters formed on her skin.

As they had previously, the characters only stayed on her skin briefly before fading.

Fumiko sighed. "I think your message was received. Loosely translated, it says the offer stands."

Zofie nodded. "As I expected. I'll continue to think about this. When the time is right, we might even be able to search for it."

Zofie then turned her attention on me. "And for us... I need to change my clothes. We have a ceremony to attend."

Fumiko replaced her necklace and left for the library. No doubt to see if she could assist Spraggel.

As soon as the door closed, Zofie stepped closer and wrapped her arms around me in a fierce hug. I returned it, and we stood for a bit in the middle of the room.

"Do you think I made the right decision?" she asked. "I may have committed the kingdom to starvation."

I considered a moment before answering. "That may be true, but I don't think so. You'll figure out something. I do not doubt my princess."

I released her. "Now, hurry up and change your clothes. You've been looking forward to this since you started planning it. I'm sure they're waiting on us by now."

She looked up. "You're right. I started this, so I shouldn't be too late."

"I'll call your maid."

She shook her head. "No need. This is the dress I'm wearing."

"But you said…"

She put a finger over my lips. "That, my future husband, was an excuse to be alone with you. I… I have something I need to tell you. I was going to tell you at the picnic."

I looked into her eyes and smiled. "And what is that, my dear."

She opened her mouth, but a loud knock sounded at the door. She sighed and muttered, "I should have known." And then louder. "Enter."

Her chamberlain, Eallair, poked his head in. He scowled when he saw me but quickly turned his attention to Zofie.

"I'm sorry, your majesty, but the guests are waiting. I'm not sure I can put them off much longer. They've become a little rowdy."

Zofie nodded. "We're coming." She put her arm through mine and dragged me toward the door. "I'll have to tell you later."

I grinned at her. "All right, I'll be waiting."

The recent events had put a damper on what Zofie had planned for today, but I was glad she was mustering up some of her enthusiasm. We had a lunch to attend. It was the start of her first project in the kingdom, albeit a small one, but still important. And she hoped it would set the tone of her reign.

Myst users were needed for any kingdom to prosper, but Wynn had depleted ours. And we desperately needed myst users. With the state of things, recruiting them was going to be difficult, which left Zofie with no other option but to train them.

So Zofie was starting a school. Something she had been wanting to do for some time now. And I knew how important this was to her.

Zofie was smiling but looked a little worried as we made our way toward the dining hall. I had been around her enough to know she was composing her thoughts. She would have to address her guests. I had been afraid she would not be able to pull this off, especially with everything else that had been going on in the kingdom. But as I learned, Zofie was a master of organization and had made it happen.

She paused at the entrance where Eallair was waiting for her. The low murmur of friendly conversation drifted from inside the dining hall just beyond. The chamberlain frowned when he saw me, but then again, he *always* frowned at me.

"Is everyone here?" she asked him.

"We are missing one from Iron Landing, your highness," Eallair said. "She took ill at the last moment, but her town sent a substitute, one Cabrina Bryst. We haven't had a chance to test her yet, but she does have the gift."

Zofie nodded. "The response was better than I expected. How about the ones that showed up without an invitation?"

His mouth tightened in surprise. "How did you know? We had one show up at the gate begging to attend."

"And did you let Lashea in?"

The chamberlain paused in surprise, then nodded slowly. "We did, as you instructed. We told her she would have to meet the entrance requirements before being accepted. Also, we would have to contact her parents."

Zofie rolled her eyes in his direction. "Only you found she was an orphan."

Eallair's mouth tightened a little more. "That is correct." He glanced nervously at me. But I just shrugged. This was new to me too.

He looked back to Zofie. "How did you know?"

She smiled. "I didn't. But I was hoping she would come. I owe her."

I gave her a puzzled look.

Zofie put a hand on my shoulder. "I'll tell you about it later. It happened before I met you." She smiled. "We sort of helped each other."

Zofie turned back to her chamberlain. "Anything else?"

"No, your highness. Everything else is in order."

Zofie nodded. "You did well." She turned back toward the chamber. "Now, let us get started."

The chamberlain smiled, pleased at the compliment. "I will announce you."

Zofie paused him. "No, I think for this lot, I would rather you didn't."

He tried to stifle his disapproving frown and nodded. "As you wish."

Zofie took my arm and then took a deep breath—but she hesitated. She looked to me, concerned. "Is this really all right? The kingdom is in such a bad place now."

I patted her arm. "It will be fine. As we well know, you have to grow your seedlings *before* you need the crops. Otherwise, you won't have them when you're ready."

She gave me a nervous smile before standing a hair straighter and slipping on her princess face. I hoped I said something right for once.

So with Zofie on my arm, we stepped into the brightly lit room. The smell of spices and food made my mouth water. We had wanted to make this special despite the short supplies, so we had been saving up for this event. Getting a free meal was part of the deal for the school. That and two years of service to the crown after they completed training. It was a deal most families jumped at.

The conversation died as soon as we entered the room. You could have heard a pin drop. There was a single long table in the room with about twenty boys and girls, all in their early to mid-teen years. These were the first ones attending Zofie's new school for myst users. Several adults sat with them, including Captain Milner and Master Rourke. Spraggel was strangely absent, and I couldn't help but wonder what he was up to.

Zofie took her place at the head of the table. I sat while she remained standing behind her chair.

"Thank you all for coming to our new school." She scanned the audience. All the faces were turned expectantly toward her.

About midway down the table, I spotted Maggie de'Glougeman—

the daughter of Mikney, the innkeeper of the Inland Sea. Zofie had spotted Maggie's budding abilities during a stay at the inn, and had been determined to have her as a student. However, Mikney was extremely protective of his daughter and at first refused. Had it not been for us being Maggie's rescuers from a potential kidnapping, the princess likely would not have been able to convince him.

Zofie continued her speech, "While we can only handle a few now, it is my sincere desire that we grow in numbers until we have to move out of the castle. I am hopeful you will learn enough to master the abilities in myst each of you have. Maybe even some of you will become teachers yourselves to help spread what you learn. You are our future seedlings. Please do everything you can to grow!"

Everyone, even the old chamberlain, applauded. She turned to give me a smug smile. She just used my words in her speech! Zofie turned a broad smile and looked at her audience. "Now everyone, eat up!"

Immediately, the servers came out and began laying out the plates of bread and bowls of vegetable stew. The girls and boys both tore into their meals. It was meager fare, but likely better than most of them had been able to get recently.

Maggie glanced in my direction, and even though she was a little ways away, I could tell she blushed. She quickly leaned over and said something to the girl sitting next to her. The girl glanced in my direction and also blushed. The two exchanged more whispers.

Coren! came Abe's booming voice inside my head. I winced.

Zofie glanced in my direction, picking up on Abe's interruption.

I hid my mouth behind my hand. "What is it, Abe? I'm a little busy at the moment."

Busy stuffing your gut and ogling the girls. If I didn't think it important, I wouldn't dream of interrupting your consumption of dead matter and looking for your next opportunity to procreate.

Zofie frowned. I don't think she appreciated Abe's remark about the girls.

At first, she had been excited about being able to talk with the ancient curse, but lately she'd been feeling a little differently. I think she was almost ready to have me remove the ability. Abe also knew Zofie was listening in and did everything in his power to get me in trouble.

Like I needed his help.

I leaned closer to her. "I was not looking at the girls that way. Why would I look at girls when I have a beautiful young woman next to me."

Because you're greedy, that's why.

I rolled my eyes. "What did you want Abe?"

I briefly smelled a curse nearby. A complex one.

"Can you show me?"

Of course.

My vision changed, and I saw the now-familiar strands of light stretching across the room. With so many myst users close by, the complexity of the glowing threads was overpowering.

On Zofie, I could see her familiar network of blue lines and the bright glow of her curse mark. And likewise, on some of the students' chests, I saw a brighter spot which had to be their own small curses, likely to protect against a more deadly one.

"I can see that a few of the students are cursed. Is that what you smelled?"

No, this was stronger—a much more complex curse.

"You mean like a Dark Avenyts trying to hide itself?"

Could be. But it could also be a curse one of these children have and are embarrassed that their friends might find out about it, so they had it concealed.

I glanced at Zofie, and she gave me a concerned look in return.

But I couldn't pick up the direction or distance. It may have even been outside.

Zofie leaned back and motioned to Eallair. When the chamberlain came over, she whispered in his ear, and he nodded once. He briskly stepped away. No doubt, Zofie wanted to alert our guards.

"Let me know if you smell it again."

Oh, I shall. Your curse bloodhound will bay loudly.

"That was not funny."

I didn't mean it to be. But someone has to be paying attention. Unlike you, I won't be checking out the girls.

"Will you stop that!" I said a little louder than I intended. Several of the students gave me a funny look. Something like, "oh, look at the crazy man talking to himself."

Embarrassed, I looked down at my unfinished meal. The thought of a Dark Avenyts in the room dampened my appetite. And I had so wanted to enjoy my food.

With the hungry students, it didn't take long for them to empty their bowls. And when they were done, Zofie stood. "Now that everyone is finished, let me introduce you to your teachers. Your first lesson will start this afternoon with Mistress Delwynwill." Zofie indicated a dark-haired woman on her right who looked like she could be the mother of any of the students. She gave a quick nod of her head and smiled. I had talked to her briefly, and she seemed to have solid experience teaching literature and mathematics, but more importantly, myst fundamentals. I had thought I might even sit in on some of her lessons since I now had to understand how Abe worked.

Zofie continued. "And to help balance out your training, tomorrow morning Captain Milner will begin showing you the basics of self-defense. All myst users should know how to defend themselves." The man gave a brief nod to the students but did not crack a smile.

This was my contribution to the planning. He very reluctantly took on the role, but I think he was actually excited about it.

Zofie smiled. "You will also receive instruction from others as the need arises. Now, are there any questions?"

A young man sitting toward the back raised his hand. "Your highness, will you be one of our teachers? I've heard you are a very powerful myst user." You could hear the hope in his voice.

If you didn't know Zofie, you wouldn't have noticed any change in her expression, but I did. The question pained her. She hated that she wasn't going to be able to participate. She *wanted* to teach them. But she couldn't for two reasons: her duties as monarch didn't allow her the time, and the other, she couldn't use her myst now. The curse from her brother was still active, and while it originally changed her into a chimera that was slowly dying, thanks to my intervention, it was now gradually turning her back to fully human. Not to mention, since Abe had taken control of it, the Dark Avenyts couldn't touch her.

Zofie shook her head. "I may appear in your lessons occasionally, but I will not be one of your teachers." She paused. "Are there any others?"

A young woman who looked older than most of the others raised her hand. "Will the Cursed Knight be teaching us?"

I groaned. There was that name again. I really wanted to put a bad curse on the minstrel that wrote that ballad.

Zofie glanced my way and smiled. "Sorry, but no. I need my knight close to me. He may also appear occasionally, but not as one of your regular teachers."

Another hand shot up. "Will we really get a meal every day?"

Zofie nodded. "Yes, in fact, you'll get three a day. It will not be as nice as today's, but you will not go hungry."

There were a few more questions in that vein, and she dutifully answered each one until they went silent. Sensing she had satisfied them, Zofie raised her head just a little straighter. "I must go now. Once again, welcome to our little school. Make us all proud. You are dismissed."

There was a moment of silence, and then the students began to move. Some clustered around the teachers, while others started to make their way out.

I stood and leaned close to Zofie. "You did wonderful."

She turned to me. "I hope so."

"Ah, your highness? Coren?" said a new voice. Zofie and I turned to see Maggie approaching us. She had a wide smile and was blushing furiously.

It had only been a couple of months since we last saw her, but she must have had a growth spurt. She was nearly as tall as Zofie now. With her hair pulled into a tight braid, and wearing what appeared to be a new dress, she looked much more mature than the young serving girl that had spilled a cup of ale in my lap on my first visit to the inn.

And with her stood another girl about her age. I did not recognize her, but she appeared to be one of Maggie's friends. Like Maggie, her brown hair was pulled back in a single braid, although of a more complex braiding. She wore a dress of simple design, which seemed just a tad large for her. It gave her a younger appearance than her friend. She held her clasped hands in front of her but didn't seem to share Maggie's nervousness.

"Hello, Maggie." Zofie smiled.

Maggie bowed her head. "Princess, I had no idea you were who you were when you stayed at our inn. Creator," she rolled her eyes. "I can't believe you slept in my bed, and I told you all those things."

Zofie reached forward and pulled her into a gentle hug. "And I enjoyed every minute of it. Our midnight chat was most enlightening." And they both giggled. I was going to have to ask Zofie about that one.

Zofie looked over Maggie's shoulder at the other girl standing there. "And who is your friend?"

Maggie turned to introduce her. "This is Cabrina Bryst, the youngest and only daughter of the Bryst family. One of the other students couldn't come, so Cabrina took her place."

I nodded. So this was the one Eallair had mentioned earlier.

Cabrina blushed and gave a formal curtsey. "It is an honor to meet you, Princess Zophia." She turned to me and gave me another curtsey. "And you too, Sir Coren Hart."

I returned her greeting with a bow. "We are well met, Mistress Cabrina." She grinned.

Maggie cleared her throat. "Coren..." She paused a moment. "I guess I should start calling you Sir Hart."

Zofie laid a gentle hand on Maggie's arm. "You can call him whatever you want." She rolled her eyes in my direction. "For myself, I call him different names depending on what trouble he's gotten himself into." They exchanged a quick laugh and a knowing look. Something was going on between these two.

"Why don't we compromise," I offered. "Just call me Sir Coren."

Maggie nodded, then stood a little straighter. "Princess Zofie. Sir Coren. I have not properly thanked you for saving me from the slavers.

I had nearly given up hope when the two of you showed up." Maggie looked to Zofie, complete admiration on her face. "And the way you transformed into that griffin... it was so majestic."

Cabrina leaned toward Maggie and gave her a gentle nudge with her shoulder.

Maggie's eyes went up. "Oh, yes." She reached into a pocket in her dress and pulled out two small boxes, each tied with a neat bow: one pink, one blue. She presented them to us on her palms. "Please accept these small tokens of appreciation. I made them myself, so they are not much, but I hope they will please you just a little."

Zofie smiled warmly. "Maggie, you shouldn't have." Zofie reached for hers. "May I open it now."

Maggie blushed. "If you're not too embarrassed."

Zofie shook her head. "For my friends, never."

I hesitated in reaching for mine. It wasn't that I didn't appreciate the gift. I was just unsure of protocol. I had never received a gift like this before. I hesitantly reached for it. "Is it all right? I've caused your father a lot of trouble over the years."

Maggie smiled. "Please. This is from me. Not Father. And don't worry about him. He still hates you."

"Well then," I took the small box and opened it.

Zofie and I both saw the contents at the same time. She gasped and pulled out a tightly woven bracelet in shades of pink. It was braided with a beautiful pattern and had a highly polished wooden heart affixed in the middle. I was impressed. It had been done meticulously. Maggie must have worked hard to make it.

For mine, it was of similar design, but was a dark blue, and instead of a heart, had a small white river stone which the color set off nicely. "Thank you. This is a splendid gift."

Zofie nodded. "Indeed it is." She held out her wrist to Maggie. "Would you do me the honors? I've heard that if a friend ties it on for you, you will be friends forever."

Maggie blushed again. She took the bracelet and began to tie it around Zofie's left wrist. "I made Cabrina and myself one too." Cabrina smiled and held hers up for us to see. Maggie continued, "But I have somehow misplaced mine. I'm sure it will turn up."

Cabrina stepped forward. "Would you like me to tie yours on, Sir Coren?"

Maggie looked up from her work. "Cabrina helped me with them, so it's all right."

I nodded and Cabrina stepped forward. She took the bracelet and pulled out my arm, stepping closer than I would normally have been comfortable with.

She glanced up at me as she began to tie it on. She smiled sweetly. "I guess this means we'll be friends for the rest of our lives."

Something about the way she said it struck me as odd. A feeling of wrongness began to tug at the corner of my mind.

Coren! I can sense the presence of that complex curse again.

"Where is it?" I looked up, scanning the room.

It's... right in front of you. The girl! She is cursed with one of the Dark Avenyts!

She turned her face up to me and smiled. Only it wasn't the innocent smile of a young girl. It was the smug look of someone having just gotten exactly what they wanted.

I jerked my arm back, but it was too late. The bracelet had already been tied. I glanced at Zofie and hers was also in place.

Cabrina held up her own bracelet-covered wrist and touched it with two fingers from her other hand. I felt myst begin to build. A lot of myst. This was not some simple spell, but a very sophisticated charm.

I yelled to the guards, but it was already too late. All three bracelets started to glow a bright pink, which swiftly transitioned to a deep red.

Cabrina gave me one last look as her smile began to fade, a look of sad resignation on her face. I felt my own perception begin to fade, and suddenly my world went black.

And out of that darkness, I heard a voice. Deep and seeming to resonate inside me yet coming from far away. It was Abhulengulus, but he spoke strangely. *It's not yet your time, little one,* he said. *You are everything I hoped for.*

The darkness suddenly broke, and I watched as Cabrina collapsed in front of me. Maggie gazed at us in horror. She bent over her friend.

Coren! Abe screamed in my head. *Something's wrong. The charms! They...*

Then a longer pause before he said something much weaker.

Help....

And then he was silent.

I looked to Zofie. "Something's wrong with Abe!"

But I did not receive an answer. My eyes went wide in horror as I saw Zofie's face—it was completely expressionless. Her arms hung limp at her sides.

"Zofie!" I called. I gently turned her face toward me.

Her beautiful blue eyes swept in my direction, but they did not see me. They held no recognition.

It was like no one was home.

CHAPTER FIVE

Forced Hand

I stepped up to the bars of the holding cell and considered its single occupant. Cabrina sat on a stool in the center of the room and smiled back at me innocently. She looked down and smoothed a wrinkle on her dress.

I watched her silently. I was unsure of how to approach an interrogation. She acted just like a young girl. Yet I knew from experience, she was much more. I wanted to be angry at her but punishing the body would do nothing to the other intelligence inside her. It was like beating up the coat of a thief. The garment had no choice in the matter and couldn't help that it had been worn while a crime had been committed.

Fumiko would be joining me in a moment. She was overseeing Zofie's examination by the healer and Master Rourke. She had pushed me out of the room, saying I needed to quit walking around in a daze and find out what had happened. She was right, of course. I was having trouble dealing with this.

When the charm had activated, all of Zofie's bright intelligence had been yanked from her. She would walk if pulled forward, sit if placed next to a chair, eat if food was pushed in her mouth. But nothing more.

Unfortunately, Zofie wasn't the only casualty. Abhulengulus wouldn't answer. I had called his name several times, but he had been deadly silent since his plea for help. The charm had to be interfering with him too. Rourke had examined me after looking at Zofie. He said my curse was still there, and even looked to be operating on some level. But he couldn't tell me if Abe was truly broken or was just being suppressed. He did admit that combining curses and charms could have unexpected effects. While both used myst and could do similar things, they operated quite differently. I began to suspect that maybe the charm had actually been intended for me, but because of that strange charm to curse interference, Abe bore the entire cost.

Funny, I had wanted to be rid of Abe since I first got him, but over the last couple of months, we had come to an understanding. Now that he was broken, I had to say I missed him.

I shook my head and tried to focus on the problem in front of me. We had to figure this out.

Cabrina loosened her braid and began to redo it. She seemed utterly unconcerned that she sat in a dungeon cell and had just harmed the kingdom's ruling monarch.

A moment later, Fumiko strode into the dungeon with a guard and Master Rourke in her wake.

"How is she?" I asked. Fumiko glanced briefly at our captive before turning her gaze back to me. Her expression was unreadable. "The same."

I looked to Rourke. He shrugged. "The charm somehow interferes with mental processing. Her mind appears to still be there, after a fashion. But it's like she has been separated from her body."

I frowned. "It's got to be the bracelet. Can we remove it?"

Rourke cleared his throat. "I'm not sure that taking it off is a good idea. At least until we can learn more about how it operates. I hate to admit it, but it's a very complex charm, far beyond my abilities. I might study it for years and not fully understand it." He pointed to my wrist.

"Oh, and one other thing. It's also connected to yours, and I believe, one other charm."

"A third?" I turned toward Cabrina, who was watching us with interest. "Your bracelet is the third one, isn't it?" I asked her.

Cabrina smiled at me but said nothing. She finished her braid and sat up straight, once more smoothing out her skirt. The youth finally pulled up her dress's sleeve to show us the bracelet she had displayed earlier. "I told you already," she said. "Take the bracelets off, and our bodies die. *All* three of us."

"You too?"

She nodded.

I looked to Rourke for confirmation, but he just shrugged. "I can't say whether she's right or not. The princess may have been able to tell, but I have no idea."

I shook my head and glared at Cabrina. "Why? Why did you do it?"

She didn't answer.

I frowned and turned to Fumiko. "Were you able to find out anything?"

Fumiko snorted. "Spraggel has been a whirlwind of investigation. I think he's called in every favor anyone has ever owed him. According to what he's found so far, Cabrina is exactly as she appears—a girl with myst abilities attending school. Her parents are extremely loyal and noticed nothing unusual about her behavior. Same story from her friends. Nothing extraordinary, except for the substitution. The day before the girl originally chosen was to leave, she took ill and nearly died. It left her too weak to come." Fumiko took a deep breath and let it out slowly. "She was diagnosed with food poisoning. Not surprising since our supplies are in such bad shape. But it could have easily hid a different type of poison." Fumiko turned her gaze on our captive. It was cold as ice. "Couldn't it, Cabrina?"

Cabrina just smiled and shrugged.

I sighed. "What about Maggie?"

Fumiko frowned. "We've confined her to her room. She is very distraught over what happened and has cooperated with us as best she

can. More importantly, she is not possessed by a Dark Avenyts."
Fumiko shook her head sadly. "No, it appears she was simply used to
get close to you and the princess."

"Maggie had nothing to do with this," Cabrina interjected. "I'm the
one that put the charms on the bracelets." She sat up straighter and
leaned forward on her stool, showing the first concern I had seen in
her. "It was all me. I'm the guilty one."

I grasped the bars of her cell and leaned against them. "You realize
Maggie is technically an accomplice. She made the bracelets and carried them inside the castle. That's enough to execute her right there."

Cabrina sat back in thought. After a moment, a slow smile came to
her face. "If you want me to answer your questions, you will release her
and bring no charges. She was my tool. Nothing more. She worships
both you and the princess, so there is no way she would knowingly
cause you harm."

"I'm not sure the magistrate will go along with that."

"You're the Cursed Knight. They will listen to you. It is the only way
you'll get your questions answered."

"How do I know you'll keep your word."

She shrugged. "I will keep my word, as you will keep yours."

"Are you sure?"

She smiled. "You're the Cursed Knight. Maggie has told me enough
about you that I have a good idea of your character."

I sighed. "All right. I'll speak with the magistrate to dismiss the
charges."

Cabrina sat forward. "*And* she stays at the school. She wants to
attend very badly."

I nodded. "And she stays in school."

The youth smiled. "Now what would you like to know?"

I thought for a moment. "Why did you do it?"

She shrugged. "I assume it was to make it easier for my kind to take
over this world, but other than that, I'm not sure. I was just given the
bracelets and instructed on what to do. I am of low *cothe,* so they did
not tell me what this was for."

"*Cothe?*" I asked. "What is that?"

Fumiko answered for her. "There's no word for it in Ellish. It's a combination of caste and rank. She's basically saying she's young, low-born, and a common foot soldier."

I glanced in Fumiko's direction, but her face was expressionless. Fumiko had been possessed by one of their kind for a few months. She never spoke of the experience, but we knew it bothered her greatly. Not only had it taken control of her body, but it had also riffled through the knowledge in her brain as one would the books in an archive. But I hadn't considered that knowledge may have also flowed the other way.

Cabrina smiled at Fumiko. "You must be the one whose *exemplar* was murdered. I bet you feel naked now with no one to whisper to you."

Fumiko glared at her but did not answer.

I looked back to Cabrina. I had to ask the obvious question. "Why didn't you just kill us instead of incapacitating us? Risten just the other day seemed pretty intent on it."

She shrugged. "I'm not sure, but it does seem strange even to me. Killing would have been more efficient."

I considered Cabrina for a moment. "And why didn't you just switch to a new host after giving us the charms. You could have gotten away and left the girl behind."

Cabrina nodded. "Moving from one body to another is fairly quick, but not instantaneous. Besides, I ran out of myst when I activated the charms. They were very myst intensive. And when my kind doesn't have enough, we lose consciousness."

"Where are the others? Who helped you?"

She shrugged. "Last I saw them, they were headed into the woods close to this girl's house. She was standing outside, hanging out laundry for her mother when they approached her. They simply used a silence charm and then I *perfected* her." She leaned closer. "It's amazing what you can do between the sheets, even if they're hanging up." She chuckled.

"What are their names?"

"They never told me. It was a man and a woman. Their bodies were just a few years older than this one, but their *exemplars* seemed very experienced."

"How about Wynn or Risten's location?"

She shrugged. "No idea. I know of no Wynn other than the one that was the previous king, and I had not heard of Risten until you mentioned her."

"You might know of her as Lilith."

Cabrina frowned. "That name, I know. I was told to stay clear of her. No reason was given."

"And your base of operations?"

"Don't know. I came straight from the cross-world portal."

Fumiko fixed her gaze at the girl. "This is getting us nowhere. Perhaps we should torture her a little. It might loosen her tongue."

"We can't take a chance on it hurting Zofie." I rubbed my face. The day wasn't that old, but I was already feeling exhausted. "All right. What do you want from us to remove these charms?"

Cabrina gave a quick shrug. "I wasn't told to bargain. Besides, I don't have a way to remove them. I was only told how to get them started."

I stared at her in frustration and ran a hand through my hair. She was just being so casual about this. "Aren't you at least afraid of dying? The other lords could decide it's too risky to keep you around and kill you even if it meant it killed us too."

She shrugged. "I'm not really afraid. I've had the chance to *perfect* a body far better than I could ever expect and in a land where everything is clean and beautiful." She spread her arms to indicate the cell around her. "Even being in this dark, dingy place is better than my starting point. I would go content." She lowered her arms and shook her head. "Although I would be sad that the girl would also die. She is a nice person."

I thought for a moment. First, she was concerned about Maggie, and now about the body she possessed. This was totally unlike the others I had encountered. To them, we were nothing more than articles of clothing to be worn and discarded at their whim. But this one didn't seem that way.

I had a sudden thought. "What is your name?" I asked.

"Cabrina."

I shook my head. "Not your host's name. Your name."

To my surprise, she blushed and looked down. "I... I don't have a name. I am of low *cothe*. We aren't given names because we usually don't survive that long."

I blinked at her as what she said sunk in. She was disposable. I almost felt sorry for her. They never intended for her to survive, which meant she would not tell us anything useful. I didn't think she was lying. She just didn't know anything to tell.

Sighing, I turned to Fumiko. "We're done here."

She nodded and we turned to leave, with Rourke following behind.

"What are we going to do now?" Fumiko asked.

I shook my head. "I'm not sure. But praying for a miracle is high on my list."

I slowed as we entered the wing of the castle leading to Zofie's quarters. As it does this time of year, evening had come quickly, and the corridor ahead was lit only with only a few myst lanterns. The dim light reflected my own dark mood.

I drew to a halt at the turn leading to Zofie's room. "Why don't you two go ahead," I said. "I need a moment to think."

Fumiko nodded sadly. She gave my shoulder a reassuring pat before turning down the hall. Master Rourke glanced my way, looking grim, and followed behind her. As I watched, the pair paused in front of the door—a guard on either side of it—knocked and then were admitted.

A big sigh escaped me as I leaned against the cold stone wall, a complete sense of loss coming over me. *What was I going to do?*

I rubbed my face. The simplest solution would be to cut the bracelets off and have Rourke and a healer standing by to treat us. But that was risky. There was no guarantee that they could treat us in time, and one or more of us could die.

Why had they done it? Was it to stop us from rebuilding the kingdom? Or perhaps it was because they were afraid of us stopping their invasion. But incapacitating Zofie and my curse seemed such an odd move. I couldn't help but think this had somehow been botched. That the effects we were seeing were not what had been intended.

I looked down the darkened corridor. *What were we going to do without her?* Zofie was a genius of organization and leadership. Under her, the kingdom had started to rebuild. The people had begun to have hope. When word got out their ruler was unable to lead them—what would they do? And Zofie had no heirs, which could send the kingdom into chaos as the lords fought for control.

There was really only one answer. Get these bracelets off us.

And soon.

I gave another sigh and pushed myself off the wall. I couldn't put this off any longer. I walked up to Zofie's door, nodded to the guards, and knocked. Permission to enter made my heart jump into my throat.

Opening the door, I found Zofie sitting in her favorite chair with Fumiko standing beside her. The princess sat perfectly straight, staring off into the distance, with her hands neatly folded in her lap. I couldn't count the times I had seen this familiar scene. She even still wore the dress from our earlier lunch. But she did not turn as I entered. There was no smiling welcome, no asking how I was, no reaching of her hand to take mine. Not the slightest hint of recognition. It tore my heart apart.

Fumiko was talking to her quietly, reporting to her everything we had learned. At first this seemed odd, but then as I thought about it, it made perfect sense. We didn't know if Zofie's mind had been removed or if it was being suppressed. She could be listening to us and just not able to respond. Giving her updates would surely provide some comfort to her.

Spraggel was already in the room, sitting in another chair by the fire. He looked grim. Rourke stood by the window with his back to us, rocking nervously back and forth on the balls of his feet.

When Fumiko had finished her report, I knelt beside Zofie's chair and took her hand. I kissed it gently. "I'm sorry, Zofie. It doesn't look like this will be fixed quickly. I don't have much to add. Our captive is not going to tell us anything useful." I sighed. "I think our best option is to search for someone that can safely remove the charm."

I bowed my head over her hand. "If Abe still worked, I could modify your curse. We might be able to hit on something that would work around the charm. Or better yet, be able to see how to remove it." While I fought so hard not to, I felt a tear come to my eyes. "I've failed you," I said softly.

Fumiko put a hand on my shoulder.

Unexpectedly, a strange voice interjected: "Forgive me, may I have an audience?" The accent was familiar.

I immediately leaped to my feet and reached for my sword. Master Rourke gathered his myst, and Fumiko whirled to face the new-comer—only no one was there.

"Down here," said the voice.

I looked closely and then finally spotted it: A lone, earth-colored cricket sitting on the carpet. And I also recognized the voice. It was Imperial Advisor Tusita Yonge. Which meant he was using a cricket for his avatar this time.

Fumiko moved between us and the insect. "Leave!" she shouted. "The princess gave you your answer." She moved to squash it.

"I can remove the charms," it said calmly. Fumiko's descending foot froze in mid-air.

I grasped Fumiko's arm. She looked up at me, conflict clearly on her face. But at a gentle shake of my head, she reluctantly stepped back.

I put away my sword. "How did you find out? Fumiko is no longer your eyes and ears."

The antenna on the cricket moved excitedly, and it hopped forward. "Although the view of the toilet is quite striking, surely you don't be-lieve the great Kuiojia Empire has only one set of eyes and ears at its disposal."

The insect paused while we considered each other. I finally spoke. "Aside from the issue of spies, how can you help Zofie?"

"Charms are my specialty. There is no one in the empire, maybe even the entire world, that is better. I felt it my duty to offer my assistance. At the least, it might offer a challenge to analyze a charm created by the Dark Avenyts. But from what I've heard so far, it is a simple mind capture charm with a death removal sequence. It should be simple to take off... if you know how."

"Are you sure?" Rourke asked. "These are very complex charms. Plus, the removal sequence has a lot of protections built-in. If not removed exactly the right way, it will kill them."

"Ah, you must be Master Rourke. It is a pleasure to meet you. While I cannot confirm or deny what you say, I can assure you. I am quite the expert in charms. This avatar before you is proof."

I looked to Zofie who sat passively in her chair. *What question would she ask? What would she instinctively know to do?* I turned back to the cricket. "And what would be the price of your assistance?"

He didn't hesitate. "In compensation, we would like to borrow the Griffin's Key. And you would need to bring the princess and the bearer of the other charm so I can examine them and determine the best path of removal."

Spraggel leaned forward. "Since you want this key so badly, why don't you come and retrieve it?"

"Alas, such is not possible. I am unable to leave the palace. My physical condition does not allow it. Not to mention, I have to be close to my emperor at all times. Ask Fumiko. She can explain."

I glanced to her for confirmation. She looked away and nodded.

I put a finger to my lips. "So, you want us to travel to the empire. Can you have..."

But I trailed off as Spraggel began to shake his head emphatically. Fumiko jumped to my side and pulled me urgently toward the window. She leaned in to whisper in my ear. "*Don't* ask him to open a portal for us," she breathed. "It's not only a breach of protocol, but it's dangerous. You could be transported directly into his dungeon, or even the bottom of the sea. Besides, it makes us look weak. We have to provide our own way to at least the empire's borders. We have no choice."

Despite my puzzlement, I gave her a quick nod. I wanted to ask her how we would get there with all our myst users gone, but I'd leave that for later.

Spraggel and Rourke stepped over to join us. We huddled close.

I looked at each of them. "I say we take a visit to the empire and give the key to Yonge. Anyone disagree?"

Rourke shook his head.

Spraggel looked thoughtful but also shook his head.

Fumiko frowned and crossed her arms. "I do not like this. It has the smell of a trap."

I glanced toward where the cricket sat. "It does. But what choice do we have?" I nodded toward Zofie sitting silently in her chair. "I can't turn down even the slightest chance of bringing her back."

Fumiko sighed, her shoulders dropping in acquiescence.

I went to stand before the cricket again. The others flanked me. "We will have to find the key first. This may take us a bit since we have no idea where it is."

The cricket gave a little hop. "For one of your abilities, I'm sure it will be a simple matter."

I was not so sure. Simple matters sometimes turned out to be quite complicated.

The cricket gave another little hop. "I hope you will excuse me. I must leave now. This avatar is at its limit. Use Fumiko to contact me once you have the key. I look forward to seeing something other than a messy toilet closet."

And with that, the cricket stopped moving.

"Is he gone?" I asked.

Rourke nodded. "The connection to the cricket is no longer there."

Fumiko turned toward us. "Be careful dealing with him. His offers always have a catch."

Spraggel nodded. "I agree. We do need to be careful. There is something about him that disturbs me."

I went and looked down at the deceased cricket. "Why does he pick insects for this?" I asked. "Especially ones out of season?"

Fumiko looked at us sadly. "Because he loves to torture bugs."

CHAPTER SIX

A Hidden Talent

I hovered in that strange place half-way to dreams. I was exhausted. But in spite of that, I had positioned a padded chair beside Zofie's bed and diligently taken my post within easy reach of her sleeping form.

While I had fought it, my eyelids had begun to drift and my body to relax. But my mind was active. And in my half-consciousness, I could hear a whispered conversation, only it was an improbable discussion between Zofie and Abhulengulus. But I couldn't make out the words.

Then suddenly, I heard Zofie's voice softly call me. *"Coren?"*

I struggled to answer.

"Coren?" she called again, a little louder.

I tried to get my mouth to move, to make a reply.

"Coren!"

I desperately wanted to answer her. The words of her name were on my lips—

Fumiko's hand came down on my shoulder, startling me. "You should get some rest," she said. She had come up to stand by my chair.

I blinked as the vestiges of the dream left me. *Had it been real?* I glanced at Zofie's sleeping form and was struck by a wave of sadness. It had almost been like she was talking to me.

I looked up at Fumiko. "You should take your own advice."

She shrugged and turned her gaze toward the slumbering princess. Fumiko's expression was hard to read. The room's only light came from a dimmed myst lantern across on her other side, and it cast her in a dark silhouette. "I'm used to long nights," she said. "Sleep and I are not friends. Haven't been for many years."

We both watched quietly as Zofie slept. The only sound was her soft breathing and the occasional crackle from the smoldering coals in the fireplace. The castle's silence was deep and pulled me further into the depths of loneliness and despair.

After our guest had left his avatar, Zofie's small staff had pulled together a rough plan on how to proceed. The first step was to begin making preparations to visit the Kuiojia Empire. We couldn't afford the attention, nor the cost to properly outfit a full escort, so we decided to travel incognito, fast and light. Captain Milner had volunteered to oversee the travel preparations. He said he would have everything ready to leave on a moment's notice.

The second step was to locate the Griffin's Key, and I prayed we could get to it quickly. Spraggel and Rourke were going to individually consult whatever sources they had to see if there was any hint of its location. Unfortunately, Spraggel didn't have much hope of this working.

Which meant our best bet of locating it was to use the most powerful finder in the kingdom—the Wayward's Finder. This happened to belong to Lord Dewi Merrick. Neither Merrick nor Zofie were on the best of terms. Mainly because he had been running brothels—recruiting his workers through questionable means and not entirely with their permission. If it hadn't been for his son Galvyn and the way we borrowed the finder, which involved breaking a lot of things and putting giant holes in his manor's wall, Lord Merrick might be in prison right now. That, plus he had quickly agreed to correct the error of his ways and compensate those involved. Zofie made sure that he did.

Which made answering the next question even more important. *How did we get him to let us borrow it?* That problem was assigned to Fumiko and me. And while we had discussed it, we had not come up with a solution.

I glanced up at Fumiko. She was deep in thought. Not for the first time, I wondered how much I could trust her. And if one of her secrets was going to bite us.

"Lord Merrick won't let us use the finder without Zofie's royal authority," she said. "He's as slippery as an eel. He'll come up with some kind of excuse unless Zofie goes to him and demands it directly."

I snorted. "I agree, but Zofie can't do that right now. And he of all people, can't let know about her condition."

Fumiko looked off into the distance, seemingly conflicted. But she took a deep breath, and her expression hardened as she came to some sort of decision.

She turned to face me. "I know of a way."

"How?"

She motioned me to stand and led me over to the fireplace. She glanced over to Zofie before turning her gaze on me. "You have to swear you won't tell anyone about this. No one. Not even Zofie."

I glanced in her direction. "But she's...."

Fumiko shook her head. "Don't worry about that for now. Can you keep this just between us?"

I rubbed my face. "That's a high price. Why can't we tell her? Zofie's a very accepting person, and I'm sure she would not be offended by anything you've done."

"True." Fumiko nodded. "Don't get me wrong. I love Zofie. She's been very kind to me. I'd give my life for her in a heartbeat, and I count her as my closest friend. But still..." She searched my face. "She's also a ruler. And sometimes, they have to do difficult things. Maybe even things they don't want to do." She looked down. "Some rulers might find my skills... useful."

I shook my head. "I don't think Zofie is like that."

She shook her head. "Neither do I." She looked to Zofie's sleeping form. "But I don't want to take the risk. You, on the other hand..." She looked back to me. "I know you would never force me to do something horrible."

I began to feel a little uncomfortable. She was obviously hiding some deep scars, and I didn't feel I deserved the level of trust she was giving me. But if she had a way to find the key—

"All right," I said. "I swear I won't reveal what you show me. That is unless it somehow becomes a threat to Zofie herself."

Fumiko nodded. "I can accept that."

"So, how can you get Lord Merrick to let us use the finder?"

Fumiko turned her back to me and took two steps away, before pausing and then looking over her shoulder. Only, it wasn't Fumiko anymore. Zofie was smiling coyly, looking back at me and wearing the same dress she had worn earlier in the day.

"What do you think, Coren?" the vision of Zofie asked, in her familiar inflection. She smiled with that same sweet smile my love always used.

My heart leaped into my throat. I glanced to the bed and saw the real Zofie laying on her back, covers pulled up to her chin, and her eyes closed.

"How...?"

Suddenly Fumiko was back to her normal self. She turned away. "I'm a myst user, nowhere near as strong as Zofie or Rourke, but I can craft illusions to conceal myself. One as detailed as that, I can't hold for long, maybe an hour at most, and a detection device can see through it."

"Still, that's pretty impressive. But why would you not want Zofie to know about this? It seems perfectly harmless."

She turned slowly to face me, her expression sad. "You are much too trusting." And suddenly Fumiko wasn't there anymore. My eyes darted around the room. "Where did you go?"

I heard Fumiko's voice from in front of me. "It's another type of illusion. This one of shadow."

I looked closer, trying to detect some sign she was still there. I stiffened as I felt a single finger poke me in the back.

"I can use it to conceal my movements," she said. "I can sneak up on someone quite easily."

Fumiko walked around in front of me, her hand trailing along my shoulder. "I can hold the shadow illusion for two or three hours, provided I can keep my focus. That's plenty long enough to sneak up on someone unawares." She looked down. "And the reason I wasn't worried about Zofie hearing us is that I've surrounded us with a circle of silence. Sound won't travel outside it. It easily covers voices..." and then she whispered. "Or a scream." She shivered.

I suddenly understood why she had been reluctant to tell Zofie. Fumiko's skills could easily be turned toward a dark purpose. "But why would you need to learn something like that?"

Fumiko didn't answer. She crossed her arms and took two steps away before turning back toward me. From her demeanor, I could tell I wasn't going to get an answer.

"So," she said. "I can pretend to be the princess for a short while. Hopefully, her presence will be enough to convince Lord Merrick. We'll just have to keep the visit short. I haven't practiced in a while, so the shorter, the better."

I smiled. "I don't think that will be a problem. He hates us. We'll be out before you know it."

Fumiko nodded. She stepped closer and rested a hand on my arm. "And please Coren, don't tell anyone. No one can know."

I tried to make light of it and gave a short bow. "Your secret is safe with me, Mistress Fumiko."

But instead of a smile, Fumiko looked at me sadly. She seemed to catch herself and quickly turned away. "You're much too trusting."

The carriage bounced hard and I was startled awake. I sat up, looking around and trying to get my bearings. Across from me, Fumiko sat with her eyes closed and her head leaning against the side. I shook my head. Even asleep, she still looked composed. I wondered how she did it.

I pulled the window shade aside and saw that we were close to Lord Merrick's manor. I nervously rubbed my palms on my knees. I sure hope this worked. If Merrick suspected anything, it would not only mean we wouldn't get to use the finder, but he would know something was wrong with Zofie.

I tried to rub the tiredness from my eyes. Neither Fumiko nor I had gotten much sleep. Zofie had slept quietly through the night, so we were quite startled when at dawn, she had opened her eyes and sat up. But to my disappointment, she took no further action. Zofie simply sat there in her nightdress until Fumiko directed her to take care of her morning business. Seeing her emotionless face in the dawn light did nothing to ease my heart.

And so mid-morning, leaving Zofie in the care of her trusted maid, Fumiko and I took the royal carriage to call on Lord Merrick. It was a couple of hours away, so both of us had used the opportunity to grab a few moments of rest.

I looked to the carriage's other occupant. Fumiko's revelation the night before was fresh in my mind. Not only could she use a sword on par with Risten, she could also use myst to craft illusions. Which meant someone had received a lot of training in their youth. Imperial Advisor Yonge had mentioned something about her being a daughter of the emperor, so maybe such training was normal for those of that rank. Maybe she had been groomed to be an officer in the empire's army. But why had she insisted I keep it a secret?

As I looked at her, I began to revise my opinion of how she acted. I had always considered her very shy. Around us, she was reserved and maybe a bit aloof. But now, as I thought back on it, I don't think that was right. She had acted *guarded*. Like she was afraid to let anyone get too close to her. She obviously had some deep scars. And I couldn't help but feel there was much more to Fumiko than I ever dreamed.

I glanced out the window again and saw we were nearing the manor. I reached across and touched Fumiko's knee. "We're almost there," I said.

Her eyes opened immediately, and she sat up completely alert. I wondered if maybe she had been pretending to sleep.

"Are you nervous?" I asked.

She shrugged. "A little. I have met him only twice. I'm concerned that he might ask me something that only Zofie would know. Or worse, he drags out our visit for longer than I can maintain the illusion."

I pointed to her usual dress. "Would it have helped to wear one of Zofie's outfits?"

The carriage began to slow.

Fumiko shook her head. "Surprisingly, no. Clothes that are close, but not exactly right, are much harder to cover. It's almost like reality wants to overrule the illusion, so my own clothes work best." She cocked her head to one side. "The only thing that would be better would be a blank slate."

"Blank slate?"

"Yes, without any clothes at all."

The carriage stopped, and I heard the driver talking to someone.

"You mean *naked*?" I asked, in near panic.

She leaned forward. "You wouldn't mind, would you? Escorting me through the manor, knowing I wore not a stitch under my illusion."

What? My mouth fell open.

She gave me one of her rare half-smiles. "Don't worry. I chose not to do that because it's too damn cold."

The carriage door swung open, and suddenly the vision of Zofie sat across from me, finely dressed in one of her travel dresses. But her eyes had a twinkle I wasn't sure was Zofie's or Fumiko's. "Besides," she said in Zofie's voice. "I knew you couldn't handle it."

I blinked at her in surprise, frozen to the spot.

She smiled back innocently, then waved her hand toward the door, indicating we should get out.

I opened my mouth to say something, but in my embarrassment, words abandoned me. I finally shook my head and exited. I held out my hand to help her down.

Still smiling, she accepted my hand and gracefully stepped onto the cobblestone pavement. She appeared to be Zofie in every respect.

We had sent a message earlier that morning, so the doorman was expecting us. We were shown to Lord Merrick's study and asked to wait while he finished up some other business. He would join us shortly.

As the servant closed the door to the study, I couldn't help but notice that the room had no chairs. There should have been at least one by the desk, but it was mysteriously missing. It was also interesting that we were not offered any refreshments. I couldn't help but smile. No doubt, he just wanted to subtly remind us that this was his territory, and we were not exactly welcome. I also did not doubt someone was listening, hoping to catch some unguarded moment between us. Maybe even some juicy gossip he could turn to his advantage. I shook my head. The nobility and their power games. I never would understand them.

I expected we would have to wait a while, so I was surprised when there was a knock at the study door. Lady Nadine Merrick, Lord Merrick's wife, breezed in.

She was a slender woman, a tad taller than me, and appeared to be in her early mid-years. Her shoulder-length hair was blonde with streaks of white highlights. Today, she wore it with a band of delicate pearls holding it back from her face. And she was dressed in an elegant, but functional white blouse and black skirt.

I owed her. When Galvyn and I had 'borrowed' the finder, she hid us from Lord Merrick's men and helped us make our escape.

She smiled and gave us a bow from the door. "Good morning, your highness and Sir Coren. I hope you don't mind me joining you for a moment." She quietly closed the study door.

"Not at all, Lady Merrick," I said with a slight bow. "I trust you are well."

She chuckled. "The best I've been in years. My little hobby of collecting fine wines over the years is finally starting to pay off. Since my husband's business ventures have recently turned into a liability, I'm able to provide for us while we rebuild. After all these years, my husband is finally starting to realize I have a brain."

I smiled. "That is most excellent to hear."

Lady Merrick stood straighter. She went to the disguised Fumiko and grasped both her hands. "Your highness, I wanted to congratulate you on your engagement." She glanced at me and smiled. "I think you've chosen a fine young man."

"Thank you," said the vision of Zofie.

Nadine stepped back and clasped her hands in front of her. "I do hope you will invite me to the wedding. I know my husband has made it difficult for us to be high on the guest list, but I, for one, would love to attend."

The vision of Zofie hesitated. I could tell Fumiko was unsure how to respond.

But Nadine shook her head and held up a hand. "There is no need to answer now. I realize you are months away from making your list, and you must choose carefully who you invite. But if not my husband, please do consider me. I would so love to see you and your attendants walk to meet your groom." She smiled. "I bet you're going to choose that bodyguard of yours as your first. What is her name? Risten, isn't it?"

I tried not to show any reaction. Risten had been born a bastard child of the king's brother, Bernard Xernow, and she had never known her birth mother. The woman's identity was a mystery. However, when Lady Merrick had hidden Galvyn and me, I had put the pieces together and figured out Nadine was Risten's mother, and that over the years, she had been watching Risten from afar. It was yet another secret that I carried. I wondered if I would break under their burden.

Zofie's illusion gave a chuckle. "Risten is indeed the one I was hoping to pick. But I'm not sure she could tolerate being in a dress for that long."

Nadine smiled. "That indeed could be a problem." She paused. "I had heard she was away. I hope everything is all right with her. You need your bodyguard back." She looked over at me. "Nothing against your knight, of course."

Zofie's illusion smiled. "While he's nowhere near as good as Risten, I still plan to keep him."

Then Nadine suddenly grew serious. "And please be careful, your highness. I heard there was an assassination attempt on you. So don't wait too long to bring your bodyguard back soon. You must be protected."

Zofie gave a nod. "I will indeed be careful. Plus, I have my trusted knight, which I plan to keep constantly by my side."

Nadine turned to me. "And you too Coren, please be careful." She surprised me by pulling me into a motherly hug. "And don't forget your promise." With that, she disengaged and stepped toward the door.

"While I would love to chat longer, my husband will be perturbed with me if he finds me distracting his guests too much, so I must leave."

And with that, she slipped out of the room.

Fumiko and I looked at each other. That had been strange.

But we didn't have time to ponder it as Lord Merrick himself strode into the room. He gave a perfunctory bow to Zofie and completely ignored me. "Apologies for keeping you waiting, your highness. Business has been challenging lately, as I'm trying some new ventures. Now, what can I do for you today?"

The disguised Fumiko spoke. Her voice the perfect commanding tone Zofie used when dealing with troublesome subjects. "I would like to use the Wayward's Finder. There is an ancient artifact I need to locate."

Merrick considered her for a moment. "I'm assuming you're aware of the fee for using the finder. It has been customary for generations. Your father knew, but I wasn't sure if he passed down that information."

I tried not to show any emotion. Zofie had been holding tightly to our remaining gold since we were so short.

The disguised Fumiko didn't say anything at first, merely stared at him. "How is your export business coming?" she asked softly. "I had heard a rumor that a person was found inside one of your company's shipping crates. I assured that person it must to be a mistake. That Lord Merrick had surely learned his lesson on dealing in humans."

The tension in the room shot up. As the two stared at each other, Lord Merrick's face stayed unconcerned. "For past royal consideration, I would be willing to let you use the finder for a mere token of a few gold royals."

I swallowed. A single gold royal was worth a smallholding by itself. I think our treasury only held a few now, if that many.

The disguised Fumiko remained still, not moving a muscle. I glanced down at her feet and noticed a slight waver. She was tiring. I counted up the time since we had stepped out of the carriage. It had only been half an hour ago, so Fumiko must be more out of practice than she thought. We had to wrap this up quickly.

Fumiko fixed him with her gaze. "Perhaps what your businesses need is someone to help with your accounts. I could lend you my secretary. She is excellent at ledgers. I'm sure she could help you find missing inventory or lost funds. Making correct entries can be so difficult. And we both know the value of keeping good accounts. Especially when one has loans to the other lords. I imagine they would be quite outdone if your accounts were ever discovered to be less than accurate."

Merrick remained expressionless; however, a bead of sweat on his forehead betrayed him. "That won't be necessary, your highness. In fact, what are a few royals among friends? Why don't I just let you use it? You never know, I might need a favor in the future."

The disguised Fumiko gave a cold smile. "I think that is an excellent idea. Gold should never come between friends."

Merrick started moving toward the door. "I will be back in a moment." He left, and only a few minutes later returned with the finder. He held it out to us. "Would you like to do the search?"

The disguised Fumiko smiled. "Would you be so kind as to do it for me? I'm sure you're much more capable than I am."

Merrick gave a pained smile. "Of course. Now, what are you looking for again?"

"The Griffin's Key."

Merrick closed his eyes and held the finder out. "Please show me in what direction the Griffin's Key is located."

The finder immediately started to glow. We waited for it to begin to move. But after a few moments, the glow died.

He tried it again. But with the same result.

Merrick looked at us a bit fearfully. "I'm sorry. But it can't locate an object by that name."

I glanced to Fumiko and our eyes met. Even though it was Zofie's face, her disappointment was perfectly readable.

What were we going to do now?

As we rode back to the castle in the carriage, I kept the shade up and watched out the window at the passing scenery. The late afternoon sky had become cloudy, and the air had developed more of a cold bite. By evening, we would likely get either freezing rain or possibly snow. The grayness matched my dark mood. We hadn't been able to learn what we needed.

Lord Merrick had been uncharacteristically patient as we tried a few more combinations, but the finder stubbornly refused to home in on the key. He had explained to us that we had to have the exact name of the artifact. And like the Mirror of Bygone Tears we had searched for previously, some things were just blocked from being located. In desperation, we even tried finding Wynn and Lilith, but they didn't show up either. Also likely concealed. We finally had to stop because Fumiko signaled she was reaching the end of her endurance. So we had thanked him and quickly left.

What were we going to do? It all seemed so hopeless. Hopefully, Spraggel and Rourke had located some lead. I sighed. But before we had left, they had said things did not look promising—there were only a few more places to check. If it wasn't for the fact that Lilith had been prepared to kill for it, and Advisor Yonge had reached out all the way from the Kuiojia Empire, I would have thought it was all make-believe.

I rubbed my eyes. I glanced over at Fumiko across from me. She had turned sideways in her seat with her back against the carriage's sidewall and curled up into a ball, with her head resting on her knees. It was hard to tell if she was asleep or not. The moment we had entered the carriage, she had dropped the illusion and fell back into her seat completely exhausted. She had done an almost perfect job of impersonating Zofie. But watching her in action led me to believe there was more to her skill than just looking like the person. She *became* that person. As I watched her, I couldn't help but ask the question: *Exactly what were you trained for?*

I shivered. It was getting cold in the carriage. Blankets were kept under our seats, and I was tempted to pull one out. Maybe even try to catch a nap myself. Tonight promised to be another long one. But I resisted. If Fumiko was sleeping, I might disturb her.

So I stuffed my hands into my jacket pockets and was surprised to feel something inside one of them. Pulling it out, I discovered a piece of carefully folded paper. That was odd—my pockets had been empty before. What was even stranger was that it had my name written on it in a flowing feminine penmanship I did not recognize.

Opening it revealed a brief note from Nadine. She must have slipped it into my pocket when she hugged me. It was carefully written, and I noticed there was not a single cross-out.

Dearest Coren, it read. *Apologies for this hidden note, but it is the only way I could get this information to you discreetly. My sources tell me, Risten has been scouring the eastern part of the kingdom for one of the ancient artifacts. Something to do with a key. She seems quite determined to get it. So determined she's been leaving a trail of blood in her wake. But recently, she's shifted strategies and appears to be waiting for something. She was last seen in Iron Landing and in the company of a man named Wort. Please be careful and stay away from that town.*

I am not sure what Wynn did to my Risten, but it's like she's a different person. She's become heartless. I've also heard she was the one that made the attempt on the princess's life. This is totally against her character, and something must be driving her to do this. Something horrible.

I know you have other challenges at the moment, but I beg you to hear this mother's plea: please save Risten. You of all people I am confident can do this. It was not signed.

I sighed. Nadine must have been watching Risten closely over the years to notice the change in behavior. And she was right. Something horrible had happened—a Dark Avenyts. I would definitely save Risten if I could, but I wasn't exactly sure how. She was far too dangerous to even get close to.

But what really surprised me was the man with her. Lord Wort Dilyston. Risten had a death grudge against the man and had sworn to kill him. He had murdered her master. The Risten inside likely raged every time he was near.

I frowned. While I wanted to save Risten, and it hurt me to even think it, but I had to get Zofie back first. Assuming we could ever find this Griffin's Key. There had to be something we were overlooking.

I glanced at Fumiko only to find her eyes open. She still rested her head on her knees, but had turned her head in my direction, her face impassive.

"We should interrogate our prisoner again. I believe she knows more than she's telling us. Maybe apply some *motivation* to help her remember."

"Motivation?" I asked.

"Nothing that would kill her, just make it uncomfortable." There was a coldness to her voice I did not like.

"You mean torture her?" I shook my head. "While I have no love for the Dark Avenyts inside her, the girl is just that—an innocent girl. Torturing one, tortures the other." I glanced out the window. "Besides, she didn't give even a hint she knew anything more. I'm not opposed to questioning her again, but torture is out of the question."

She gazed at me a moment longer. "You're too trusting."

I thought she might pursue the argument, but she hugged her legs tighter and nodded toward the paper I held.

"Is that a note from Lady Merrick?" she asked. "I thought I saw her slip something into your pocket."

I nodded, surprised she had noticed while I had not. "Apparently, Lilith is anticipating our next move and waiting for us in Iron Landing. We'll have to be careful we don't run into her."

Fumiko gazed at me without speaking. I couldn't help but feel I was being assessed.

"Lady Merrick was right," Fumiko said. "You can't protect Zofie against her."

I considered her a moment before answering. "I know. I practice every day, and I am getting better, but my skills are nowhere near what would be required to beat her. It could be years before I'm good enough, if ever."

She watched me quietly for a moment. And then she surprised me with her question. "How far would you go to protect Zofie?"

I shrugged. "I would give my life for her."

Again the long pause. She glanced out the window and then returned her eyes to me, fixing my gaze with hers. "Dying is easy. Living with a tainted soul can be quite difficult." She paused. "Would you be willing to taint your soul for her?"

I leaned forward. "I would do whatever it took to keep her safe."

"Would you?" she asked, her expression cold. "Would you even be willing to get your hands dirty? To do those things that must be done no matter how distasteful? Would you be willing to give up even the one thing in the world you truly love?"

I didn't like this turn in the conversation. "Of course, I would protect Zofie," I said a little more harshly than I meant to. "I'd do whatever it takes."

She continued to hold my gaze. Uncomfortably long. I sensed she was dissatisfied with my answer.

She finally looked away and put her forehead back on her knees. "Coren, I will help you as best I can. But at some point, you're going to have to decide exactly what you're protecting and how much you're willing to give up to do it."

She paused. I crossed my arms and looked out the window. I thought she was done.

But Fumiko had one last thing to say.

"Living with a tainted soul can be more painful than you can ever imagine."

CHAPTER SEVEN

Interrogation

W hen we arrived back at the castle, it was nearly dark. A cold rain had settled over us and had just begun to turn freezing. Snow, I didn't mind. It was beautiful to look at and brought pleasant memories of playing in it with my father. But I hated it when the rain turned to ice. My curse had frequently used it to make some calamity happen. Evidently, slippery surfaces were perfect for recharging my luck.

As we passed through the castle's doors, I had intended to head straight for Zofie's room, but Fumiko stopped me just inside the entrance.

"Let's go to the kitchens and get something to eat," she said. "We missed our midday meal."

I shook my head. "I'm going to pass. Instead, I think I'll check on Zofie."

She frowned. "Did you even have any breakfast?"

I hadn't. "I'm not hungry," I explained. I looked up the stairs just inside the door. "My stomach is in knots. There is no way I can eat now."

I could sense her disapproval, but she changed topics. "We should update the rest of the council on our failed mission this evening."

I nodded. "Yes, we should. Let's meet in Zofie's study in an hour. Hopefully, Spraggel and Rourke have been more successful in digging up clues than we have."

Fumiko gave a slight bow and turned to leave. "Agreed. That will give me time to let the others know." She quickly walked away and headed down a side corridor.

Something struck me as odd as I watched her head off, but I couldn't put my finger on it. I shrugged.

I went straight to Zofie's room. The guard at the door admitted me with no hesitation. And when I saw her, my heart broke all over again.

The princess was sitting in her chair close to the fire with her hands in her lap. Vidonia had dressed her for the day and done up her hair in an elaborate coiled braid. She looked beautiful. But she still wore the blank expression I was coming to loathe.

Vidonia looked up from her needlework as I entered. She had drawn up her chair next to Zofie's with a small myst lantern between them.

"Any change?" I asked.

She shook her head sadly.

I knelt before Zofie and took her hand, raising it to my lips for a brief kiss. I missed her so much.

"The finder didn't work," I told Zofie. "The others are coming later to figure out what to do." I kissed her hand again. "I'm sorry."

I laid my head in her lap, just feeling her warmth. What I would give to feel her fingers running through my hair.

Vidonia stood up and stretched her back. "Since you're here, Sir Coren, do you mind if I fetch the lady something to eat. It will give me a chance to stretch my old legs."

I nodded, and she left on her mission, while I moved into the chair she had vacated. I took Zofie's hand and leaned back.

I had gotten very little sleep the previous night and been too keyed up to rest in the carriage, so it was no wonder I began to drift. Sleep claimed me before I knew it.

Coren.

I became aware of a voice. Was it Zofie?

I suddenly realized I was dreaming. But it was fuzzy. I had to focus to see any details. I stood on a plain of all gray, which stretched for as far as I could see in all directions.

Coren.

Came the voice again. It seemed to originate behind me. I turned and saw Zofie standing there. And behind her stood Abe, with his stick-figure body and completely round head. The one eye of his curse mark was open and looking at me. I reached for them, but there was some sort of barrier preventing me. I tried to speak, but no words would come out.

Coren, she called again. *Can you hear me? We're trapped...*

I jerked at a knock on the door. "Enter," I called.

Rourke opened the door. He noticed me blinking and rubbing my eyes. I wondered how long I had been out.

"Sorry," he said. "I didn't realize you were asleep. Fumiko said we were gathering here. I came early to deliver the charms we talked about."

I blinked up at him. "You did?"

The dream echoed through my mind, and at first, I couldn't figure out what he was talking about. Then it hit me—the control charm for Cabrina.

I nodded. We had talked about this the previous evening. If we did end up traveling to the Kuiojia Empire, Cabrina was going to have to come with us. So the problem was how to keep her under control with the few people we'd have with us. Rourke had offered to make a set of charms that would help.

He seemed especially pleased at completing his task. "I've already placed the controlling charm on the prisoner. I even explained to her how they work. Surprisingly, she took it without complaint, saying she didn't want to cause any more trouble for her host. Of course, now that it's activated, she can't take it off. And don't worry, I made sure it won't interact with the other charm she's wearing." He grinned. "To use it, all you do is touch the master amulet and give one of four commands. Oh, and I also included a locate ability."

I nodded. Rourke had outdone himself. It was exactly what we had talked about. "Where is the master amulet?"

Rourke grinned. "I gave it to Mistress Fumiko. I passed her in the hall a little while ago. She seemed most pleased." He looked up. "She mentioned something about testing it and asking the prisoner some questions."

I suddenly got a bad feeling—the conversation about interrogating Cabrina echoing through my mind. I got up and headed for the door. "I'll be back in a minute."

When I arrived at the dungeon entrance, the guard on duty gave me a worried look. "Sir Coren, Mistress Fumiko is with the prisoner."

I couldn't remember the guard's name, but I had frequently seen him in the dungeon. Technically as the queen's knight, all the guards in the castle were under my command. However, I had not exercised that authority since I was still new to my role.

The guard grimaced. "Sir, she asked not to be disturbed."

I grew uneasy. "And?"

The guard looked like he had just eaten something foul. "I'm not sure sir, but..."

He paused at the sound echoing from inside the dungeon. It was a young girl's voice, and she sounded in pain.

My eyes went wide. "Open up," I commanded.

The guard jumped to his task, and I strode in.

As I entered the corridor to the cells, I could hear Fumiko just ahead around the corner.

"Where are the others?" she asked, not a trace of emotion in her voice. "You have to know."

"But I don't!" yelled Cabrina. "I told you they..."

I rounded the corner just as Fumiko gave the command, *"Bind."*

Cabrina was in her cell. Her hair was in disarray, and tears were streaming down her face. Fumiko was outside of Cabrina's cell and was touching an amulet around her neck. It flashed blue, and immediately, Cabrina's wrists came together, and she dropped to her knees on the stone floor. Hard.

"Owwwww," she sobbed. She bent forward and put her head on the floor. "I told you I don't know."

"What are you doing?" I asked, not believing what I was seeing.

Fumiko looked up in surprise. "I was just testing Rourke's charms."

"It looks like more than just testing. I thought we had agreed we would not torture her."

She shook her head. *"You* had agreed to it. Not I." She looked back to Cabrina. "Besides, she's not hurting. She's merely not happy with it."

"Sir Coren, please," she sobbed. "I don't know anything."

Fumiko touched the amulet. *"Silence."*

Suddenly Cabrina sobs disappeared. Her mouth moved, but no sound reached us.

"Release her, Fumiko,"

She turned to me, her expression cold. "Coren, I'm only doing what must be done. She is one of the enemy, and all they know how to do is lie. I've been under one's control and seen first-hand how they operate. She's using you. You're simply too trusting to see it."

I stepped closer until she had to look up at me. I was furious. "Release her," I repeated. "She's admittedly been possessed by a Dark Avenyts, but she's also a victim. You can't separate one from the other. Torturing her is... wrong."

Fumiko held my glare for almost a full minute. I almost didn't think she was going to back down. She finally touched the amulet. *"Release,"* she said.

The amulet flashed blue again. Cabrina's wrists separated, and the sound of her sobs returned. "...don't hurt Cabrina anymore. I've told you all I know."

Fumiko looked me squarely in the eye. "Sometimes, you have to do the hard things. You'll never be able to protect Zofie like this."

I couldn't remember when I had been so angry. I held out my hand. "The amulet."

She looked up at me a moment more before lifting it over her head and placing it on my palm. We held each other's gaze a moment longer, and then she stepped away, quickly moving toward the exit. But she paused at the door and turned. "Remember this conversation when she's got a knife at your throat." Fumiko left the dungeon.

I unlocked the cell door and knelt beside Cabrina. "She's gone."

Cabrina leaped into my arms and cried into my shoulder. "I told her I didn't know anything," she babbled. "I really don't." She swallowed. "We were so scared."

I hesitated. Was she using me? Was she manipulating me to her designs? Maybe I *was* too trusting. Then again, was that a bad thing? I put my arms around her and let her sob into my shoulder.

After her tears had died down, I helped her stand. That's when I noticed the small rips on her dress around her knees. They were bloody. I couldn't help but wonder how many times Fumiko had made her slam down on the rough stone floor. I helped her sit on her bed and then went out into the small area outside the dungeon proper and asked the guard if he had anything for cuts. He gave me a small clay jar of some kind of healing salve.

Cabrina watched me warily as I reentered her cell.

I held out the jar. "I brought something for your knees."

She hesitated but took it. She hiked up her dress to just above her knees. They were bloody and bruised, confirming my fears. She winced as she gingerly applied the salve.

As I watched her, I couldn't decide if she was putting on an act, trying to gain my sympathy, or was really hurt. I just wasn't sure.

"I begged Mistress Fumiko to stop," she said as she dabbed on the medicine. "Cabrina's body was being damaged, and the one inside could feel everything. And neither of us understands why Mistress Fumiko would hurt her. I've already told her everything I know."

"She considers you an enemy and believes you've not been completely honest. You did attack someone close to her."

She looked up. "Then why are you helping me? You are even closer to the princess. She's your future mate. Am I not an enemy to you too?"

I sighed. "To be honest. I would like to see you punished for what you did. But there is a difference between being punished for a crime and hurting someone who is innocent. The Cabrina inside you did nothing to deserve a punishment."

The youth finished with the ointment and held it out to me.

"I was just following my directives. While I knew how the charms were made and who was supposed to get them, I did not know what they did."

I took the salve from her. "Directives. Are they like orders?"

She nodded. "Only stronger. It's impossible for me to go against them."

"What are your directives now?"

She shrugged. "I don't have any. I'm not sure why they didn't give me more. All I have is just the basic one all of my kind has."

"Which is?"

She gazed up at me a moment before answering. She finally said, "Serve."

I gave her a puzzled look. "Serve who?"

She shrugged again. "Basically, anyone with a higher *cothe* than me. But for now, without a higher directive, I serve Cabrina."

I looked at her doubtfully. "And what does Cabrina want?"

She sat up and smiled brightly, seemingly quite pleased with herself. "She wants to mate with Master Rourke," the youth said matter of factly. "She thinks he is quite handsome..."

The youth broke off and winced. She looked up as if talking to someone else. "What do you mean I wasn't supposed to tell? It's true!" She looked back to me. "I think I embarrassed her."

I blinked at her in confusion.

Cabrina cocked her head to the side. "But in my opinion, you are much more worthy of mating with..."

She winced again and looked to the side as if listening to someone else. She finally looked back to me and blushed. "I apologize. I apparently have said something inappropriate. Cabrina inside is yelling at me, but I'm not sure why."

I couldn't help but smile. "That was just a little inappropriate, especially for a young maiden. But I'll take that as a compliment."

She sighed. "Human courting rituals are so hard to understand. I'm surprised you manage to reproduce." She winced. "Cabrina yelled at me again."

I shook my head in disbelief. "Anyway, I had best be getting back. I'm supposed to be meeting with the other advisers."

"You're taking us somewhere, aren't you?"

I couldn't see a reason to hide it. "To the Kuiojia Empire, assuming we can find an ancient artifact he wants." I had a sudden thought. "Did your people mention anything about the Griffin's Key?"

She shook her head. "No. I was told only the bare minimum."

"Nothing about any of the ancient artifacts?"

She shook her head again. "Sorry. The only thing I've heard came from your ballad, *The Cursed Knight*."

I cringed. "That account is not exactly correct."

"But you did find the Mirror of Bygone Tears. Can't you do the same thing you did before to find it?"

I considered her. I wasn't sure how much I wanted to reveal. But I gambled. "We've tried the finder, but it didn't work."

"Then what about the mirror itself. Didn't you use it to prove the princess was innocent?"

"We did, but it only shows a myst user's memories. It doesn't show how to find an inanimate object."

She shrugged. "Then why don't you ask it to show you the memories of the last person to visit the key's location."

I stared at her. "That's actually a good suggestion. However, I have to use Abe to unlock it, and your charm has made him stop working."

She looked puzzled. "Can I see your curse mark?"

I thought it an odd request, but I pulled up my jacket and shirt sleeve so she could see it. She examined it intently. "Your curse is very different from us, similar but different. But one thing I can say for sure is that it still operates."

I looked at the curse mark myself. "How... how do you know?"

She shrugged. "Because I can smell him. The closest analogy I can think of is feeling a person's breath, or maybe the scent of their body. But I can definitely say he's alive, and at least on some level, is working."

My eyes went wide. Then I might be able to start the mirror.

I took her hand and gave it a gentle squeeze. "Thank you. I'm not sure why you're helping me, but I appreciate it."

She blushed. Deeply.

I turned to leave. "I have to try this out."

As I was leaving, I heard Cabrina talking to herself. I guess it was actually to the girl inside of her.

"I told you he would make the better mate."

I strode into Zofie's study, brimming with an exuberance I hadn't felt since she had been attacked.

Rourke was in his usual spot by the window while Captain Milner and Spraggel sat in chairs closer to the fire. Fumiko stood before them and seemed to have just finished explaining about our attempt with the finder. She regarded me coolly.

Spraggel brightened when he saw me. "There you are. I was wondering if you were going to join us."

The princess sat to one side with that same blank expression I hated. I went to Zofie and knelt before her. I took her hand and gave it a kiss before turning to the others.

Spraggel rubbed his chin. "So the finder didn't work. I'm not surprised. Otherwise, it would have been found by now. And our research came up empty."

Captain Milner cocked his jaw to one side in irritation. "So what do we do now?"

I smiled. "I want to try using the Mirror of Bygone Tears."

Rourke frowned. "But doesn't that just show a myst user's memories? We've tried it on other things, and you have to have the context for the memories to make sense."

"True, but it might give us a clue."

Captain Milner shrugged. "What have we got to lose?"

Rourke likewise agreed while Fumiko remained silent.

I held out my hand. "Spraggel, the mirror please."

Spraggel frowned. "I hope I can remember where I put it." He reached into his strange pocket up to his elbow and began to search around.

Rourke looked at me in disbelief. "You gave one of the most important ancient artifacts to Spraggel?"

I shrugged. "What else could I do? I thought it was a better hiding place than the bottom of my linen drawer."

Rourke shook his head but said nothing more.

A moment later, Spraggel reached further down into his pocket. "Ah-ha!" he exclaimed. He pulled out a shiny black orb just slightly smaller than my fist. It was totally black—its darkness seeming to almost eat any light touching it. The mirror was considered one of the most powerful of the ancient artifacts. It could show any event from a living myst user's life, whether the person granted permission or not. But it had serious limitations. Plus, there must be some way to block its effects since we had not been able to use it on Wynn or Risten.

I took it from him and then touched it to the curse anchor on my wrist. We all held our breath as we waited for it to start. But nothing happened. Disappointment flooded me as the mirror remained its lifeless black. I shoved it against my wrist harder. "Abe, you foul-mouthed, good for nothing curse. If you can hear me, please make this thing work."

To all of our surprise, Zofie gave a soft groan. We all looked to her in surprise.

Suddenly, I felt it move of its own accord. I released the mirror, and it remained floating in the air. As we watched, it unfolded like a flower into a larger, bowl-shaped object of the same deep black.

I nearly danced. "Show me the last person to visit where the Griffin's Key is kept," I asked it.

It hesitated, but then I felt a rush of excitement as a pull of myst went through me. The world began to fade away, and I felt myself heading toward a dream. It was a shared memory. I had done this before with Zofie, but I don't think I would ever get used to looking out through someone else's eyes—

With the back of my wrist, I pushed a strand of hair out of my face being careful not to let the flour on my hands touch anything. That included my dress, which loved to become dusted in the stuff.

I added a few more drops of goat milk to the bowl and mixed it together with my hands. This was the last of the flour. After this, I wasn't sure what we would do. I guess eat what was left of the cheese and drink goats milk until that too ran out. Poor old Nibbles had already been giving less milk.

I carefully mixed everything and then scraped every last morsel on to a mixing board and began to form it up into a loaf. I almost cried. It was so small, especially for four people. I sighed and pushed the annoying strand of hair behind my ear again.

Father had gone to try to sell one of our precious goats to purchase more flour, but I had my doubts there was any to buy. Rumors were that even the princess couldn't afford to have any.

I guess we were lucky to have any goats at all. The soldiers had come over the summer and confiscated everything. The only reason we had what we did was because Father had hidden some in the nearby forest.

Unfortunately, he hadn't hidden me. And when they hadn't been able to find goats, they turned toward something else—

I jerked my thoughts away from that dark path.

Finishing with the dough, I put the tiny loaf into the oven. I took care to place it in just the right position—I couldn't afford to burn our last loaf of bread. I then went to see if our supply of cheese had miraculously grown overnight.

I heard footsteps behind me and turned to see my little sister enter. She carefully shut the door behind her. She was only seven and bundled from head to toe in a thick coat, with a rough wool scarf covering her face. "I think Rotha might be getting upset with me. She keeps expecting me to give her more feed."

I looked back down to the cheese. Unfortunately, it was the same size as yesterday. "Is Mother all right?" I asked.

"Yes, she's got her bow and is watching the goats like a mother bear watches her cubs."

I smiled. "I feel sorry for whatever tries to steal one of her animals, be they beast or human. They will surely suffer a fate worse than hell."

She giggled at the remark. She was an ordinary girl with plain brown hair and a slim build. Unremarkable in every way, except for her smile. It lifted my heart every time I saw it. However, her dirt was another matter.

"Floria!" I yelled at her. "Clean your boots off. Don't dirty my floors."

Floria looked down at her boots and lifted one up to inspect it. "But I did Docila. I did!"

And then I smelled it—something burning. "I gasped and turned back to the small oven. The bread was just starting to burn...."

I blinked as the vision cleared, as did the others in the room.

Master Rourke shook his head. "It's hopeless. Those people could be anywhere in the world! That's worse of a problem than we had before."

Spraggel shook his head. "Perhaps we should try again. Be a little more specific to get it to show us a location."

I, on the other hand, started laughing. I couldn't help myself. After days of not knowing, of worrying over what to do, the laughter just rolled out of me.

They all looked at me like I had finally lost it. And maybe I had.

Spraggel leaned forward. "Are you all right, my boy?"

I nodded, wiping a tear from my eye. "I couldn't be better."

"Then could you share the joke with us?" he asked. "I could certainly use a good one right now."

I nodded. "I think Abe has somehow been influencing my luck again because this is unbelievable."

Spraggel looked at me warily. "And how so?"

I shrugged. "I know those people. In fact, I know exactly where they are."

Captain Milner asked, "And?"

"That's my stepfather's house. Those were my sisters."

CHAPTER EIGHT

Homeward Bound

The next morning, as the sun rose a finger's breadth above the horizon, we gathered in Zofie's study where we would begin our trip. Of the five who were traveling, all save one was present. And we expected her shortly.

I fidgeted next to Zofie's desk resisting the urge to go through the small pack resting on it one last time. I had double-checked it three times, so I doubted a fourth was going to make a difference. I wore my regular clothes but had added a hooded cloak, which was slightly too warm even in the chill room.

Spraggel, one of those traveling with us, sat in a chair against the wall and was hunched over a binder with ink and quill in hand. He claimed to be making an official royal record of our trip. After all, how often did someone from our kingdom visit the Kuiojia Empire? I had told him that it sounded like an excellent idea. But when he turned away, he mumbled something about the minstrels needing new material. I began to suspect I knew where the accursed performers had been getting their information.

Like me, Spraggel had also been given a pack, but he had merely stuffed it in his bottomless pocket. I really needed to see about getting one of those.

On the other side of the room, perched on the edge of a chair, sat Fumiko. I was afraid that she would try to wear her simple dress, but she surprised me by choosing close-fitting pants, a warm shirt, and a hooded cloak. The young woman stared silently ahead with hands clasped between her knees. She had been making a point of not looking my way. I think she was still miffed at me over Cabrina's interrogation.

Rourke again stood by the window and gazed out across the castle grounds. He had released the myst barrier keeping out the frigid air and basked in the cold sunshine. From the way the young man gripped the window's ledge, I think he was nervous. He was going to give our journey a head start by opening a portal. He claimed it would be the farthest he had ever attempted. I just hoped he didn't run out of myst as one of us was passing through it.

And finally, Zofie sat in her chair. Vidonia had dressed her simply, but warmly in a shirt, vest and pants, along with her long cloak. She sat there unmoving with hands in her lap. I couldn't help but study her face for some infinitesimal showing of expression, but there was none. We had considered bringing Vidonia along with us to help with her but decided against it. I just hoped I'd be able to care for her properly during our travel.

I jumped at the knock on the door. Captain Milner joined us, and with him came the last of our party. Cabrina.

She too had been dressed in practical shirt, pants, and boots, with a heavy hooded cloak. Her expression was wide-eyed. It was like she was going to her first party.

I sighed. It was time.

We decided to go with the smallest number of people we could get by with: Zofie, Cabrina, and myself because of our connected charms, then Fumiko as our guide, and Spraggel... well, because he was Spraggel.

We would also be going in secret. The official story was that Zofie had been injured in an assassination attempt and was in bed recuperating. Fumiko had already canceled all her appointments and forbidden anyone but her council and Vidonia from entering her room. Master Rourke and Captain Milner had agreed to stay back and keep things running until we returned. Which meant we had to travel quickly before our ruse was exposed.

Unfortunately, Xiangwei City, our ultimate destination within the Kuiojia Empire, was roughly a third of the distance around the world. Which meant we had a lot of ground to cover, and the only way to quickly do that was to use portals.

To get us started, Rourke had volunteered to open a portal to Iron Landing—the first major town along our path. I had initially argued against this move based on Lady Merrick's letter concerning Risten. It could be deadly if we encountered her. But, unfortunately, Iron Landing was the only town along our path that held a *correspondor*—a specialized myst device that could communicate with another pared with it. Or in our case, it also served as an anchor for the remote end of the portal. Zofie commissioned it to be placed in the town just in case she needed to travel there quickly.

So I had reluctantly agreed to pass through Iron Landing despite Lilith being there. Going overland by horse, or even upriver by boat, would take several days and expose us to discovery. We would just have to keep a low profile so as not to attract attention.

From Iron Landing, we planned to take a barge up the Nortesy River to Dunomhir. My family didn't live in the town but were within riding distance.

Fortunately, Dunomhir also happened to host a retired myst user by the name of Master Oddfrid Vandobarre. We were hoping to get him to open a long-range portal all the way to the Kuiojia Empire. However, this might take some convincing, having left the king's service rather abruptly a few years back. Since then, he had become a recluse and refused to have anything to do with the royal court.

I had asked Rourke why he couldn't just do it himself and quickly got an indignant lesson on myst portals. Apparently, there are two kinds—short-range and long-range. Rourke could only use the short-range kind, and despite 'short' being in the name, it required a huge expenditure to open it. The one he planned for Iron Landing would nearly deplete him and put him out of commission for at least a week.

However, a long-range portal worked differently. It could, in theory, be opened to anywhere in the world. But to do it did require a unique ability called *wayfaring*—something only a few people had. These wayfarers were highly sought after and generally very well compensated. Unfortunately, the royal one had vanished along with most of the other myst users in the kingdom. That left Oddfrid as our only option other than going overland.

"It's time," I announced. Each of the others moved to their assigned positions while I helped Zofie stand and take her place in the circle. I took a deep breath, looked at each one of our small group, and then nodded to Rourke.

He returned my nod. "The portal will be small, barely large enough for you to pass through. I will put it on the floor so you can drop inside, but you must do it quickly. I can only hold it open for less than a minute." He looked at us levelly. "And if I say to hold, do not enter the portal. You do not want to be caught in it should I have to drop it."

We nodded. All of us looked nervous, except Spraggel. He unexpectedly slapped me on the back. "Don't be so serious Coren. It's only Iron Landing."

"I know, but this is the first time I've traveled like this."

Spraggel leaned closer. "You have nothing to worry about. Mikney doesn't know you're holding Maggie under house arrest... yet. Once he finds that out, you might have something to worry about."

"What?"

With a grin, Master Rourke closed his eyes, took a deep breath, and let it out slowly. I then felt him gathering his myst. On the wooden floor in front of us, a light blue circle began to glow, almost a cyan color, and barely large enough for someone to drop through. It grew in intensity, and then suddenly, the boards beneath it seemed to disappear.

"Now!" he yelled.

I went first. I hopped forward and fell a good five feet onto another wooden floor. I quickly moved to the side, barely avoiding getting hit in the head by my and Fumiko's packs. I pulled them to one side just before Fumiko dropped through. She wheeled to the side and began to check our surroundings. A moment later, Zofie's feet appeared. I quickly grabbed them and helped lower her down and away. Spraggel came next and then finally Cabrina. I held the words for her control charm ready, but she stepped to the side and knelt as instructed. She looked around in fascination. Another pack came through with some spare items, and then the portal snapped shut, leaving us in darkness. But it wasn't total. There were gaps around the shutters letting in a little of the morning light.

The room we were in looked familiar. The exact location of the correspondor was a secret, but if I was right...

We heard steps outside the door to the small room. Fumiko pulled her knife and moved to the side of it. It opened, and her knife went immediately against the person's throat.

Mikney de'Glougeman's eyes went wide. I held a curse detection charm toward him. It did not react, and I relaxed. "It's him."

She stepped back and sheathed her knife. She gave a short bow. "Apologies, innkeeper."

Mikney glanced at her warily before locking on me. "I should have known it would be you up to something. When I agreed to allow the placement of that myst thing in my attic, I figured you would eventually show up." He huffed. "Is my daughter all right?"

I smiled. That would be his first concern. "She is well. One of her friends dragged her into a bit of mischief, but her involvement has been resolved. And don't worry, it won't affect her schooling."

He nodded before giving the rest of us a brief appraisal. He gasped when he recognized Zofie. "Your highness. I had no idea." He immediately dropped to one knee. Then he noticed her lack of response.

"She can't reply," I said softly. "She was the victim of an attack, and we're on our way to find a way to remove it. We were hoping to get your help to speed our journey."

He nodded and stood. "What do you need? I'll do anything to help her. I owe you both for saving Maggie and myself from those slavers. Not to mention getting my daughter into the queen's school. I'll do whatever is in my power."

"We need a barge going upriver. A fast one. And we need to keep this quiet."

Mikney rubbed his chin in thought. "Going upriver this time of year will be difficult. So far, it hasn't frozen solid, but the water level is down, which makes navigating it tricky." Then he grinned, evilly. "There is someone who owes me a favor, so let me check with them first. Still, it might take a bit to arrange."

I nodded. "We'll wait. But the faster we leave, the safer it will be for everyone."

Mikney turned to leave. "In the meantime, while the attic might not be the nicest room I have, it is the most isolated. Staying here until I return would be best."

Spraggel smiled. "Then would it be possible to get some of your fine ale while we wait?"

Mikney smiled apologetically. "The last of my ale ran out two weeks ago. All I can offer you is some water."

Spraggel's smile faltered. "None at all?"

Mikney shook his head. "Not a drop. I don't think you'll find any left in all of Iron Landing."

Spraggel's shoulders slumped. He looked like he had just lost his best friend.

I looked from Mikney to Spraggel. I knew my old master took his ale seriously, but they were talking like someone had died.

Mikney patted him on the shoulder. "But there is hope. An old friend of mine is braving the winter seas."

Spraggel looked up hopefully. "Southern ale?"

Mikney nodded. "The bastard is overdue, but if anyone can get through the storms, he can."

Spraggel took a deep breath. "I'll say a prayer for him."

Mikney gave Spraggel another pat on the shoulder. "As will I." And they both then bowed their head and paused in silence.

I shook my head in disbelief and glanced at Fumiko. She just shrugged.

A moment later, they both looked up. Spraggel wiped a tear from his eye, and Mikney gave his shoulder a reassuring squeeze before leaving on his mission.

I knew these two took their ale seriously, but this was just a little much.

We settled down to wait, making ourselves as comfortable as we could in the cramped attic. It seemed like weeks, but Mikney returned in only an hour. Apparently, luck was with us. The innkeeper had found a loaded barge waiting on one last container that was due shortly. The barge-master said if we could come now, he would give us passage to Dunomhir.

We quickly gathered our supplies and went with him out to the river docks. The streets were bustling with people in heavy coats, but the crowd began to thin as we approached the docks. The cold air blowing from downriver was frigid and would tug and pull at one's coat seeking warmth to steal. I shivered and turned to see my companions had also settled further into their cloaks.

As we rounded the last corner, I paused to make sure Zofie's clothes were keeping her warm while Mikney and Spraggel went on ahead. Cabrina was so involved with looking at those around us she ran into the back of me. She blushed and looked away.

As I fussed with Zofie's cloak, Fumiko and I scanned the few people on the streets and the surrounding buildings. The wharf itself was almost deserted, likely driven away by the cold. I saw no barges out in the river itself, but there were quite a few of them covered and tied to the wharf. It didn't look like they would be moving until spring.

Mikney and Spraggel looked to be headed toward the only one with people on it.

Unexpectedly, I felt something hot on my wrist. I looked down and pushed back my cloak. The charm that Cabrina had given me was hot. Not enough to burn, but warm enough to be uncomfortable. This was really odd. The last time a charm had acted like this was back before Abe had introduced himself. Early on, I had been given an amulet to wear that would dampen my curse's bad luck, and in effect, limit Abe's ability to protect me. One time, when I was fighting a monster and was just about to be eaten, the amulet got unbearably hot and cracked. And thus breaking the charm so Abe could help me.

I was puzzled. Did this mean that Abe was trying to break the charm? I certainly hoped not since that could kill us. I looked to Cabrina and was surprised to see her staring at two people farther down the wharf. One wore a deeply hooded cloak, while the other had a broad-brimmed hat pulled tightly over their head.

Up until a moment ago, the youth had been smiling, but now she looked disappointed.

"One of them has been perfected," she said quietly.

My eyes went wide. Abe was trying to warn me.

"Fumiko, the two people approaching on the left."

She nodded but didn't look in their direction. She nudged me toward the barge. "I'll guard Zofie. See if you can get them to follow you. Just walk slowly until the fighting starts."

"Fighting?"

But in reply, she just gave me another nudge.

I took Cabrina's hand and pulled her after me. "Don't stare," I admonished the girl. I expected resistance, maybe an attempt to escape, but she came willingly and simply looked down at her feet. Side by side, we walked leisurely toward the barge.

The two people approaching didn't change their course but continued to walk at a steady pace. I could hear their measured steps scraping on the cobblestones as they drew near. One was quite a bit taller than the other, but the taller's hood and the shorter's hat hid their identity. I couldn't even tell if they were armed. I released Cabrina's hand and laid it on the hilt of my sword.

While still several paces away, we passed in front of them, and I thought they might rush us at that point. But they maintained their maddeningly steady pace and passed behind us.

Just as I thought perhaps we had made a mistake, I heard the rustling of a cloak. In one motion, I started to pull my sword and wheeled to face—a knife inches from my chest. From beneath her hat, Lilith smiled wickedly up at me.

Her companion threw back his hood and slowly drew his rather large sword. My eyes went wide when I recognized him. Lord Wort Dilyston. The cloak's sleeves were large but seemed to strain to contain the man's massive arms. I'd once thought them the size of small trees. Last we met atop Mount Eternal, he had been in Wynn's employ and very nearly killed us.

"Hello, Coren," said Lilith. She put a hand on the arm holding my half-drawn sword and tugged downward until the sword rested back in its scabbard. She leaned closer. "You're too slow. You'll never be a match for me in a million years. So be a good boy and don't do anything stupid. I'm here for Zofie, but I'll take you too if you insist." She leaned forward. I could feel the point of her knife even through my clothes. "Now where is she?"

I grinned back. "Do you honestly expect me to tell you?"

Lilith shrugged. "One could hope." Then she smiled. "But there are other ways."

Her other hand shot out and grabbed Cabrina.

"NO!" yelled Cabrina. Suddenly, her shoulders slumped, and her head fell forward.

"What did you do to her?"

"She is of low cothe. Easily readable and will do everything I say." She glanced in Cabrina's direction. "Now why don't you tell me where Zofie is? Or perhaps you'd like me to dig through your host's brain to find it. I probably wouldn't have to damage her too much."

Cabrina shook her head and slowly raised an arm, pointing to the corner we had left Fumiko and Zofie. Lilith smiled and glanced over her shoulder. I followed the gaze—only they weren't there.

Wort suddenly pointed with his sword. "She's already on the barge. How did she sneak past us?"

Lilith cursed. She released Cabrina and shoved me hard to the side. I stumbled about to fall when Cabrina, of all people, caught me and steadied me.

"Sorry," she whispered. Then she shoved me after them.

I broke into a run. Cabrina would likely take the opportunity to escape but saving Zofie came first. I ran after them. But to my surprise, the youth ran just behind me.

Up ahead, the bargemaster and his two crew were frantically casting off ropes. Zofie stood in the center of the barge, and Spraggel was helping her to sit. With wide eyes, he noticed Lilith and Wort running toward him and began to dig in his special pocket, no doubt looking for his long lost sword.

But where was Fumiko?

In answer, she leaped from behind a crate sitting beside the departing barge, planting herself between the attackers and the departing vessel. She held her sword before her in both hands, using a defensive form I did not recognize.

Lilith swapped her knife for her sword as she ran and raised it high. Fumiko held her stance, her expression emotionless. Just before they impacted, Lilith switched to another form, but Fumiko followed, swiftly altering her own to match, countering it perfectly.

Lilith stepped back in shock. She frowned and launched herself again, raining down blows only to have Fumiko counter each one.

Wort ran past the fighting pair heading for the barge. I leaped toward him in a flying tackle and knocked him to the ground. I tried to pin him from behind, but he was too strong. He threw me off, and before I could react, grabbed me by the throat and lifted me off my feet. Wort pulled his sword back to finish me off.

Suddenly, Cabrina was next to us, tugging on his massive arm. "Please Lord, spare him," She begged.

Wort glared at her. I tried to tell her to run, but his grip was so tight, I could only make choking sounds.

Then she did the strangest thing.

She kneed him in the groin.

Wort gave a surprised 'oof' and crumbled to his knees.

"Get on the barge!" yelled Fumiko. Still rapidly exchanging blows with Lilith. They were evenly matched, with neither being able to advance or get away from the other.

I grabbed Cabrina's hand and ran for the barge. We managed to leap aboard just as it was pulling away. Fumiko and Lilith continued to fight as we backed away from the docks. A bargeman was trying hard to push us out using a long pole, while another was hastily trying to raise a sail.

I looked on helplessly as the two women fought. The distance between the dock and the barge was slowly increasing. As I measured the gap with my eye, there was no way Fumiko could make it.

Just then, Fumiko gave a spinning kick toward Lilith's face. Not expecting it, the other woman staggered back, giving Fumiko the chance she needed to break away. She took off running in our direction with Lilith in fast pursuit.

Standing now, but with still wobbly legs, Wort made a grab for Fumiko, but missed. Lilith slowed, confident her prey had nowhere to go. She and Wort spread out to trap her against the edge. There was no way she could jump the growing gap.

But Fumiko didn't slow down. Instead, she put on a burst of speed as she approached the edge of the dock.

I quickly moved to the corner of the barge closest to the edge and braced myself in the hope I might be able to catch her. But I didn't see how.

Everyone on the boat held their breath as she approached the edge at full speed. My eyes went wide as I felt a sudden pull of myst. Then Fumiko leaped high into the air, the jump carrying her higher than should be possible. And of course, it was. But not if one used their myst to boost their jump.

With arms wheeling, she sailed toward the barge for a full two heartbeats before crashing into me and knocking me to the deck. As she lay atop me, trying to catch her breath, she leaned up and kissed me on the cheek. "I haven't fought like that in a while." Then she realized what she had just done and blushed. "Apologies... I forgot myself."

I helped her up, and we looked toward the docks. Lilith and Wort were standing at the edge of the wharf glaring at us. Lilith turned to Wort and shoved him. I couldn't make out the words, but I don't think it was anything nice.

A group of the Royal Guard trotted out from a side street, no doubt alerted to the fight happening on the wharf. Lilith and Wort took off in the opposite direction, but not before Lilith gave us one last look.

It seemed to say, *this is not over.*

Our progress upstream was faster than I had expected but slower than we needed. The dock men would pole us through the slower currents, use the sails if the wind was right, or would pull out paddles if they had to. They kept a small fire in an iron pot in the center of the barge, which we positioned Zofie close to. My heart ached when I looked at her and saw her impassive face staring out into the distance. I tried to make sure she was as comfortable as I could make her and constantly fretted over her being too hot or too cold.

After we were sure Lilith wasn't an immediate threat, Fumiko had settled down with her cloak tightly wrapped around her, pulled her hood up, and went fast asleep. These fights seemed to take a lot out of her. When I considered it, it must be hard using your myst while fighting—no doubt exhausting. And that jump. It took a lot of myst to physically move an object, so she had likely drained herself.

Spraggel chatted amiably with the bargemaster, and they discovered they had several acquaintances in common.

Which left Cabrina. She quietly sat close to Zofie without saying a word. But her eyes were going everywhere—watching the bargemen going about their work, observing the passing riverbank, even just staring up at the cold blue sky above.

I sat down beside her, and she gave me a guarded look.

"I think you know what I'm going to ask," I said softly.

She didn't say anything.

I sighed. "Why did you help us? Why didn't you try to get free?"

She shrugged. "I explained before. I have no directives, so I try to do what the Cabrina inside wants. And she wanted to protect you and the princess. She feels guilty for the harm we have done."

I considered her for a moment. "What did Lilith do to you when she took your hand."

Cabrina looked at me sadly and then glanced away in shame. "She overrode my will. I am unnamed and of low cothe. There is no way I can resist someone so ancient." She shivered, and I didn't think it was from the cold.

"Any idea on what her... *directives* are?"

Cabrina glanced back up at me. She shook her head. "No, I only know what I've overheard. But she has to be looking for this key too."

"Was she one of the those that helped you... *perfect* your host?"

Cabrina shook her head. "No. While one was a man and the other was a woman, their bodies were younger." She glanced at Zofie. "I also don't think Lilith knows the princess is like this."

I nodded. I had gotten that same impression.

She continued. "Which means she wasn't behind it."

I frowned. "Then this isn't a two-way struggle. We have a third party involved."

Cabrina gave a most girl-like sigh. "I would agree with your conclusion."

I looked away in thought. A third party. Another group competing with Lilith. This did not bode well. I had thought the Dark Avenyts were united in their thinking. But perhaps they were more human-like than we thought and had groups with conflicting interests.

In the brownish water beside us, a double-handful chunk of ice floated past. I glanced at Cabrina, who was studying the ice intently. I almost felt sorry for her. Not only was she disposable, but she was treated like a slave to the others of her kind. I shook my head. Regardless, she was a Dark Avenyts. I had to be careful I didn't begin to trust her.

I decided to try a different tact. "Perfecting. You said the Dark Avenyts possessing Risten had perfected her. You've also said that about yourself. Perfecting means to make better. How can stealing someone's body make them better?"

Cabrina turned her focus on me. "We do not steal their bodies. We form a partnership with them. We were created to help our hosts be better than they naturally are. We provide them with knowledge, skills, and perspective that they would not normally have."

"Even if the person doesn't want it."

She smiled. "How can they not want to be perfect?"

I considered her for a moment. "Can I speak with Cabrina? The one inside? Without you... *perfecting* her?"

She gazed at me for several moments. I could almost hear the whispers of an internal conversation going on. The odd thing was, she didn't blink the whole time.

"Yes," she finally said. "She will speak with you as long as you promise not to yell at her. She's afraid you hate her."

"She's a victim. How could I possibly think that about her."

Cabrina leaned forward and touched my arm. "And she is extremely shy. Please be gentle with her."

And then Cabrina's expression changed. I had seen this before, but it still amazed me. The very barest change in expression, the slight curve of her lips, the way she held her eyes. I couldn't say for sure what it was, but a completely different personality animated her features.

She immediately looked down, and her hands began to fidget. "I-I-I am... sorry. W-w-we've c-caused so much trouble."

My eyes went up in surprise. She had a pronounced stutter. No doubt made even worse by what had happened to her.

I shook my head and gave her a gentle smile. "There is nothing for you to apologize for."

She gave her head a small shake. "I should have tried h-h-harder to stop her. I told her not to do it." Still looking down, she glanced up before returning her gaze to the deck. "B-but she c-couldn't stop. She had to follow the orders." She drew herself in tighter. "I should have tried harder."

I reached across and touched her hand. "Don't worry. We'll get that Dark Avenyts off of you as soon as we can."

She looked up in horror. "P-p-please don't hurt her. She's not so bad. I w-wouldn't be able to see all this if it w-wasn't for her." Her gaze quickly returned to the deck. "I'm not the b-bravest person, and I have this stupid stutter. Even though my father made me apply for the p-princess's school, my fear is so bad I w-wouldn't have been able to show up." She squirmed in her seat. "B-but she helped me. Told me w-what to do. Calmed my fears." She slowly shook her head. "I've never had a c-close friend before. One I could talk with and share secrets. And... and she's almost become one."

I was shocked. "But it's a Dark Avenyts?" I said, a little more harshly than I intended.

Her eyes widened in sudden terror...

And then she was gone.

I could tell control had shifted. The Dark Avenyts inside of her was back. Cabrina sighed. "I told you not to scare her. You made her cry, and now she's gone to her deep dark place."

I leaned closer. "What have you done to the girl inside you to make her trust you so?"

She frowned. "I haven't done anything. You, on the other hand, scared her."

What?

She leaned forward. "You don't understand. She's had it pretty tough over the last year, and her stutter is only part of it. Puberty came late for her, changing her overnight from a skinny girl to a pretty young lady. Unfortunately, the young lady attracted the attention of one of the bastard soldiers raiding their farm. Her father ended up with a broken arm and a cracked head in stopping him. And on top of that, she's just come into her myst abilities—which she hates. Her neighbor, about her age, went missing during the summer, disappearing to Creator knows where like all the other myst users in town. She keeps wondering why her powers came so late and why she survived, but her neighbor didn't." She paused, her expression stern.

I didn't know what to say.

She continued. "You still don't understand, do you? She's eat up with guilt, Sir Coren. In her view, it's all her fault. That she's caused nothing but trouble for her loved ones and that everyone hates her. When I came along, she had already picked out the tree she planned to hang herself from." She sat back and folded her arms. "So be nice to her. If anyone deserves to be treated kindly, she does."

I blinked at her. Being scolded by a Dark Avenyts was not how I expected this conversation to go.

She stood. "So please excuse me, Sir Coren. I need to talk to my host for a bit." She turned and made her way toward the front of the barge, seating herself on a tall crate and gazing out at the water.

Still reeling from my conversation with Cabrina, I decided a talk with Spraggel might be in order. Cabrina was not acting like any of the few Dark Avenyts I had encountered.

I turned to Zofie and checked that she was warm enough. My movement must have disturbed Fumiko, because she opened her eyes and sat up, quickly taking in her surroundings. She yawned.

"Is Zofie all right?" she asked.

I nodded and squatted beside her. "She hasn't changed. I just keep checking to make sure she isn't too hot or too cold. I've been changing her position about every quarter-hour."

She nodded and yawned again.

I looked down. "Thank you again for saving us. You really are skilled. You were fantastic back there."

She looked up at me a moment—her face unreadable. "And you are terrible. We're going to have to do something about your skills before you get us all killed. As her knight, you're supposed to be responsible for protecting the princess."

I looked down. "I know. I thought I had gotten a little better. In time, I will catch up."

She squinted at me. "Time is something we don't have."

I got a little miffed, my voice rising. "And how am I supposed to change that? I practice every day. I'm doing the best I can."

Fumiko considered me for a moment. "The best you can do is not good enough."

I frowned in disgust. "Then what am I supposed to do?"

Fumiko looked at me levelly. "We're going to have to cheat."

CHAPTER NINE

A Lesson Shared

We made good progress up the river and arrived in Dunomhir in only five days. To save time, as well as maintain our security, we slept on the boat and only went ashore for supplies. Thankfully we did not see any more of Lilith or Wort, but I was afraid that was only temporary.

It was late afternoon when we stepped off the barge, so we sought out an inn to pass the evening. There had been little to do while traveling other than sit. But it was tiring none the less. Not only did we have to stay alert for any sign of pursuit, but there was also the need to keep a constant eye on both Zofie and Cabrina. Zofie to make sure she was warm, fed, and had her other needs taken care of. And Cabrina to make sure she didn't fall out of the boat while examining a leaf in the water.

The bargemaster recommended the *Thirsty Boar*, one of the few inns still open in the town. Dunomhir was smaller than Iron Landing and had done even worse under Wynn's rule. It had gotten so bad that open rebellion had broken out, which was put down with the full might of the royal army. The evidence was in the several burned-out buildings we passed as we made our way into town.

The inn itself had seen better days, but the proprietor was delighted just to have customers and did his best to make us welcome. We later learned we were his first overnight guests in a week, and only a few locals would buy his admittedly heavily watered ale.

Rooms presented a minor problem. I didn't trust Fumiko to be alone with Cabrina, and I needed Fumiko's help with Zofie. Plus, both of us had to keep an eye on the Dark Avenyts.

So we decided to let Spraggel have his own since he snored worse than a storm in high summer. For the others, Fumiko and I thought it best if the rest of us stayed together. Although it meant I slept on the floor again.

After Zofie was bedded down and Cabrina sound asleep, Fumiko came to me as I knelt on the floor arranging my blankets.

"Coren, may I speak with you for a moment."

I looked up at her, puzzled at her unusual formality. She knelt across from me, her expression one of resignation. The room's single myst lantern shed a dim light, leaving the room cast in shadows. One fell across Fumiko's face only partially illuminating it and giving her eyes a strange sparkle.

While I tried not to notice, Fumiko was really an attractive woman. I had seen her draw the eye of many a young man. Rourke himself was proof of that. But she ignored the attention. The fact she rarely smiled spoke to something in her past that had hardened her heart. I couldn't help but wonder what tragedy had caused it.

She sat back on her heels, back perfectly straight, and put her hands in her lap. "Coren, I have been thinking of how to quickly improve your fighting skills. While they will work against an untrained attacker, they are..." she searched for the right word. "*Insufficient* to protect against someone of medium skill, and especially against the princess's cousin."

I sighed. "I know. Before Risten was possessed, she told me the same thing. I've been practicing, but I don't know what else to do?" I hung my head. "Maybe we should find someone that can better protect her."

Fumiko took a deep breath and let it out slowly. "There is a way to quickly get the skills you need."

My eyes went wide. "How?"

She licked her lips, looking very uncomfortable. "There is a technique to speed up your training. It is a closely guarded secret and requires a significant amount of myst to do it. But I was trained in its use. However..." She paused, searching my eyes. "It is forbidden."

I gave her a puzzled look. "Forbidden? You mean as in not a good idea, or forbidden as in you'll be hanged?"

She gazed at me levelly. "Both. Not only are there risks with the process, but it is also forbidden by the Council of Sages. They have the power to execute anyone caught using it."

I leaned forward. "And what is this secret technique? How could it possibly help me?"

She looked down. "I can transfer my sword skills directly from my brain into yours."

I considered her. "Zofie has shared her memories with me before. It was a little disorienting, but it didn't seem dangerous. Is this technique something similar?"

She rubbed her palms on her thighs. "It is similar in process, however not in scope. You see, sharing the memory of an experience is simply putting the sights and sounds of that into your head. It's the same as listening to a story or reading it from a book. But transferring a skill is different. It resides not just in your head, but also in the organs, nerves, and muscles of your body. So all of those must be transferred too."

I looked at her skeptically. "Sounds too good to be true. What's the catch?"

She nodded. "There are several. For one, you could die. Sometimes, the body rejects the skill refusing to take it, yet not be able to get rid of it. This can cause a wasting of the body until the person dies. However, if done properly, that rarely occurs."

"That doesn't sound encouraging. What are the others?"

"Well, it takes a lot of myst and requires several sessions to transfer all that is needed. It will take at least a day to rebuild my myst for the next session. And also the techniques I would give you are mine. The skills transferred are only as good as the source. So any mistakes or bad habits will come with it. And finally, you will still need to practice what is transferred, or they will quickly fade. You have to practice them to make them your own."

She paused. I could tell we had reached the part she really wasn't sure about.

I looked at her levelly. "That's not all, is it?"

She hesitated in her answer. "There are... side effects. The skills themselves are tied to my own memories of when I learned them. You will see things that I'm not really comfortable showing you." She looked down. "Things that will make you despise me."

I looked up in surprise. "Fumiko, I don't want you to do something that makes you feel violated. If you're not comfortable with it, then don't do it. We'll just have to think of another way."

She shook her head. "I don't want to lose any more of my precious people. I only ask that you not tell my secrets. Not even to Zofie. What I'm about to share is more intimate than being lovers."

I leaned back. "Fumiko, I don't know about this. As you would say, I don't feel worthy of this gift."

She turned her face toward me, and she gazed squarely into my eyes. I could see a mixture of dread, hope, and sadness. "Will you accept my offering? It is the only way I can help you and the princess. Both of you mean more to me than life itself. You've given me a home, friendship, and a purpose. You have no idea how grateful I am."

I glanced over to the bed where Zofie lay. In the silence of the room, I could hear her softly breathing. I thought back to the conversation Fumiko and I had in the carriage. How far would I go to protect Zofie?

Pretty damn far.

I turned back to Fumiko and nodded. "What do I need to do?"

She ran a hand through her hair. "This will be exhausting for both of us. I suggest you lay on your pallet since you will fall asleep immediately afterward. It's part of the brain's process to absorb the information. I'll kneel beside you and manage the flow."

I laid back on my blankets while Fumiko took her place beside me. She took my hand and raised it to her forehead. I felt her myst gathering.

"You don't have to do this," I said softly.

"Oh, but I do, precious person Coren. I most certainly do."

And then the world began to fade, and I suddenly saw the world through Fumiko's eyes.

The man that I faced seemed huge. Dressed in dark gray with a face and head completely shaved, he had to be one of the largest men I'd ever seen. Of course, most people were larger than me. I was already twelve, but I still looked like a child.

"Again!" he commanded.

The room was filled with over thirty students, boys and girls, all dressed in gray pants and a belted shirt. The air was filled with the sounds of grunts and yells and carried the smell of sweat and exertion. Like me, all were practicing the new form with a stick sword. Only most of the others were paired with other students. I was still with the teacher. Thank the Creator we weren't using real swords. He would have cut off a leg by now.

I assumed the initial position of the form we were practicing. I tried to ignore the stinging pains in my thigh. I had been unable to follow the form one time too many, and the teacher had issued motivation in the form of hits to my thighs and buttocks.

We started again from the base form and then proceeded slowly through the routine: turn, step, point, stab—

Wack! The stick was immediate. I blinked and refused to give up my tears.

"Your stab is too low. It needs to be higher."

The room was full of children and teachers going through similar motions. I had not been the only one to receive motivation, but for most, they had become sufficiently motivated that they didn't need it anymore. I, on the other hand, was not doing so well. And being last in this class frequently resulted in one disappearing.

No one knew where.

The instructor considered me a moment. My battered leg began to tremble, but I ignored it.

He sighed and stroked his chin. "You're normally better than this," he mumbled.

At the words, several in the class cut their eyes in my direction. They were forbidden to outright stare, less they also end up being punished.

The instructor seemed to have an inspiration and looked around the room. "Jiaying!"

She was practicing with another student across the room and instantly froze. She stepped back and turned to face the instructor. "Yes, master."

"Take this girl through the new forms. You're free to issue motivation if she doesn't do it perfectly." He leaned forward. "And I'll issue motivation to you if she doesn't."

"Yes, master."

Jiaying stepped in front of me under the watchful eyes of the instructor. We each took the beginning forms. I had practiced with other students before, but only a few times with Jiaying. She was the best in our group. The instructors rarely issued motivation to her. All they had was praise. Most of our group hated her.

We were dressed in the same loose-fitting pants and shirt, and even in the same shade of pale gray. And as I readied for the first movement, I noticed even our black hair was cut the same length. It was almost like looking in a mirror.

"Wait!" she barked. I held my place. She leaned toward me and jerked me one way and then the other. "Like this," she said loudly. And then she brought her face close, coming within a finger of my ear. She breathed, "It's your monthly, isn't it?"

She stepped back, and I tried to keep my face impassive. Was it that obvious? While I may have the chest of a boy, my insides were changing into a woman. The cramps had been especially bad this morning. So bad, my concentration had lapsed, and I missed some of the initial demonstration. I gave a tiny nod.

She nodded back. "We'll go through this very slowly, so watch closely."

And Jiaying began to move. Slowly, so slowly. I had to fight to move that slow. My muscles screamed at me to go faster, but I ignored them and followed Jiaying's lead: turn, step, point, stab, block, slice—going through the entire routine. It was like watching another me—until we reached the end.

I blinked in surprise. I had made it all the way through.

"Again, faster," she said.

And we did it again, it was still slower than I would have liked, but I made it through.

Three more times, we went through the routine. The instructor came back over and observed the last time. When we finished, he nodded in satisfaction. "Ten more times. Both of you."

As the instructor turned away, Jiaying moved close to adjust my stance. "Next time, signal me," she whispered. "I can show you an herb in the garden that will help."

And when she stepped back, she did the oddest thing.

The side of her mouth curled up ever so slightly.

I couldn't stop my own mouth from mirroring her.

I awoke slowly, feeling the presence of a comforting warmth beside me. My groggy brain was balking at the idea of actually letting me think. It almost felt bruised.

I slowly opened my eyes, expecting Zofie to be slumbering against me. Only it wasn't. Fumiko lay curled up at my side sound asleep, her head resting on the edge of my shoulder, and her arm draped across my chest. I blinked, trying to clear the cobwebs and remember why she was there. Then it came to me—the skill transfer.

I rubbed my face, exhaustion washing over me. I was so tired. My arms and legs felt like I had run all night long, carrying a load of lead on my back. I desperately wanted to go back to sleep, but my thigh hurt too much from the teacher's hits...

My eyes went wide. Fumiko had been the one hit, not me. I ran my hand down my leg and could feel the sore spots just under the skin. I shook my head. She had warned me about the after-effects, but I hadn't thought they would be that strong. I think I had bruises.

I felt someone looking at me and glanced over at Cabrina. I found her sitting cross-legged on her pallet, watching me intently. "Did you have sex with her last night?"

I immediately sat up and regretted it—my head was pounding. "No, we did not!" I rubbed my aching temples. "Why in the world would you even ask that?"

"Well, you and Mistress Fumiko are lying on the same blanket. Isn't that customary after having sex? My host is very inexperienced on human reproduction, and both of us are very curious."

"No!" I shouted. "We were just... sleeping."

Cabrina looked at me skeptically. "My host says it's only done in private, and it's typical for partners to deny it. Why is that? If you're going to reproduce, why don't you just do it!"

"We did not have sex!" I yelled.

My shout awoke Fumiko, who realized we were lying a little too close to each other. She refused to look at me and immediately got up. "I'm going to get breakfast for Zofie," and grabbing her boots, she was out the door.

For myself, I kicked my blankets to one side and grabbed my sword. I pulled it and held it before me. It felt different—wrong, yet right. Remembering the routine from Fumiko's memory. I tried to mimic it, only to find my body moved by itself, flowing effortlessly through the motions. I went through them again much faster and was amazed at what I could do. The blade almost sang as I went through the form. The technique had worked. All I had to do now was practice.

My mind drifted to the other parts of the memory. To me, it felt like it happened just hours ago, when for Fumiko, it was half her lifetime away. I understood why she had chosen that memory, being exactly what I needed to learn those forms. But what exactly had been happening to her? She was being trained for something. Something difficult. And harshly. But what? No wonder she rarely smiled. I could still feel the echoes of the inflicted pain.

And that girl Jiaying, I sensed emotions attached to her. Strong ones. But they were too vague to make out. I shook my head. Fumiko had asked that I keep her secrets, so I best not even think about it. I had been warned of the intimacy of the memory, but the reality was more than I had expected. I was seeing her closer than I'd seen any person. Even Zofie. It made me uncomfortable. I couldn't help but wonder what it must be doing to Fumiko. I sighed. She was indeed giving me a very precious gift. I had to make sure I used it wisely.

I looked over to Zofie. Her eyes were open, but she just lay there, unmoving. For some reason, I felt guilty. Like I had been unfaithful. Something I would never do. Yet Fumiko's memory haunted me. And I could never tell Zofie about it. Wasn't that a form of cheating?

I frowned. But I had to do it to protect her. It was the only way. I just hoped it was enough. We still had a long way to go, and Lilith was not going to leave us alone.

Spraggel entered without even knocking. "Good morning." He pointed over his shoulder. "I just saw Fumiko, and she was a bit on the grumpy side. Did you do something to her?"

"They had sex!" yelled Cabrina.

Spraggel shot me a knowing look. "Really."

I decided right then that Cabrina might not live through the day. I swear. That girl was starting to sound like Abe.

After a quick breakfast, we set out for Oddfrid Vandobarre's estate. The carriage we finally hired was a rickety affair with a roughly patched hole in one side and a broken step. It also only held four, so Spraggel volunteered to sit with the driver.

We had more trouble than expected hiring a ride. For one, our destination was far outside of town, surrounded by farms and forest. Quite isolated. The driver would take most of the day getting there and back.

Plus, Oddfrid had a bit of a reputation—several turned us down flat. They said the man was insane. From my standpoint, that just meant he would get along well with our group.

Under Zofie's grandfather, Oddfrid had kept the kingdom supplied with long-range portals, and according to Spraggel, was quite powerful in his day. Some said one of the best. Rumors had it that the past king had begged him to save the villagers in the path of a forest fire. He only had minutes to do it, so he opened not one portal, but two, each leading to different locations. He held it until all the villagers were able to escape. No one had been able to do that since.

But now Oddfrid was quite advanced in age and long since retired. However, his leaving the royal service had been abrupt and clouded with rumors of strange circumstances. Some said he'd suddenly lost his powers and had been forced into it. But others spoke of trying to open a portal too far and killing someone. Exactly what constituted too far was a bit of a mystery.

It was late morning when our driver stopped at a branching of the road, saying he was as close to Oddfrid's estate as he intended to go. He pointed up an overgrown path saying the house was just a short walk away. I eyed the indicated route. Had it not been winter, we might not have been able to follow it.

We walked up the path and discovered it led to a large house hidden from the road by tall unkempt pines and flanked by two massive oak trees. In its earlier years, the house would have been quite magnificent. But now it was showing its age. The faded paint was cracked and peeling, with dead vines having taken over the left side. On the roof lay a heavy branch split from one of the oaks, which looked to have knocked off the top of the chimney.

We paused at a gate in front of the house. It was open, hanging by only one rusty hinge, and allowing entrance to a walled yard, filled with generations of dead leaves courtesy of the massive oaks. I left the others at the gate and picked my way to a small stoop, which groaned and popped when I stepped on it. I could feel the board sag under my weight. The door, worn and cracked, had a dull brass knocker, which I tried to use, but it fell off.

I knocked. "Hello," I called. "Is anyone home? We're here to see

Master Oddfrid Vandobarre. Princess Zophia Xernow requires his assistance. I am Coren Hart, her knight."

There was no reply from inside. I began to wonder if anyone lived here anymore. Then I heard a squeak from above, followed by a gravelly voice. "Go away," it said. "I have no use for royalty."

I looked up and noticed a worn shutter on a window high above the door had opened. I took several steps back but didn't see anyone inside.

I looked over my shoulder at Spraggel with a questioning look, but he just shrugged.

"Please, sir," I called again. "It is a matter of life and death. The well-being of the kingdom is at stake."

Croaking laughter drifted toward me. But it came from a different direction: my left and from around the side of the house. "You have no idea how many times I've heard that same line. I can't count the times I *saved* the kingdom." All the mirth drained from the voice. "I don't do that anymore. I have nothing left to give. I just want to live out my remaining days in peace."

"Sir!" I shouted. "I beg you, please listen to us. We need to go to the Kuiojia Empire as quickly as we can."

"Leave," came the gravelly voice, only this time from behind me. I wheeled to see no one there.

Spraggel frowned and stepped forward to join me on the stoop. "Good man," he said. "Will you please stop with the parlor tricks. You're scaring the young ones."

"Then maybe you *should* be scared. How do you know I'm not a ghost, and I'm trying to capture your soul."

Spraggel snorted. "Not very likely. All you're doing is opening up tiny portals and speaking through them."

Suddenly, swords and spears appeared sticking up from the ground around us. And from their base, blood began to seep from the ground.

"Now leave before I take your blood too."

Spraggel rolled his eyes. "Please. At least be a little more original.

You pushed those weapons through a portal. And the red water is likely from the nearby ironworks."

Suddenly a naked man appeared in front of us, with his feet hovering at about head height. "Oh really, then how do you explain the apparition before you? Now leave before I eat you!"

Spraggel waved a dismissive hand. "Another parlor trick. You're just teleporting between you standing somewhere and being in the air. You're just doing it so fast you're not falling. And put some clothes on dammit. We've got ladies here."

The naked man disappeared. A few moments later, the front door opened and slowly swung inward. The previously naked man came out wearing a worn cloak. He looked to be even older than Spraggel, and I thought Spraggel was ancient.

"That was most disappointing. All that work and you saw through all of them." He examined Spraggel closer. "Do I know you?"

"Spraggel van Deviante," he gave a short bow. "You've transported me several times over the years."

Oddfrid nodded. "I remember now. You pissed off that myst user, and she transformed you into a cat."

Spraggel nodded sheepishly. "That would have been me."

He considered Spraggel for a moment longer and then harrumphed. "She should have left you." He turned back to us and straightened. "But none of this changes anything. I won't help you. My days in service to the kingdom are long past."

I was starting to get a little miffed. "I noticed you said won't, not can't." I marched down the path to where the rest of my party stood and took Zofie's hand. I led her forward. We stopped in front of the man. "This is Princess Zophia. Now tell her that you won't help. That you won't help her get her mind back."

Oddfrid ignored her. "I told you I won't get involved in the affairs of nobles ever again. I don't care if she is the princess." He glanced her way and then immediately looked again. His expression softened. He then leaned forward and gently pushed back her hood. She stared at him blankly.

"What happened to her?" he asked softly. "The last I heard, she had reclaimed the throne."

"She did," I said. "However, a Dark Avenyts put a charm on her leaving her like this. Her intelligence, her personality, are just not there."

Oddfrid reached for her hand and pulled it toward him. Her sleeve fell back to reveal the charmed bracelet. "This must be the culprit. It's quite a bundle of twisted threads. Far beyond my ability." He turned troubled eyes in my direction. "I can see a powerful curse on her already, which is why the charm." He gently lowered her hand. "Dark Avenyts, you say? That's impossible. What really happened?"

Spraggel brought Cabrina forward. "Oh really. Take a look at this one."

Oddfrid turned unbelieving eyes toward the girl and then shook his head. "Her curse is indeed extremely complex, but I can't say for sure it's a Dark Avenyts."

I frowned. "Maybe we should let her possess you so you can see for yourself."

He took an involuntary step back. "No, I don't think that is necessary." He sighed. "Assuming I were to help, what exactly do you want of this old man?"

"We need you to open a portal for us to the Kuiojia Empire. We have spoken with a myst user there who says he can remove the charm."

His eyebrows went up in surprise. "That's quite the distance. I haven't done a long-range portal that far since..." he paused for a moment, looked up at us, and then seemed to think better of what he was going to say. "Since before you were born."

Spraggel stepped forward. "You're the only wayfarer left in the kingdom. Without your help, we'll have to make the trip overland, and you know how dangerous that is, even in the best of times."

He considered us for a moment. "I can't open a portal into the empire. No one can. It is protected by their huge myst barrier, which stops all curses and portals. The best I can do is place you at its border. And even then, it will take at least three portals with a minimum of one day rest between. Which means I have to come with you at least that far."

I grinned. "We would be most appreciative. If you can get us to the borders, we'll figure out something from there."

He glanced again at Zofie. "I can't believe she's all grown now. I remember when she was just a baby in her mother's arms. Seems like it was only yesterday." He sighed and looked back to me. "I assume you're in a hurry?"

I nodded. "We have one more item we need to collect before leaving. And I'm praying it won't take that long."

He paused and looked at each of us in turn. He finally gave a deep sigh. "I'll help you. Just this once." He glanced at Zofie. "Come back this evening and be prepared to leave immediately. In the meantime, I'll start making preparations and review my maps. Short-range portals are very forgiving, but long-range ones are not." He grinned. "I've got to be sure I don't accidentally put us inside a mountain."

I agreed a little research might be a good idea.

CHAPTER TEN

Family

It was early afternoon when the carriage slowly drew to a halt at the next stop in our journey. Although I longed to stretch my legs, I didn't immediately move. Instead, out the carriage window, I examined the footpath we had stopped beside and the house beyond—farther up the hill and barely visible through the dense trees. It was little changed since my last visit. Unlike Oddfrid's, this path was well-maintained. It was even marked with a small wooden sign, expertly embellished with the picture of a goat and the owner's name.

Lauremarius.

It was my family's home.

Cabrina impatiently shoved her head beside mine to also see out the window, and I realized I was blocking the others from exiting. I glanced back to see Fumiko giving me a curious look. I think she sensed my hesitation. With a sigh, I steeled myself and opened the carriage door.

As we were leaving Oddfrid's, I had tried to persuade him to speed up our travels by opening a portal for us to my family home. But he had refused, saying it was too dangerous. He had no beacon to affix the far end of the portal. Instead, he gave me a round crystal orb about as large as my palm, which would open a return portal to his front yard. He made it clear that it contained only enough myst for one trip, so to use it carefully, and not leave anyone behind.

So, we took the carriage to the next destination. One which I was not looking forward to. My step-father's house.

I would always think of it that way. Mother had been forced to sell the horse stables shortly after my father had died. He had been the one with the business sense, so when he wasn't there to take the reins, it quickly went downhill. So after a brief courtship, she threw in her lot with my stepfather, Mellen Lauremarius. I guess he was a decent fellow in his own sort of way. He was always nice to Mother, but he and I never really hit it off. It likely had something to do with the way he reacted to my curse, treating me like some kind of diseased person. But it was home. I tried to make the best of it and get along with my new step-sister.

But I guess over that first year, my bad luck had pushed my stepfather just a little too far. I would never forget the late-night conversation I'd overheard when he thought I was asleep. Mother was already well into the pregnancy of what I would later learn was my younger sister. He was quite blunt about it and demanded that she find somewhere else for me to live. It wasn't long after that I was apprenticed to Master Spraggel.

I was a little bitter about that. Not so much at my stepfather, but with my mother, Octavia. She hadn't protested one bit at his demand. It was probably the reason I had visited only once since I had been apprenticed and that had been at my baby sister's first birthday. She was seven years old now.

As we walked the winding path up the hill, the house came into better view. The structure itself was nothing fancy being partially dug into a sharp rise in the land behind it. The house's flat roof was topped in soil and built to be an extension of the hill. In warmer times, both the hill and the top of the house would be covered in green grass. I grinned. The goats loved it up there. I remembered my first visit and my amazement at the goat looking down on me as I walked in the front door.

But there were no goats in evidence now. They were likely in the barn atop the hill to protect them against the cold and perhaps even predators. Especially the two-legged kind.

We were nearing the house when a woman atop the roof stood up. She was in her mid-years wearing a plain dress and heavy coat. What hair peeked out from her cap looked to be tinted with gray.

And she was aiming a small crossbow at us.

"Halt!" she called. "State your business."

Fumiko immediately reached for her sword, but I held out a hand to pause her.

I took a step forward. "Hello, Mother," I said.

She blinked at me in surprise. "Coren? Is it you?"

"Indeed, it is I." I opened my arms toward her.

She lowered her weapon, but the look of surprise didn't leave her face. "I can't believe you're here. It's been so long." She glanced at the others. "I had heard you were doing well."

"May we approach?" I asked.

She put her weapon down and stepped back, disappearing from our sight atop the roof. But she reappeared around the side moments later and came forward to give me a fierce hug. "It's good to see you after so many years." She gave a short laugh. "You're taller than me now. And from what I've heard, a knight. I would never have believed it." Worry crossed her face. "What about your curse?"

I smiled. "Under control for now. I'll tell you about it later." I extended an arm toward the rest of my party. "Mother, let me introduce my friends. You remember Master Spraggel. This lady here is Fumiko, and the one just behind her is Cabrina." I didn't give any further explanation about Cabrina—hoping Mother would accept it as part of the queen's business.

Then I indicated the silent Zofie beside me. "And this is the one I'm engaged to, Princess Zophia."

A look of horror came over my mother. "You brought her here! The princess?" Her voice squeaked. She fell to one knee before Zofie. "I'm sorry, Princess, I didn't know you were coming. I would have prepared better."

"Mother," I said sadly. "She can't answer you."

My mother gave me a questioning look from where she knelt.

I sighed. "She's under the influence of a charm that's robbed her of her will. We're on a mission to break her out of it."

Mother slowly stood and looked at Zofie more closely. Her eyes flicked between us.

Suspicion suddenly crept into her voice. "You aren't running from one of the lords, are you? We can't protect you, Coren. We lost almost everything...."

I touched her hand. "No, it's nothing like that. We need an ancient artifact, and when I cast for it, it pointed me here. I need to talk with Docila."

Mother nodded her head toward the house. "She's inside." A look of concern on her face. "And please don't fight with her. She's had a rough time recently." Her voice dropped. "A really rough time."

I wondered what had happened but decided not to press it. Docila and I had butted heads the moment our households had merged. She was a couple of years older than I and thought she ruled the kingdom, while I, being an only child, had a slightly different opinion. I think she was one of the reasons I was apprenticed off so young.

We turned toward the house. The front door burst open, and a child of about seven, wearing a thick coat too big for her, ran to Mother and stood bashfully beside her. She turned big eyes toward us.

I squatted down beside her. "Hello, Floria."

The girl looked up at Mother.

"Go ahead," Mother urged. "You can talk to them. They're not soldiers."

"Hello," she said timidly.

I grinned. "I'm your big brother, Coren."

She digested the information but made no further comment. I couldn't blame her. I hadn't seen her since she was a babe.

I felt something brushing on my leg and looked down to see a rather large cat rubbing against me. I smiled. I scooped him up and scratched him behind the ears. "Hello, Mischief. I see you're living up to your name." He purred loudly and made sure I knew I was not to stop.

"Coren," said Spraggel behind me. "I hate to rush, but we do have an appointment later."

I put Mischief down. The cat gave me a displeased look before turning and sauntering off.

I stood and nodded.

Mother took Floria by the hand and turned toward the house. "Mellen has gone to try and trade a goat for some grain. The problem is that while most are more than willing to take the goat, they have little to offer in return. And the ones that do, are more likely to slit your throat than part with their coin." She gave a soft chuckle. "Which is why I'm watching the path. We had a run-in with some people that thought our goats were free. We had to change their minds rather forcefully."

Fumiko looked around warily. "Coren, I should probably wait outside."

Mother shook her head. "No need for you to stay out in this chill. Come inside where it's warm." She turned to her child. "Floria, go watch for us."

The young girl nodded and ran toward the back of the house. A few minutes later, she reappeared standing on the top of the roof. She knelt there, scanning our surroundings. It broke my heart that things had come to this in the kingdom.

Inside was the simple dwelling I remembered. It even smelled the same with hints of spices, bread, and simmering stew. It only had one room where the cooking, prepping, and eating occurred. And overhead was a loft where everyone would sleep, as well as another door which opened atop the hill.

In the middle of the room rested a large table with the preparations for a meal scattered across it. And behind it was a stone hearth with a crackling fire and an iron pot hanging from a hook over it. Docila stood before it with its glow framing her. She stood behind the table like one would a shield, and she did not seem inclined to come out from behind it.

She had matured since last I had seen her. Like her father, she was tall with blond hair and light-colored eyes. She wore a simple earth-colored dress with a shawl of a slightly darker hue around her shoulders. Her expression was tight—of one terrified of something yet having nowhere to run.

"Look who showed up on our doorstep," Mother said proudly.

Docila quickly searched our faces. "I don't..." Then she locked on me. "Coren?"

I grinned and nodded. "Hello, sister."

She stayed where she was. "What are you doing here? We can't take any more bad luck." She sounded accusatory. "Aren't you with the princess now? Her knight even?"

Mother looked at her and frowned. "Be nice. He has the princess with him."

A look of fury came over Docila's face. "Get out!" she yelled and grabbed up a cooking knife lying on the table. Fumiko reacted immediately and put herself in front of Zofie.

I held up my hands. "Wait! We just want to talk with you."

Docila came slowly around the table, moving with a pronounced limp. "That's what the soldiers said. They were the king's soldiers. But when I wouldn't tell them where the goats were hidden, they hit me." Tears came to her eyes. "And when I tried to get away, they hit me some more, and tore my clothes... and... and..." She turned away and rubbed at her eyes with the heel of her hand. "I have no use for royalty. Leave me alone."

Mother shouted, "Docila. Put the knife down. These people had nothing to do with that."

Docila looked at the knife, seemingly puzzled why she even held it. She set it carefully down on the table and then turned to tend the fire with her back to us.

Mother pursed her lips. "Forgive her. She's had it rough."

I gave her a questioning look.

But Mother shook her head, her eyes pleading. I guess the soldiers had done their worst to Docila. And the wounds were still raw—especially the emotional ones.

Damn Wynn. Not only had he bankrupt the kingdom, he had also stolen its soul.

I looked to Zofie, standing silently beside me. What would Zofie do? Her heart was ten times bigger than mine and always knew just the right things to say. I considered her a moment. Then perhaps she should say it.

I turned to everyone else. "Mother, would you show my friends the goats. I bet they would love to see them. Since I've seen them before, I'll take a moment to talk with Docila."

Fumiko shot a puzzled glance my way. Spraggel, on the other hand, gave me a brief nod of approval and dropped a hand on Cabrina's shoulder. "I bet you'd like to see the goats, wouldn't you?"

The youth grinned. I thought she was going to jump up and down.

Mother froze for just the barest second, then she caught on. "All right, everyone. Like my son says, we have the finest goats this side of the mountains." And she began to lead them out.

Fumiko reached to take Zofie's arm, but I shook my head. Fumiko gave me a puzzled look but went out with the others. A moment later, the door closed, leaving just the three of us alone.

I tugged on Zofie's arm and she followed. I guided her to a bench beside the table and seated her there. She sat with back straight and blank eyes staring straight ahead.

"Docila," I said. "I have someone I want you to meet."

My stepsister looked up from bruising herself with the fire. Her eyes were damp, and they flicked from me to Zofie. While Docila watched, I took off my companion's mittens and cloak, leaving her in just her regular travel clothes of shirt and pants. I placed her lifeless hands into her lap and sat beside her.

Docila took in the whole scene. She rose, and frowning in disapproval, limped around the table to stand over us. She studied Zofie a moment before waving a hand in front of her face. Zofie didn't even blink.

"What's wrong with her?" Docila asked.

I reached for Zofie's hand and held it up to show her the bracelet encircling her wrist. "This charm is robbing her of her will. Those behind it are trying to stop her from saving the kingdom. I'm doing my best to get the charm off without it killing her."

Docila frowned. "Would serve her right. All the royals, playing with us like we're insects."

I shook my head. "Not Zofie. She was trying to figure out a way to feed everybody. She's been begging the neighboring rulers and lords to please share. But they've all turned their backs on her. She fears that they are merely waiting for us to grow even weaker so they can attack us." I kissed her hand before returning it to her lap. "She spent every last piece of gold in the treasury buying food, not to mention selling what was left of her jewelry. She thought it might help a few extra days."

Docila looked troubled. "Why are you telling me this?"

"Because she needs your help. The price for getting the curse off her is something called the Griffin's Key. And when I used a myst device to search for it, it pointed me to you. Do you know anything about it? I think I can safely say, the fate of the kingdom depends on us finding it."

Docila sat down beside me. "I have no interest in helping her kind. The lot of them can burn in the Creator's darkest hell for all I care."

I shut my eyes in frustration. What could I say to get her to help me? I glanced at Zofie. Even with no expression, she was beautiful. But what I really loved was the wonderful person inside. How could I make her see that?

"Did you know," I said abruptly. "She keeps a small stuffed dog on her bed." I chuckled. "It's completely worn out. She says her mother gave it to her the year before she died as a Day of the New gift. And..." I could feel my heartache swelling. "She loves picnics. She and I tried to have one just a few days ago in the family crypt no less. She did it to remember her parents, trying to stay connected to them. And..." I could feel dampness coming to my eyes. "Did you know she can complete my quotes? She's the only person I know of that can do that. I'll say the first part, and then she'll complete it. And I can do the same for her. It's unnerving and wonderful at the same time. And... and..." I looked up at my sister with tears in my eyes. "I love her, Docila. I know you and I have had our squabbles, but please... help her. Every time I see her like this, my heart breaks just a little more. She means everything to me."

Docila considered me for several heartbeats. Her eyes flicked to Zofie and then finally back to me. She placed her hand on mine. "I won't help her," she said softly. "But I will help you... if I can."

I grasped her hand and gave it a gentle squeeze. "Thank you."

She stood up abruptly. "But it comes at a cost." She cocked her jaw and limped back toward the fire. "Mother talks about you all the time. How you're a knight now and doing so well. She hangs off every letter she gets, pouring over them for some tiny detail she might have missed." Docila turned to look at me. "It gets annoying. Not that she talks about you, but you don't even acknowledge she's there."

"But she wanted me out when I was just a child."

She stabbed her finger in my direction. "Listen Coren. She feels deeply guilty for making you leave. I guess we all do. And Floria asks about her brother all the time, which doesn't make it easier for her." She shook her head. "Even though I'm not her flesh and blood, she treats me as if I'm one of her own. As I've grown, I've come to understand her a lot better." Docila stood erect and clasped her hands in front of her. "So my price is for you to visit Mother at least once a year."

I shook my head. "She seemed pretty eager to get rid of me."

She sighed. "Coren, you have no idea what it was like living with you. I was in constant fear that I would get seriously hurt." She took a deep breath. "Mother was afraid too. And just think, she was pregnant with Floria. What if you made her miscarry, or she died in childbirth, or even caused the new baby to be stillborn. With your curse then, it could have caused a thousand things to go wrong. Which is why she felt she had to choose between her oldest son and her unborn child. She knew her oldest could take care of himself, but her unborn..." she trailed off.

I hadn't thought of it that way. "How do you know this?"

"We talk. Father means well, but he's a man and doesn't really understand. So she talks to me." She looked away. "Creator knows I've needed to talk with her lately."

I shook my head. "Are you sure that's what she wants?"

"I'm sure, but ask her. It would go a long way to easing her guilt. Just don't tell her I'm blackmailing you into it."

"And what about you, Docila? Do you want me to visit? I still have my curse."

She shrugged. "As long as it's not for too long, I guess I could handle it. Besides, it would be nice to make fun of you again."

I couldn't help but chuckle. "And what will you do if I refuse."

She grinned wickedly. "I'll tell the princess about the time you wrecked the privy."

My eyes got big. "You wouldn't dare."

She just smiled.

I held up my hands. "I surrender. I've been outmaneuvered."

Nodding in satisfaction, she took a large spoon and stirred the pot hanging over the fire. "Now back to this *thing* you need to find. What exactly do you need from me?"

"To show me the Griffin's Key. Other than being something of legend, I have no idea what it looks like."

She gave me a sad look. "Coren, I don't have anything resembling a key. For that matter, we don't have any locks. I don't know how I could possibly help you."

I sighed. "It's likely something very old. Ancient. And it might not look like a key. I had to find something called a mirror, and it looked like a ball of glass. Have you run into anything like that? Or perhaps it might have acted strange or be protected somehow."

Docila gave me a funny look. "Ancient, you say? Well, there was the place I hid the goats. It had some ruins in it and sort of qualifies as strange."

I leaned closer. "How so?"

She tucked a stray strand of hair behind her ear. "It was back in the spring. We'd gotten word the soldiers were coming, and they were taking everything of value. Father sent me into the woods to hide the goats. I thought I'd take them up to a small clearing about a mile from here, but the goats were being stubborn, as they frequently will, and before I knew it, I had lost my way. I thought that if I cut due north, I would cross the stream that runs close to our house. As I led the goats, I found I kept veering east while they tended to stay in the northern direction. I stopped and restarted several times but kept veering off.

"I finally got angry and made a conscious effort to go north. It got harder and harder, like something was pushing against me. But you know how stubborn I can get. I knew I had to get the goats to safety, or we would not have enough to make it through the winter.

"Then suddenly the resistance just stopped, and I almost fell into a break in the woods. And it had ancient ruins in it. The goats loved it because it gave them big rocks to climb on, and the grass there was wild and tender. I figured if it was hard for me to find, then it would be doubly difficult for the soldiers. So the goats and I bedded down right there and stayed overnight." She licked her lips. "But the really strange thing was at night. There was this glow coming from some of the stones. It wasn't scary or anything, but strange." She sighed. "I returned to the house the next day to find the soldiers had come but had not been able to find me. They had searched the woods, and even found my trail, but couldn't follow it."

I leaned forward excitedly. "Can you take me there?" I asked. "That might be it."

Docila opened her mouth to reply but didn't get the chance. Just then, I heard the back door open and Floria come flying in. She came down the stairs until she could jump the rest of the way down. Her face flushed from running. "There are two people coming up the path," she said breathlessly. "A man and a woman."

My heart leaped into my throat, and I prayed it wasn't so. "Was the woman wearing a wide-brimmed hat?"

The little girl nodded. "And they have swords too."

"Creator!" I ran my hand through my hair, trying to get my thoughts together. It was Lilith and Wort.

And we'd led them right to my family.

CHAPTER ELEVEN

Hidden Ruins

I went to Zofie and pulled her up, hurriedly jerking on her cloak. "What is it, Coren?" asked Docila.

"It's Zofie's cousin. She's trying to kill her." I pulled Zofie toward the steep stairs hoping I'd be able to get her up quickly.

Docila's eyes went wide. "You involved us in their royalty games!"

After a couple faltering steps, I managed to get Zofie climbing up them. I glanced at Docila and shook my head. "Not now. You can beat me up later. We have to get to the others and find somewhere to hide."

Docila cocked her jaw like she wanted to say more, but instead grabbed Floria and followed right behind us.

We headed out the loft door and toward the barn. We were fortunate it was located on the back of the hill and not visible from the path leading to the house. It would give us a few more precious minutes.

Docila and Floria trotted ahead since all that poor Zofie could manage was a fast walk. Fumiko met me at the door, and I quickly explained about our unexpected guests. She took Zofie while I went to close the barn's double doors. They would be no barrier to what was coming—they didn't even have a bolt. But it might buy us a few more seconds. I turned toward the group huddled in the middle of the barn. Fumiko stood with Zofie, and we exchanged a glance. This was not good. My family made excellent hostages, and all it would take would be capturing one to stop me in my tracks.

"Should we fight them?" I asked.

Fumiko looked pained. "I can't beat both of them, and if you try to take one of them, you will die."

"But my new skills..."

Fumiko shook her head. "It's too soon. You need much more to be effective, especially against her."

I glanced at each of the ones in my group. Cabrina nearly bubbled with excitement, and Spraggel was digging in his pocket again. I prayed he didn't find his sword. In sharp contrast, Docila and Floria clung to each other looking horrified.

And of course, there was Mother. She pulled out her crossbow and stomped toward the door. "I'll get rid of them."

I grabbed her arm. "No, you won't. Those people won't hesitate to kill you if they even suspect you might know where Zofie is."

"I'm not afraid of them."

"You should be," I shot back. "Risten's a sword-master. You'll be dead before you can feel the cut."

Fumiko quickly scanned the interior. The barn was completely enclosed with the door at the front as the only exit. With the doors shut, little light reached us from outside, coming mainly from gaps around the frame and the places in the side walls where the boards didn't completely meet. At the back of the barn was a loft used for storing hay and other items they didn't want the goats to sample. A simple ladder was used to climb up to it. On the barn's right side were two fenced pens, which ran the length of the barn. About a dozen goats were in the back pen staring at us hopefully. Normally, they would be out foraging, but with the cold and predators, they were being kept mostly inside. I sighed, seeing how few my family had remaining. Usually, there were several times that number, and I couldn't help but wonder how many would survive until spring.

Fumiko shook her head. "We'll never get Zofie up the ladder." Then she spied the blankets hanging on the wall just high enough not to attract the attention of the goats. She strode over to them and pulled them down. "Quickly," she said. "Over here." She climbed into the empty pen and moved to the side closest to the door.

We followed.

"Shouldn't we go to the back?" I asked, pointing to the rear of the barn.

"No," she said. "They'll be less likely to search close to the front."

Fumiko shook out the blankets. "Everyone get down here in the corner as close to each other as you can. And don't say a word when the door opens—we should be in its shadow."

My head jerked in her direction, suddenly understanding what she intended. She was going to use her myst to hide us. This would also risk revealing her ability to others, something she had been trying to avoid. Her gaze caught mine, but she dismissed me with a simple shake of her head. I guess she deemed the risk necessary, and I couldn't help but appreciate the gift she was giving to protect my family.

We did as she instructed, and I took my place on one end with Zofie between Cabrina and me. Fumiko quickly covered us with the blankets and took her place on the other end. Then she closed her eyes and concentrated.

No sooner had Fumiko started when we heard steps outside. The barn doors flew open, and Lilith strode inside with Wort just behind. She wordlessly pointed to the loft, and Wort stepped to the ladder, quickly climbing up. He was out of my line of vision, but I could hear his steps on the boards above us.

Lilith came further into the barn and looked closely at everything. She even lifted the feed bin to make sure it was empty.

Behind Lilith, Mischief sauntered through the door. As cats do, he walked along the wall, uncaring of human affairs.

A moment later, Wort came down the ladder. "No one," he said.

Lilith shook her head. "They must be close by. There was a fire in the hearth, and it had been recently tended."

"Do you think she's here?" asked Wort.

"I'm not sure," answered Lilith. "Our source saw her headed in this direction. Also, there were carriage tracks on the road. Someone came here not long ago."

Lilith turned toward the door. "Let's go back toward the house. They likely circled back around us. Maybe we can pick up a trail."

Mischief strolled under the bottom board of the pen and meandered in our direction.

Oh no.

The illusion of shadow surrounding us might have fooled Lilith and Wort, but Mischief had no problem with it. He walked over to the hidden blanket and began to rub on it. I didn't dare try to shoo him away. That would out us sure as anything. I could only imagine what it looked like with him sliding against something that couldn't be seen. I could even hear him purring.

Lilith gave one last look around the interior. My heart leaped in my chest as she glanced at the cat. But to my great surprise, her gaze moved on. After a moment, she simply walked outside, and I heard her steps recede into the distance.

I quickly yanked Mischief under the blanket. He seemed most pleased with himself as I stroked his fur.

We waited for a few minutes, and then I slipped out from under the blanket. Motioning for the others to remain where they were, I shoved Mischief at Cabrina. She stared at the cat as if it was some strange beast, but steeled herself and began to carefully stroke his fur. Mischief didn't care whether she be human or Dark Avenyts. He just welcomed the petting and purred loudly.

I crept to the door and checked outside—no sign of them. I went back to the others and knelt close.

I turned to my mother. "Is there anywhere you can go to hide. Maybe old Fendrason's place?"

She shook her head. "Fendrason's burned down last summer, and there's been some unsavory fellows hanging out in what's left. The forest would be the best bet."

I glanced to Zofie. Going anywhere quickly with her was going to be a problem. I sighed. "I'll check to see if we can sneak out and hide...."

Mother cut me off. "I'm not leaving the goats. We've worked too hard to keep what's left."

I shook my head. "But there's no way we can get all of them out, *plus* all of us, without attracting her attention."

Mother folded her arms across her chest, looking quite determined. "I'm not leaving them. I'll fight first."

Fumiko and I exchanged a glance. I knew from experience that when my mother dug in her heels, she could be very stubborn.

"Mother, you're..."

Fumiko abruptly stood and brushed off her pants. "Hiding here is our best option. Besides, moving the princess is slow. We'd never outrun her if she started chasing us. I'll stay behind and keep everyone concealed."

"Behind?" I asked.

She nodded. "While you sneak out and try to find the key."

I frowned. "Are you sure?" She was running the risk of revealing her illusion ability.

She gazed at me levelly. "No one notices the shadows."

I took a deep breath considering the options. None were great. "All right," I finally said. "Just be careful. I doubt Lilith is going to give up easily." I turned to Docila. "Can you show me where you hid the goats? I think it might hold what we're looking for."

Unfortunately, Docila was not taking this well. I could see fear on her face. "But what about those people?" she asked apprehensively. "My limp will slow us down, and they might see us." I could hear her voice shaking. She was just a fingerbreadth away from balking. I had to do something.

I raised my eyebrows in mock surprise. "That shouldn't be a problem. Unless that is, you've forgotten how to make yourself vanish?"

She cocked her head to one side in puzzlement. "Vanish?"

I nodded. "When I came to live here, I was certain you could. Because when it came time for chores, you were never around."

A faint smile spread across her lips. "Only because you would disappear as soon as the topic of work came up. Wouldn't show back up until dinnertime."

I smiled and held out my hand. "Then it sounds like we won't have a problem. With you vanishing and me disappearing, we will be just fine."

After a moment's hesitation, she took it. "I guess you're right."

While everyone else huddled quietly in the corner of the pen, Docila and I slipped out the door.

Moving as fast as she could with her limp, she led the way across the pasture and into the forest bordering it. During my short time living on the farm, I had frequently played and watched over the goats in the open field, but I had been forbidden to enter the woods. Of course, I had—but only the fringes. Even then, I could see how easy it would be to lose one's way. For me, there had always been something unnerving about the tall trees.

But not so for my older sister. She fearlessly entered them to rescue some wayward goat, gather firewood, or forage for tasty mushrooms.

So it was with a bit of envy that Docila led us into the forest along a faint trail. We followed this until we reached a huge pine tree and then turned onto an even less distinct path. We made good progress, but I could tell this was costing her. Even though her limp was gradually becoming more pronounced, she didn't complain. As I walked with her, I couldn't help but wonder if perhaps she had never been the villain I had imagined as a child. Maybe, she had just needed to grow up too.

After what seemed like half an hour, Docila stopped and pointed up the trail. "Just a little further in, you're going to start to feel like I'm heading in the wrong direction. Just ignore it and follow behind me."

I nodded. "I've encountered something like it before back when we climbed Mount Eternal."

Her eyebrows went up in surprise. "You mean that's true? I thought it was just a made up part of the song."

There was that ballad again. I shook my head. "No, it really happened. Only it wasn't quite as dramatic as they portrayed it."

"What about the other parts?"

I sighed. "Some of them are sort of true, but blown way out of proportion."

She smiled wistfully. "I can't believe my little brother has a ballad written about his adventures." She patted me on the shoulder. "Maybe one day you'll tell me what really happened."

I smiled. "I think I'd like that."

She turned and led me deeper into the woods.

Just as she said, the feeling came on slowly—a sense of wrongness. I frequently caught myself at least a pace to the right or the left of where Docila led. I would correct it, only to once again find myself off course.

"Aren't you affected?" I finally asked in frustration. "I'm not doubting your direction, but it feels so wrong!"

She shrugged. "I've been here a couple of times, and I've just learned how to ignore it. I focus on the landmarks instead. It helped that during the first trip, the goats didn't seem bothered by it."

I focused on following her and tried to shut everything else out. It was difficult, but thankfully, we didn't have much further to go. The feeling suddenly vanished as soon as we crossed some invisible line. We emerged a few paces later into a clearing utterly devoid of trees and brush. Instead, it was filled with clusters of huge broken stones, with some having pieces of ornate figures carved on them and others appearing to be chunks of broken statues. There were even a few that could have been columns toppled on their sides and covered in vines. It looked like a giant hand had swept across them and knocked everything down.

I wandered among the fallen giants, amazed that everything had been broken. All the other works of the ancients had been in near perfect condition.

"What could have happened?" I asked aloud.

Docila came to stand beside me. "When I was a girl, I heard an elder tell of a strong earthquake when his grandfather was just a boy. I thought that might have done it."

I nodded. That sounded reasonable. I guess even the ancients couldn't stand against the forces of the earth. I just hope it hadn't also destroyed the Griffin's Key.

Docila watched me patiently while I stood in place and turned in a circle, trying to get a feel for how everything had been arranged. I tried to imagine what it looked like before the earthquake.

There had been a life-size statue in the center, which now lay broken on the ground. It reminded me of the Myst Siphon that had protected Ruin's Shield and nearly killed Zofie. And indeed, when I looked closer, I could see that there had been a short circular wall around it. Also within the circle rested a jumble of stones, which must have been some type of building.

I picked my way to the remains of the building and circled its perimeter, searching for a way to see what might be hidden under it. But nothing was evident. I was about to go back to the house and see about getting a shovel when I noticed a dip in the ground. It was slight, but definitely there. I knelt down over it and used a loose rock to try to dig a little.

Suddenly the ground underneath me gave way, and I plunged through. I dropped about five feet and landed painfully face down in the dirt. I lay there, momentarily stunned. Thankfully, a sizable pile of loose soil had broken my fall.

"Coren!" Docila called from above. I rolled over and looked up to see her staring down at me. "Are you all right? I thought you were dead there for a moment."

I sat up, groaning as my battered body protested. I brushed dirt from my coat, creating clouds of dust. "I'm a bit bruised and a few scratches, but nothing broken."

I examined my surroundings. The afternoon sun was peeking through the hole above and provided ample illumination to see what lay immediately around me. The familiar shape of stairs emerged from underneath the pile of soil I sat on, one side going up and blocked by several large stones, and the other leading down into the darker depths.

"I seem to be in some kind of stairwell," I called up. "It must have been covered over in the earthquake." I scooted toward the darker portion of the stairs. "I'm going to see what's down here."

"Be careful," Docila called back. "You don't know what horrors could be lurking in the dark."

I thought back to the stone men and the giant crab that had protected the Mirror of Bygone Tears. Yes, there definitely could be bad things down here. I pulled out my sword and held it ready.

I carefully picked my way through the debris on the steps and down the stairwell. Once I was beyond the initial cave-in, the wreckage quickly cleared, leaving only a thick layer of undisturbed dust.

The darkness grew as I moved away from the collapsed ceiling and farther down the stairs. I reached inside my jacket and pulled out my trusty amulet. It had originally protected me from the worse of my bad luck. But since Abe had broken it, all it was good for was producing a dim light. But even that had proven quite useful.

I didn't have to go too far before the stairs ended at an arched doorway. The moment I passed through, a bright light from above sprang to life, making me shield my eyes. When I could finally see again, I realized I was in a large circular chamber, completely empty and with no other doors.

An elegant mural, painted directly on the curved wall, adorned the chamber. It was exceptionally well done and in the same style as the ones I had seen before in the crypt of the Mirror of Bygone Tears. And even after the passing of a thousand years, the picture's colors were crisp and bright. It looked like it had been finished just yesterday.

I studied it, thinking it might provide a clue to the key's whereabouts. The mural's subjects were eight life-size pictures of men and women wearing stately robes and evenly spaced around the room. The background behind each varied but seemed to be some sort of court scene. The renderings were so lifelike it looked like they could start talking at any moment. A master artist had indeed painted them. I could easily imagine myself appearing before them in a great hall.

All but two of the figures were standing. The seated man and woman wore crowns and perched on what looked like finely crafted thrones. There was no doubt the seated pair were rulers, maybe even king and queen. To my surprise, I thought I recognized at least a couple of the faces from a vision I had received on Mount Eternal. But it was the seated woman that drew my attention. I stepped forward and examined her closely. I had seen an older version of her in a dream I'd had only a few weeks ago. I knew with absolute certainty who it was.

Evelend. The genius behind all the ancient artifacts and weapons.

And Abe's creator.

At the time of the portrait, she was in the prime of her adulthood with brilliant red hair, gentle eyes, and a confident smile. I couldn't help but wonder what she was like. While I hadn't noticed it in the vision, I could faintly see a resemblance to Zofie in this younger version. She could very well be one of Zofie's ancestors, a thousand years removed. No wonder Zofie was so damned smart.

It also begged a larger question. Evelend must have been a queen, yet why was there no record of her? It didn't make sense. There was definitely something amiss. I sighed. But that would have to wait for another day.

As I counted through the portraits, I noted an irregularity. I had initially thought the figures evenly spaced along the wall, but that wasn't entirely correct. One section of the mural on my right had a gap, as if the artist had allowed enough space for one last person, but never included them. It reminded me of the missing symbol on the entrance to the crypt of the Mirror of Bygone Tears. There, the empty spot had been reserved for the Thief of Curses. Could this also be the case?

I moved to the spot and cautiously touched it, but nothing happened. I ran my hand across the wall but found it perfectly smooth, without a hidden seam or crack that might conceal another door.

I sighed in frustration and turned once more to scan each of the pictures. I had expected there to be at least some clue as to the key's location. But no such luck. Other than the portraits, the room was empty.

Was this chamber just to honor those long dead? While the explanation didn't seem exactly right, I couldn't think of another purpose. I guess I needed to look elsewhere. This room was a dead end. As I was leaving, I paused at the doorway and gave the room one last look. My eyes flicked to each of the portraits before turning away.

I froze and looked again. Evelend's figure frowned back at me. I blinked. Hadn't she been smiling a moment ago? I shook my head. I must not have been paying attention.

I glanced into the darkness outside the entrance. This had been a waste. I hoped there were other clues in the ruins above. "Well," I said aloud. "At least there's no monsters."

"Oh, there might not be a monster, but there is a murderer here," came a female voice from behind me.

My eyes went wide. I drew my sword and whirled about. To my amazement, the picture of the queen had changed. She now stood beside her throne and glared at me.

And then she moved, pointing an accusing finger at me. "And that murderer is you."

CHAPTER TWELVE

Unpleasant Visions

That was enough for me. I tried to run, but for some reason, my legs were frozen to the spot. I couldn't move. I looked up at Queen Evelend. She now stood with hands clasped before her.

"Why have you trapped me?" I asked.

"Because you are a truly heartless murderer. And not only that, but a thief of other's good fortune. You steal their luck to save yourself, even if it means their death." She spread her arms, indicating the others in the room. "And now it's time for you to be judged by my council." She raised her voice. "I declare my court in session."

Suddenly all of the mural figures surrounding her started to move.

Some of the figures slipped to their neighbor and whispered in their ear, others turned an admiring gaze on the queen, while the king leaned forward and slit his eyes, examining me closely.

This was some kind of myst trick. I struggled to pull my feet free.

Queen Evelend moved toward her throne, and with a flick of her skirts, sat down on it. She turned to the king, "Your majesty, I charge this man with murder. Murder of the worst kind—premeditated and cruel. Even his family was not spared."

The king lifted his chin. "Coren Hart, Thief of Curses, what say you to this charge?"

How did he know my name?

"I'm not a murderer," I said. "I merely seek the Griffin's Key. I need it to restore my princess."

The queen smiled cruelly. "Such a noble cause," she said sarcastically. "But all villains say such."

I spread my arms. "Then who have I killed? I have not harmed anyone."

She sighed dramatically. "Lies already? Did you not kill your father? Cause him to be drowned, so you could live?"

My head shook in denial. "No, it was Abhulengulus. He..."

The queen waved her hand.

I found myself a child lying on the wet ground beside the swollen river coughing up water. A strange man knelt over me, and he was saying something, but I couldn't make out the words. I turned my head to the side and saw my father lying next to me. Only, he was white and still—and he wasn't breathing.

I looked to the man leaning over me in shock.

"You're lucky to be alive, boy...."

I jerked as I came back to the present, my mind and heart reeling from the memory.

The queen did not pause in her accusations. "And did you not kill your mother's unborn child. Your very own brother."

I again shook my head, not understanding. "I don't have a brother."

She leaned forward. "But you would have, had you not killed him in the womb." She smiled cruelly. "Your mother quickened with child right after taking her new husband. But she miscarried."

"I didn't..."

The whispers from the others on the wall grew around me. I could barely make out what they were saying, *"Guilty..."*

The queen waved her hand again.

I was my child self again, a year after my father's passing. I was kneeling beside my mother. She sat on the edge of her bed with tears slipping down her face. "What's wrong Mother?" I asked.

She merely shook her head.

I reached out to hug her, but she pushed me away. "Don't touch me!" she yelled, obviously angry. "Just leave me alone!"

I found myself back in the queen's chamber. I remembered the event, but at the time had no idea what had happened. My heart filled with guilt.

The queen continued her onslaught. "You stole your brother's luck before he could take his first breath!"

"No, it..."

The whispers from the other figures grew in volume. "*Guilty... murderer....*"

"And what about the others. While you may not have killed them, you have certainly made it so they wished they were dead... like your step-sister."

A man wearing the king's livery had Docila pinned to a large oak tree, a big hand around her throat. Two others held her arms, bending her back painfully against it. I somehow knew it was Docila only a few months ago.

"Where are the goats!" he demanded.

His grip wouldn't let her breathe, little alone answer. She shook her head.

The soldier frowned. "So be it." He grinned evilly and leaned forward until his face nearly touched hers. "Then I'll have to take something almost as valuable." He then grabbed the collar of her dress and ripped it open to her waist...

I fell to my knees. "I didn't..."

"*Guilty... murderer... thief....*"

But the queen didn't stop. The scene changed.

Risten sat on the floor of the dungeon, chained to the walls, her face bruised and her lip bleeding.

Wynn was smiling at her. "I think I have just the one for her," he said. "One that doesn't require as much myst as some of the others." He cocked his head to one side. "Send for Lilith."

Wynn turned back to her. "I think this will be educational for both of you. Lilith tends to drive her hosts insane...."

I gasped for breath.

The murmurs from the figures on the wall continued to rise. *"Guilty... murderer... die...!"*

I shook my head.

It was laundry day, and Cabrina's mother had insisted that everything be washed, including the bed linens.

The young girl stood outside, smoothing the white sheet across the drying line. She slid the clothespin into place and then reached for another, only to notice the world had gotten strangely quiet. Curious, she looked up to see a man and a woman standing next to her. The man smiled and unexpectedly grabbed her, wrapping his arms tightly around her and lifting her bodily off the ground. The woman then stepped forward and touched a dark red crystal to Cabrina's forehead.

Cabrina suddenly felt another presence inside her mind. And that presence shoved her aside and took over her body—

"Please stop," I begged.

"Guilty... he must die...!"

The visions came faster, rolling from one to another.

"Spraggel! Get back!" I yelled.

The horse stumbled and the girth holding the elder's saddle broke, throwing him to the ground—

Mikney turned from the keg of ale he was moving to answer a question. He suddenly lost control of the barrel and it rolled back across his leg—

Fumiko stood in her master's cottage and tried to free herself from the woman holding her. The woman grinned. "I curse you," the woman whispered. "To become me."

Fumiko screamed as the entity entered her mind—

I knelt on the ground, tears in my eyes. *Had I caused that much pain? That much suffering?*

The queen frowned. "There's not a single one of your family or friends that you haven't affected. Even the one you said was your true love, Princess Zophia—"

Wynn touched a finger to her chest. "Zophia Olwenna Xernow, Princess of Brethnach, I curse you. I give you the curse of Eternal Transformation!"

A blue glow surrounded her, and she began to change. She screamed in agony as bones crunched and warped, organs came undone and moved inside her, and her skin seemed to melt and reform.

And she felt the excruciating pain of each and every change—

Hot tears slid down my face to land in the dust before me. I couldn't believe the pain I had caused.

"Die... you must be punished...."

The queen gave a sad shake of her head. "Your crimes are obvious. You should be put to death."

I nodded. I picked up my sword and turned the blade so the point rested just under my rib cage.

"Die... you must die...."

I took a sobbing breath.

And then an angel spoke. *"Don't listen to her, Coren."*

It was Zofie's voice, a flash of brilliance within my darkened heart. I shook my head. I must be imagining it.

"Hurry, Princess. I can't hold it." That was Abe.

"Hang on, my dearest knight." Zofie spoke again. *"Help is coming. Just remember who you are. And know that I will always love you."*

I shook my head again. There is no way Zofie could love someone like me. Someone so evil. I had to be punished for my crimes. I tensed to press the blade into my chest.

I suddenly felt arms around me. Hugging me close. Real arms. Real fingers pushed the sword away, and I turned my head to face her. "Stupid brother," said Docila. "What do you think you're doing?"

And suddenly, the spell broke. The bracelet on my wrist was searing hot, but immediately began to cool.

I looked up into Docila's concerned face and then to the chamber walls around me. The mural was as it had been, with all the figures returned to their original places. "How...?" I croaked.

"I got worried about you when you didn't come back. Then I just got this feeling I needed to find you."

Realization struck me. I had nearly killed myself. I wrapped my arms around Docila and gave her a fierce hug. "Thank you. You saved my life."

Embarrassed, she pulled away. "Yeah, yeah. Wouldn't be the first time."

We stood, and I faced the image of the queen. "You failed. I have committed no crimes. Yes, my curse can change luck, but certainly not with the intent of hurting others."

The queen leaped from her chair. "And now, we will have to take her too. Yet another innocent killed in an attempt to save yourself."

The bracelet flashed hot again, and I took reassurance from it.

"No!" I yelled. "I won't let you."

I looked around the room, and my eyes froze on the empty spot along the wall. What had Zofie's voice said? *Remember who you are?*

In sudden inspiration, I grabbed Docila's hand and pulled her with me toward the empty section of wall.

"What are you doing?" demanded the queen. "Admitting your guilt and trying to run?"

"Guilty..." the chant began to rise around me again. I could feel the guilt starting to grow in me once more. Only this time, Zofie's words warmed me. *Know that I will always love you.* Leaving the guilt with no power.

I examined the wall.

"Coren?" asked Docila, concern on her face.

I released her hand and then slapped the wall as hard as I could. "I am the Thief of Curses. And in the name of Princess Zophia Xernow, I command this chamber to open."

And suddenly, a new picture appeared on the wall. I staggered back in surprise. It was a man dressed in plain clothes and giving me a one-sided grin. "Let him pass," he announced loudly.

My eyes went wide. While I did not recognize the face, I knew the voice. It was Dughall from the same vision I'd had when I saw Evelend. The original Thief of Curses.

The one that had betrayed her.

To my surprise, the figures on the mural vanished, leaving only the circular wall with its paint cracked and peeling. A moment later, the section of wall I faced disappeared, and I found myself in front of another arched entrance.

Beyond was again nothing but darkness. I reached behind me and took Docila's hand before stepping inside.

A single light snapped on just ahead of us and provided enough light that I could make out another chamber about the same size as the previous one. A single cone of light illuminated a raised platform—just a step above the floor, roughly oval in shape, and carved out of the same stone as the walls. In the very center of the platform, a slender, cylindrical pedestal rose from the floor—almost a high table—made of highly polished white marble and elegantly carved in an intricate weaving pattern. I gasped. It was identical to the pedestal that held the Mirror of Bygone Tears.

We moved cautiously forward, kicking up dust from the floor with every move. On the stand, resting in a shallow impression, was a silver cylinder about a foot long and a fingerbreadth thick.

Is that the key? I wondered to myself.

"What is it?" Docila asked.

I shook my head. "I'm not sure. But I know we can't touch it yet."

I moved to the side furthest from the door and had my suspicions confirmed. The pedestal had another part on the back, not readily visible from the front. A small square of marble extended out from it with the imprint of a life-sized hand carved from the stone. It looked as if someone had pressed it into the marble. But the real surprise was on the wrist of the impression. It was a symbol I knew quite well.

"That's your curse!" Docila exclaimed.

I nodded. I pulled back the sleeve on my left arm, baring it to the elbow. "Stand back," I said. "Last time I did this, it set off a trap."

Docila prudently moved closer to the door before turning to watch me. I aligned my hand and wrist with the impression and pressed down. The stone was cool to my skin and had a gritty feel from all the dust.

Suddenly, my world changed. I was standing in a place of all gray: everything around me, as far as the eye could see, was a dull color—like a thick fog on a brightly lit morning. And it was deadly quiet—as if sound didn't exist in this realm. My eyes widened in surprise. This was a place I had been in before.

It was the place curses lived.

Standing before me was a stick figure, arms and legs nothing more than simple lines. Its head was much larger than a human's and perfectly round—a flat circle instead of a sphere. Inside the circular head was the image of a pedestal, so detailed I could make out all its intricate parts. And if I looked really closely, I could almost make out tiny gears moving along its boundary.

The being seemed to be waiting for me. "I hoped to never see you, Thief of Curses," it said, which was surprising since it had no mouth. "If you are here, then something is wrong."

"I've been told we need to move the Forever Nexus Shadow. And for that, I need the Griffin's Key."

The being nodded. "Then take it. I'm tired of watching it anyway."

He turned away. "Wait!" I yelled. "Abhulengulus is broken. Can you tell me how I can fix him?"

The being turned back. It gestured off to one side. "You mean them? I was wondering what their problem was."

I looked where he indicated and saw another stick figure standing a short distance away. Inside its perfectly round head was a stylized eye which I instantly recognized.

Abe!

He was beating on what seemed to be an invisible wall. But what utterly shocked me was the person beside him.

It was Zofie.

She too was beating on the wall and seemed to be shouting, but I couldn't understand her.

I ran to the wall and joined them in beating on it. But the barrier did not yield.

"They're trapped," I said. "How do I release them? Would the key work?"

The being shrugged. "I have not seen the like of this before. All I can say is that the key opens many things. To say more would go against my making. When the ancient weapons were sealed away, *HE* decided to separate the knowledge from the item. So while I have the key, I cannot tell you how to use it. I would give you the information if I could." He gave a deep chuckle. "*HE* really was a bastard."

"Please!" I begged, resting my hands on the barrier and gazing at Zofie longingly. She was so close.

He turned and waved me away. "Begone. My watch is done."

I suddenly found myself back at the pedestal. I blinked and looked around, pulling my hand away and rubbing my wrist. It felt numb.

Docila was standing directly beside me. "Are you all right? You were standing there for so long, I was afraid you weren't coming back."

I shook my head, trying to clear the jumbled thoughts. Zofie had been in the world of curses. But why there? I glanced down at the sealing charm around my wrist. How had this charm done that? I would have to talk with Spraggel.

"I was talking with the curse on this pedestal," I said distractedly. "He said I could have the key."

She drew back. "You can talk to curses?"

I smiled. "I can steal them too?"

She shook her head. "So you really are the Thief of Curses, just like the ballad said."

There was that stupid song again.

I then reached out and wrapped my fingers around the silver bar. It was frigid to the touch, and when I lifted it out of its cradle, felt much heavier than it looked.

I glanced around, half expecting something to jump out, but nothing did. That was a pleasant change.

We left the way we had come in, with the light going out behind us and returning the ancient chambers back to darkness. It was almost anti-climactic as we climbed out of the hole and walked back to the farm. But I couldn't shake the feeling that it could not be this easy.

We stopped at the edge of the woods and searched for any sign of Lilith or Wort. But there was none. I took Docila's hand and started forward, but paused. The charm on my wrist suddenly grew uncomfortably warm. If last time was any indication, then something was up. I scanned the area again but saw nothing amiss.

Not seeing anyone, we made our way to the barn but found it empty. *Where was everyone?* My heart sank. Something must have happened. Fumiko wouldn't have moved them without a good reason.

"I'm going to go check the house," I said to Docila. "Wait here. If I don't come for you, go back to the ruins and wait for help." I pulled out the Griffin's Key and handed it to her. "Hold on to this for me just in case."

Her brow furrowed in worry, but she took it and nodded.

I moved to the back of the house and found the door barred. Since we had left it open, it meant someone had at least been inside. I couldn't argue with that. It seemed prudent to lock the doors.

I moved to the front of the house and cautiously opened the front door, peering inside. Suddenly, the door was flung open and my eyes went wide.

Lilith sat on the bench beside the kitchen table.

And little Floria was sitting on her lap.

CHAPTER THIRTEEN

Goats and Cats

"Hello, Coren." Lilith gave me a wicked smile. She was braiding Floria's hair. The little girl was perched stiffly on Lilith's lap, and while unharmed, didn't appear too happy.

Spraggel sat nearby on a stool, calmly taking in the situation. I noticed his hands were tied in front of him. Having run out of places to sit, my mother stood horrified by the hearth. Her wide eyes were fixed on her youngest daughter.

Cabrina sat huddled in the far corner. She was unbound, but her nose was bleeding, and her cheek seemed to be swelling. There must have been some disagreement between them.

Wort, the small room making him seem unnaturally large, held the door while gripping Mother's crossbow in his other hand. I knew there was no point in running. I wouldn't make it two steps down the hill.

But the worst, and no doubt staged for effect, was Zofie. She sat beside Lilith with a totally blank expression and held the kitchen knife pointed to her own throat.

The odd thing was that Fumiko wasn't among them. Either Lilith had already killed her, or she had managed to slip away. The latter more likely, I decided. If Lilith had killed her, she would be proudly displaying the body. Fumiko might be hiding somewhere nearby using her shadow ability.

Those in the room watched in horror as Lilith calmly finished braiding Floria's hair and tied it off with a pink ribbon. Her motions were slow and deliberate, calculated to instill maximum fear. The only sounds were the crackling of the fire and the rustling of Lilith's clothes as she worked. In the distance, I could hear the goats bleating.

Lilith patted the girl's shoulder. "There now, that will hold better. You can't go around with a loose braid." She looked over to me and pulled the girl higher into her lap. She put her arms possessively around her. "You know Coren, the Risten inside is loving this. She's always wanted a little girl. Someone she could teach all the things that her master taught her. Likely something to do with not knowing her own mother." She shrugged. "Why you humans want to populate the world with little versions of yourself is a complete mystery to me. Perhaps if I *perfect* enough of you, I'll figure it out one day."

"Let them go, Lilith," I said. "It's Zofie and me that you want."

She shook her head. "That doesn't make sense Coren. Why would I let my leverage go? If I kill one or two of them, then it will ensure you assist me in order to save the others." She put a finger to her lips. "I can't kill Zofie since I might need her to unlock some of the artifacts, plus she'd be useful in getting to those troublesome Keepers. And you, of course, I can't kill. We need to examine the curse you carry. It has some attributes that we might be able to incorporate into ourselves. Especially that ability to change luck." She gently stroked Floria's hair. "And this one is also off-limits. The Risten inside would become most troublesome should I attempt to hurt her." She looked up at the others in the room and smiled. "But that still leaves me with at least three to use, not counting the eastern bitch." Her mouth drew into a frown. "She dies regardless."

I wasn't sure what to say. Dreadful silence hung heavy in the room. Cabrina shifting her position sounded painfully loud.

Lilith glanced in her direction. "But one thing I don't understand is why you have that unnamed one with you. She is of no value that I can see."

At the mention of her name, Cabrina shuffled nervously and continued to stare at the floor.

Interesting. As Cabrina had suggested, Lilith doesn't know about the charms linking us three.

Despite the situation, I couldn't resist digging for more information. This could be important. I held up my arm and pulled back the sleeve to reveal the bracelet charm. "It's because of this," I said. "Cabrina tricked us into putting these on, and it made Zofie as you see her." I decided not to mention Abe's silence.

Lilith nodded in understanding. "That explains a lot. It smells of something Wynn would do. You're no doubt trading the key to get the charm off." She laughed. "I have to admit Wynn is a wily one."

I tried to keep my face impassive, but she picked up on some subtle hint.

Her smile slowly faded. "It's not Wynn, is it?"

I just stared at her.

Lilith gave me a smug smile and moved Floria to sit beside her. She gave the girl's hair one more loving stroke and then slowly stood, leisurely stepping over to Cabrina.

The older woman looked down at the youth for a moment before violently grabbing Cabrina by the hair and jerking her head back painfully. She howled in pain.

I took a step forward but was instantly blocked by Wort with the crossbow pointed point-blank at my chest.

Cabrina tried to pull herself free. "You can't hurt me!" She blurted out. "If this body dies, so does Sir Coren and the princess." She held out her own bracelet as proof.

"It's true Lilith!" I shouted. "Don't hurt her."

Lilith turned her head in my direction and grinned evilly. "I don't need to kill her. Isn't that right, *no name?*" She gave the girl a shake to emphasize the point. "I'll just root around in your host's memories until I find the answer. And believe me, I will find it, even if I have to turn her brain to mush to do it."

"Please," Cabrina moaned. "This girl has done nothing to deserve that."

Lilith's eyes went up in shock. "Don't tell me you're empathizing with your host? I can't believe you're so foolish. It's like these farmers empathizing with their goats." She smiled evilly. "Just remember that sometimes, their goats become their next meal."

I got the impression she was saying that for the benefit of the person inside Cabrina. No doubt trying to stoke her fear.

"Stop it Lilith!" I shouted. "I'll tell you."

A confident smile spread across her face. "You're so weak Coren. I knew it wouldn't take much to persuade you."

She roughly released Cabrina and wandered back to the bench beside Floria.

I was unsure how much Lilith knew, so I didn't dare lie to her. "We made a deal with the Kuiojia Empire. We give them the Griffin's Key, and they remove Zofie's charm."

Lilith pursed her lips and nodded thoughtfully. "Which explains the trip to Oddfrid Vandobarre's place. You need a wayfarer." She looked up and tapped her lips in thought. "Risten inside has always wanted to visit the empire." But after a momentary pause, she shook her head dismissing the idea. "Better not. Business first."

The charm around my wrist suddenly began to warm considerably. I folded my arms across my chest to hide my discomfort.

Lilith leaned over and pulled Floria against her, giving her a hug. The woman smiled. "Enough of this. Give me the item you salvaged."

My face must have betrayed me again.

"I know you've got it." She gazed up at me smugly. "Of course, you'll need to tell me how to use it and explain how it relates to the Forever Nexus Shadow."

The charm on my wrist continued to heat up. I could almost smell it smoldering, and I couldn't let Abe burn through the bracelet. It would kill the three of us.

I glanced around the room. On the far end of the table were two buckets of water, likely carried in that morning. They were still mostly full.

I held up a finger. "Can you give me a moment?"

Lilith watched with interest as I eased over to the buckets, pulled up my sleeve, and submerged my hand into it up to the wrist. There was a hissing sound and instant relief from the pain. Lilith blinked in surprise and then broke out laughing. "Your curse is trying to break free of that charm by pulling an excessive amount of myst through it. Amazing! We've definitely got to examine him closer."

I leaned over the bucket. *What was I going to do?* I couldn't let Lilith kill my family. And if she got the Griffin's Key, it could give the Dark Avenyts access to a most powerful ancient artifact.

I glanced into the unused bucket and saw how it reflected the light from the open door, mirroring the view of the wall and rafters.

My eyes went wide. Scowling back at me was a dimly lit face in the shadows of the room. Fumiko! I tried not to let my excitement show. I slowly raised up and used my body to conceal my other hand. I pointed to the hostages in the room. Fumiko nodded.

I sighed. It was time to bring out my deadliest weapon. Sometimes it worked well, and others, it just made things worse. But I had to try it.

My big mouth.

I turned to Lilith, keeping my wrist in the water. It was starting to bubble around the charm. "If I give you the key, what do I get out of it in exchange?" I asked.

Lilith snorted. "How about the lives of your family." She grinned. "And maybe a kiss."

I felt the heat on my wrist suddenly stop. It hit me that Abe hadn't been trying to break free, so much as trying to change my luck. And he must have been waiting for something. But what?

Cabrina huddled in her corner just beyond Lilith, staring at the floor. At Lilith's mention of a kiss, the youth's eyes came up in surprise.

An idea began to form. Cabrina was fascinated with human courting. Could it be a characteristic shared with other Dark Avenyts? Something they didn't understand and were intensely curious about?

Only one way to find out.

I wiped off my hand on a nearby towel and then stepped over to Lilith. I gently nudged Floria toward her mother before sitting in her spot. Lilith's knife appeared in her hand as I leaned closer. I heard Wort shuffle a step in our direction, but she waved him back. He pointed the crossbow in my direction, signaling he was watching.

"All right. The lives of my family and a kiss. But..." I brought my face within an inch of hers. "How about you give me my kiss now to seal our deal."

Lilith's face grew red. "You would do such a thing in front of Zofie? Isn't that referred to as cheating?"

"I've always cared for you, or at least I have the Risten inside. You're a very beautiful woman."

She seemed unsure.

I reached forward and played with one of the ties on her shirt. She looked down at my hand and seemed unable to take her eyes off it.

"Don't believe me?" I asked. "Look into Risten's memories of our time on Mount Eternal. We shared a blanket, didn't we? She told me a man and a woman have to wed if they share a blanket."

Lilith gave a tiny shake of her head. "It was only talk. Nothing more."

I moved a fraction closer. Our noses were almost touching. "Really?"

I closed the distance, slowly pressing my lips to hers. Momentarily, she froze in shock, then violently pushed me away. I fell backward, landing hard on my butt. She glared at me and wiped her mouth with the back of her hand. "You humans are so disgusting! It's no wonder we had to assume control."

"Hey!" shouted Wort. "Where did they go?"

Lilith leaped to her feet. As I picked myself up, I looked along with her. Cabrina still huddled in the corner, but Spraggel, Floria, and my mother were gone.

Lilith cursed and glared at me, knowing I had provided the distraction. Her fury turned to Wort. "Go look for them!"

Wort started for the door but drew up short as a goat kid appeared in the entrance. It gave a bleat in protest and leaned forward to nibble on his pants. Wort shoved past it and trotted out to search. The kid, undeterred, sauntered into the room. It gave another bleat and then stepped over toward us.

Having become familiar with goats from my time on the farm, something about its walk just didn't seem natural. Also, I would surely have noticed a kid in the goat pen, but there had been none. To me, its gait seemed more like... I grinned in understanding.

Lilith pointed to the kid with her knife. "Do something with that."

I nodded and slowly bent down to pick it up. As I lifted the animal, I had my suspicion confirmed.

"Uhh... Lilith dear. I think this is actually for you."

She wheeled to face me. "What?"

But I simply threw the kid at her face. Fumiko's illusion fell away to reveal one very pissed off cat.

And then, my curse's bad luck took over.

Lilith struggled with the animal, quickly shoving it away, where Mischief deftly landed on his feet. The movement caused Lilith to stagger back, catching the bench with the back of her knees. She lost her balance, tittered, and fell backward, colliding hard with the table. The table decided to give up and collapsed, spilling its contents onto the floor—which included the two buckets of water. She tried to catch herself but stepped on a cup which rolled under her foot. She staggered again, and stepping into the pool of water, slipped with both of her feet flying out from beneath her. She landed hard on her back, with her head bouncing off the stone hearth. Momentarily stunned, she lay unmoving.

That was interesting, I mused. My curse hadn't caused that kind of calamity in quite some time.

Lilith groaned and rolled her head. I grimaced in disappointment. *Creator!* That wasn't going to hold her for long.

I immediately went to Zofie and grabbed the knife she held to her throat. Glancing down at it, I briefly considered using it on Lilith. But Nadine's plea to save her daughter sprang to my mind. That was Risten's body. Killing one would kill the other. There was no way I could do it. I threw away the knife.

Cabrina showed up right beside me. I didn't hesitate to put Zofie's hand in hers and shove both of them toward the door. "Get to the woods!" I whispered.

Cabrina nodded once and pulled Zofie behind her.

I looked around the interior, wondering how Fumiko had managed to get them out. But despite their head start, it would not be enough for Zofie. I needed to give them a few more seconds to get away.

By the time I turned around, Lilith was already getting to her feet. And there was death in her eyes. She pulled her sword and charged.

I didn't dare engage her with a sword. I trusted Fumiko's assessment that I couldn't beat her. I looked around for something to use as a shield, when I spotted Lilith's hat hanging by the door. It was the same one she had used to open the portal to escape from the castle's crypt. I briefly considered it. *Would it work for me?*

I quickly grabbed it and stepped out the door. Lilith was right behind me, raising her sword to strike. I tossed the hat on the ground just in front of her. As soon as it hit the floor, a person-sized portal opened on the floor...

And a very surprised Lilith stepped into it. She landed hard against the lip closest to me but was unable to find anything to hold on to. She slipped inside. I could hear her cursing as the portal closed after her.

I immediately turned to run after the others. Zofie had said that it was only a short-range portal, so Lilith was likely still nearby. We weren't out of danger yet.

As I ran, I had to admit that having one's luck bent for you certainly did have its advantages. I just prayed that there wasn't something horrible coming to balance things out.

It didn't take long to catch up with Cabrina and Zofie. Fumiko had joined them and was trying to urge them faster. Only, she wasn't doing so well herself. She grimaced with every step and was favoring her right side.

"What happened to you?" I asked.

"Later." Fumiko pointed toward the pasture. "I sent Docila and the others on ahead. She said you'd know where to meet her."

And indeed, I did. The ruins. With its protection, it would be difficult for them to find us.

Assuming we reached it in time.

Unfortunately, Wort was still out there somewhere looking for us. And Creator knew where Lilith was right now. My bracelet was warming on my wrist again, which meant trouble wasn't far away.

Fumiko echoed my thoughts. "We need to move faster."

I did the only thing I could think of. I stopped and pulled Zofie toward me. "Forgive me, Princess." I then bent and put her over my shoulder. She was heavy, feeling more like a sack of potatoes than a person, but I thought I could manage.

We then resumed at a fast trot and quickly made it to the forest. I thought we were in the clear, when the bracelet on my wrist blazed red hot.

I immediately grabbed Cabrina and ducked behind a tree. Fumiko didn't hesitate and followed my lead. Only a heartbeat later, I heard a thunk as an arrow shaft embedded itself in the tree where I had just been standing. If Abe hadn't warned me, that very well could have been in my back.

"Thank you, Abe," I muttered.

"You're welcome," whispered Zofie.

My eyes went wide. I looked to Cabrina and Fumiko to make sure it hadn't been them, but they appeared as shocked as I was. *Was Zofie back?* No, I didn't think so. She still hung loosely over my shoulder. I heard the crunch of leaves and knew I didn't have time to figure this out. Fumiko looked exhausted and had a hand on her ribs. But she pulled her sword anyway, ready to take him on. I caught her eye and signaled her to wait. Wort had surely reloaded by now, so he would shoot her as soon as she emerged.

"We need a distraction," I mumbled as I resettled Zofie's weight on my shoulder.

"We're working on it," Zofie whispered.

The bracelet flashed blazingly hot, and I almost cried out. It hurt. Which meant there was likely some weird luck thing going to happen.

And it did. I heard a loud growl come from my right. I looked up to see a rather large black bear ambling in our direction. I shook my head in disbelief. *Shouldn't bears be hibernating now?* For the Creator's sake, it was the middle of winter! This was fringing on the impossible.

The bear stopped and sniffed the air, rising up on its hind legs. Its head swiveled in our direction, and it gave a low growl. I think if it could have smiled, it would have.

I couldn't help but wonder if I had overdrawn on my good luck. That there was no more to give, and it had chosen this moment to balance things out. I prayed it wasn't so. I grabbed Cabrina's hand and prepared to make a run for it.

Just as the bear dropped down onto all fours, a bolt grazed its side. It growled in anger, then wheeled toward the new threat. I glanced around the tree to see Wort desperately trying to reload my mother's crossbow, but it was being finicky. The bear must not have liked the looks of the man and charged. Wort dropped the weapon and pulled his sword.

I did the only logical thing. I took off into the woods, pulling Cabrina along with me. Fumiko came along behind. In my hurry, I lost the faint trail Docila had used, so I turned in the direction I thought the ruins would lie.

"Head more south," Zofie whispered.

How were they doing this? But I didn't hesitate to follow the instructions. I changed my course, pushing aside small trees and brush to make a trail.

When I didn't think I could carry Zofie any longer, I called for a break. I stopped and set Zofie down to stand in front of me. Then with trembling legs and aching back, I collapsed and sprawled against a tree. My two companions were relieved to have a short respite and sat beside me. I noticed that Fumiko was favoring her side.

I leaned my head back and shut my eyes, trying to get my heart and breathing to slow down. I knew we couldn't stop for long. My bracelet was still warm on my wrist, which meant trouble had to be close by.

I looked up at my beloved standing before me. I had to ask the question. "Princess, can you hear me? Is it you that has been speaking to me?"

Zofie's face kept its blank expression, but her mouth began to move. "Unfortunately, no. Rather, it is I, your devoted curse, that is actually sending the words. Although I wouldn't be able to do it without help from the princess. So I guess you could call it a combined effort."

Hearing those words lifted a huge burden from my heart. I had been so worried that perhaps the charms had left her body intact only to kill her mind. "So, she is all right?"

"Well, considering she's been kicked out of her body, she's doing pretty good. In fact, she's been trying to find a reliable way to communicate with you since this whole mess started. The attempt to get into your dreams didn't work, and the working she used back in the queen's chamber can't be used again. She broke it getting to you."

"Can I speak with her?" I asked.

"No, she can't," he said disgustedly. "This damn charm has that wrapped up tightly. In fact, the only way Zofie and I are communicating with you is because the charm maker didn't anticipate a few things. Quite sloppy really."

"What things?"

"Well, I don't want to get too technical—because your slightly smarter than a monkey brain wouldn't be able to understand—but let's just say he didn't anticipate my myst connections to Zofie. Remember, I control her curse, and you asked to share the pain of her transformations. And on top of that, you had me make it so Zofie could listen in on our conversations. Because of those connections, the damned charm got confused and did some weird stuff. We're still trying to figure it all out. She thinks she might be able to fix things from this end."

"Fix things? How?"

"Your damn woman is a *Creator forsaken myst seer*. She thinks she can rearrange my workings *from the inside!* It took her a bit to figure it out, but she was able to fix things so I could use her mouth. Oh, and by the way, don't blame me for all the weird stuff that's been happening. She's figured out how to use my ability to change luck and has been using it a lot. I've warned her that things have to balance, but she's pretty much ignoring me... *Ouch!* That hurt." There was a pause. "What do you mean I deserved it? I'll be so glad to get you out of my workings."

I couldn't help but smile. Zofie was so determined. I think I just fell in love with her again. I shook my head. But now was not the time. "Can I transform Zofie?"

"No," she said softly. "Those skills are still sealed because your woman... *Ouch!* Will you stop that?" There was a pause. "Really? You're kidding me. All right, if you say so. Anyway, those skills are sealed. Let's just leave it at that."

Something was being concealed from me, but I didn't have time to worry about it.

"What about my curse ability?"

"The same. The princess says these charms are different from anything she's encountered. Quite sophisticated, in fact. Curses and charms are not compatible, which is why the Dark Avenyts don't normally use them. I can't imagine where they got these from."

I glanced at Cabrina, who was intently inspecting the underside of a rock. If the Dark Avenyts didn't typically use charms, then why did she? I shook my head. Another mystery, but for another time.

I stood. "We need to be moving. I'm sure Wort is out there somewhere looking for us." I went to put Zofie over my shoulder again.

"Oh, one last thing. I can only talk to you while you're in danger, so I'll lose the ability when you get closer to the ruins. The princess says it has to do with how everything is connected up."

I sighed and touched her face. "At least, I know she's still around somewhere. Would you tell Zofie, I love her."

"She heard you. What...? Now don't start crying. Tears aren't good for my insides... I'm a what...? *OUCH!*"

I couldn't help but smile as I picked Zofie up and put her back across my shoulder.

I think Abe had finally met his match.

It was only a short while later that we began to feel the effects of the ruin's area of misdirection. For me, it seemed easier the second time, and I followed Docila's advice to focus on the landmarks. It worked fairly well to keep me on course. However, Cabrina and Fumiko were more affected and kept drifting off. I finally had to take Cabrina's hand and make Fumiko hold my cloak.

Fumiko continued to favor her right side as we walked. I finally asked her about it.

"You're injured, aren't you? And don't tell me nothing because I can see that it's not."

She stepped around a bush. "I was careless. Wort gave me a good hit and with a shovel, no less. I might have a broken rib. I'm lucky he wasn't using his sword."

I stopped, bringing both of them up short. I sighed. "You should have said something. Do you need to rest? Is there something I can do for you?"

She glanced behind us and shook her head. "No, we don't have time. Maybe later, I'll get you to help me bind it."

Cabrina piped up. "She was so brave." The youth was nearly bouncing with excitement. "While we were hiding, your mother decided we should make a run for the forest. We couldn't stop her, and as we were leaving, Wort surprised us. Fumiko fought him, and she even managed to knock his sword away." Cabrina got a little dreamy-eyed. "She was just like the heroes in the books my host was telling me about."

I glanced to Fumiko. She just shrugged and looked away.

Cabrina frowned and continued. "But while she was distracted, Wort picked up a shovel and managed to get a hit in. It knocked her back at least ten feet. Then Lilith showed up and threatened to kill us all if we didn't go in the house. Only Fumiko managed to escape. I tried to fight too..." she looked down. "Only, Wort punched me, and I fell down." She unconsciously rubbed her face. "He hits pretty hard."

I touched Fumiko's arm, and she looked up in surprise. "You protected my family. I can't thank you enough."

She blushed and opened her mouth to say more, but paused and slowly shook her head, clearly deciding against it. Instead, she pointed up at the clouds starting to obscure the late afternoon sun. "We better get going," she said. "I think the weather is going to change."

A chill wind slipped around us to emphasize the point. I nodded and forged ahead.

The pull of the ruin's misdirection got worse, and I had to correct myself a few times, but we somehow managed to make it through. Like before, the pressure to turn away suddenly stopped, and we stepped out into the clearing...

And I nearly tripped over a goat.

I glared at it in surprise as it gave me a curious stare and chewed on some dried grass. *They brought the goats?*

Spraggel, my sisters, and my mother rushed over to us.

"You made it," my old master sounded surprised.

I set Zofie down and collapsed to all fours. My legs felt like water.

"What about Lilith and Wort?" asked Spraggel.

"I helped Lilith fall into her own portal, and thankfully, Wort caught the wrong end of a bear."

I tried to rise to my feet, but my legs were none too happy at the prospect. I staggered, and they trembled but held. I looked to Zofie. We had Oddfrid's orb portal, so now that we had the key, we could leave at any time. I shook my head. But while it would be nice to rest and leisurely return, we didn't have that luxury. If we stayed here, or they even thought we were, they would keep trying until they figured out my family's hiding place. I'm sure we left lots of clues for a determined someone to find. No, we had to lead them away. And in such a way that they didn't come back.

I looked to Mother. "Would it be safe for you to stay here for a while? We need to deal with those following us."

She nodded. "We'll be fine. A little cold maybe, but there are plenty of places to shelter."

Docila nodded. "After I found this place, I stashed some supplies here in case the soldiers came back. There's also plenty of dried grass for the goats. We can last a couple of days, maybe even a week if we stretch it."

I nodded. "Hopefully, you won't have to wait that long."

I sighed. "We'll do our best to get them to follow us away."

She gave me a worried look as only a mother could. "You're not going to face that woman again, are you?"

I shrugged. "I certainly hope not. But there's no other way."

She shook her head. "You could stay here with us until she gets tired and leaves."

I shook my head sadly. "No, I can't take that risk with my family." I glanced at Zofie. "Besides, I need to get my princess back to normal."

She nodded. Clearly not liking it, but understanding.

And so, I retrieved the Griffin's Key from Docila and gave it to Spraggel to store in his ever deep pocket. Then we said good-bye to my family. They gave us each a hug and especially thanked Fumiko for saving them. I couldn't help but smile at her embarrassment.

And of course, I kept my word to Docila and promised my mother I would visit her in the spring. My mother teared up, Floria bounced, and Docila gave me a sly smile. I guess they weren't perfect, but then again, they were mine.

So with Spraggel, Fumiko, Cabrina, and Zofie in tow, we headed back. Gray clouds obscured the sky as we entered the vicinity of the house. We were also losing our daylight, which would make this even more difficult. We used the barn for cover as we paused and carefully surveyed the area for signs of Lilith and Wort. Although we saw no trace of them, there were a thousand places between us and the road that they could be hiding.

With little choice, I motioned us forward but abruptly stopped when my bracelet suddenly flashed hot. I stepped back.

"Coren," whispered Zofie unexpectedly. "They're close and will chase you as soon as you show yourselves."

I glanced at my party. That was exactly what we wanted, but we also needed a way to outrun them.

Zofie continued, "However, the princess has an idea."

There must be enough danger that Zofie and Abe were able to talk to me again. I couldn't decide if I was relieved or not.

I leaned closer and whispered, "What is it?"

"The princess says..." There was a pause and then some mumbling. There seemed to be another conversation going on in the background. "...that won't work, I tell you... Anyway, she says... *Hey!* Don't mess with that... *Ouch!* ...You're going to hurt yourself..." A pause. "See, I told you you'd get hurt. Serves you right." There was a longer pause. "Well, I guess that might work... *Ouch!*"

"What is she doing?"

"Your damn woman is once again messing with my insides. And I'm not liking this one bit. Creator blasted myst seers don't think the universe's rules apply to them. Hey! Don't touch that!"

I nodded thoughtfully. "Yeah, that is Zofie."

"Will you stop..." A pause. "All right! I'll tell him. The princess says, go to the road. And don't be surprised at what happens."

I rolled my eyes. Oh no, what was she up to now.

And sure enough, the sky opened up, and it began to snow.

Hard.

A chill breeze stirred the air making the snow swirl around us. I pulled my cloak tighter and checked to make sure that Zofie's was bundled tight. I wasn't sure this was a good idea. The ground was already cold, so the snow immediately began to accumulate. Which meant it would be easy for them to track us. Then I realized Zofie's reasoning.

That was the whole purpose. So they *could* track us. Lilith would see our trail and know we weren't there anymore. She didn't care about my family, so she'd come after us.

I motioned the others to follow me and headed down the hill toward the path leading to the road.

We hurried as fast as we could through the snow. I couldn't believe how fast it was piling up. Cabrina got so distracted staring at the white covering that she slipped, and would have fallen, had Spraggel not caught her.

And sure enough, just as we reached the bottom of the hill, we saw two figures coming after us. Only the snow seemed to be hindering their progress. I saw Wort slip and fall. Lilith didn't even pause, intent on leaving him, but she too fell.

The wind suddenly rose, grabbing at our cloaks and pelting us in the face. My first thought was that my luck had suddenly shifted, but then I realized it had helped clear the path ahead, and at the same time, push it toward our pursuers.

But the snow wasn't the only surprise. When we came to the road, a large carriage, completely enclosed and crafted of highly polished wood, sat there with the horses still harnessed to it. Definitely not the shabby one we had used to get here. It seemed to be waiting.

I trotted up to the driver who was checking his horses. "Hello," I called. "Why are you just sitting here on the road."

The man frowned. "I's won't be fer long. It's almost even'n, and I needs to be get'n back." He turned toward me. "I carried a pair here's earlier, but they said they'd gives me double if I waited. But I's haven't seens hide nor hair of them since."

I smiled. "Would you be willing to take us instead? That couple decided to stay. You might say, we had a bit of a falling out."

The man's eyes narrowed. "They still owes me at least two silver. Ones for the trip and ones for the wait."

I reached into my coin purse and pulled out four. That was going to seriously hurt my travel funds.

I put two of them in his hand. "This is to take my friends and me to Oddfrid Vandobarre's place." I then placed the other two with them. "And this is to not stop for anything."

He glanced over my shoulder and saw our pursuers in the distance. "Anyth'n?"

"Not even the Creator himself."

He smiled. "I thinks I can do that. She t'was a bit of a bitch anyways."

While the driver climbed up on top of the carriage, we hurriedly piled inside. He started forward before I could even get the door shut.

Like the outside, the interior of the carriage was much plusher than the one that brought us. I would say it almost rivaled the royal one. The inside was also much more spacious, so we all fit comfortably.

I leaned out the window and looked behind us. As quickly as it came, the snow stopped, and we were soon on bare road. I could easily see Lilith and Wort not too far behind us as they won free from a snowbank. Lilith didn't hesitate to launch herself after us, with Wort trailing behind.

I had seen Risten run before and knew she could sprint pretty fast. I had to assume Lilith would take advantage of that. The driver had urged the horses to their fastest pace, but that was only a fast walk. No way could it match her speed. If Lilith could maintain her pace, and I knew she could, she would catch us in just a few minutes.

I held out my hand to Spraggel. "The portal orb Oddfrid gave us. I need it now!"

Fumiko looked at me like I was crazy. "It's not safe to open a portal while moving. Our forward momentum will also be transferred."

I pointed behind us. "Got a better idea? She's almost on us."

Fumiko stared at me a moment and then shook her head.

Spraggel sat up straighter and smiled. "I'll get it." He immediately began to search in his pocket.

I groaned. "You put it in your pocket? I told you not to."

He gave me a disgusted look. "Of course I did. Where else would I put it."

He dug deeper—up to the elbow. He muttered to himself. "Well, I think I put it in here."

I looked out the window. Lilith was close and gaining fast. I could see the whites of her eyes.

And she looked pissed.

I leaned back in. "Spraggel...? Any time now."

He shouted in triumph and pulled it out.

I immediately grabbed it and squeezed the orb three times between my hands as Oddfrid had instructed. I then yanked off one of Zofie's mittens and set it on the floor with the orb on top, so it didn't roll away. After a moment, the orb began to slowly pulse with a pale blue light. We had ten pulses before the portal activated, and I began to count them.

One... Two... Three... Four...

The carriage unexpectedly rocked, and I knew Lilith had caught up with us. I could hear her climbing across the top, and then our ride began to slow. Apparently, she had convinced the driver it was the right thing to do. Probably with the aid of a knife at his throat.

Five... Six... Seven...

I huddled us together around the orb, praying the portal had enough room to operate inside the carriage. It was tight, and we had to hunch over, but we were able to pull close. I hugged Zofie to me tightly with one arm, and Cabrina the other.

Eight... Nine...

The carriage was still moving when the door flew open. With knife drawn, a grinning Lilith stood looking in.

Ten...!

Suddenly, the portal opened beneath our feet.

The look on Lilith's face was worth gold. "No!" she yelled.

I smiled and waved at her as we dropped through.

CHAPTER FOURTEEN

First Portal,
Second Memory

We landed hard in front of Oddfrid's house. Unfortunately, as Fumiko has said, the momentum we had while in the carriage also came with us. Slight as it was, it was like we had suddenly been tossed off a walking horse, which I guess in a sense we had. We rolled and came to a halt in a pile of slightly embarrassed humans.

I quickly knelt beside Zofie and patted over her arms and legs, making sure she wasn't hurt. Thankfully, our heavier winter clothing provided a limited measure of padding. The other point of thanks was that Lilith and Wort had not been able to follow. But that didn't mean we could dally.

Not a moment later, Oddfrid opened the door and surveyed us critically. He didn't look happy. "How close behind you are they?" he asked abruptly.

I turned from helping Zofie stand and blinked at him. "How did you know we were being chased?"

He frowned. "That's the way it always is with nobles and their games." He folded his arms and leaned a shoulder on the doorframe. "So, how long do we have?"

I scratched my head. "If they drive the horses hard, they could be here within the hour."

He sighed and held the door wider for us. "Come inside. I'm almost done."

We started forward, but Fumiko held back. "I'll stand watch," she stated. "That woman may have a way to catch up to us more quickly."

I shook my head. "Not before I bind your chest."

Cabrina jumped up. "I'll watch!" she offered. "I've never done that before. This body has good eyes."

Spraggel put a hand on her shoulder. "Why don't we go watch together. If you stay with them, you'll be saying they've had sex again."

Cabrina turned to Spraggel in indignation. "But they did!"

"We did not," I stated flatly.

The youth didn't appear satisfied with the answer.

"Come dear," said Spraggel. "Let's do a quick check of the perimeter." He then pulled her after him.

I ushered Zofie and Fumiko inside. We found ourselves in a wide foyer with stairs on the right, a door to what looked like a study on the left, and an open doorway leading into the back. Except for a few worn chairs that had seen better days and one dust-covered table, the room was bare.

I settled Zofie down into one of the less dusty chairs and turned to Oddfrid. "Do you have any bindings? My friend has been hurt."

He frowned at us again and exited out the back doorway, but returned a moment later with some strips of cloth. He shoved them at me and then left, mumbling about having to finish his preparations.

Fumiko carefully removed her cloak, wincing as she raised her right arm. She released the ties of her shirt and went to lift it off, but was unable to. She gave me an embarrassed smile. "It hurts more than I thought."

I stepped behind her and helped her gently raise her shirt. She slipped it off, and while modestly holding it in front of her, stood with her back fully exposed.

I remembered hearing that you can tell a lot about someone from their back. And as I stared at Fumiko's, it whispered of a difficult past. She was of slender build but not skinny. Under her pale skin, I could see well-defined muscles across her back and shoulders—not a trace of fat on her. But marring her smooth flesh were a host of small scars starting mid-way and spreading down to her waist. They looked old, having long since healed. But what caught my eye was high on her right shoulder and completely unexpected—a small tattoo of a butterfly, beautifully done in reds and blues. A work of art all by itself, which seemed slightly out of place against the sea of scars further down.

Realizing I was staring, I slid my eyes to her side. I grimaced. Mid-way up her torso, I could see the injury—it was turning a deep blue. I gently probed it, and she hissed and jerked away. The skin had been broken in a couple of places, but there was no major bleeding.

"He sure got you good. I guess you're lucky it was a shovel," I said as I started to wrap her chest. I was careful to keep my eyes on her back and away from the more private places in front. I couldn't help but notice how warm her skin was.

"True." She said through gritted teeth. She looked over her shoulder at me. "Coren, you're going to have to make it tighter."

I frowned. "If I make it too tight, you won't be able to move."

"And if you don't make it tighter, it will hurt too much *to* move."

She dropped her shirt which pooled at her feet. Maintaining her back to me, she held her arms away from her body. "This will make it easier."

I glanced at Zofie, feeling a little better at having her close by as a chaperone. I unwound the little wrapping I had done and started again going a little tighter.

"Higher, Coren."

"But..."

She sighed. "I know I'm a woman, and you're embarrassed, but you've got to do this right. Would you rather I get Spraggel?"

I shook my head. "No, I'll do it."

I started once more, moving higher up her chest and making it tighter. I tried not to think about the feminine parts I was touching.

I glanced at the art on her shoulder and tried to distract myself. "Where did you get the tattoo? It's beautiful. Does it mean something?"

She was silent for a moment, and I thought she was going to pull one of her 'I don't want to talk about it' diversions. But she answered a heartbeat later. "The emperor's royal artist did it. I was quite proud of it at the time. It's nothing myst related, but more of a sign of my previous station. Only the elite got them."

"Is it related to the training I saw in your memories?"

She gave me a worried glance over her shoulder. "Yes."

I smiled. "Then it must be a sign that you graduated."

She was silent a moment. "I guess you could say that." She looked back forward and didn't speak further. I sensed a delicate topic and just worked in silence.

I tied off the binding and diverted my eyes as she pulled on her shirt. She rolled her shoulder tentatively, smiled, and nodded. But her expression fell as she faced me, turning to one of sadness as she searched my eyes.

Suddenly the room went eerily quiet, and I realized Fumiko had just covered us in an area of silence. Which meant Zofie would not be able to hear what came next. "That tattoo says I was once part of a special group in service to the emperor. Only a select few graduated, and we received only the most difficult of assignments. But while I left that life behind…" She reached up and gently touched my face. "I can never escape it."

Fumiko abruptly turned away, and the room's sound suddenly returned. Oddfrid strode back into the room carrying a well-used leather satchel. He plopped it down in the center of the floor. The satchel was faded and worn, tired almost, and like its owner, looked to have made this trip many times before.

"Gather everyone together," he said. "It's time to go."

I did as he asked, and moments later, we stood nervously in the foyer. Oddfrid gave us a quick inspection and nodded. He stood erect and put his hands behind his back. "Our destination this evening will be a town called Piredrop in the kingdom of Zeveiltia. It's about a third of the way to the Kuiojia Empire and is much colder than it is here. In fact, at this time of year, they will likely have a lot of snow."

He paused for a moment looking at each one of us in turn. I somehow felt this was a well-practiced lecture. "Now," he continued. "Going through a long-range portal is very different from a short-range. The difficulty and amount of myst required for any portal doubles with the distance traveled. So the amount of myst to transport you back from your family's home was about five mystumns..."

Spraggel held up his hand. "What is a *mystumn?*"

Oddfrid blinked at Spraggel like he had been thrown off his lecture. "A mystumn is a unit of myst usage. I don't have time to go into the details about it." He cleared his throat, looked up, and seemed to find his place. "In any case, if I were to open a short-range portal from here to Piredrop, it would require over two hundred thousand mystumns, which is far beyond what a normal human could do. So, you might ask, how do we do it?" He leaned forward and smiled conspiratorially. "We actually don't. Instead, we use a naturally occurring portal that happens to open close to our destination. You could almost think of them as tunnels in the universe. This greatly reduces the effort required."

I gave him a puzzled look. "Naturally occurring portals? But wouldn't that mean people would be falling into them all the time?"

He smiled like this was his favorite question. "Ah, just because they're naturally occurring doesn't mean they're readily accessible. I have to make a short-range portal to reach into it, then another to pull us out when the time is right."

Spraggel stroked his beard. "This is all well and good, but why are you telling us this?"

He nodded. "To simply let you know... you're in for a very bumpy ride. Don't be surprised if you feel nauseous or can't tell up from down. That is all normal." He started to turn away. "Oh, and you'll be in absolute darkness the whole time, which may last a few minutes."

He clapped his hands together and rubbed them briskly. "But don't worry, I've done this hundreds of times and only had something go wrong a few."

I had to ask. "Did anyone die?"

He shrugged. "I'm not sure. We never found them."

I sighed. "Dear Creator. Can we just get on with it?"

He grinned in reply.

He had us all gather close together and tied a rope securely around all of us, and then he had us hold hands. He explained it was critical that we not lose contact with one another. I took Zofie's hand on my right and held it firmly while Cabrina grabbed my left.

Once we were ready, he closed his eyes and began to hum. I felt myst gathering, and a glowing bubble of blue light grew up from the floor to completely enclose us. I wanted to ask him why he hummed but didn't dare at this point. I had time to check Zofie one last time before the floor vanished, and a pool of blackness appeared beneath my feet.

Then we fell.

The room we were in slid by as one would expect when falling into a hole. Then everything changed. As Oddfrid predicted, we entered total darkness. No, it was more than total. It seemed to suck up any light that came with us until we were picked clean. And then suddenly, I couldn't tell up from down. I felt like my head suddenly switched with my feet, and now I was falling up. There was sound too. Like we were in a huge bell which rang and rang, but it had tones that I couldn't always hear, but more felt in my chest. And the smells and tastes... At one moment, it was the scent of dandelions in spring while chewing on iron nails, and then next the stinking odor of sulfur while eating sour pickles. There were just too many conflicting sensations for my feeble brain to process. I gripped Zofie's hand tighter. Someone groaned.

And suddenly, we were through. We dropped onto soft-packed snow. Zofie staggered beside me in our uneven landing, but I quickly steadied her.

We stood on top of a small hill with a rough wooden fence

encircling us that was more ornamental than functional. Fresh snow had piled up against it, signaling a recent storm. But thankfully none this night. Over our heads, the night sky was completely clear and full of stars. The half-moon illuminating the white field around was us had shifted to a position closer to the horizon, indicating we had indeed traveled far to the east.

But the thing that struck me most was the bitter cold. Our breath came out in cloudy puffs, while the air greedily pulled at what little heat we possessed. I shivered. We would need to get to shelter soon.

We quickly untied from one other while Oddfrid pulled out some instrument from his pocket and looked at it. Its feeble glow bright in dim light. He pointed to the west. "The town is just over that hill."

"Couldn't you open a portal for us?" Spraggel asked, his teeth chattering.

Oddfrid shook his head and started forward. "I've exhausted my myst. At one time, I could have, but as I am today, no."

We followed, struggling with the snow. It wasn't that far, but having to push through was difficult. When we topped the next hill, we saw a small town below us, too small even to have a wall. However, I took heart at its windows, shedding golden light across the white covered ground and promising some much-needed warmth.

Oddfrid led us to what appeared to be an inn. The occupants glared at us suspiciously when we entered. The people, almost to a one, were of a stocky sort and wore thick furs and knee-high boots. Oddfrid didn't hesitate to walk up to the innkeeper and speak to him in a language I didn't recognize. It was vaguely similar to Andronise, but I couldn't make out the words. I think he asked about someone named Joesphi, but the innkeeper shook his head and pointed skyward. Apparently, that person had passed away. Oddfrid shook his head sadly and said a few more things before passing him some silver pieces.

He turned back to us. "I have gotten myself a room, which I would greatly appreciate if you stayed out of. For the rest of you, you'll be staying in the barn. It's the only thing he has left. The snow has caused many of the travelers to pause their journey."

I nodded. "All right. Could you help us get something to eat before you go?"

Oddfrid gave me a puzzled look. "What? No protest that since you're royalty, you should have the room?"

I shrugged. "You're the one that needs the rest. It makes perfect sense that you would take it. Plus, Zofie's the only royalty here, and she has never been picky about where she sleeps."

He looked at us a moment more before turning to the innkeeper and saying something to him in that language I didn't understand and then pointing to us.

The innkeeper nodded and pointed to a large table to one side. He then called over a serving boy, about Cabrina's age, and gave him some instructions.

Oddfrid led us over to the table. I carefully helped Zofie sit, and the others filled in around us. A moment later, the young lad returned and served us each a steaming bowl of some kind of stew. I couldn't help but notice that he kept glancing at Cabrina—to the point where he nearly dropped her bowl in her lap. Naturally, she was oblivious to it until Spraggel leaned close and whispered in her ear. The young girl's eyes went wide in surprise. Afterward, she began to discretely glance in the boy's direction. I couldn't help but smile. For someone so interested in human courting, she had to have it pointed out when it happened to her.

After we were done, the serving boy led us outside to a barn. A couple of horses and a cow watched us curiously from a pen to one side as we entered. I had been a little concerned about staying in a barn, but this one was well maintained and thankfully kept heated using an iron stove in the center. There was also plenty of fresh, clean straw to lay down on. It actually wasn't bad at all. We were all tired, so everyone quickly settled for the night.

I had just gotten Zofie bedded down when Fumiko touched my arm. I turned to face her.

"It's time for another lesson," she said.

I looked around at the others. Burrowed into a pile of straw,

Spraggel was already softly snoring. Cabrina was lying under her blanket, but I could see her eyes still open, watching us with interest. No doubt hoping for another hint on human mating practices.

My shoulders slumped. "I'll be honest, I'm exhausted. Can't we wait until tomorrow night?" It was true I was tired, but there was another reason to delay. The last memory had been so personal. She had not lied when she said this process was more intimate than being lovers.

Fumiko just stared at me a moment. "If you say so." She started to turn away but suddenly wheeled and aimed a punch at my face. I instantly reacted and perfectly blocked it using a technique I had received from her. But she quickly followed with another to my stomach. I was totally unprepared and didn't even see it coming. She pulled the hit, so it barely made contact. But her message was clear. I was nowhere near ready.

Fumiko straightened, face unreadable. "Not bad, but that will not be enough to stop Lilith next time. And you know she's coming. It's just a matter of time."

I sighed. "All right. But I have to say I'm not comfortable with this. It's just so... personal. I see things about you that I probably shouldn't."

She held my gaze for a moment before answering. "You're right. I'm not comfortable with it either." She nodded toward Zofie. "But for her, I will do anything." Fumiko turned her gaze back to me. "Will you?"

I gave one last deep sigh and finally agreed. "All right. Let's get this over with."

I laid down on my blanket, and Fumiko knelt beside me. Once more, she took my hand and raised it to her forehead. I felt her gathering her myst.

I glanced over at Zofie sleeping beside me. "I wonder what Zofie thinks of us doing this."

Fumiko's lips grew into a half-smile. "I think she would be jealous that I'm taking all of her man's attention."

"Zofie?" I asked in surprise. "She doesn't have a jealous bone in her body."

Fumiko looked sad. "Ahh, you may be right." And then softer, in a faint whisper, "But then again, you never know what truly lurks in a woman's heart."

A moment later, the world began to fade, and I was thrust into Fumiko's past.

My stomach twisted in knots as I waited my turn.

I knelt on the highly polished wood floor with my knees on the edge of the contest area. The others of my group, identically dressed in gray pants and a belted shirt, were lined up beside me, motionless, all of us with backs straight and hands in our lap.

The windows were open today, letting in the scents of spring flowers and providing a gentle breeze to cool the room. However, it could do nothing to alleviate the smell of sweaty exertion, and maybe a bit of fear, that permeated the room.

In front of me, two of my group were fighting. Their swords flashed in the bright sunlight streaming from the open windows, and the clang of metal against metal punctuated their strikes. The blows they traded were deadly. Should either one of them make a misstep...

I closed my eyes and tried to center myself. I needed to be calm. My turn was next, and I had, unfortunately, drawn a girl who was as close to a friend as it came in my group. We were only fifteen, but this was the sorting. One of us would leave the group today, never to return.

No one knew what happened to those that lost, but rumor had it that slavery was the best outcome. And we didn't talk about the worst.

I opened my eyes and tried to focus on the fight. Tried to analyze their movements and dissect their weaknesses. But at this point, there were very few. Those who consistently made mistakes had been weeded out long ago.

Not for the first time, I wondered why my father had forced this on me. Forced me to be part of this group of children and receive such brutal training. The Emperor's Butterflies, as we were called. They said we were special, and we should be honored. But from the way they treated us, it didn't seem that way.

I couldn't understand what I had done to deserve it. I couldn't have offended Father. I had only met him the one time, and he didn't even know who I was.

And I certainly didn't pose a succession threat. I was so far down the line that it was laughable. I wasn't even suitable to be some allies' concubine! Even the relatives on my mother's side refused to acknowledge me.

The only reason I could think of was due to the scandal my mother had been involved in. Maybe it was to punish her. Whatever the reason, I would likely never know.

But one thing was sure about the Butterflies. Once entered, there was only one way out.

"Hold!" came the shout of the referee.

I jerked myself back to the present.

The red seeping through a slash in one of their shirts caught my eye. It was just a flesh wound—nothing serious in of itself. My eyes slid up to the boy attached to the injury. Duong was his name. He was always joking and made us smile, even though we tried not to. But now, his expression was hard and full of anger. I could see his lower lip tremble.

The victor was named Weisheng, and he gave no expression, merely moved to attention with his sword lowered. I was close enough that I could see a drop of blood run down its razor edge and gather at the tip. I couldn't help but watch in horror as it dripped to the floor. My eyes wouldn't leave the spot. It looked so red.

The two boys bowed to each other. They turned to their seconds and bowed again, extending the swords to them on the flats of their hands. The seconds received the weapons in the same manner before turning and presenting them to the masters.

Relieved of their swords, the two combatants once again faced each other and bowed. Despite his win, Weisheng looked like he was going to cry. But Duong shook off his earlier anger and gave his opponent a confident smile before turning with head held high and walking out of the room. For a moment, Weisheng swayed, like he might run after him, but he held firm and then went to his place and kneeled with the other victors.

"Fumiko! Jiaying!" announced one of the masters. My heart pounded in my chest. Now it was my time.

We stepped out onto the floor. When we reached the center, we briefly faced each other before bowing. Jiaying avoided my eyes. As I looked down, I couldn't help but notice the spot of blood on the floor, perfectly round, and so, so red. For some reason, it made me shiver.

Rising, I turned, and our seconds brought over our weapons—highly polished steel, the kind some ladies of court used for a mirror. It was hard, smooth, and cut like a razor.

I bowed to my second and took the sword in my two hands before turning to face my opponent. We bowed again, and then for the first time since stepping onto the floor, we looked into each other's eyes. I guess I knew her better than I thought. Her gaze held nervousness, yet also a fierce determination. Many years ago, I had thought of her as my twin, and as we stared at each other, I knew it was true. Her eyes mirrored mine perfectly.

I had sparred with her many times before. She was good. Very good. The best in our group. And in one way or another, this would be the last time we fought together.

We moved into our opening forms and waited for the signal. I felt a bead of sweat run down the side of my face.

"Go!"

And we moved.

We swung at each other. No holding back. The sharp clang of our swords coming in quick succession. Forward, back, left, right. Moves so fast, they were hard to follow. She feinted, I countered. She attacked, I defended. The muscles in my arms and legs, conditioned over many hours of practice, responded before the thoughts could form in my brain. Our deadly dance was horrifying. Yet, it was beautiful. I noticed my opponent's smile. And to my horror, I smiled back. Her movements were graceful, beautiful, an honor to behold. In that moment, I loved her. My sister. My twin.

But perfection could never last. We were after all, just young girls. Our limbs grew tired. Our concentration began to break. A slip had to occur. As we drew to our conclusion, I knew I couldn't let her die.

"Hold!"

We each froze instantly in place and took a step back. I cut my eyes to my left arm and the new rip in my sleeve. Red was seeping through it. My stomach knotted. Had I made the right decision? Was I about to find out what lay beyond the sorting?

A hush fell over the room. Not even the spring breeze dared break the silence. Out of the corner of my eye, I saw the masters quickly gather and begin to whisper among themselves. They hadn't called a winner.

I looked across to Jiaying, and she stared back in wide-eyed surprise. The reason was easy to see. She also had a cut on her arm in nearly the identical place as mine. It appeared we had wounded each other at exactly the same time.

I understood the consternation of the masters. This could not be a coincidence. It had to be arranged somehow, and it took great timing and skill to pull it off. One of us had created an opening, while at the same time, offered one. Only someone of exceptional skill could do it. Even the masters would be hard-pressed for such a feat. But which one of us? The wrong choice would eliminate a genius.

And that they dared not do.

Jiaying realized this too, and a slow smile crept onto her face. We both began to hope.

The masters broke apart. "Draw!" announced the referee. "Both return to your places."

We bowed and passed off our blades to our seconds, before kneeling in our previous spots. We each wore the only red sleeves of those remaining. It was amazing how similar the wounds were. Like they mirrored each other.

I cut my eyes in her direction. She was having trouble concealing her relief, as I too was having difficulty hiding mine. A coincidence had saved us both. Or so it seemed.

But even at my young age, I already knew...

Coincidences didn't exist.

CHAPTER FIFTEEN

Cabrina's Gift

I awoke to a warm weight on my chest and the sound of someone banging a metal pail. I could tell the pail's operator was trying to be quiet, but it just wasn't working. As for the weight on my chest, Fumiko lay partially across me. She must have also passed out after sharing her memory. She lay atop me, dead asleep, her head resting on my chest and her arm thrown across me. I watched her face for a moment as she slumbered—a rare unguarded moment for someone so reserved. Her mouth hung partially open, and her mussed hair spread across her cheek and across her eyes. I ached to brush it back, but I dared not, lest I wake her. Not for the first time, I noticed her smooth skin and delicate lips—she was every bit the beauty. I understood why Rourke was so enamored with her. It would be quite easy to fall under her spell.

Too easy. I thought of Zofie and looked away.

The memories of her fight hung in my mind. It was as fresh as if it had happened yesterday. What had it been? She had referred to it as the sorting. But, exactly what was it? Why had the emperor ordered her to be part of it? And most importantly, why had they put her in that impossible position of choosing between her friend and her own life? So many questions. Now that she had shared her memory, maybe she would be willing to talk about it.

The pail rattled again, and Fumiko's breathing changed. Her eyes slowly blinked open and flicked around the barn's interior before finally settling on me. And then she smiled. It was like the sun had suddenly risen. But she seemed to catch herself and bolted upright. "Sorry," she mumbled and immediately stood. Without looking up, she grabbed her cloak and was out the door.

I sighed. I must have embarrassed her. I would have to apologize later.

I turned toward Zofie and found her sitting up, eyes staring straight ahead. Which meant she was ready to be taken to the privy. I immediately felt guilty. I had spent a couple of extra moments staring at Fumiko when I should have been helping my princess instead.

"Good. You're finally awake. I can get some breakfast."

I turned to see Spraggel standing with his backside to the stove. He was impatiently rocking back and forth on his heels. Behind him, on the other side of the stove, Cabrina sat on a pile of straw with her knees pulled up to her chest. She was intently watching the other occupant in the room—the serving boy from yesterday. He was the operator of the noisy pail and was using it to water the animals.

"Breakfast?" I asked, running a hand through my hair.

Spraggel nodded. "Yes, you know the meal you have after the sun comes up. The one I've been dying to have while you've been sleeping with your other woman."

I looked up in surprise. "She's not my woman."

Spraggel frowned. "Judging from the way she was snuggled up to you, I'm not so sure." There was a note of irritation in his voice. "I'm beginning to wonder if Cabrina might be right."

I shook my head. It occurred to me that Spraggel didn't know about the nightly memory transfers. And I couldn't tell him either. I guess it must look a little suspicious. He's seen us wake up in the same bed two nights in a row. "There is nothing between Fumiko and me. She is just... helping."

Spraggel's eyes went up. "I imagine she could be very helpful to a young man whose fiancée is incapacitated." He stepped forward and placed a hand on my shoulder. His expression softened. "Be careful, Coren. Playing with the hearts of young ladies can be painful for everyone involved. Take it from me. I know." He smiled. "It's why I spent almost a year as a cat."

I blinked at him. *A year?* He had mentioned something about pissing off the wrong myst user in his younger days. But a year?

I shook my head. "There's nothing between us. Zofie is all I need."

"I trust you, Coren. Just remember that Zofie does too." He gave my shoulder a reassuring squeeze. He then clapped his hands and went to get his cloak. "Now, for some long-overdue breakfast."

"You didn't have to wait."

He gave me a surprised look. "Oh yes, but I did. Someone had to keep an eye on Cabrina."

I picked up my blanket and started folding it. "You could have taken her with you."

He pointed a thumb over his shoulder at the girl. "I tried, but she was too intent on watching someone..." He rolled his eyes in the direction of the serving boy.

I glanced at Cabrina. She was watching the boy with hawk-like intensity. The young lad would occasionally glance in her direction, but then quickly divert his eyes in the 'I want to look at you, but I'm too embarrassed' way youths do. And her attention wasn't helping. I could almost see the boy's nervous sweat.

Spraggel opened the door, the chill air drifting in around him. "That's why I'll leave dealing with her to you." He grinned mischievously and then slipped outside.

I couldn't help but smile. I guess I had helped create the situation. I had forbidden her from speaking to anyone, or we would further restrict her movements. It looked like she was dying to talk with him but was trying to honor our agreement. Or at least the letter of it.

"Breakfast does sound good," I said and went to Zofie and helped her stand. I pulled a few bits of straw from her hair. I leaned in and kissed her on the cheek.

I turned toward the young girl. "Want to come with me, Cabrina?"

Her eyes flicked from me to the boy and back. She knew she had to come with me, but didn't want to leave.

I motioned her over. She gave me a curious look but quickly rose and came up to me. I bent and whispered in her ear. "Do you want to talk to the young man?"

Her eyes went wide in surprise. She nodded.

"You've done what we've asked, so I'll let you for just a moment. Just remember not to embarrass the young lady inside of you."

She nodded. "She's the one that wants to talk to him, but she's too embarrassed. I don't think I'll ever understand humans." She shook her head. "You have to talk with someone to find out if they're a suitable mate, yet you're afraid to talk to them because they might be." She shrugged. "Maybe I'll understand one day."

I smiled. "If you ever figure it out, please explain it to me."

She grinned. Then she almost skipped over to where the young man was bruising himself with cleaning the animal's pen. "Hello," she said.

He didn't pay her any attention. Cabrina went to stand in front of him, so he had to notice her.

"My name is Cabrina. What's yours?"

He shook his head and made an exaggerated shrug. He then said something in his language which none of us understood.

I sighed sadly, realizing she was going to be disappointed.

Cabrina gave him a puzzled look and then looked toward me.

"He doesn't speak our language," I said.

"Can you teach it to me?" she asked.

I shook my head. "I don't know this one. Besides, it takes a long time to learn a language, and we won't be here that long."

Cabrina's face fell. Then surprisingly, she looked to the side, which meant she was having an internal conversation with the girl inside. She suddenly smiled and refocused on the boy. She reached out and grabbed his hand. He looked up at her in surprise before a bright violet light gathered around her.

My eyes went wide in shock. "Don't!" I yelled, dropping the bag I held and starting toward her.

But she didn't stop. Instead, she whispered, "I curse you... with myself."

The violet glow intensified, nearly blinding me and enveloping both her and the boy.

I touched the restraining amulet around my neck, the words to activate it forming on my lips.

The glow hadn't even faded, before the boy whispered in perfect Ellish, "I curse you... to return."

The violet glow flared again, once more enveloping them.

"Bind!" I yelled. Her hands instantly went together at the wrists, and she fell to her knees.

"Oww!" she wailed. "What did you do that for?"

"You cursed him!" I yelled back. "I thought I could trust you."

She looked up at me angrily. "It was *her* idea. Not mine. Besides, I was only there a moment." She lowered her head. She sniffled and spoke more quietly. "Can you loosen these up a bit? They're hurting her."

Behind me, I heard the boy saying something. "What just happened?"

I turned to face him, and he was looking at me quite puzzled. "I'm sorry. Our companion is a myst user, and she did something she wasn't supposed to."

He looked down at his hands. "I felt something in my head for a moment. Something hot. It was really strange." He gave me a puzzled look. "So both of you actually can speak my language."

Then it hit me. I shook my head in disbelief. "I'm not speaking your language. You're speaking mine." I looked to Cabrina. "You gave him our language?"

She looked up from where she knelt. "Of course I did, you stupid human!" There were tears in her eyes. "How else was I supposed to talk to him? I can perfect people, so I perfected him. You said I could talk with him, and *she* told me to do it."

"She?" I asked.

"You know, the Cabrina inside. Talk to her if you don't believe me." And suddenly, Cabrina's expression changed. I instinctively knew I was talking to the owner of the girl's body.

"Don't b-b-lame No-name," she said. Her stutter was worse due to the excitement. "It's my fault. I'm the one that told her to do it."

I blinked in astonishment. "She's doing what you tell her?"

The youth shrugged. "W-w-why wouldn't she? It's my b-body, and she has no other d-directives. She's tried to give control to me several times, but I've... refused." She looked down. "I don't stutter if she talks."

I considered her for a moment. "Release," I finally said, and Cabrina's bonds let go. She sighed in relief and sat up, rubbing her wrists.

I looked up at the boy, who was concerned, but unsure what to make of our exchange. "Everything is all right now," I said. "Consider the ability to speak our language a gift. Our companion wanted to talk with you and decided that giving you our language was the fastest way."

He grinned, clearly delighted. "Thank you very much! This is a great gift! I've been trying to learn it since we have travelers from your lands. But it's been hard for me to wrap my tongue around your words. My father will be most pleased. In fact, I'm going to tell him right now." The excited boy ran to the door and was out only a moment later.

I bent over Cabrina and offered her my hand. She looked at it a moment before gingerly taking it so I could help her stand.

"Are you all right?" I asked. "I'm sorry I bound you, but I was afraid your Dark Avenyts was going to make a run for it."

She shrugged and looked down. She was avoiding my eyes. "I'm fine. No-name has w-withdrawn for now. She's very frustrated and w-won't even talk to me. She d-didn't like that you p-punished me for something she did."

I patted her shoulder. "Well, don't worry. We'll get No-name off of you soon."

And then she said something that surprised me.

"I'm not in a hurry. I kind of like her." She glanced up at me before returning her gaze to the floor. "I w-was scared at first, but after she c-completed her mission, she's b-been... sort of... nice. I haven't had very many friends and w-w-we talk all the time. She helps me be the p-person I've always w-wanted to be." She looked down with tears in her eyes. "It's nice."

I put a finger under her chin and lifted her face to look at me. "What will you do if she gets a new directive?"

She shrugged. "As long as she's with me, I don't think I'll care."

I stared at her in disbelief. "You know she's a Dark Avenyts. An enemy to humans. She could kill you."

She looked down and stirred the straw on the floor with the toe of her boot. "Yes, I know." She took a deep breath and then looked up fully into my face. "But is that so different from the princess ordering you into battle against an enemy? You might not want to hurt the people you go up against, but you'll still do it." She paused and searched my face. "It's the same for her. She'll have to do it, but she won't like it. It doesn't change that she's still my friend."

We stared at each other for a moment. A nagging thought occurred to me. *Was there more to the Dark Avenyts than I originally thought?*

My stomach growled, and we both smiled. The tension in the room eased. "I guess we've waited on breakfast long enough."

She nodded and went to get her cloak.

I looked to Zofie, standing close by patiently waiting. Would I go into battle if she ordered? Would I be willing to kill a friend?

I shook my head. It bothered me that I didn't have an answer.

We spent the day resting. Not that I minded. The last few days had been a whirlwind, and I needed the time to regain my strength and compose myself.

But resting was not the same as relaxing. Even though we were over a thousand miles from our home in Brethnach, I still couldn't help but feel a twitch at my back. Lilith was coming. I knew it as sure as I knew the sun would rise tomorrow. The only question was when.

I practiced with Fumiko later that morning and was surprised at my new sword skills. We cleared a spot in the barn large enough to spar and be out of the snow. When we were ready, I launched into the same attack I had seen her use against her friend. Naturally, she defended against it perfectly. Back and forth, we traded blows until Fumiko called a halt. I stepped back breathing hard. This was really difficult, but exhilarating. I had been able to hold my own. I grinned at her. "That was fantastic. I feel like I could take on an army now."

Fumiko didn't seem winded at all. It reminded me of practicing with Risten before the Dark Avenyts took her. She had likewise never seemed fazed.

She shook her head. "You have some skills now, but they are still *my* skills, not yours. You still have much work to do."

I shook my head. "Surely, it can't be that bad."

Fumiko cocked an eyebrow. She raised her sword and moved into position. "Again."

I grinned and moved to my first position. We launched at each other, and I was able to counter her every move. Then Fumiko varied the flow, and I suddenly didn't know what to do. My nimble blade became awkward and slow. The next thing I knew, my weapon was flying across the room, and her sword was pointed at my throat.

"See," she said. "You have a copy of my skills in your brain. But there are still some things you don't know." She stepped back, sheathing her sword. "Also, your muscles haven't incorporated all the knowledge yet. Your arms are about to fall off, aren't they?"

I smiled sheepishly. "Pretty much. My muscles are quivering." I stepped over to pick up my sword.

She pursed her lips. "You need to practice. Go through the forms by yourself, as many times as you can stand. Five hundred would be a good number to start with."

"Five hundred?"

She nodded. "You won't remember them for long unless you practice. Remember, they are my skills, and while your brain has temporarily accepted them, it will soon figure out they are not actually yours and purge them."

"But Zofie has given me bits of her memories before, and I remember them just fine."

Fumiko sighed and rubbed her side. Her ribs must be hurting her. "Those are different. She set a context for remembering them, plus they were likely short. Skills are a different matter. They have no context, so I have to give you one of my own memories to attach them to."

I nodded. That explained why I was seeing Fumiko's past. She was giving me strong memories to cement the skills to my brain.

I looked down at my hands. "But still. You could use this to train an army of sword-masters in no time."

Fumiko shook her head. "While it will work for some, it will not work for the majority. The instructor is giving up a piece of themselves to their student, who must receive it unconditionally. It's not something one can do with everyone. They have to have some sort of bond."

I looked at her levelly. "In other words, they have to trust each other."

She stepped closer and put a hand on my chest. "Totally. You saved me from the Dark Avenyts. I trust you completely."

"As I do you. You've saved my neck more times than I can count. So, I guess we do have something not everyone has."

She nodded. "Indeed, we do." She paused, staring up into my eyes. I felt her lean just a hair closer—

Then she abruptly turned away. "I think I'm going to rest for a bit." Fumiko rubbed her side. "That practice made my ribs hurt again." She made her way over to a pile of straw and carefully reclined against it.

I nodded. "I'm going to go check on Zofie."

She closed her eyes. "Don't stay too long. You need to practice."

I stepped to the side to wipe the sweat from my face. But as I thought about it, I became curious. I turned back to her. "Where did you learn to do this? Share your skills, I mean. Was it at that school I saw?"

She didn't answer at first. She slowly opened her eyes and turned to look at me with that neutral expression. "No," she finally said. "It wasn't. Myst training was excluded. I was taught that before I was inducted."

My eyes drew up in surprise. "Then where did you learn? I don't know much about myst usage, but don't you come into your abilities at puberty? You couldn't have been much older than that in the first memory you gave me."

"You're right." Her expression did not change. "My mother taught me."

"She must have been an excellent teacher for you to learn everything so quickly."

Fumiko propped herself up on her elbows and gazed at me levelly. "I was forced to learn quickly. I had just come into my powers when they notified my mother of my induction. That only gave us five days to prepare."

I shook my head in disbelief. "How is that possible? Your skills are so advanced."

Fumiko raised her head, her eyes locking with mine. And I knew—
The forbidden skills.

It's the only way she could have gotten training so fast. Myst or sword, a skill was a skill.

Shock spread across my face. I slowly shook my head. "Your mother... she didn't?"

"She told me it was the best way to help me survive. Provided I kept my new skills hidden."

That explained why she swore me to secrecy. "But you were only a child," I protested. "You would be receiving a grownup's memories. Things a child couldn't understand. It was like she was forcing you into adulthood."

Fumiko stared at me a moment longer. "True," she said. "But she knew my childhood had ended the moment the Emperor's letter was delivered. It was the best she could do to protect me."

I could only stare in shock, thinking of the toll only two lessons had taken on me. "It must have been extremely hard on you."

Fumiko laid back down and shut her eyes. "No. Receiving the skills wasn't too bad, nor the secret practices afterward. I adapted well." She was silent for a moment. "The hard part was her weeping over me before every lesson."

As I made the trip from the barn to the inn, I tried to shake off the weight of what Fumiko had told me. I used to think I had a difficult childhood, losing my father, being cursed with bad luck, and then being sent away from my family. But based on her revelations, I think hers might have been even worse.

Inside, I discovered Spraggel sitting beside Zofie and talking to an obviously bored Cabrina. Seeing him lifted my spirits. My old master could be strange sometimes, but he had taken in a cursed young boy and gave him an education. For that, he had my eternal admiration.

Spraggel smiled when he spotted me. "Ah, Coren. How's the practice going?"

I went over to Zofie and kissed her on the cheek. "Pretty good so far. I still have a ways to go, though." I sat down beside her and glanced at the leftover sausages on her plate. "Has Zofie eaten yet?"

Spraggel shook his head. "She wouldn't."

I turned to him, puzzled. "She's never refused before."

Spraggel shrugged. "I offered her a bite of sausage, but she kept her mouth closed and would turn her head. I even tried some porridge, but she refused that too."

I looked over at the sausages. They did look a little greasy. Maybe they weren't agreeing with her. I would have to keep an eye on her to make sure she got enough.

I turned to Cabrina. "Where's the young lad?"

She immediately brightened. "I talked to him for a bit earlier as he washed the tables and floors. But he's got chores elsewhere and..." She rolled her eyes in Spraggel's direction. "I couldn't go."

"I'm sure you'll have other chances to speak with him."

She nodded but was clearly not pleased with that answer.

Over her shoulder, I could see the innkeeper pouring ale for another of his patrons. He caught my eye and motioned me over. I sighed. It was likely to complain about what happened to his son. He led me over to an empty table. I took one chair, and he took the other across from me.

He gave me a mug of ale, which he said was on him, and introduced himself as Eviek. He was a friendly enough individual, a little on the gruff side, and spoke slightly broken Ellish. However, I couldn't help but be a little suspicious at his friendly banter. He was not acting like a father upset over his son. There had to be something else.

He put both of his hands flat on the table and leaned closer. He spoke softly. "Your girl. She gave Ellish language to my youngest, Troy. What girl did..." He looked down. "...is great gift. Knowing it will be a big help to him. And me too. We get many travelers from lands near you."

I leaned forward. "Is Troy all right? It didn't affect him, did it?"

Eviek shook his head emphatically. "No, he fine. He talking my ear off now." But I sensed that was not all.

I nodded. "That's good. What Cabrina did can create problems. I'm glad he didn't have any." I was assuming that what Cabrina did carried some of the same side-effects and risks as what Fumiko and I were doing.

Eviek considered me for a moment. "Can she make him read and write Ellish too? Or maybe do numbers? He a smart boy. Can even do some myst things. But out here, there is no one to teach him. His mamma showed him a few things before she died, but I don't know enough to teach him more. Mamma always wanted him to go to university in Khartiva, maybe work the King's books and numbers. Even tax collectors make good coin."

I drew back in surprise. This was not how I thought the conversation would go. "What Cabrina did could have hurt him badly, and your son is fortunate it didn't. We've had to punish her for it." I didn't want to tell him that his son had been briefly possessed by one of humanity's mortal enemies. That might get us kicked out of the inn, or worse, killed.

Eviek sighed. "So you won't allow it?"

I shook my head. "Allowing isn't the question. Your son could end up injured."

He clasped his hands and placed them on the table. He looked at me earnestly. "I need to find something good for Troy. My eldest will be taking the inn when I die. Plus, traffic along this route is slowing. Trade not like it used to be. That means Troy has to find something else." He looked away. "Mamma asked me to send him to university, on her deathbed no less."

Just then, Troy came in carrying a heavy load of firewood. Cabrina practically leaped up to help him with the door. They chatted as he stacked the wood by the hearth.

Eviek gave me a pleading look. "What if I offer gold? How much would it take?"

I understood the problem. Not everyone managed to learn to read and write. If trade really was dying along this route, then it could mean the difference between a good life and a life working as someone's indentured servant.

But while I sympathized, he had no idea how risky it was. What if the next time there were some of the side-effects Fumiko had mentioned. Or even worse, what if Cabrina decided not to move back to her body. Then there really would be a big mess.

"I'm sorry, but we dare not try it. The risk is just too high. It could ruin him."

Eviek looked down, disappointed. "If you change mind, I will pay. I'll give you three gold coins."

I was not familiar with the coin of this land, but gold was gold. It seemed a substantial offering. I slid my chair back. "I'm sorry. I can't."

He slapped the table's top, his face turning red with anger. Everyone looked over at us. "Is it because we're filthy heathens to you! Is that why my coin isn't good enough!"

Troy looked up at his father's outburst and came running over. He spoke to him in their language. The big man turned away, and grabbing his coat, left the room.

Troy turned to me. "I'm sorry. Father gets a little excited at times. I told him to accept what you had given us as a gift and not press for more. But he wouldn't listen." He shook his head. "I better go after him." He then went out the door.

Spraggel wandered over. He patted me on the shoulder. "Coren, you certainly have a way with people."

I sighed. "What was I supposed to do?"

Spraggel shook his head. "Not piss him off." He looked toward the door. "I've got a feeling this isn't over yet."

I had expected Eviek to ask me about it again, but he said nothing more. He only regarded me with a deadly silence whenever I was near. I tried to stay out of his way.

Oddfrid had been notably absent most of the day. We had started to become a little concerned, but when we knocked on his door, he had simply yelled from inside that he was resting. We didn't see him until mid-afternoon when he emerged still looking exhausted. He was also uncharacteristically subdued as he explained he needed another day to recuperate. Our journey's next leg was the longest, and he needed to be well-rested before trying it. However, he thought he would be ready by morning.

For me, I took Zofie to the barn, sat her on a stool, and under Cabrina's watchful eye, talked with her as I practiced. I really missed her—the way she would smile, the twinkle in her eye, the sound of her voice. All of it. Not only was she my beloved, she was also my closest friend.

I needed her back in the worst way.

When evening finally rolled around, we began to settle for the evening. Spraggel wandered in and immediately went for his pile of hay.

He was snoring in only a few minutes. He had been drinking a lot of ale, so I guess it caught up with him.

Troy came to do one last check on the animals, although I suspected it was more to have one more word with Cabrina. While he was there, Fumiko begged some fresh bindings and salve, which he was more than happy to fetch.

Fumiko turned to me after he was gone. "Would you help me again?"

I nodded. "Let me take Zofie to the privy first."

Cabrina piped up. "I can take her," she offered. "Besides, I need to go myself."

I paused and considered her.

Cabrina rolled her eyes as only a young girl can. "What? Do you think I'm going to run off with her or perhaps kill her? I've had plenty of chances to do that if I wanted to. Besides, where would I take her in this weather and in the dark?"

She had a point there. "All right. But come right back."

Cabrina went to Zofie and took her hand, pulling her toward the door. "Come on, Princess. Let's take care of our bodily needs. I swear I don't see how you humans put up with it." She kept up a constant stream of words as they went outside, headed for the privy.

"Are you sure that's wise?" Fumiko asked as she turned away and slipped off her shirt, exposing her well-toned back to me. As I unwound the old binding, it suddenly hit me that I was alone with a half-naked woman. I shook the thought away as I began to apply the salve to the dark bruise on her side. I tried not to notice how warm and smooth her skin felt. She hissed at the touch.

"You think she's a danger to Zofie?" I asked, more to distract her from the discomfort than being concerned.

Fumiko shook her head. "No, that's not what I'm talking about. You're beginning to trust her. That's what is not wise. She's a Dark Avenyts and doesn't think as we do." Fumiko looked at me over her shoulder. "Although I have to admit, she's not acting like the one that possessed me. Maybe it's because she's so young for her kind."

I finished applying the salve and moved to put the fresh binding on. I carefully began to wrap it around her chest.

"Could be," I said. "Cabrina and No-name do seem to be about the same maturity level. They make quite the pair."

She nodded, but said nothing more.

The binding came up shorter than I expected and I had to reach around Fumiko to tie it off. I leaned close, trying to touch as little of her as I could.

"There. That should do it," I said when I finished. But when I went to pull away, she grabbed my hands and pulled them against her stomach, making me lean closer. "Hold me for just a moment." She leaned back into me and sighed contently. "Please. Your hands are so warm."

I felt very awkward and wasn't sure what to do.

After a moment, she released me and put on her shirt. She turned and looked into my eyes. "Zofie is so lucky. I love her from the bottom of my heart, but I have to admit I'm envious."

I gave her a nervous smile. "It's probably just my curse altering our fate so that you'll help me. I wouldn't read too much into it."

She leaned closer. "Perhaps you're right." Then her hand shot out, grabbing me behind the neck and pulling me into a brief kiss.

My eyes went wide in shock.

She pulled away and took a step back. Uncharacteristically, one corner of her mouth pulled up. "Your curse made me do that." She turned away. "I better go check on those two. Knowing Cabrina, she's decided to urinate in the snow just to see what it does."

Fumiko pulled on her cloak and left.

I got our blankets and spread them out. I couldn't help but wonder what all that was about. Could Fumiko harbor feelings for me? I hoped not. And I hoped I wasn't giving her the wrong idea.

Just then, the door flew open with Fumiko leading Zofie inside. "I can't find her!" she yelled. "Zofie was standing in the middle of the path all by herself. But Cabrina wasn't with her, and she wasn't in the privy." Fumiko came closer. "Not only that, but from the tracks in the snow, there appears to have been a struggle. I could make out at least three pairs of adult-sized boots."

I stared at her in disbelief.

Cabrina's been taken.

CHAPTER SIXTEEN

Hard Stop

I t had to be the innkeeper, Eviek. I immediately woke Spraggel and explained what happened. He rubbed his face and then waved his hand toward the door.

"Go," he said. "We have to find her. I'll protect the princess."

I nodded and ran out the door with Fumiko on my heels. Once outside, I reached in my shirt and pulled out Cabrina's control amulet. I thanked the Creator that Rourke had foreseen we might need something for this situation. I moved to a clear spot between the inn and the barn.

"Locate," I commanded. It flashed briefly to let me know it was active. I then started to slowly turn in a circle. When I was halfway around, it flashed. I looked up. It was pointing down the snow-rutted road in front of the inn. "Damn."

I looked to Fumiko. I couldn't see her well in the dim light of the partial moon. "I'll go ahead. Let Oddfrid know we might be leaving a little early."

Fumiko didn't move. "Whatever you do, don't fight them. You're not ready."

I grinned. "Don't worry. I'm Mister Negotiator. My preference is to talk them to death."

She returned the grin. "That does fit your style better." And then she turned and ran toward the inn.

I mumbled softly to myself. "Unfortunately, it doesn't hold up so well against swords." I turned and jogged in the direction the amulet indicated, nearly falling on a patch of ice.

During warmer times, the road I traveled was likely a wide and well-maintained thoroughfare into the village. But now, it was mainly just a path through the snow trampled down by those unfortunate enough to be out in the cold. The only thing around me was a blanket of white, broken only by a few trees and the occasional dark house. The thick snow seemed to muffle some sounds, yet amplify others. The crunch of ice under my boots seemed unnaturally loud. It wasn't lost on me that this would easily alert my presence to any potential attacker.

And Creator, it was frigid. I shivered. My breath came out in dense puffs of fog. I periodically flexed my hands to keep them limber should I have to pull my sword. We had cold and snow back in Brethnach, but nothing like this. It just made it clear that I was a long way from home.

I didn't have to go far to reach the village square. I paused beside the town's central well and consulted my charm. It pointed toward a sizable building just ahead. Dim flickers of light could be seen coming from around its shuttered windows. It was too dark to make out exactly what the structure was, but from its shape, it appeared to be a village hall or perhaps a Creator's temple.

I trotted toward it—again slipping on the ice—and quietly climbed the three stone steps leading up to the door. I could hear voices coming from inside.

It sounded like Eviek, and he didn't seem happy. "You little witch," he yelled. "I don't believe you. You gave him Ellish. You can make him able to read and do numbers."

"Pa," came his son Troy's voice. "Don't do this."

"Be quiet!" he yelled. Then I heard a meaty slap.

"Don't hit Troy!" It was Cabrina. "I've told you I can't!"

I looked back down the way I had come hoping to spot Fumiko, but I didn't see her. I really should wait for her before confronting the man. He likely had help inside, but I had no clue as to how many or if they were armed.

I heard another slap. "Why did you hit me?" yelled Cabrina.

"Give him the teachings, or you get more than just slap."

"I've told you I can't," she pleaded. "Now let me go before I get into trouble. And quit hitting Troy."

A new voice joined the conversation. Another man. "And my daughter. You said she could have it too!"

I heard another meaty slap, and Cabrina wailed.

I had to act. I reached for the door's latch—when suddenly the charm on my wrist went hot. I froze.

Coren, can you hear me? I winced at the booming voice inside my head. It was Abe.

I glanced at the door, afraid to speak. I breathed a whispered, "Yes."

Oh, goody. The princess has been working on getting my voice back inside your head since yesterday. I can still only talk to you when you're in danger, but she's most pleased that at least this much is working. I, on the other hand, would have preferred to have gone a few more years without your company.

Yeah, it was Abe.

I breathed another whisper. "What's inside?"

About that. There's a big guy standing just inside the door. And he's a little jumpy. As soon as you opened it, you would have been making a bad fashion statement with a knife sticking out of your chest.

The arguing on the other side of the door seemed to be escalating. Apparently, one of the men thought his daughter should go first.

Now, don't open the door. In this case, I think it would be better to just knock.

"Knock?" I whispered in disbelief.

He chuckled. *Trust me.*

I stepped up to the door, gave it a couple of loud raps, and quickly stepped back down to the street.

The door immediately opened, and a large fellow stepped out, brandishing a pretty big knife. As soon as his foot hit the first step, he slipped on the ice, and his feet went flying. He landed on his back and knocked his head hard on the stone steps. He lay there unconscious.

"Not terribly original," I commented.

Abe snorted. *Everyone's a critic.*

I quickly rushed through the door.

Inside was a large room dimly lit from a single lantern resting on a rough wooden table. Eviek and two other men looked up as I entered. I had seen both of them at the inn. One appeared to be unarmed, but the other had a wicked-looking club. Troy leaned against the wall dabbing at his nose.

Cabrina sat on a bench in the center of the room, plainly relieved when I entered. "It wasn't my fault," she exclaimed. "I didn't do anything this time!"

I focused my gaze on Eviek. "In this region, is it customary to abduct one's guests?"

I caught Cabrina's eye and motioned her to leave. She started to rise, but Eviek's large hand came down on her shoulder and pushed her back down.

"She stays until my son gets the teaching he needs."

I shook my head. "She can't do that. Now let her go, and I'll forget this happened. But if you force my hand, I won't go easy on you." I hoped I could back up my words.

Troy stepped away from the wall. "Pa, just let her go. This has gone too far."

Eviek pointed at his son. "You be quiet!"

I took a step closer. "Eviek, this is wrong, and you know it. Now let her go."

He frowned. "I don't want to do this, but Troy has got to go to university. It's his only chance at decent life!" There was desperation in his voice. He reached for his knife.

I heard a scraping step, and hoping it was Fumiko, I glanced behind me. But no such luck. It was the big guy I had left outside. He was holding his knife, and Creator, did he look pissed.

"Abe," I whispered. "A little help here."

But he was silent.

Then the three men in front of me and the one behind all rushed me at once.

My body reacted before I had a chance to even think. It felt wrong, but at the same time, it also felt right. My eyes went wide. Fumiko's skills. *It was working!*

I wheeled and kicked the man with the club, my leg flying up perfectly and catching him in the chin. He staggered back.

Almost magically, I spun on my heel to the big man coming at me from behind. I dodged his knife and kicked him hard in the side. His mouth made an "oh" of surprise. I punched his abdomen just below his ribs, causing him to double over and fall to his knees.

The unarmed man came at me throwing punches. I easily dodged them and slipped inside his guard, landing an uppercut into his chin. He toppled like a tree.

Eviek lunged at me brandishing his knife. From the way he moved, I could tell he was a brawler, not a fighter. I caught his descending hand and quickly twisted it behind his back. I brought my foot up to his backside and shoved him hard. He staggered and tripped over a bench, falling hard on his face.

Club man came next, swinging crosswise at my head. Of the four, this one seemed to know how to use his weapon. I ducked and leaped back, quickly drawing my sword from its scabbard. We briefly considered each other.

He charged, swinging as he came. I parried and caught the weapon on my sword. As I expected, the blade gouged the club deeply and stuck. As he jerked back, I followed and knocked him off balance. He also staggered back and fell across a bench as I freed my sword.

I smiled. This was much too easy. Fumiko's skills were unbelievable.

Eviek picked himself up and came at me again with his knife.

Almost of its own accord, my sword parried the thrust driving it away. He jabbed again and again, but each time I blocked it. With blind rage in his eyes, he swung downward as hard as he could.

I was immediately reminded of Fumiko's fight with Jiaying. She had made a similar move.

Seemingly of its own accord, my blade knocked the knife so hard it flew from his hand. And then, just like I had seen in Fumiko's memory, I wheeled and aimed for the man's throat. Only unlike Jiaying, the man had no weapon to stop me.

I didn't want to kill him, but my body refused to yield.

Troy slammed into me, making me stagger.

My body turned on its own and quickly raised to strike the unarmed youth.

"NO!" screamed Cabrina.

Immediately, a wall of brilliant deep purple sprang up between us. It had to be the thickest myst barrier I had ever seen. I struck it. The blade reverberated in my hands like I had hit a stone wall. But I couldn't stop. I struck it again and again, powerless to halt the blows.

A hand suddenly materialized and grabbed my wrist, halting the motion. "Stop it, Coren!" Fumiko was beside me, wearing an expression of concern. "You're done."

I looked at her in horror. *What had just happened?* I dropped my blade like it was hot. I had nearly killed Troy. If it hadn't been for the myst shield, I would have struck him.

I looked around at the men lying on the floor and Eviek on his knees holding his injured hand. I had done all this. It was fantastic on one level—but horrific on the other. I had nearly killed them. They weren't bad people, just desperate. But ending their lives would have come so easily, I would not have noticed.

Troy knelt beside his father. He was looking at me with terror in his eyes.

"I'm sorry," I said. I scooped up my sword and numbly followed Fumiko and Cabrina out the door.

As we walked together back toward the inn, Fumiko looked at me. "You should have waited. I told you, you weren't ready."

"I'm sorry," was all I could say. "Thank the Creator you put up that shield. I'm not sure what would have happened if you hadn't."

She shook her head. "It wasn't me."

My eyes went up in surprise.

From behind us, Cabrina spoke up. "I did it. Or at least the Cabrina inside did."

We both stopped and turned to her.

Cabrina looked up in surprise, her eyes flitting between the two of us. "What? My host just reacted. She hates using her myst, but she can use it when she wants to. It was either that or have Troy hurt."

Fumiko and I exchanged a glance. That had been no simple wall. While I knew very little about using myst, I did know that making something that impenetrable took a lot of it. That wall had been *thick*.

I crossed my arms. "You mean it wasn't you, No-name?"

She shook her head. "No. That was all Cabrina. While I could use her abilities if I wanted, she's asked me not to."

We contemplated her a moment longer. The youth danced from one foot to the other. "Do you mind if we keep going? It's frigid out here."

We turned and resumed walking back to the inn. This only deepened the mystery about the Dark Avenyts inside Cabrina. With that much myst, there is no way we could have stopped her should she have decided not to go along with us, or worse, escape. In fact, back in the castle dungeon when Fumiko was interrogating her, she could have easily stopped it, or for that matter, broken out of the cell altogether. But she hadn't used it.

Fumiko said she was acting differently. But I couldn't help but wonder...

Why?

It was well past midnight when we got back to the inn. I was relieved to see Oddfrid sitting with Spraggel and Zofie in the barn. Our belongings had been packed, and all of them had on their cloaks. I immediately went to Zofie and hugged her. She obviously could not return it, but this one was more for me. I was still shaken by what had just happened. I couldn't get Troy's terrified expression out of my mind.

I quickly explained what happened, and Oddfrid agreed we should leave quickly.

"I could use a bit more rest since this will be the farthest of the portals, but it shouldn't be a problem. I definitely think it's riskier to stay than it is to go."

He did look more rested, but I could still tell he was not up to his full ability yet. But we really needed to get away in case the local authorities decided to investigate. Since we were foreigners, there was no telling how they would treat us.

Under Oddfrid's direction, we tied ourselves together in the same order as last time. And once more, he had us hold hands and gave us the warning that no matter what happened, never let go.

I firmly held Zofie's hand, taking comfort in it even though she did not grasp mine in return. As for Cabrina, I didn't think it was possible, but she held my hand more tightly than she did last time. I was afraid she was going to squeeze it off.

Oddfrid gave us one last careful once-over before closing his eyes and beginning to hum. He was a terrible hummer. I was going to have to ask him why he did that.

Like last time a glowing bubble of blue light grew up from the floor to completely enclose us. I winced as Cabrina's sweaty hand gripped mine even tighter.

"I don't like this," she moaned.

Suddenly the floor vanished from beneath our feet, and we fell. The barn's interior slid by as one would expect when falling into a hole.

As had happened last time, we dropped into a darkness so total that it seemed light could never be bright enough to illuminate it. Then up became down, and right became left, leaving me totally disoriented. The ringing sound returned and grew to a near-deafening volume, while the smells and tastes came and went faster than I could process. However, since I knew what to expect, this time didn't seem as scary. *It isn't so bad*, I told myself.

We fell a remaining few inches onto the wooden floor of a large building. *A warehouse?* As I made sure Zofie was all right, I noticed that Oddfrid didn't drop the sphere surrounding us. I heard Cabrina gasp.

Looking up, I saw we were surrounded by a ring of quite unsavory men and women brandishing a menagerie of weapons. And standing at the forefront with her arms crossed was a figure I dreaded to see.

Lilith.

She was grinning. "You're late."

"You moved the beacon," accused Oddfrid. "That's forbidden."

She shrugged. "A girl's got to do, what she's got to do." She pulled her sword and tapped the myst shield around us. "Drop the barrier, old man. I have no quarrel with you. Cooperate and I'll let you go. Besides, what can you do? You've got to be almost out of myst."

As I eyed the mob around us, I realized there was no way out. We were caught.

Oddfrid looked at me, and I was convinced he was going to hand us over. Then his eyes fell on Zofie. His expression immediately hardened—

And he began to hum.

Oh, Creator!

I could feel the myst gathering.

Lilith's eyes went wide in alarm. She looked over her shoulder. "Stop him!"

A woman in the robes of a myst adept stepped forward. But it was already too late. The floor disappeared, and we fell through.

Once again, we were immersed into an absolute inky blackness, and I quickly lost all sense of direction.

Then Oddfrid cried out in agony.

It felt like we slammed into a stone wall at full speed—my head jerked at the impact. We emerged into an early dawn sky. I gasped at the frigid air blowing past me so fast it hurt. And suddenly, my disoriented brain realized we were falling with the wind whipping past us. Off on the horizon, I could see the sun peeking over the edge. It had been after midnight when we left, so we must have traveled quite the distance. Looking down, I could see only white puffy clouds, and below that, the ground racing toward us. Glancing over at Oddfrid, I noticed he had blood leaking from his nose, and his head rolled loosely.

What had happened?

Cabrina grabbed my arm so tightly I could feel her fingernails gouging through my cloak. And on the same arm, the charm on my wrist began glowing red hot. If it wasn't for the frigid air blowing past us, it would have burned through my cloak.

I shook off the fog still clinging to my brain and frantically tried to think of something I could do. If I still had Abe, I maybe could transform Zofie into something that could save us. I glanced at those with me. But that wouldn't work since the bird would have to be large enough to carry five people. And anyway, Zofie couldn't use her myst right now.

I saw Fumiko with eyes closed, and she seemed to be concentrating. I felt our descent gradually slow, but the resistance only lasted a moment. She looked at me bleakly and shook her head, confirming she wasn't powerful enough to stop us. Spraggel was smiling and had his arms out like he was trying to fly. I shook my head. He seemed to be enjoying himself.

I turned to Zofie beside me, expressionless as she had been since receiving the charm. This was likely going to be my last time seeing her in this world. "I love you," I said aloud, the wind eating my words.

And she loves you too. Although I can't understand why. You're such a Creator blasted trouble magnet.

It was Abe!

"Can you save us?" I yelled.

Why do you think I'm talking to you, monkey brain. The princess has an idea.

The clouds were getting closer. I wondered what it would be like to pass through one.

"Then get on with it!" I pleaded.

The fluffy clouds rose up, and we plunged into them, to emerge a moment later with the ground looming closer by the heartbeat.

Wish I could, but you've really outdone yourself this time. Even the princess agrees. We can't help you with this one...

I had time to wonder if I would feel any pain when I hit.

But Cabrina can.

"What?" I shouted.

Cabrina, you can hear me, can't you? The princess did something to let you listen too.

I looked over at her, and with her eyes wide in terror, she nodded.

The princess says that Cabrina was selected for the school not only because she is a powerful myst user, but she is on Zofie's level.

She's a myst seer. She can not only use spells, she can craft them.

And she can use myst shields.

I didn't think someone that was terrified could look panicked, but she did. She shook her head emphatically.

The princess says we're going too fast to use a portal. The momentum we carry would kill us. Instead, Cabrina will have to catch us.

"I c-c-can't do it!" she yelled. The wind was too fierce for the sound to travel, but courtesy of Zofie and my curse, I heard her in my head. And since she stuttered, it was the real Cabrina.

Abe switched to a commanding tone I had never heard him use before. *No-name! You Avenyts curse! Didn't you say your purpose was to enhance people? To perfect them! Then by the Creator, help her! It's the only way she's going to live.*

Cabrina stared at me for just a heartbeat and then closed her eyes tightly, shaking her head.

Then I heard a different voice. It sounded female, and I knew it was the curse inside Cabrina. No-name. And she was talking to her just like Abe did me. *Cabrina*, it said. *You've been practicing. You can do this.*

"I c-c-can't! Besides, putting a shield around us w-won't help!" she cried. "It'll be too hard. W-we'll be c-crushed!"

You're right. No-name replied calmly. *A hard wall won't help. But maybe a pillow would. How about you put us inside a giant pillow.*

I eyed the approaching ground. I could make out what looked like water smattered with grass and tiny islands. We only had a handful of seconds left.

Cabrina nodded. She gave a deep breath and squeezed her eyes together. The hairs on the back of my neck stood up, and I could feel the myst gathering.

"I can't," Cabrina whined.

I know you can, replied No-name. *Think of a big puffy pillow. Pink. You like that color.*

"Pink?" Cabrina asked.

Big, fluffy, and your favorite shade of pink. Do it girl! Now!

The feeling of myst gathering increased. My eyes went wide. This was big. Really big. Cabrina's hair stood straight out, not even moving in the fierce wind. I could see sparks fly around her.

Below us, I could see a bright pink glow spread across the ground. It rose toward us, and we fell into it.

We hit it hard, but it collapsed under us, gradually slowing us down while at the same time enveloping us. It was like falling through pink honey. Slowing us until we were almost stopped, the giant myst bubble popped, and we dropped the last few feet into shallow water.

I quickly untied myself and made sure Zofie was sitting up and frantically checking her for any injury. Cabrina had passed out, and Fumiko was helping her sit up. I went to Oddfrid. He was limp, and his skin was cold, but he was thankfully breathing, although shallowly.

As I cradled him, I finally looked around. We were in some kind of swamp. Tall grass, reeds, and bushes were all around us. And it was hot. Steamy would be a better word.

Spraggel stood and looked around in puzzlement. He summed it up best.

"I don't think I've been here before."

We pulled ourselves together and splashed through the water, searching for higher ground. We finally found a little bump of a hill that was only a couple of feet above the water. But it was at least dry. Although something preferred not to share it with us, slithering through the tall grass and into the water as we stepped on. It had seemed to be a snake of some sort. But of a variety much, much larger than I was used to.

While Fumiko looked over our little island to ensure no other large creatures were sharing it, I used the lower branches of the hill's only tree to get a higher perspective of our surroundings.

The stunted tree, a type of pine, didn't particularly care for my weight on its limbs, but held as I climbed up a few feet. It wasn't much higher, but it got me over the bushes and tall grass.

The land was quite flat, so even from my short height, I could see quite a ways around me. A clump of trees was not too far away to the north and looked to be relatives of the one I stood in.

Directly ahead of me, at the limits of my vision, I could make out what was either clouds or mountains. I wasn't sure which. In the other direction, the swamp spread before me with a few of the solitary trees scattered about. There looked to be a rather large lake in that direction and perhaps some open water.

As I was climbing down, I noticed a piece of cloth tied to a branch. It was a dull red now, but at one time had likely been much brighter. And it had been put there deliberately. I looked around. So there were people here too.

I plopped down beside Zofie, who sat calmly looking ahead with no expression. A flying insect buzzed around her, and I waved it away. There certainly was no shortage of those.

Cabrina huddled by herself a short distance away with her arms hugging her knees. She looked tired, but her expression was unreadable. I got the impression there was an internal conversation going on with the curse inside.

I leaned over toward her and pointed to Spraggel. He had curled up on his side and was already snoring. I swear that man could sleep through the end of the world.

Cabrina turned her gaze to where I pointed. "Why don't you take a nap too," I suggested. "I'll watch."

She nodded weakly and laid down.

We were all exhausted from sloshing through the water, not to mention having no sleep. While the sun may have been up, our bodies were still convinced it was a couple of hours after midnight. I couldn't help but wonder how far we had traveled through the portal. It had been near midnight when we had started. Since dawn greeted us when we arrived, that meant we had moved quite the distance to the east. And the warm weather indicated we were in a much lower latitude. We were likely half a world away from home now.

I took the chance to check on Oddfrid. His condition was unchanged, and he had not regained consciousness. Fumiko thought he must have myst depletion, but she wasn't sure. What she didn't say was that he really needed a healer.

Fumiko sat beside me. "Where do you think we are?"

I shook my head. "Probably one of the southern lands, but I honestly have no idea." I pointed to the tree behind me. "I also found evidence of people here. We'll have to keep watch. We don't know if they will help us or eat us."

Fumiko gave a tired nod. "I doubt they'll eat us. We don't look very tempting right now."

I couldn't help but chuckle.

We sat for a moment in silence. Off in the distance, I heard a lonely bird cry out.

"Why do you think Oddfrid took us here?" she asked. "Do you think he had this destination in mind, or was this just some random location to get us out of there?"

I shook my head. "I have no idea, but I'm sure he had a reason." I slapped at an insect on my neck.

Fumiko glanced over at Oddfrid and then to Cabrina. "I guess the bigger question is, how did Lilith know where we would come out?" She pulled up several blades of grass and began to braid them. "She's known our location three times now. That's too much of a coincidence. She's got to be tracking us. Do you think Cabrina is giving our location away?"

I shook my head. "I don't think so. Or at least, not intentionally. No-name and Lilith seem to have different agendas." I glanced over at the youth. Cabrina lay facing away from us, so I couldn't see her face. "There's definitely something about her that we don't understand. But I don't think she's in league with Lilith."

Fumiko's fingers carefully braided the grass. She pulled more blades and began to weave them in. "Then, if it's not her, who could it be?"

"Well, I don't think it's Oddfrid since he pulled us out of that trap. That leaves Zofie and Spraggel, but neither of them would do something like that." I shrugged. "I don't think we're looking at the problem the right way."

I glanced over at Zofie, sitting calmly by the water. She was sweating profusely, and her legs were caked with mud. I frowned. Just beyond her was a floating log. I didn't remember that being there before. In fact, it was drifting toward shore just in front of her.

I got up and went to move her farther up the bank when suddenly, the bracelet burned hot. Before I had time to think, the log suddenly lunged forward with a large mouthful of ugly teeth. It was some kind of giant lizard, and it was aiming for Zofie.

I dove for her, putting myself between her and the creature. Its powerful jaws snapped shut, barely missing her legs. I frantically tried to shove her farther up the bank slipping in the process.

Unfortunately, the creature didn't take the hint and drew itself farther up the bank and lunged again. I couldn't get to my weapon, so I did the only thing I could think of and kicked it. With a quick flick of its head, its jaws snapped down on my boot, the thick leather sole keeping it from closing its mouth. It started to thrash, swinging its head wildly from side to side and dragging me toward the water.

Fumiko ran to join the fight and stabbed the big lizard with her knife. She hit it several times, but the creature kept on pulling me toward the water. Her attacks didn't faze it, and none of them penetrated its thick hide. I frantically tried to get my foot free of the boot, but it wouldn't come loose.

In desperation, Fumiko pulled her sword and stabbed it first in the body and then in the head. That seemed to get its attention. The beast must have decided we were too much trouble and released me, sliding deeper into the murky waters.

I scrambled back from the edge and let my heart calm down. Falling through the sky hadn't been that terrifying.

Fumiko plopped down beside me. She then pointed to the other floating logs nearby. There were a lot of them. And if their number was any indication, it didn't look like we were going to be moving off our little island anytime soon.

She sighed. "I think I'm not liking this place."

I leaned back on the grass and swatted at another insect biting me. "Me either."

Suddenly, the bracelet on my wrist flashed hot. I sat up in alarm. Unexpectedly, Zofie spoke.

"Coren," she said, still wearing that blank expression.

Fumiko and I turned to her in surprise.

She continued. But while it was Zofie's voice, it sounded more like Abe. "Whatever you do, don't piss them off."

"*What?*" I asked.

"And the princess says, *smile*." It was the same advice she had given me when we met the keepers for the first time.

That was when I felt something pointed nudge me in the back. I swiveled to see a large, well-muscled man behind me. He was mostly naked except for leggings and a loincloth. He held a long spear tipped with what looked like a solid piece of very sharp obsidian.

And he wasn't alone. There were two others with him, likewise armed.

Fumiko reached for her sword, but I halted her with a hand on her wrist.

I then slowly rose to face the newcomers. Remembering Zofie's advice, I did the only thing I could think of.

I raised my arms and smiled.

CHAPTER SEVENTEEN

An Old
Friend

The native used deep strokes to propel the dugout rapidly through the water. The village up ahead on the shore of the river seemed to be our destination. From his well-muscled back, this must be a trip he made regularly.

While they did surprise us on the little island, they seemed friendly enough. Unfortunately, we did not share a common language. Although we had tried to communicate, their leader had finally laughed at our attempts and just patted me on the shoulder.

But it was Oddfrid they were most interested in. Their leader quickly examined him, and then directed the others in loading him into one of their three dugouts. The biggest of their number paddled away with him as fast as he could. The two men left behind split our party between the remaining dugouts and followed the first at a more sustainable pace.

After traveling out of the swamp and through a thick forest of partially submerged trees, we finally emerged into the river proper. A rather sizable village with clusters of mud and grass huts sat on the river banks. The natives paddled for a sandy beach near the densest group of shelters.

As we approached, a small gang of children, laughing and jumping, ran to the water to greet us. Boys and girls alike were shirtless, wearing only loincloths. They called out to the approaching dugouts, and the men would call back to them good-naturedly. Some of the older children even swam out and escorted us back in.

Our hosts beached their dugouts on the sandy portion of the bank and helped us get out. Several adults met us, chattering in their native language. Like the others, the men just wore loincloths, but the women were dressed in loose, colorful tunics that came down to just below their knees.

They directed us into the village and sat us down on grass mats around a central stone fire pit. Then they served us some kind of meat and vegetables roasted on a stick and some slightly bitter tea. We hadn't eaten all day, so this was a welcome treat. They watched with interest as I fed Zofie but didn't interfere or make a comment.

By the time we were done, we had collected quite the crowd. Two young girls about Cabrina's age seemed to take a particular interest in her. They seemed fascinated with the youth's light brown hair—which was in sharp contrast to their own dark curls. She was quite embarrassed with the attention.

They then took us back down to the sandy beach, gave us each a piece of floral scented soap, and pantomimed washing. They were treating us well, so I had to assume they were trying to politely say we stank. Unfortunately, we probably did.

Several of the women came forward and pulled away Zofie, Fumiko, and Cabrina. I was reluctant to let Zofie go, but Fumiko agreed to watch after her. They took them farther down the shore behind an odd partition I had seen earlier. Several of the men stood with us and continued to pantomime washing.

Taking the hint, Spraggel and I stripped down and washed at the river's edge. I noted that while the women were afforded some privacy, the men were not. Several of the women watched with amused interest. I blushed when one of them stood on tiptoe to get a better view. She winked at me.

When I came out of the water, my clothes had been replaced with a plain tunic and slip-on sandals. Then, with the sun just resting on the horizon, they took us back to the firepit, where we waited for the others. It was only a few minutes later that Zofie, Fumiko, and Cabrina joined us. They too had been dressed in long flowing tunics in a pattern similar to the other women. Their hair had also been washed, and for Zofie and Cabrina—Fumiko's being too short—had been woven into a complex braid and spiraled atop their head. The final touch was a large flower affixed to their hair. I had to admit they all looked good, but especially Zofie. I wished she could have seen it. She so loved new clothes. I stepped up to her and kissed her on the cheek. All the villagers awed in appreciation.

They then led us into one of the larger huts in the village and indicated we should all sit on the mats around the hut's fire pit, although today, there were no flames.

The sun was almost down by that point, but the interior was gently lit with golden myst lanterns. The interior carried the strong scent of flowers, and indeed there were two fresh bundles propped up against the wall on the side opposite the door. A crown made of feathers hung on the wall above the flowers, and on the ground around it were several small, beautifully decorated vases. All of them had been covered and sealed with wax. I somehow got the impression it was some sort of shrine.

Two female guards took positions outside the door, and then an older woman entered with a young girl trailing her. The dim light did not immediately reveal their features. It appeared the woman's hair was completely white and flowed down her back in what looked to be thick curling locks. The girl with her was dressed similarly, but her hair was of a vibrant yellow. The color would have put some flowers to shame.

They both went to the side of the room with the vases and knelt there. They paused with head bowed for almost a minute, before turning to face us and taking their places on the mat. But when the woman looked up, my eyes went wide.

She was not human.

Her skin had a scaly look to it, and from what I could tell in the dim light, was a yellowish-green color. And what I had thought was hair, was instead some type of down. I still thought she could be considered an elder because of her wrinkled skin, but now I wasn't sure. The girl behind her was of the same race, although a smaller and non-wrinkled version.

The woman looked up at us and gave a toothy grin. "Welcome to our village," she said in lightly accented Ellish. "My name is Kaleefah, and this girl is my daughter Haahleefah."

I stared at her, completely at a loss for words. *Exactly what was she?*

I gave a slight bow. "I am Coren Hart." I then introduced everyone. I noticed her smile dropped as she looked at Cabrina—a faint rumble coming from her chest. But she seemed to catch herself and returned to her odd smile.

It dawned on me that pulling her mouth back and revealing her teeth was not a natural behavior for her species. Instead, it was something she did to approximate a smile for her human companions. However, I'm not sure it was having the intended effect.

"I trust my people have been treating you well?" she asked.

"Very well," I managed to get out. "We thank you for your hospitality?" I leaned forward. "What of our friend? Is he all right?"

She nodded. "Oddfrid is being cared for. He is suffering from severe myst depletion, as well as a myst backlash. I'm surprised he wasn't killed. We've done all we can for him at this point. And I assure you, he is getting the best care we can offer. After all, he is an old friend. My apprentice, actually. Which is likely the reason you ended up here—somewhere he knew would be safe."

I bowed my head to her. "Thank you again for your generosity." A thousand questions leaped to mind, but Spraggel beat me to it.

My old master leaned forward, looking like he had just received a Day of the New present. "You wouldn't by chance be a *Ntipani*, would you?"

Kaleefah's downy hair gave a quick vibration, and her mouth stretched into one of her toothy smiles. She was clearly pleased. "Why yes, I am. I believe my daughter and I are the only ones left in this world. I'm surprised you know the name."

Kaleefah put a hand over her mouth in another attempt to mimic a human gesture. Her hand drew my attention. It was different from a human's with long fingers and one too many joints. It hit me that I had seen one like it before—when we had accidentally opened the portal on Mount Eternal. It had been probing the newly opened entrance to our world.

Spraggel grinned. "I ran across the description in my research a while back. Your kind was mentioned in a passage from the War with the Dark Avenyts. Scholars have been arguing about your existence for centuries."

"Well, I assure you, I do exist. For now, at least." She leaned forward and turned to me. "So tell me, Coren Hart. What brings the Thief of Curses and the Xernow heir to our village." She glanced at Cabrina. "And why are you traveling with an Avenyts?"

These people had been very kind to us, so I saw no reason to hide anything. I took a deep breath. "Oddfrid agreed to take us to the Kuiojia Empire to remove these charms." I held up my wrist. "The young lady over there tricked us with these bracelets, and now we can't take them off, or they will kill us. These charms have silenced Abhulengulus and stolen Zofie's will. A powerful myst user in the empire, Imperial Advisor Yonge, thinks he can remove them. We're trying to get there."

She looked at Cabrina. "Interesting. Avenyts don't typically use charms since they can't control them." She looked back to me. "What else? Surely, Yonge isn't doing this for free."

I leaned back. "Well, our kingdom needs food to survive the winter. He agreed to remove the charms and give us supplies in exchange...."

Kaleefah interrupted, her smile growing harder. "For the Griffin's Key. And he plans to use it to access the Forever Nexus Shadow."

I blinked at her. "How did you know?"

She waved me off. "About a year ago, his representative contacted me about it. However, I only confirmed what he already knew." She leaned forward. "But that doesn't explain why you're here. Something else must have happened."

I sighed. "When we exited our last portal, it was a trap. Risten Brightmare, Zofie's cousin, has been possessed by a Dark Avenyts named Lilith." I looked down. "She's been trying to stop us."

Kaleefah nodded and rubbed her chin. Another gesture that didn't seem entirely natural for her. "Which means this Lilith is trying to get the key for herself." She sat up straighter. "Oddfrid must have realized this and thankfully made it very difficult to follow your trail."

I hesitated but went ahead and revealed our suspicions. "That's the third time she's found us. We're afraid she's somehow tracking us."

Kaleefah shrugged. "She will not find you here unless we allow it."

Fumiko spoke up for the first time. "But hasn't that happened already? That one," she pointed an accusing finger at Cabrina. "She's got to be reporting where we are."

"Possible. But she is not the one revealing your location."

Fumiko leaned back in surprise. "Then who?"

The elder looked over her shoulder at her daughter and said something in a hissing language that I was sure my human mouth could not replicate. The girl jumped up, immediately ran to the side of the room, and just as quickly returned. To my surprise, she placed a hair comb in her mother's hand.

The elder rose and then moved to kneel behind Zofie.

Fumiko and I both jumped up in alarm.

Kaleefah gave us one of her unnerving smiles. "Do not worry. I will not harm the princess."

Under our watchful eyes, she carefully took down Zofie's hair, spread it out, and began to gently comb through it.

I couldn't contain myself any longer. "What exactly are you doing?"

She didn't look up from her task. "Combing her hair."

I blinked in puzzlement. The next question was forming on my lips when Kaleefah stopped, and with her other hand, plucked something out of Zofie's hair. The elder smiled.

"This is what's revealing your location," she said. "It's called a myst louse." She placed something on what would be the palm of her oddly jointed hand and held it out. All I could see was a tiny black dot with little fibers coming from it.

"Is it alive?" I asked.

Kaleefah shook her head. "No. It's just a tiny seed that likes to stick to things. Just perfect for someone wanting to put a locater charm on it and place it on the person they want to track."

Her daughter appeared beside her with a tiny clay pot, and Kaleefah carefully put it inside. The young one covered it and then quickly left the hut.

The elder gave me one of those unnerving smiles and then began to quickly refix Zofie's hair. "My daughter will use coals from the fire to make sure it is destroyed."

"You're a myst seer, aren't you. That's why you could see it."

She nodded, her deft fingers making quick work of the braid.

"But where did she get it from? Could Cabrina have done it?"

It only took a moment longer for her to finish the braid and recoil it atop her head, again placing the flower in her hair.

"She could have gotten it from anywhere. They are easy to place, and unless you know what to look for, difficult to find." She looked at Cabrina and stared at her a moment. "Did you place it on the princess?" she demanded.

The youth shook her head.

Kaleefah's eyes drew down. "Do you lie to me? I am of the eighth cothe," she said sternly. "You will obey."

Cabrina's eyes went up in shock. She jumped up immediately and prostrated herself in front of Kaleefah. "No, mistress, I didn't do it. My directive was to place the bracelet charms on the princess and Sir Coren. Nothing more."

"What is your directive now?"

"I have none."

Kaleefah held out her hand. "Unlikely. I must read you."

Cabrina hesitated.

Kaleefah shouted. "*Now!*"

The youth shivered and looked up pitifully from her place in the dirt. "You won't hurt her, will you?"

The elder's downy hair gave a quick vibration and then she froze. Their exchange had been so intense, the sudden stop was unnerving.

Then Kaleefah seemed to soften, giving the youth one of her toothy smiles. "No child, I will not hurt your host. Nor will I hurt you. On that, you have my promise."

Cabrina gingerly placed her hand in Kaleefah's, who grasped it tightly. The two stared at each other for several heartbeats, and then the elder let her hand go. The youth stood silently and returned to her place.

Kaleefah turned to me. "It is as she says. She did not place the louse on the princess. She also really doesn't have any directives. That is unusual, but not unheard of."

I stared at Kaleefah with wide eyes. "You're a Dark Avenyts?"

She rolled her eyes. "Hardly. I have what you humans refer to as a *Light* Avenyts. I have always thought it humorous that you refer to them as being dark and light, depending on how they go about perfecting you."

I held up my hand. "Wait, you mean to tell me there is more than one kind?"

She considered my question. "More than one kind is not really the correct way to think about it. It's more of a thought pattern. An idea. A difference in opinion. Both of which fulfill their basic purpose."

"Which is?" I asked.

She smiled. "To make the hosts better." She paused and looked at each of us in turn before finally continuing. "Of course, better is subject to interpretation."

No one spoke as the information sank in.

I licked my lips. "So which one have we been talking to? The Avenyts or the host?"

She smiled. "The host, of course. That's the difference between their thinking. The Dark Avenyts believe that the host is flawed and must be tightly controlled for their own well-being. However, the Light Avenyts do not believe in directly interfering with the decisions of the host. They also believe the host is flawed, but that the only way they will improve is to make mistakes and learn from them."

She paused, and her eyes flicked to the right. "Uy says I'm getting off track. I do tend to do that. Oh, and Uy is my Avenyts. Her full name is Uylendiseeizna." She nodded. "So tell me about this charm that is causing you so much trouble."

"Well, Zofie has lost her will, and Abe has gone silent. But they have spoken to me when I've been in trouble. For instance, right before your people found us, Abe, speaking through Zofie, warned me to be nice to you. During one of those times, he mentioned that Zofie was working on him from the inside."

She looked up as her daughter returned and again sat behind her. "That *is* interesting. Perhaps we should go visit them."

I looked up in surprise. "Go visit?"

She glanced over her shoulder to the girl behind her. "Keep watch."

The girl nodded.

Kaleefah looked back to me and gave one of those toothy smiles. She held out her hand.

I gingerly took it. Not sure what I was getting myself into.

To my surprise, she held out her other hand toward Cabrina. "You too, child. You must see the damage you have wrought."

Cabrina gave the hand a look of loathing. Her eyes briefly flicked toward the door as if she was considering running.

Kaleefah wiggled her fingers. "Are you afraid to meet those you've injured?"

Cabrina stared at her a moment. "Yes."

Kaleefah gave a broad smile. "Good, there's hope for you yet."

Cabrina slowly stretched forward, but the elder quickly reached forward and snatched her hand.

Kaleefah looked to the others. "We'll be back in five heartbeats."

The hairs on my neck rose as I felt a powerful surge of myst, and for me, the world suddenly changed. I found myself standing in a place of all gray: everything around me, for as far as the eye could see, was a dull light gray. I had been to this place before. It was the realm of curses.

In front of me stood Kaleefah, and even though she was of a different species, I could tell this was a younger version of herself. All her wrinkles were gone, and she was a brilliant yellow color. She was dressed in a pale robe of a similar shade. It was painful to look at her because of how she contrasted with the gray world. While she was beautiful, it was obvious she didn't belong here. Like me, she was visiting.

Looming beside her was the stick figure of a curse—arms and legs nothing more than simple lines, with a large circle for a head. Uylendiseeizna. And like the other curses of this realm, this one had a symbol inside her circle head—a tropical flower I was unable to identify. And as I had with other curse figures, I sensed movement inside her head from tiny gears rolling about and giving off specks of light, rapidly whirling and flashing. It was almost hypnotic.

Beside her stood a very surprised Cabrina. She was looking around wild-eyed and seemed ready to panic. On her shoulder sat a smaller version of a curse stick figure. Like the others, this one had a circle for a head, but there was no symbol inside it. It had to be No-name.

She patted Cabrina on the head. "Be calm. There is nothing to be frightened of here."

"Oh yeah," Cabrina answered. "Then w-w-why are you scared too."

I felt a presence behind me and turned to see someone I was completely unprepared to see. Zofie. She had both hands balled into fists and was beating on some kind of invisible barrier. She was yelling at me, but there was no sound.

And beside her stood a curse I knew instantly. It was Abe—a stick figure with the single eye of his curse anchor in his round head. Only, he was frozen in place. If I looked closely, I could see that the tiny gears in his head were motionless.

I ran to Zofie and placed my hands against the barrier. "I can't hear you," I yelled.

She stopped pounding on the invisible wall and gazed at me forlornly. So close and yet so far.

"This is interesting." Kaleefah came up beside me. "I've never seen anything like it."

She reached out with a single finger and touched the barrier. The tip of the digit glowed, and when she pushed, the barrier stretched slightly, but it did not break.

Uy leaned to Kaleefah and whispered something in her ear.

Kaleefah nodded. "You're right. This is some sort of charm." She looked back at it in puzzlement. "But why is it here? Curses are blind to charms. And why is Princess Zophia in there? A charm can't do that." She gave a very snakelike hiss.

Uy again leaned down and whispered.

She looked to Abe and stepped to stand in front of him. "Can you understand me?"

Abe remained motionless.

Kaleefah gave another very snakelike hiss. She suddenly reared back, her right hand starting to glow, and smacked the barrier hard. The entire wall quivered and took up the glow, but like the surface of a lake, it quickly settled.

Uy leaned down and whispered to her again.

Kaleefah turned in my direction and gave me a considering look. "Didn't you say that Princess Zophia had talked to you?"

"Yes, but it was only briefly and usually at the worst possible times—like when we were going to be killed."

She growled deep in the back of her throat. She looked over to Abe and peered at him closely. She pointed, talking to Uy. "See that part there in his making. It's off to one side. It doesn't exactly match. I think something has been added."

Uy again whispered to Kaleefah.

"You're right, there are other parts scattered about. It's like he was put together from leftover pieces." She looked up at Uy. "But what has that got to do with this barrier?"

Uy turned her head in my direction. I blinked, and she instantly stood before me. Grabbing me by the neck, I was lifted off my feet. I couldn't breathe and struggled to get free. But, while she may have looked like just someone's line drawing, she was incredibly strong. Too strong to break loose. I felt the world begin to fade.

"Stop it!" I heard Zofie shout. I turned panicked eyes toward her and saw Zofie leaning close to a small hole in the barrier.

Uy put me down. As soon as my feet hit the ground, the hole started to close.

She leaned toward it. "It's Abe's ability to change luck. It interferes with the charm. But only for a few seconds after the danger passes."

"Zofie!" I yelled and ran to the barrier. "What can I do?"

"No time," she yelled, the hole rapidly closing. "I'm fine. Abe wakes up periodically, usually when this part of him becomes active. But most of the time, he stays motionless. But whatever you do, don't cut the charms off. They're booby-trapped...."

And then the hole closed. Zofie continued talking for a few seconds before realizing no sound reached us. She slapped the barrier in frustration.

I felt a tap on my shoulder, and Uy stood next to me. I took a step back, fearing she was going to grab me again, but she put her stick figure hands together and bowed her head.

"She's saying she's sorry for grabbing you," said Kaleefah, stepping closer. "It was to see if endangering you would do something to the barrier. And it did." She made that hissing sound again. "But how this is interacting, I don't understand."

Uy leaned down and whispered in her ear again.

Kaleefah nodded. "You're right. We must leave now."

I turned to the barrier and laid my open hand against it. Zofie came forward and did the same from her side. She looked ready to cry but was fighting not to.

"I'll get you out of there," I said. I put my other hand over my heart and pointed to her. She smiled sadly and did the same.

"And now we must leave," said Kaleefah.

Suddenly, I found myself back in my body in the hut. Fumiko was beside me, a look of concern on her face. I smiled at her. "I'm all right."

She looked relieved. "You wouldn't say anything."

I nodded. "I got to see Zofie. Her will... I don't know, *soul*? Is behind a barrier. But she's all right. Abe and her both."

"I'm sorry," announced Cabrina from the side. She was looking down. "I didn't mean to cause either of you pain."

I opened my mouth to reply but was interrupted by one of our guards rushing in. She spoke urgently to Kaleefah in their native language.

The elder made a growling sound in the back of her throat. "It looks like you were followed after all."

She quickly got up and moved to the door with the girl shadowing her. We followed her outside.

It was dark now, and all the stars were out. But to my utter surprise, that wasn't the only thing we could see in the sky.

Far away, there was what appeared to be a giant glowing eye high up in the sky over the river. A beam of bright light shot out of it, and it would sweep back and forth along the ground. Even from this distance, you could tell it was looking for something.

And it was coming closer.

CHAPTER EIGHTEEN

In Plain Sight

Fumiko pointed. "What is that?"

Kaleefah didn't answer at first, studying it intently. The river people gathered along the shore with us and talked excitedly among themselves.

The elder finally turned to the leader and talked with him. After a brief exchange, he nodded and went over to huddle with his warriors.

After her discussion, she stepped toward us. "That, I imagine, is someone looking for you."

"But what is it exactly?" I glanced back toward it. "Whatever's attached to the eye has to be huge."

Kaleefah chuckled. "It's not some giant monster. Instead, it's a myst working. A type of one we haven't seen since the great war. You've definitely attracted the attention of someone with a lot of resources."

I cocked my head to one side. The great war? Just how old was she?

Ever the practical one, Fumiko asked. "Do we need to run or defend against it?"

252 ※ Jessie D. Eaker

Kaleefah shook her head. "No, we just need to..."

Loud drums interrupted her. I jumped at the sound. Four of the villagers had set up large drums close to the central fire and were beating them to a spirited rhythm. The villagers began to gather around them.

"What are you doing?" I leaned toward Kaleefah. "Are you calling for reinforcements?"

The elder shook her head and pulled her mouth back into her version of a smile. "No, when you want to hide something, the best place to hide it is out in the open."

Some of the villagers had started singing. It was getting hard to hear Kaleefah.

"I don't understand."

Spraggel clapped me on the shoulder. "My boy, don't you see. We're going to have a party!"

A villager woman, one of the honor guards, ran up with several necklaces. She passed them out to us.

"Put those on," instructed Kaleefah. "It will help you blend in."

I put it on as instructed but felt no different. I then did the same to Zofie, and to my surprise, her appearance—hair, skin coloring, and fascial structure—changed to that of a young village woman. Spraggel, Fumiko, and Cabrina quickly donned theirs and became villagers of similar ages and heights.

Kaleefah nodded at her handiwork. "Those will also mask your myst signatures. Now all that's left is to have a little fun and wait for those things to pass."

"What about Oddfrid?" I asked.

She nodded again. "Already taken care of."

Fumiko leaned forward. "Won't they be suspicious that we haven't noticed them?"

Kaleefah shook her head. "On the contrary. They'll be suspicious if we *do* notice. That thing would normally be invisible, but we're able to see it because of the barrier around the village. It shows all invisible things."

"Barrier?"

She nodded. "It's how I earn my keep. Keeping all the pests away." She grinned and pointed at the giant eye. "Even the myst ones." She pushed me toward a knot of people around the fire. "Now mingle. No more than two of you together at a time. And leave the princess with me. I'll have her sit at my side. She'll look like an attendant."

I turned to say something to Spraggel but found he wasn't there. Looking around, I saw him holding a clay cup, and using hand gestures, was trying to talk with one of the older ladies. I couldn't help but smile. Spraggel may be older than the Creator himself, but he definitely knew how to get around.

Fumiko leaned close. "I'm going to patrol the perimeter. I'm not comfortable with this subterfuge, and I want to be ready in case it goes bad."

I nodded. "I'll keep an eye on Cabrina."

She was immediately off toward the edge of the activities.

I didn't have to look far for the youth. She was glued to my side. Even through her disguise, it was evident that she was nervous.

I glanced up at the eye. It was nearly on us, and I didn't want to give it the least indication we didn't belong.

I leaned toward Cabrina. "Kaleefah says we'll be all right. I don't think we have anything to worry about. So try to relax a little."

Cabrina shook her head. "You misunderstand. Those don't frighten us. We're afraid of all the gathered people." She licked her lips. "Neither of us have experience with this sort of thing."

I smiled. "Then, the appropriate thing to do is to face your fears." I grabbed her hand and pulled her toward the crowd standing around the firepit. She reluctantly followed.

The gathered crowd made room for us, and those close by were smiling. They didn't seem very concerned about the watcher above.

Closer to the firepit was a wide, open space. A group of the villagers had formed a circle, holding hands and dancing to the beat of the drums. I did a double-take. Spraggel was in the midst of it, laughing with the older woman I had seen earlier.

I sighed. That man.

At some signal, the ring in the middle broke apart, and the younger girls all ran to join it. Another young girl about Cabrina's age took her hand and pulled her forward. She nervously looked over her shoulder at me, and I motioned for her to go. She reluctantly let herself be hauled away.

The steps were simple, and Cabrina easily mimicked them. And while her expression was more restrained than the others, she too smiled with her new friends.

I had moved so that I could keep watch on Cabrina, as well as the approaching eye. It took every ounce of control I had not to look at them when they arrived over top of us. The eye paused, seeming to watch us closely. But after several agonizing heartbeats, it finally moved on. I sighed deeply, realizing I had been holding my breath.

After the giant eye had moved down the river, I sat next to Kaleefah, who was intently watching the dancing. Zofie, in her disguise, knelt beside her. I couldn't resist taking her hand and kissing it. "Do you think they will be back?" I asked.

Kaleefah bobbed her head. I think she was attempting to shrug. "I'm not sure, but I doubt it. The amount of myst needed to maintain the eye is huge, especially from a distance." She turned to look at me and grew serious. "But you must leave in the morning."

I had expected this. They had granted us a tremendous courtesy by protecting us. But there had to be limits. We had just put the entire village in danger.

"I understand," I said. "But will Oddfrid be well enough to travel by then?"

Kaleefah looked back to the dancers. "My student will not be going with you. It will take him weeks to recover enough to even think of using his myst."

She reached her large multijointed hand over and patted my own. "Fear not. I will not make you walk all the way to the Kuiojia Empire." She leaned forward and pulled back those teeth in the semblance of a smile. "I will open a portal for you." Her smiled faded. "I also need to give you some information. I debated about letting you know this."

The elder considered me for a moment. She then signaled over her shoulder to the young one behind her. The girl immediately got up and then knelt between us. She looked nervous.

Kaleefah ran her hand down the younger's head, smoothing her downy feathers. I could tell this was a gesture of affection for her.

"My daughter has something she needs to tell you," said Kaleefah. "You see, I had planned to accompany you to the Kuiojia Empire, but this one has forbidden me. When I asked her why, she didn't want to tell me at first, but it eventually became too much for her to bear, so she finally did."

I waited for her to proceed. I couldn't help but wonder what was so important.

Kaleefah stroked the girl's hair. "Why don't you tell him," she urged.

Haahleefah looked up at me. "I have reached the age of..." and then she said something which had a lot of hisses and clicks in it—a word no human could pronounce. She continued. "This means I can catch glimmers of the futures to come."

"A foreteller?" I asked in disbelief. They were things of legend.

Kaleefah nodded. "For a few females of our kind, there is a brief period of time, just before we grow old enough to reproduce, where we can see what might happen. Haahleefah has that ability. And she saw something in your future."

I looked to her expectantly, wondering what it could be.

She paused and turned big eyes up to me.

"One of your party is going to die."

I stared at the ceiling of the hut, trying to see into the shadows flickering there. A dim myst lantern provided the slight illumination needed for them to frolic in the corners of the supports. I was too exhausted not to rest, yet my brain too full to even consider sleep. The implications of Haahleefah's foretelling kept running through my mind.

Outside, I could hear the sounds of night creatures around us and the occasional movements of the villagers in the huts nearby. A child cried out in the distance, but it was quickly answered by a mother's soothing shush.

One of your party is going to die.

Beside me, I searched for Zofie's hand and grasped it tightly. She couldn't acknowledge the gesture, but I drew what comfort I could from it. I prayed it wasn't her. And then immediately felt guilty. Did I want to wish it instead on someone else of my group? My master perhaps, or even steadfast Fumiko? Could I even allow myself to think of sacrificing Cabrina?

I had immediately asked what would happen if we abandoned our quest. But she said the result was the same. All the paths into the future converged at that point. We might change who it was, or exactly when it occurred, but the outcome would be the same. Which was why she could tell me. Her words wouldn't change anything for me or my party. The one change that could possibly occur had already happened—by telling me her mother would be saved. She had apologized for her selfishness. Not that I could blame her.

I heard one of our attendants shuffle outside, thinking Spraggel might be returning. There were whispers in their language and then steps away, so evidently not—just a changing of our escort. I grinned. Spraggel must have found someone more interesting to spend time with.

Upon entering our assigned hut for the night, Cabrina had collapsed exhausted onto her mat and instantly fallen asleep. I could hear her softly snoring.

I heard movement on the other side of Zofie and saw Fumiko sit up. She rubbed her side where she had been injured. I sighed. It was hard to believe it had only been three days since that had happened.

She glanced in my direction and saw I was awake. She whispered, "Sorry to disturb you, but I'm having trouble sleeping. My ribs still hurt."

I shook my head and whispered back. "You didn't bother me." I thought of a line from a play Zofie liked. "'*Darkness may fall and sleep elude us...'"* I paused, hoping Fumiko would complete it. But she just shook her head.

I sighed. *"But dawn waits for no man.'"*

Fumiko rubbed her side. "Sorry Coren. I know you're trying to get me to complete it, but I don't know what it is. Only Zofie can do those."

And I knew she was right. It made me miss her all the more.

Fumiko pulled at her bindings. "Could you loosen these? They rebound me after my bath, but they got them too tight."

She knelt on her mat while I sat behind her. She tried to lower her tunic but couldn't get through the opening. "Turn away for a moment," she asked.

I did and heard rustling cloth.

"All right," she said.

I turned around to find she had taken off her tunic and wrapped it around her waist but left her bare back facing me.

I set about my task, unwinding it while she held up her arms. I then reversed course and felt around trying to get the binding restarted, but something didn't feel right.

Fumiko chuckled. "A little lower Coren, or I'm going to think you're trying to seduce me."

My face burned hot. I was far from an expert in female anatomy, but I quickly figured out what I was touching. "Sorry," I mumbled and shifted my aim. I worked in silence, basking in my embarrassment.

"How does that feel," I asked when the last wrap was secured.

She rotated her arm. "Much better. Not nearly as uncomfortable."

She held the tunic to her chest and shifted around to kneel facing me. I couldn't help but notice the slender curves of her shoulders. She smiled. "Thank you. You have good hands."

Zofie sighed in her sleep, and I suddenly realized how near Fumiko was. How little she wore. And how beautiful she was.

I looked away. "I guess I'll try going to sleep now."

But she put a hand on my knee keeping me from rising. She searched my eyes, and her expression grew serious. She leaned closer. I froze, a rabbit caught in a myst light.

Then she seemed to catch herself and slowly straightened and clutched the tunic tightly to her chest. "You need some more skills. If you're not too tired, I can share some more with you."

I glanced to Zofie and then back to Fumiko. "How many more until I'm done."

"At least one more. You're a sponge for the information. But from here on out, you'll need to practice harder to cement the skills. Otherwise, the transfer will evaporate."

I was tired, but if all went to plan, we would be at the gates of the Kuiojia Empire tomorrow. There wasn't much time.

"All right," I said. "Let's do it."

Fumiko made a twirling gesture, and I realized she needed to put her tunic back on. I blushed and once again turned away.

Once dressed, she knelt beside my head as I lay on my mat and put her fingers on my temples. She had her back to the dim myst light in the room, so her face was nothing but a shadow.

"Coren, the skills I'm giving you tonight are tied to a memory you will not like. I beg your forgiveness, but I cannot change the past."

I shrugged. "It can't be that bad."

I felt her myst gathering. "Coren, you severely underestimate me."

And then I was sucked into Fumiko's memory.

I paused in the dark corridor, my back to the wall, and listened to the small sounds around me. I heard the light steps of a guard in another part of the building, a light snoring in the room up ahead, and as expected, a much heavier snoring from one floor up. No one was close by. I quietly crept down the corridor—the placement of my feet deliberate and entirely silent.

It was three years since the sorting. After that event, our training had changed. The basics had been learned, so instead, we were taught how to apply them. To deadly effect.

After the sorting, I had received two things, both of which I was extremely proud of. The first was a small tattoo in the upper corner of my back—a butterfly, beautifully done in reds and blues. The second was a pair of daggers of unsurpassed beauty and utility with blades of an unusual dark forging—to better hide with the weapons drawn. I kept them sharp enough to cut your finger if you lightly touched them. And this night was my first mission. I would be handsomely rewarded if I completed it successfully. Or killed if I didn't.

My deadly blades were now strapped to my back within easy reach, but so they wouldn't move as I walked. It would be only a few more minutes before I needed them.

I made my way to a set of stairs and silently climbed them, flitting from shadow to shadow as I moved. This opened into another corridor, which unlike the one below, was lit with a dim myst lantern.

I could see two guards standing at the room's only door. Up until this point, the map I had memorized and the information I had been given had been completely accurate. That information had said there was only one guard at the door. Unfortunately, it was doubly wrong. I wondered what other pieces of information were incorrect.

But I could not afford to hesitate. I used my myst to cloak myself in shadow and crept forward. I pulled my knives and before they knew it, slammed both blades into their throats. Neither made a sound as I eased them to the floor.

Being careful not to step in their blood, I listened at the door. There was only snoring. But listening closer, there was also another even fainter breathing. Another piece of information omitted. I had not been warned that he might have a bed partner.

I silently lifted the latch on the heavy door and slowly, oh so slowly, pushed it until its opening was barely large enough to admit me. I slipped inside and quickly stepped into the shadow offered by the lee of the door. Then ever so quietly, I eased the door shut.

The inside of the room was almost totally dark. There were no windows, and the walls were of dense stone. The only way in or out was through the door behind me.

I pulled out my special myst light, which provided a dim but narrowly focused illumination. I used it to quickly scan the interior.

My intelligence had been vague on the room. Not many people were allowed inside. I had been assured there was a large bed, a high ceiling, and a door leading to a bath. But that was all they had been able to discern. Even the servants had been tightlipped. Of course, it was because if they revealed any details of the room, they would be executed. And they were tested regularly.

Clothes had been carelessly thrown about the room. I frowned. One was a ripped woman's blouse—someone had certainly been eager.

I stepped toward the bed, careful of the soft carpet I tread on, and using my light to closely watch for any sign of a trap. It would have been easy to hide a myst alarm within its plushness. I froze. Something didn't look right. I reversed the step and went to one knee to look closer. And indeed found something. While it used a myst concealment, a tiny ridge ran the perimeter of the bed.

I stared at it. If I crossed it, it would likely set off all manner of alarms. I swung my light back and forth over it. The carpet was indeed plush, and my feet sunk into it. But if I looked closely, I could tell there was a path where the fibers were trampled just a bit more than the others. It was a path that led from the bed toward the bath. I smiled. Someone liked to come straight to the bed after their bath.

I moved to that path and noticed there seemed to be a gap in the bed's protection. I followed the path exactly and came to the edge of the bed.

Peering down, I could see my target. I knew he was a powerful lord, but otherwise, I knew little else. All I had were my orders. It was all I needed.

In one smooth stroke, I put a hand over his mouth and slit his throat. He died quietly. His awful snoring dying with him.

The bed's other occupant groaned and sat up—female by the sound. I froze in place and readied my knife. She swung her legs over the other side and stood. I heard fumbling and realized she was going to turn on a light. My eyes went wide. I could not be seen.

As fast as I could move, I came around the perimeter of the bed to confront her. My knife quickly found her throat, but not before the light started. She gazed at me wide-eyed as she died.

To my horror, she was only a girl at least a handful of years younger than me. She was barely more than a child. Her face was covered in bruises, and dried blood came from her nose. I carefully eased her back to the bed. I clenched my fists as guilt flooded me. She had been no wife or concubine. But a victim. Beaten and raped, only to then be murdered because she was in the wrong place.

I extinguished the light returning the room to blackness.
But I could still see her eyes.

I was jerked out of Fumiko's memory.

Disoriented, I looked around the interior trying to figure out where I was. I gradually realized I was in one of the village's huts and not in some lord's huge manor. But the memory felt incomplete. I hadn't received any skills.

Fumiko still leaned over me, her hands trembling. I felt something wet hit my cheek. She jerked her hands away from me and wrapped them around herself. With her change in position, I could see her eyes rimmed with tears and her face a mask of sorrow.

I turned and put a hand on her knee. "Are you all right?" I asked.

She didn't respond at first. She took a deep breath before looking up at me through her hair. "I'm sorry," she said shakily. "I couldn't finish. I thought I had buried those feelings, but apparently, they're still there."

I moved to sit cross-legged before her, processing what she had just revealed. The implications were hard to accept.

"You were an assassin." It wasn't an accusation, but a statement of fact.

She nodded. "I've killed so many people, I don't remember them all." She took a ragged breath. "Although there are a few, I can't seem to forget." She gazed at me levelly for a moment and then suddenly stood. "I'm sorry. I can't continue tonight. I've lost focus. Maybe we can try this again tomorrow."

"Of course," I mumbled as my eyes followed her.

She returned to her mat and then lay down, her back to me.

I laid back down on my own mat. My brain swirled. Fumiko had been trained as an assassin. A lot of things fell into place—her sword skills, her ability at stealth, even the fine dagger she carried around. The calm, shy, intellectual girl I knew—was a cold-blooded murderer.

I suddenly wondered if perhaps there had been another reason for

Fumiko sharing her memories with me. The normally cool young woman had trouble expressing her feelings, so maybe this was her way of sharing her misery.

She had told me previously that sleep was not her friend. I now understood why.

Because now, the eyes of that young girl haunted me.

CHAPTER NINETEEN

Reunion

A fitful sleep finally found me, but I awoke the next morning, unrested and groggy. My slumber had been interrupted several times by the nightmares of a young girl's shocked face. But in the final dream, it had been Cabrina. I gave up after that.

Fumiko was already gone from her mat.

I hadn't been up too much longer when two of the villagers quietly brought our clothes back to us. I thanked them and proceeded to get Zofie up and dressed. Cabrina refused to budge, grumbling, and turning over when I nudged her. I finally gave up and just left her to sleep.

Spraggel, accompanied by the older woman I had seen him with the evening before, came in half-way through getting Zofie dressed. He was chipper and bright, talking incessantly about the people and their culture. He claimed to have already learned some of their language. He patted the arm of his companion, explaining he had an excellent teacher. She practically beamed at him.

I couldn't handle all the cheerfulness and grabbed my sword, heading off for a few minutes of practice. Spraggel promised to make sure Zofie got fed and to get Cabrina up. I looked to the youth deep in slumber and wished him luck.

I was hoping a little exercise would clear my mind, and I was not the only one with such thoughts. I found Fumiko in a nearby clear spot at the edge of the village. A few of the villagers were watching as she practiced.

I had never observed Fumiko going through her forms before. She tended to practice in private, and now I understood why. I watched as she went through a series of moves I remembered from the first memory she had shared. And just like Jiaying had, she was going through them agonizingly slow.

I know she saw me approach, but she deliberately ignored me. And I thought I knew the reason. She was expecting rejection.

Instead, I stepped up beside her and picked up the form with her. She cut her eyes in my direction, but otherwise gave no indication I was there. Together in perfect synchrony, we went through the form—turn, step, point, stab, block, slice. We went through the whole routine. Then without a pause, did it again, only this time at a slightly faster pace. And finally again, going faster still. I had never moved so well. I was still rough, but the skills she had shared with me were unbelievable. And then I realized that each and every memory she gave me had cost her dearly. It was part of a life she no longer had wanted. But she had been willing to dig those awful memories up to give me a few pieces of gold. It was indeed a rich gift.

When we had finished, covered in sweat and out of breath, I turned to her, and as I had seen in her memory, bowed from the waist. She hesitated a moment but returned the bow. When she stood, she started to turn away, her expression frozen. But I extended my right hand toward her.

"Thank you," I said simply. "For everything. This has cost you greatly, and I am forever in your debt."

She hesitated, looking down at my hand and then back up to my face.

"Fumiko," I said, looking into her eyes. "Will you still be my friend?"

Her lower lip began to tremble, and her eyes grew moist. But she did not break her frozen expression. As someone drowning and reaching for help, she grasped my hand and gripped it tightly. I pulled her forward and gave her a friendly hug, only to have her openly weep into my shoulder. And I understood why.

There was no more hiding. No more pretending to be someone she wasn't. She had shown me her worst, and I had accepted it.

When she stepped back, still wearing that frozen expression, I thought I saw the corner of her mouth curl up into the glimmer of a smile.

At a little before noon, we gathered in the center of the village and prepared to resume our journey. I had already briefed Fumiko and Spraggel on Haahleefah's foretelling and asked their opinion on whether to proceed or return home. Neither of them hesitated and said we should continue. We would just have to be careful.

To see us off, they brought out Oddfrid on a stretcher. He looked better than he had but was still pale and very weak. I thanked him for what he had done and promised to reward him when we returned. He seemed surprised at my heartfelt thanks.

Kaleefah, and the ever-present Haahleefah, stood with us. "Be careful," said the elder. "I will open a portal near the gates of the empire. But near is a relative term. I haven't been there in... well, longer than I care to talk about. So I will have to open the gate somewhere I'm fairly confident will still be there. If memory serves me right, you will still have a two-hour walk to get there."

I smiled. "That will certainly be closer than we are now."

Off to the side, Spraggel was talking with the lady I had seen accompanying him during our stay. He took her hand and kissed it, saying something in her language. She threw her arms around him and hugged him so tight I thought I heard his joints crack.

Fumiko and Cabrina stood to one side along with Zofie. All of us were dressed in our travel clothes and had been provided refreshed provisions by our hosts.

I bowed to her. "I can't thank you enough for all your help. If there is ever anything we can do for you, please let us know."

Kaleefah gave one of her toothy grins. She reached over and pulled Haahleefah against her in a very motherly hug, which the younger one didn't seem to especially care for. "I have heard that the princess has opened a school."

I was surprised. "How did you know that?"

Kaleefah stroked her daughter's head. "I have my ways. I've learned to keep an eye on the ongoings of the Xernow's."

"Yes, the princess started one, but it's very small now." I looked over at Zofie. "And with her like this, things have been put on hold."

Kaleefah nodded. Haahleefah squirmed, but her mother held her tight. "This one has not dealt with humans outside of our village. It might be useful for her to be educated elsewhere for a while."

I smiled and nodded. "I'm sure Zofie would be honored."

The elder released the younger, who immediately stepped back out of hug range.

Kaleefah nodded. "It is time. Are you ready?"

I looked at my party and nodded. The elder turned and made some rapid hand gestures.

I was surprised since it was different than what Oddfrid had done. "I didn't think hand gestures were needed for myst workings."

She looked at me over her shoulder and gave one of her wide smiles. "They're not. But I was always one for theatrics."

"Oddfrid had us drop through the floor."

She shrugged. "It is a little bit more myst efficient, but I suspect he does it that way mainly because he likes to scare his guests."

Suddenly, the air in front of us wavered, and a vertical portal appeared, dark and black, with cold radiating from it. I even could feel a gentle flow of air coming out of it.

"Hurry," she said. "I can only hold this for a few minutes."

The crowd of gathered villagers began to shout good-bye in their own language. We waved and stepped through.

As I moved inside, the light left us completely, and I lost all sense of orientation. But it seemed only a short amount of time passed before I stepped out into the light of day. Not nearly as bad as when Oddfrid did it.

The portal snapped shut behind us, and we found ourselves on a large expanse of rock high up on a hill. The air was much drier and cooler than our previous location. I shivered as a chill wind assaulted us. Quite the difference from the tropical heat we had just stepped from.

The sun looked to have moved to early afternoon, which meant we had moved a bit more eastward. However, from the change in temperature, we must have moved much farther north.

From atop the hill, we had a clear view of the valley below us. The terrain was rugged with rocky crags, mostly bare of vegetation. Going down the center of the valley was a wide well-used road. I noticed there were a few carts scattered along it, as well as the occasional cluster of people. In the distance to the east, there were patches of greenery and what looked like a city. That had to be Da'Meigoxi, the west's entry to the Kuiojia Empire. For just on the other side was one of the few gates through the colossal myst barrier that protected it: *The Grand Tapestry*.

It was said to be the largest myst barrier ever constructed. So large in fact that it completely encircled the region. Quite the engineering feat that took over seventy-five years to build. Its actual name had long since been banished to the dusty volumes of history. But in recent times, it had simply become known for how it appeared at night—a giant glowing tapestry of color stretching into the distance. I was looking forward to seeing it myself.

The barrier had been put in place shortly after the war with the Dark Avenyts. At that time, the region was made up of eleven separate kingdoms, and they had been hit particularly hard by the war. The kings of the region had united to erect the barrier and prevent any future attacks. Then hundreds of years later, the separate kingdoms had been united rather forcefully into the Kuiojia Empire.

I did have one nagging worry about the gate—no one with a curse was allowed to pass through. That meant Zofie, Cabrina, and I would be prevented from entering. Until recently, I had never understood why. But it made perfect sense once you understood that the Dark Avenyts were actually curses. However, we had been invited, so I had to assume there would be some sort of accommodation made for us.

We found an unused trail leading downward and soon joined those on that dusty road heading toward the city. Having to guide Zofie slowed us down, but as Kaleefah had predicted, we arrived at the gates of the small town late afternoon. We decided to spend the night in the city and tackle The Grand Tapestry in the morning.

Fumiko, in her native language, easily negotiated our entrance toll with the city guards. She had explained before that the fee would be high, but I wasn't expecting outrageous. It claimed a good chunk of our remaining silver.

The sun reached toward the horizon and cast long shadows down the city streets as we searched for an inn. A merchant standing in line with us had assured us a good one lay close by. I had expected the city to be bustling with end-of-day activity but found it was surprisingly light. Only a few merchant stalls were open, most having already closed, and the ones remaining had questionable merchandise.

I quickly noticed that everyone had one thing in common—they watched us with hungry eyes.

I leaned toward Fumiko. "Why do I feel like we're being sized up for dinner."

Fumiko's expression didn't change. "Because we are. Although they would more likely consider us just a snack."

"But with the tapestry gateway located here, I thought there would be a rich trade."

She shook her head. "At one time, you were right. But things have changed. The city's tariffs have continually grown over time so that no goods enter. With the high tariffs in the city, most of the real goods never reach here. They instead pass directly through other portals just outside the gateway. It has made for some strange economics." She sighed. "The situation in the city tends to attract those who don't mind using their knives to get a morsel or two."

I glanced around, suddenly uncomfortable.

Under the watchful eyes of the town, we eventually reached the recommended inn. While the innkeeper scowled at us when we entered, the common room was full of laughter and the murmur of conversation. Judging from the gathered crowd, I doubted there would be a room for us. However, the food being served smelled delicious, and my stomach reminded me that my last meal had been over a thousand miles away.

A thin woman, in simple shirt and pants, sat cross-legged in the far corner playing some type of lyre. Her hair was long and loose and concealed her eyes as she played an unfamiliar tune. At least it wasn't *The Cursed Knight*. The performer was built nothing like Fumiko, but something about her reminded me of my friend. I couldn't figure out what it was.

Fumiko approached the innkeeper and began talking with him in her native language. The performer finished her song and carefully set her instrument aside. Fumiko had her back to the performer, so the innkeeper leaned around her to yell something at the woman. Apparently, he wasn't pleased that she had stopped.

She shouted something in reply and held up her empty mug. He rolled his eyes, clearly frustrated, and turned back to Fumiko to resume their negotiation.

The woman stood, going from sitting cross-legged to standing in one smooth, elegant action. It was a familiar movement. *Where had I seen that before?*

Carrying her mug, she stepped toward Fumiko and the innkeeper. I glanced down and saw the woman's feet were bare. Nothing unusual about that. I had seen a lot of barefooted people in the streets. No, the way her feet moved—

My eyes went wide.

A mug suddenly shattered against the far wall and all eyes in the room went in that direction—except for mine and the woman's. Our gazes locked.

Her eyes were ice cold.

I shoved Fumiko out of the way, stepping up to catch the woman's descending arm. The dagger her hand now held stopped inches from my chest. Surprise flashed across her face. She reversed and brought up her knee, but I shifted my hips to block. We danced. She tried to break my hold while I doggedly hung on. With a sudden jerk, she won free and launched herself at Fumiko.

Fumiko didn't even blink. She spun and gave the woman a swift kick to her head. The woman staggered back against one of the tables, knocking it over in the process, before proceeding to collapse to the floor.

The room immediately broke into confusion. The customers that had been sitting at the table jumped up and began yelling at her. The innkeeper nudged us aside, grabbed the woman by the collar, and hauled her out the door. He returned a moment later to retrieve her lyre, but when he bent to pick up her fallen dagger, he found Fumiko's foot on it. He wisely decided not to argue. With a wary eye on those in the room, she bent to pick it up and tuck it in her belt. It was of the same dark forging as her own blade.

The innkeeper made shooing motions and herded us out the door.

Spraggel sighed. "That was a record even by my standards. They usually don't kick me out until I've had at least one."

We stepped outside to find the woman sitting on the ground with her back propped up against the inn's exterior wall. Her nose leaked blood, and there was already a bruise beginning to darken her face. The innkeeper set the instrument beside the woman, before giving both Fumiko and me a last glance and retreating inside.

I was surprised when Fumiko held the dagger, handle first, out to her assailant. The woman looked up at her through her long hair. She took it carefully from Fumiko and made it disappear into her clothing.

"What happened to the others?" Fumiko asked, without a single trace of emotion in her voice.

"Gone. Most dead. A few like me living on scraps and memories," she answered in thickly accented Ellish. The woman glanced at me and then the rest of our party. Her eyes finally moved back to Fumiko. "It would be better for them if you let me kill you."

"I will decline the offer."

"There will be others. They have not forgotten."

"I will deal with them."

The woman grabbed her lyre and stood but paused to gaze levelly at Fumiko. "No one can deal with *him*."

Fumiko returned the gaze. "If you try again, you will die."

The woman gave a bitter laugh. "Then you might be doing *me* a favor." She turned and walked away.

Fumiko stared into her back as she went down the street. She gave no hint of emotion, but when I glanced to her right hand, she was gripping it so hard it was white.

Fumiko suddenly turned, and we fell in behind her, heading in the opposite direction of the woman.

"What was that all about?" I asked. "You had said there was a bounty for you."

Fumiko looked at me with sad eyes and shook her head. "No, that one had been for revenge."

"Revenge for what?"

"I destroyed them," she stated flatly.

"What?"

But she would say no more. I glanced at her stoic face as we made our way to another inn.

What exactly had she done?

CHAPTER TWENTY

Love and Death

As I expected, Fumiko approached me as we were preparing to sleep. And honestly, I was dreading it. We had quickly found another inn and decided it best to only get one room, both from a funds perspective and for protection. The room was small and had no bed, so there was not much space for us to spread out our blankets.

Spraggel was snoring within a heartbeat of lying down. I didn't think he got much sleep the previous night, and combined with our long walk, had completely tired himself out.

We settled Zofie down on her blanket next to me with Fumiko on the other side. Cabrina, who had been silent most of the day, took a spot by the door and agreed to take first watch. Considering the attacker today, we thought it prudent to keep our guard up.

I too was exhausted from our journey, because at least from my reckoning, we had traveled half the world in only three days. I had been hoping for a reprieve, but no such luck.

Fumiko knelt beside my blanket and patiently waited for me to finish with Zofie. I looked up at her with tired eyes and almost asked if we could wait. I had to admit, her method was effective. I was quickly mastering skills that I would never have dreamed of only a few weeks ago. Fumiko and I had spent time practicing just at sunset, and the results were noticeable. But each session took a toll, leaving me feeling a little shaken. Especially the last one. Even though it wasn't my memory, I could not get out of my mind the battered and bruised face of the girl Fumiko had killed.

As we considered each other, I could tell she was reluctant to share further memories. She was baring her soul to me. I would never again think of her as a mousey girl who liked books and quiet evenings by herself.

"I apologize for this, but we will be in the palace by tomorrow. I need to reinforce some of the skills you've received."

I nodded. "I understand."

She shuffled around to kneel beside my head. When she touched my temples, her hands were cold, and I could feel a slight tremble.

"Are you all right?" I asked in concern.

Her eyes held sadness. "You wanted to know why I have a price on my head. This memory will explain it."

I shook my head. "Fumiko, if it's that painful, you don't have to...."

She put a gentle finger to my lips. "You need to know. And at the right time, you are free to share this with Zofie. I release you from your earlier promise not to share. It was unfair of me." She looked away. "I was going to tell both of you anyway. I just hadn't found the right time. I was afraid you would hate me."

"Fumiko..."

She ignored my protest, raising her eyes to look into mine. "I was taught to be a killer, so I became good at it. I far exceeded my master's expectations. I became... death." She drew a deep breath and lightly brushed a lock of my hair to the side. She smiled sadly. "You remind me of him."

"Who?"

"My first love." I felt her myst rising. "Not so much in the way you look. No offense. He was more handsome." She shook her head. "No, it's in your personality. Something similar inside each of you. Something that makes people love you."

"What happened to him?"

Fumiko put her fingers on the side of my head. I could feel her memories drawing me in. "As you would expect... I helped kill him."

"Killed?" I began to fight the plunge. I sensed this was going to be too painful to bear. But the current of her myst was too strong, and I was sucked deep into them.

With back straight and head held high, I walked stately down the corridor with two heavily armed guards at my back. Today, I carried no weapon, and my face was unmasked—open for all to see. My dress was the magnificent robe of a daughter of the emperor, and I wore rouge on my lips and blush on my cheeks. This was a different costume than I typically wore, but suitable for the role I played today.

Lady Fumiko.

My target was a powerful lord—the second most powerful in the empire. Lord Shengli Luoyangei. His lands were rich, and his people strong. It was said that he could call out thousands of loyal fighters at a moment's notice. He was young too, having recently inherited his position. But it was already clear he was a shrewd and competent leader. One that had pointed out the corruption in the empire. But as most found out, it was not wise to make ripples among the nobles.

One attempt had previously been made on my target's life, but it had failed miserably. The assassin had nearly been caught and had been forced to resort to the poison we all carried.

But this time my role was not to kill, but to gather intelligence. I was to visit as the emperor's daughter on the pretext of becoming one of his wives. Were it to happen in reality, I would be reaching far above my station. Since I was the product of a disgraced concubine, and so far down the line, my pedigree was practically useless, this would be seen as a desperate move by my family. However, it would be just enough to open a door.

As I walked down the hall, my eyes noticed the guards' position, accessible windows, and potential shadows. I drew a map in my mind of each of these. I could see why the previous attempt had failed. It would be extremely difficult for someone to slip inside without being detected. The manor's walls were thick, and every entrance was heavily guarded. I had already spotted several strategically placed myst alarms and far-eyes. No, getting in this way with an army, little alone a single assassin, was nearly impossible.

We stopped in front of an unmarked door. Two additional guards were stationed on either side of it. They fingered their swords as they eyed me. I ignored them, pretending to be the princess and utterly unaware of how they assessed my potential threat. But as they observed me, I did likewise, noting their armor, their polished swords, and the way they stood. Both were well equipped and appeared highly trained.

A grizzled man in his mid-years opened the door. He gave me an appraising look and then frowned as if disappointed. He sighed and opened the door further, allowing both myself and my guards to enter.

I expected this to be a small dining room or perhaps lounge, but I was surprised to find the large room empty except for a single writing desk to one side. There were no windows, nor draperies, and the floor was polished marble. A picture of the previous lord and another of a woman I didn't recognize were the only decorations on the walls. The room made me feel lonely.

The chamber's only other occupant, a young man, sat at the desk with a stack of papers, writing brush and inkwell. It was devoid of anything else, except for a small board game in the far corner—Waring Generals—with the pieces already set for their next game. The young man was deep in concentration on the paper he was reading and didn't appear to notice us as we entered the room. What was odd was he had somehow managed to scrunch up his face to hold his writing brush between his upper lip and nose. He looked quite comical.

The young man didn't even glance our way until the grizzly one cleared his throat.

The young man's eyes jerked in our direction, and then he immediately grabbed for the brush, yet missed. In his haste, he sent it flying... toward me. I reacted without even thinking and caught the wayward brush between two fingers, saving my dress from the threatening ink stains.

I nearly panicked. I wasn't supposed to show any of my skills and to disguise my walk, so no one knew I was practiced in martial arts. I made a show of awkwardly removing the brush but was unsure what to do with it since I dare not approach the desk yet. So I just held it.

The grizzly old man sighed. I nearly breathed a sigh of relief since he didn't seem to notice anything.

"My lord, this is the woman we discussed. She is Lady Fumiko of the Zhang-junen family."

The young man looked nervously at his aide. "Is she the one from Lord Zhiqiang?"

The aide sighed. I got the impression he did this a lot.

"No, my lord. Imperial Advisor Yonge recommended her."

"Oh," he said. He looked back down at his paper, and then eyed the pile beside him, before looking back at me. "Then you can tell them I've met her. I've got too much to do today to be distracted." He held out his hand toward me. "My brush, please."

I hesitated. I was surprised at his abrupt dismissal. I needed at least a few days of access to gather my intelligence. I was supposed to be allowed several meetings to determine my compatibility. He might suspect me already, but I didn't think that was the case. No, it was something else.

He impatiently wiggled the fingers of his hand. "My brush."

My mind raced. He was used to being obeyed. He was used to girls dressed up and competing for his attention. From the room's lack of decorations, he had no use for frills, and if I had to guess, thought the women trooped in front of him were mere decorations. Yet, his soldiers loved him, and he had already out-maneuvered one political rival. Plus, this man had somehow evaded a previous assassin and was thought to be a threat. I somehow sensed this man concealed a bright, yet disciplined intellect. And going with the script my masters had carefully constructed was not going to work.

His aide went to pluck the brush out of my hand, but I suddenly stepped forward and over to the game board. "If you wish your property returned, you are going to have to take it." I picked up a red soldier piece from the board and moved it in a classic opening.

The guards squirmed behind me, uneasy at my undignified tone. "Lady..." started his aide.

The young man blinked at me in surprise. He held up a hand for the aide to wait. Then he stood and moved to stand on the other side of the board. He picked up a blue soldier and moved it in the classic response.

I reached for the piece that would be the classic reply to his move. He likewise started to reach for his piece in anticipation of the expected move—eager to put this to a quick end. But at the last moment, I shifted to one of the moves that was less than classic. It was considered to be—aggressive—and against a skilled player would do nothing but extend the game.

His hand froze over the board. Then continued with his classic response. He likely thought I was merely moving pieces around—the game was not popular with females, and I had only been taught as a way to practice planning against an opponent. I was no master, but I knew the basics.

My next move was to lead with the archer. He quickly followed with the next classic move—another soldier. My archer then took his soldier. His eyes went up in surprise, and he then looked at me—to really see me—for the first time. I had just disproven his belief that I was not a player. The room was deadly quiet. One of the guards shifted, and it sounded like thunder. I tried not to look at him and instead focused on the board.

The young man brought up his monk, which indicated a shift in strategy. I nearly laughed. I had played out this same plan against Jiaying, so I knew it well. She had stopped playing with me because of it. I moved my archer to endanger his general.

He leaned forward and put both hands on the desk. It was several minutes before he moved a piece. I quickly responded.

Back and forth we went, he gained advantage, then I took some back. But eventually, he surrounded my general.

I straightened and looked into his eyes. Then held out the brush to him. He carefully took it, while not taking his eyes off me. I turned to leave, my guards trailing me. As I reached the door, he called after me. "Join me for dinner this evening...."

His security was tight as I traveled down the same corridor I had before. The guards were alert as ever, but there was a different glint to their eye.

Respect? Wariness? Disbelief? I wasn't quite sure. The servants that assisted me in getting ready for dinner were almost twittering and kept exchanging knowing looks. Apparently, I had set the household on end. I sighed. If it helped me with understanding the security of the place, that was fine. He would likely be dead before the end of the month. I wondered if I would have to play the bereaved concubine. For some reason, the thought tightened my stomach.

This evening, I had dressed simply, in a white blouse, vest, and dark skirt. I realized an elaborate dress would do nothing to impress him, so I had to get creative in matching the few pieces I had. My hair was down with two small combs pulling it back from my face. I couldn't help but wonder what my masters would say—I was severely deviating from the script. But it was the only way I could see to get the information I needed. My hope is he would invite me for a walk in a nearby garden, or even better, back to his chambers where I might find some weakness in his defenses.

The guards guided me to a different door deeper inside the manor. I was not surprised to find another austere room, with a single table and two chairs in its center. The only decorations on the walls were portraits of the same man and woman from the office. Beneath the pictures sat a small table adorned with a simple bowl candle. Surprisingly, it wasn't a myst lamp, but an actual candle. I couldn't help but wonder who those people were.

But the great surprise was that the young lord was already there waiting for me. His face was expressionless as I entered, but his eyes went up like his face wanted to smile, but wasn't quite sure how to unlock the expression.

He indicated the place across from him. "Thank you for coming."

The guards took their places by the door, and I went to the only other place at the table. I couldn't help but notice there were no servants visible. Usually, the nobility liked to show off their wealth by having their staff line up against the wall and then fall all over themselves serving you. I had to admit, it was nice to see a noble restrain themselves.

"Thank you for having me, Lord Luoyangei," I said with a polite smile and a bow of the head. "You look well this evening."

"As you do you... look well, I mean, very healthy in fact... glowing actually... really pretty." He blushed. "I like your combs too." He clearly had no idea how to talk to me.

I looked down to hide my smile. "My lord is too kind."

And as surely as if I had put a knife in it, that's where the conversation died. We stared at each other for at least three awkward minutes. I never realized that three minutes could last so long. I glanced down occasionally, playing the bashful innocent, hoping he would take the lead. But nothing happened, except for the beads of sweat on his brow.

Thankfully a servant appeared from a doorway in the back, bearing a tray with our soups. The young man straightened as we were served—the gentle tinkling of the dishes loud in the room.

I had to help him out.

And then we spoke at the same time.

Twice.

We laughed nervously, but it seemed to break the tension.

And for the first time since I'd met him. He smiled. I got the impression it was not a frequent thing. And for some reason, the smile warmed me.

"You go first. Please," he insisted.

I nodded. "I was just going to say that the soup is quite good."

"Ah, yes, my master of the kitchens is excellent. Although, I would prefer he added a bit more salt. But he insists too much salt weakens the constitution."

And so the conversation went—sort of like starting a fire with damp kindling—I would give a spark, it would want to light, but then quickly fade. Oh, but the sparks—those brief insights into his life were fascinating. The quickness of the time took me unawares.

"Go with me on a ride tomorrow," he asked as our time came to a conclusion.

That was not exactly what I hoped for. I needed to find out more about this fortress of a manor. But I had to go with what was offered.

"Of course," I answered.

Early in the morning, we rode out. His escort and mine were swapped for two mounted soldiers—one male and one female. I couldn't help but smile. It meant I had graduated from just someone, to a woman he wanted to make comfortable with him.

We hadn't been traveling long when we stopped at a tiny house just outside the city's gates. An old woman came out to meet him, and they gave each other a warm hug. They exchanged pleasantries over the weather, her aching hip, and how she missed her husband. He nodded as she talked, seeming to hang on every word. He then pulled out a tiny bundle, the size of a few coins wrapped in a white kerchief, and tied with a ribbon. He placed it in her hand and folded the fingers over it. He then thanked her.

When he remounted and turned away, he explained she was the widow of his father's master at arms. The man had died while protecting his father. So he visited her every week and gave her a few coins. It was the least he could do for the years of service the man had given his family.

We continued along a well-worn path, but then he turned onto a trail less taken. We chatted along the way. Compared to the previous evening, he was a chatterbox, explaining about the path, the woods, his childhood visits. Dreadfully boring stuff—only it wasn't boring. The light in his eyes when he spoke and the gentle smile which occasionally curved his lips were more deadly than my sharpest dagger. I realized I was in mortal danger and entering territory an assassin should never enter.

I was starting to like him.

At mid-morning, we emerged onto a hilltop meadow, with woods to one side, but otherwise grass all around and an excellent view of the countryside below us. A blanket had been spread in the meadow's center, and as we rode up, a servant began to set out a light lunch. I couldn't help but smile. Why that little charmer. Someone had to be helping him.

The servant withdrew, as did the guards with the horses, to a safe distance. To my surprise, he began to serve me himself. While I appreciated the honor, he was seriously out of protocol. I was merely being presented as a concubine, not a full wife. He had no reason to court me like this.

Mid-way through our meal—as he chatted about how the crops were doing, how the harvest looked, and his plans for a new irrigation system—I noticed there was a knife placed between us. It had been used to cut a few vegetables. I looked down at the thing like a monster. It was not exceedingly sharp, but would do a good job of entering a man's body. I could easily jab it in his throat, and he would die soundlessly. I could then quietly ride away. My hand itched to take it.

And at the same time, I was revolted at the thought.

I tucked my hands underneath my legs as if to restrain them. It was not my role to kill him, I told myself. I was only to gather information. And for some reason, I was exceedingly grateful.

He paused for a moment as if considering something. "What do you think of the emperor?" he asked.

Now that was a dangerous question. To the people, he was supposed to be their moon and stars. Almost their god. To say anything less out loud was to be branded a traitor and be immediately executed. But to me, he was a man who had bedded my mother and then cast her aside when she became inconvenient. The same man who had sent me to bathe in darkness every day.

I smiled and shrugged. "He is the emperor. The one and only. What more is there to say?"

He looked off into the distance. "I think something is wrong with him. The empire is falling apart, rotting from inside, and yet he does nothing about it. My father originally supported him, but came to distrust him. He said the emperor had changed."

I shrugged again. "I do not know," I said, looking down. He was talking treason. Anyone could turn him in for saying such.

He slowly turned to look at me. His expression neutral. But his eyes... they were bright with determination. "I plan to find out. I plan to overthrow him, if I must. But the empire can't continue like it is." He paused. "I thought you might want to know before you became more involved with me. I plan to challenge the world."

We stared at each other, not saying a word. I didn't know what to say. If I were to reveal his thoughts to the other nobles, he could easily deny it. There were no witnesses. So it was likely a test to see if I would cause him trouble in the future. Or...

He could really intend to overthrow the emperor. If that was the case, it would easily explain why he had become a target.

Thankfully the servant appeared behind me and cleared his throat. Lord Luoyangei was due back for a visitor.

The gentle breeze that had been playing with his hair paused, leaving the meadow silent. And then I heard it. A sound only one accustomed to weapons would understand. The creak of wood being bent and leather being stretched

Someone had a bow.

Then I heard it release.

Instinctively, I dived forward toward the young lord, but I was too late. A heartbeat before I could reach him, an arrow struck him solidly in the chest.

"No..." I wailed.

But he just sighed and pulled the arrow out of his clothes. "Damn. And I just got these too."

The guards were already in pursuit.

I ran my hands over him in disbelief, and he chuckled at my panic. "No need to worry. It is a myst shield. Arrows and knives can't get through it."

And I could feel he was right. While I was touching him, I wasn't actually touching his body. There was some kind of barrier around him, molding to his shape. No wonder the first attack hadn't worked.

Then it occurred to me. The knife laid in plain sight had been no accident. It was to test me.

He was subdued as we rode back. I think he was embarrassed at me finding out. Or perhaps he was afraid he had pushed me away. But when we reached the stables, he quickly jumped down and came around to help me to dismount.

"Will you join me for dinner this evening? If you're not afraid of me, that is."

I smiled. "You do not frighten me."

But as I turned away, I realized he did. I was terrified.

Just not for the reason he thought.

A week later, and after several more dinners, he finally took me for a stroll through his manor's gardens. It was the last piece of intelligence I needed.

The evening was pleasant, with spring flowers in bloom and their fragrance lightly scenting the air. To my surprise, he took my hand. It was such an innocent and charming gesture, I blushed despite myself. We sat on a convenient bench, close to each other, and were quiet for a time, listening to the night insects.

"This garden was my mother's," he said, breaking the silence. "She loved flowers. And I've tried to keep it just as she would have wanted. I can remember coming here and playing while she sat on this bench and watched."

I knew from our earlier conversations that he sorely missed his parents.

Unlike mine, they had been kind and understanding people. "Your mother must have been a great lady," I offered.

He nodded. "She was. I can remember when I was about nine or ten, sitting on this very bench and declaring I hated girls." He smiled wistfully. "She brushed my hair out of my eyes and explained that one day, I likely wouldn't feel that way. But when I chose, I had to choose someone that was not only beautiful but someone intelligent and wise." He looked at me levelly. "Someone like you..."

And then it happened, most unexpectedly. An attack that took me completely unawares.

He kissed me.

I had expected him to try to seduce me. But a kiss? It was too intimate, too close... and totally disarming, especially since I liked it.

And I fled.

I immediately went back to my room and packed my few things. I then put on my travel clothes and sat down to wait for sunrise. I was too close to him. If I were asked to return with a more sinister objective—I'm not sure I could do it.

I had just sat down when there was a knock at my door. A servant entered with a tray, and on it was a small envelope. When I opened it, I saw it was from him. And like his personality, it was written in quick, strong strokes. "I frightened you. Please come see me."

I sighed. I nearly declined on the spot. I had my intelligence—I knew his weakness. There was no further reason to stay. But leaving too abruptly might raise suspicions. I needed to say good-bye.

So I went with the servant, and my ever-present guards, to his personal chambers. To my surprise, the guards and the servant were instructed to remain outside. Under no circumstances were they to interrupt.

Only I was allowed to enter.

As was the rest of the manor, the room was sparsely decorated. It was of average size and dimly lit by a single myst lamp in the corner. I was impressed with how ordinary it appeared, having only a functional bed, a small writing desk, and the ever-present tribute to his parents. Only this one was different. A single portrait was displayed on the wall—a man, a woman, and a young boy I recognized as the lord himself. On either side of the picture were two shelves.

One held a well-worn book propped up for display, and the other a ceremonial knife resting on a red velvet pillow.

Lord Luoyangei stood by the room's only window.

He turned when I entered and immediately noticed my change in clothes. "So you are leaving," he said. He turned to look back out the window. "Life's ironic," he said. "Since my parents died, there has been a long procession of potential concubines, wives, and mistresses. All of them were sure they could win my heart, and if not that, at least share my bed. But as you have seen, I have no use for pretty trinkets, and I sent them all away." He turned back toward me. "But the one woman that I desperately want to stay is leaving."

I was frozen to the spot. He couldn't be saying these things to me. He had no idea what a terrible person I was.

He stepped toward me. "You've done something no other woman has done. My heart had stopped after my parents were murdered, but you..." he took a step closer. "You made my heart beat again." He took another step.

And I retreated the same. I wasn't sure what to do.

"I have frightened you," he said softly. "What can I do to ease your fear?"

He was right. I was terrified of him. My heart was betraying me.

He closed the distance between us and again took my hand, clasping it tightly and bringing it to his chest. I could tell he was not wearing his myst shield this evening. He had completely opened himself to me.

"Don't go," he whispered and leaned in to kiss me. His gentle lips touched mine...

My eyes went wide. I felt another presence. And then his lips gave a shiver. NO!

I caught him as he collapsed. His eyes wide, his body unmoving. I lowered him to the floor, kneeling beside him and continuing to hold him as I did. I instantly recognized what had happened. Paralysis poison. Without the antidote, he would die within minutes. I looked across his body to the window, where a new shadow knelt on the sill. The assassin lowered their blowgun. "Took you long enough."

I instantly recognized the voice. It was Jiaying. The best of us. The most cold-hearted. My old friend.

And as soon as she said it, I knew I had been deceived. I had been sent not to gather intelligence. They had already known about his myst shield. No, I was to get him to lower it. It had been intended all along that I was to lead him to his death.

Jiaying stepped lightly to the floor and drew her dagger. She held it out to me and pointed to the motionless man. "Quickly, end it."

All the frustration. All the loneliness. All the pain. All the bound up guilt of more deaths than I could remember...

It all came crashing down on me.

And I grew sick of it.

"No," I whispered. I clutched him tightly to my chest and said louder. "No!"

Jiaying chuckled. "And what does your refusal mean? If you don't kill him, I will. And if I don't, another will come and another and yet another."

I clutched him tighter.

"Stupid girl. Always the bleeding heart."

Her leg flashed out and would have caught me in the chin had I not been expecting it. I grabbed her foot and shoved her back. She stumbled, giving me time to release him and roll to my feet on the opposite side of his prone body.

Jiaying bent to slice his throat, but I grabbed her wrist and pushed her back, stepping over him to put myself between them. She struggled to pull her wrist from my grip, but I held on. Her lithe and powerful leg swept at my knees, and I stumbled backward, my heels catching on the young lord's body. I had to release her wrist as I leaned backward, bridging over his body, and using the momentum to bring my foot up and to catch Jiaying in the chin.

She stumbled back, and we stared at each other ready to attack.

"Give me the antidote," I said, not daring to take my eyes off her, yet scanning my field of vision for something I could use against her dagger.

"No," she replied. Her dagger disappeared to her belt, and in one smooth motion, she pulled her sword, assuming her favorite form. One I knew quite well. I had fought with her enough to be able to guess her every move. But that also went the other way. She knew mine just as well. We had played out the scenario of fighting an unarmed opponent many times.

And the sword always won.

"Don't go rogue," she said through tight lips. "Step out of the way, and I'll forget your interference."

But even as she spoke, she was moving.

As was I.

She swung at me, and I dodged—I could hear the blade's song as it passed a hair's breadth from my ear. But she had expected that and caught my wrist with her free hand and rolled backward, sending me sailing through the air to land hard on my back. I gasped for breath as her blade stabbed at me. I barely managed to roll from beneath her and regain my feet.

We regarded each other.

"The teachers treated you special," she said, coldly. "You thought yourself our better. But I always hated you." I was surprised at the venom in her voice.

She changed her grip, and her foot slid soundlessly across the floor as she moved to a different form. One she knew I had trouble with. The change in her stance spoke volumes. Before, she had only intended to wound. But now, she intended to kill.

Weapon! I needed something—<u>anything</u> I could use against her sword. And I was running out of time. The poison in his system was slowly killing him.

"How you survived the sorting is beyond me. I even slept with Master Xiao to make sure you were my opponent. I knew you would not be able to go full out against me. Your friend." She slowly leveled her sword as she readied her next attack.

Jiaying smiled coldly. "But I have never been your <u>friend</u>."

Her eyes flicked.

I read them and moved instantly, throwing myself in front of the young lord as she shifted to stab him through his chest. I dodged her blade and slammed into her, knocking her weapon from her hands and sending us both sprawling. I rolled on top of her, intending to pin her arms, when she punched me in my exposed face.

Hard.

I must have blanked for a moment. My world swam, and I blinked to clear my vision. I tasted blood in my mouth, and there was something wet on my nose. Jiaying was slowly rising and stepping to retrieve her sword.

A weapon! I needed a weapon!

I pulled myself up and staggered against the portrait of his family, knocking it to the floor. I snatched up the book and flung it at her. She knocked it aside and raised her sword.

I grabbed the ceremonial knife and the pillow it was lying on. I was surprised at the pillow's weight, noting it must be filled with sand or beads. I charged.

The knife was far shorter than her sword. She thrust and I caught it with the pillow, skewering it, but allowing me to spoil her aim and shove it to one side. It barely missed me. I closed the distance, and we grappled. My shining knife catching and reflecting the light while her dark one seemed to absorb it. Her lips turned up into a cruel grin, confident she had me. My heart ached at what I knew I had to do.

She broke free and thrust.

I gave her a surprised expression as she felt the blade sink into my chest. I staggered back as my ripped shirt sprouted blood and ran in rivulets down to the floor.

With a grim expression, she took aim to thrust through my heart and end it. She thought she was doing me a favor.

But when she thrust, I wasn't there. I stepped to the side and sank my blade into her own heart. I caught her as she collapsed and lowered her to the floor. She looked up at me in shock, her eyes glazed, and her lips trembling.

"Who set this up?" I demanded.

She looked at me dully. "Master Xiao," she whispered. Her lips moved like she wanted to say more. Her arm came up, wavering between us, and came to rest on my chest. "I hated you," she breathed. "Because... you were so nice to me."

And then she died.

I hugged her to me and fought the tears. "I'm sorry," I whispered. "I'm so sorry."

She had no doubt been surprised when my blood and wound had disappeared. Because it had never happened. Illusions could be quite powerful.

It was ironic. The illusion that had saved her life so long ago would lead to her death. Because during our duel, I had actually wounded her. And through a myst illusion, I had duplicated it on myself.

I gently laid her down and then searched her belt for the antidote, finding the tiny vial at the bottom of one of her pouches. Then, going to the young lord, I knelt beside him and carefully raised the vial to his lips—

Only he wasn't breathing.

I gasped and felt for his pulse, but there was none. And when I checked his eyes, only death looked back.

I was too late.

I cradled him in my arms, and in my misery, rocked back and forth. I raised my head.

And wailed.

CHAPTER TWENTY-ONE

Gates of
The Empire

I bolted upright as I awoke. The strong memories from Fumiko's fight echoed in my mind. For a moment, I expected to see the dead bodies of Jiaying and Lord Luoyangei.

Instead, I found the room softly lit by the rising sun. Spraggel blinked at me in surprise and pulled back his arm. He had been reaching to awaken me since we had agreed to leave just after dawn.

He chuckled. "Are you all right? You look like you've seen a ghost."

I rubbed my face. "I think I just did."

Zofie was sitting upright next to me, awake, and likely ready for a trip to relieve herself. Cabrina was curled up in a ball in the corner and snoring softly. As expected, Fumiko was missing. I touched her mat and found it cold.

We got ourselves together and went to see about breakfast. We found Fumiko already there nursing a cup of hot tea. She refused to look at me as we joined her. Her eyes were red and puffy. I didn't think she had slept any at all.

As we sat at the table, Cabrina leaned in and whispered to me. "Did you hurt Fumiko? She left crying last night. My host tells me that you should be nice to them after you've had sex."

"We didn't have sex!" I said a little more loudly than I meant to. Spraggel and Fumiko's eyes went up, and several people sitting at a nearby table glanced our way.

I leaned down to her and whispered, "Will you quit doing that! We're not having sex."

Cabrina shook her head. "I'm not so sure. My host is convinced you're cheating on the princess."

"I'm not," I shot back. "Fumiko and I don't have that kind of relationship."

Cabrina shook her head and narrowed her eyes. "I'll be watching you just in case."

As she settled back in her seat, I had to wonder when Cabrina transitioned from being our prisoner to one of our party. Even stolid Fumiko had started to treat her differently. Something about Cabrina's energy and naivety was endearing. She didn't seem to be a bad person. And the two of them, human and Avenyts, made quite the team. The relationship reminded me of the one I had with Abe. I sighed. I hated to say it, but I missed the pain in the ass.

The rest of our meal was mostly uneventful. Once more, Zofie only ate a few bites before refusing to eat more. I hoped she wasn't getting sick.

After finishing, Spraggel left to visit the privy, and Fumiko said she wanted to shop for a moment. When I offered to come with her, she glanced at Cabrina and suggested I stay behind. I was puzzled but didn't press her on it. She assured us it wouldn't take her long.

That only left the youth and me alone at our table. I quietly sipped my tea while she distractedly stirred her uneaten porridge.

"Can Cabrina talk to you?" she asked.

I shrugged. "She's welcome to at any time."

The youth looked up uncertainly. "It's about me."

This was a switch. Cabrina usually insisted No-name take the lead. I grinned. "The answer's the same."

She nodded, took a deep breath, and let it out slowly like she was stealing herself for some unpleasant task.

The girl looked up, and her expression subtly changed. As before, the change was slight, and I only noticed it because I was looking for it.

She licked her lips. "Sir Coren, No-name is afraid."

"Why?" I asked in surprise.

She resumed stirring her porridge. "B-b-back at the village when you and Mistress Fumiko were practicing, Kaleefah and No-name talked. And it didn't go well. She said No-name is on the path to becoming a Dark Avenyts." She sighed. "She said that since No-name is young and of low cothe, she will pick up the ideas of those that control her. Every time she is assigned a directive, she will move closer to becoming one of them." She dropped her spoon in her bowl and gazed at me levelly. "But she doesn't want to be one."

I shrugged. "Then don't become one. Stay true to the light."

Cabrina shook her head. "It's not that easy. Right now she doesn't have a name, which means she's an open book. Anyone can write into it. And to fix that..." She sighed. "She needs a name."

I shrugged again. "Then name her."

Cabrina looked out the open door. "I can't. Only an Avenyts can give her one, and it has to be one of high cothe."

"What about Uy? Kaleefah's Avenyts?"

Cabrina shook her head. "No-name asked her, but Kaleefah refused, saying she was afraid I might contaminate her daughter. Even with a name, my Avenyts could still turn to dark. It's a decision No-name has to make every time she interacts with her host. How much direction does she give? At what point does she move from advising to controlling? It's a slippery slope, and once you go too far, it's hard to get back."

I put down my teacup. "But why would Kaleefah stop her? She's not the Avenyts, Uy is."

She leaned back in her chair. "It's one of those things about the Avenyts I don't understand. Since she's of the light, she won't do it without her host's permission." She gave a bark of a laugh. "Ironic, isn't it. The one Light Avenyts in the world, and she isn't allowed."

"There must be a reason?"

"Oh, there is. If Uy names No-name, then she and her host sort of take responsibility for her."

"Like an apprenticeship?"

She nodded distractedly.

I took a sip of my tea and considered the youth. "Cabrina, why are you telling me this?"

She looked up at me. "No-name is afraid she's going to turn dark and that she'll turn against me. She wants to know if there is any way to remove her."

I was surprised. But based upon how protective the Avenyts was of Cabrina, I could understand it. It made clear No-name's devotion to her host.

I smiled. "When I get Abe back, we'll ask him. Maybe he knows how."

This did not make her any happier. She slumped on the table and propped her head on her hand. "I'm against this, you know. I believe in No-name. She's a good person. I've never had a friend like her before." She paused and ran her finger around the top of her bowl. "It's just not fair."

I glanced over to Zofie, sitting beside me and staring ahead with unseeing eyes. "No, it's not."

We sat in silence for a moment. Each of us lost in our thoughts.

A smiling Spraggel rejoined us. He patted his belly. "I feel so much better." But looking us over, his smile faded. "Did someone die? You two don't seem very lively."

Cabrina and I both looked up at him in annoyance.

He continued. "We're almost to the gates. What could possibly be wrong?"

At that exact moment, Zofie leaned over the table and threw up.

I had heard that you would feel the gates long before you saw them. The barrier consumed a vast amount of myst, so even those not sensitive to the ethereal substance could feel it. For me, I felt a general sense of unease creep up my neck as we walked up an incline toward the gates.

I glanced at Zofie. Maybe it was the gates that made her throw up. She was a myst seer and likely much more sensitive than I was. After she had emptied her stomach—which wasn't that much—she had seemed a little perkier. I hoped that was what it was and not something more serious.

Traffic was heavy on the road with carts and groups of people trudging toward and away from the gates. The houses and buildings quickly thinned along the well-worn stone road until there was only wild grass and rocks along the edge.

When we topped the hill, I had to pause to just stare at it. I had expected something grandiose, but I was not prepared for just how grand it actually was.

Two giant stone dragons made up the sides of the gates, with their bodies firmly planted on opposite sides of the road and their long necks stretching out until their heads touched, forming an arch. Overtop of them and extending out from them as far as we could see was a wall of rainbows that gradually shifted and shimmered with a subdued power. Its beauty was hypnotic.

The entire empire was protected by the high myst wall at least fifty feet or more. No living thing could pass through it. So to protect the wildlife and to warn the unwary, it was made to radiate with color and feeling so they would know to keep away. It also had the effect of making people naturally avoid it.

We joined the flow of people through the gates until we came to stand in an exceedingly long queue just outside them. It only made sense, considering there were only five entrances to the empire on this side of the continent.

It wasn't until noon that we finally were able to arrive at the base of the gate and take our turn talking to the uninterested official.

We were surprised to find he spoke fluent Ellish. We deposited our required toll, and I explained why we were traveling. "We're here at the invitation of Imperial Advisor Yonge."

The man gave us a knowing look, clearly not believing me. "I'm sure the emperor himself is waiting for you just on the other side. Now hurry along."

We did as he said, but after only taking a few steps into the gate, a gong sounded. Soldiers immediately surrounded us with some very sharp looking spears and shuffled us off to a dark and dingy room to one side.

Another official, a short round fellow, entered with some kind of handheld device which reacted with a similar gong when pointed to Zofie, Cabrina, and me.

He stepped back and looked at us suspiciously. "Curses are not allowed inside our great empire." He took a deep breath and launched into a well-practiced speech. "If you wish to enter, you'll have to remove them. If you can't, then I can arrange for someone to remove them for you. If you attempt to enter again without removing them, you will be charged with attempted smuggling." He paused for dramatic effect. He clearly liked this part. "And the penalty for that is death."

"I tried to explain this outside," I said. "We are from the Kingdom of Brethnach, and we are on our way to see Advisor Yonge. He invited us here."

"What proof do you have?"

I held out my wrist with the bracelet. "He told us through his avatar that he could remove these."

The man gave it a dismissive glance. "I'm sorry, but you are not allowed to pass until you remove your curses. The law is quite clear."

Fumiko sighed and turned her back to the man. She took off her cloak and loosened her shirt. Then, slipping it down her shoulder, she revealed her butterfly tattoo.

His eyes went wide. "Come with me." There was a sudden tremor to his voice.

The man quickly led us outside and up a set of stairs. He knocked on a door at their top, eyeing Fumiko nervously as he pulled out a kerchief to wipe his sweaty brow. There was a muffled reply from the other side, and we were ushered in.

A man in a fine robe, holding a paper and writing brush, stood in front of a large window overlooking the gate. He turned at our entry, clearly displeased at the interruption. Our escort spoke with the official for a bit in their language before quickly leaving the room.

The official cleared his voice and spoke something to Fumiko. She turned and once more exposed her shoulder to reveal her tattoo.

He sighed. He reached in his pocket and pulled out a small piece of carved jade about as big as his thumb. My eyes went up in surprise. It was a beautifully done butterfly from a dark green stone. He then placed the carving in the center of his extended palm and blew on it.

Nothing happened at first, but a heartbeat later, the butterfly began to softly glow and gently pulse. The man licked his lips nervously.

"Hello Administrator," came a rich, male voice from the orb in near-perfect Ellish. "I take it our visitors are with you?" I instantly recognized the voice.

The administrator immediately gave a short bow. He likewise replied in Ellish. "Imperial Advisor Yonge. It is my honor to speak with you. These people match the description you gave me."

"Excellent. Please admit them at once. I will have a portal to the palace opened for them on the other side."

The man's face drew up in horror. "But Advisor, they have curses."

"I'm aware of that. I will take responsibility for them."

"Advisor...."

The voice from the orb took a darker tone. "Administrator, do I need to have the emperor speak with you directly. He will not be pleased with you impeding his guests."

The man's face went white. "No Advisor. I will admit them immediately."

"Good." And the jewel went dark.

The administrator tucked the butterfly away in a pocket. He then led us from the room back down to the gate, where he personally escorted us through.

On the other side, we waited only a few minutes before a long-range portal opened. It was vertical and man-high. A knight, outfitted in the traditional heavy armor of the region, emerged from it and motioned us forward.

I turned and gave the administrator a bow. "We thank you for allowing us through."

He waved it off and eyed the knight nervously. "Enjoy your visit to the palace," he said flatly. "Yonge makes sure you never want to leave." And with that, he turned away.

What was that about? I shook my head. Perhaps it was an expression that didn't translate well into Ellish.

Impatiently, the knight motioned us forward.

My companions looked at me, yet I hesitated. This was it—our final portal. Soon, we would get the charm off Zofie, and we could return home. I swore after this, I was never going to travel again.

Unbidden, young Haahleefah's prophesy came to my mind. *"One of your party is going to die."*

I clenched my fists. But what choice did I have? Forward was the only path.

I glanced one more time at my companions and couldn't help but feel a deep sense of pride. We made a good team. And I loved each one of them in my own way. I could not afford to lose any of them. I would just have to do my best to make sure it didn't happen.

With renewed determination, I took Zofie's hand and led my party into the gate.

The trip through the portal was uneventful, and it snapped shut behind us the moment we were clear. We found ourselves in a beautiful garden. Lush green shrubs and carefully manicured foliage lined the wide stone path before us. I was surprised to see the occasional flower despite the chill air and the winter season.

Two rows of brightly dressed servants, about a dozen total men and women, stood on either side of the path before us. Their smiles were as bright as their clothes. At some signal, the servants bowed in unison and said something together in their native language. I started to bow back, but Fumiko caught my arm and leaned close.

"Dignitaries don't bow to servants," she whispered.

I nodded in understanding, glancing her way. I couldn't help but notice how tense she looked. Her expression was so hard, I thought it might crack.

One of the older servants came forward. She spoke in heavily accented Ellish. "My name is Yanmei. And I welcome you to Jianhu Palace." She bowed deeply. "Please follow me. We have prepared special rooms for you while you are visiting with us."

"What about Imperial Advisor Yonge?" I asked, eager to get my Zofie back.

Yanmei smiled warmly. "He is busy at the moment but will be calling for you shortly."

Accompanied by the entire troop of servants, Yanmei led us to a magnificent set of chambers just off from the garden. There was a common room with heavily stuffed couches and chairs. Leading off from it were five individual bedrooms and an equally large bath. However, my eyes were instantly drawn to a table under a large window overlooking the garden and heavily laden with all sorts of unfamiliar dishes and beverages.

Unfortunately, before I could reach it, the servants redirected us toward the bath. Fumiko pulled me aside and explained it was customary to bathe before visiting with an important official.

I reluctantly went along with them. I was surprised to see the baths divided with movable screens. The females in our group were led to one side, while Spraggel and I were led to the other.

I then had a brief moment with a servant when he tried to remove my clothes. Language did prove to be a barrier, but I managed to get him to leave me to my own bathing.

We all emerged awhile later in fine robes and slippers. Zofie, Fumiko, and Cabrina's hair had been done up with combs, and their faces dabbed with some kind of red coloring on their lips and black highlighting their eyes.

I sighed when I saw Zofie. She looked so beautiful. But while Zofie was beautiful, Fumiko looked every bit the eastern princess. The clothes, combs, and face coloring seemed so natural on her. It made her look... breath-taking. Any man would fall for her.

I quickly turned away, chiding myself for even thinking of her that way. I had Zofie. I took my princess's hand and kissed it, glad I wouldn't have much longer until she was back to her normal smiling self. I had already prepared a quote for her to complete.

Feeling the surprising weight of a stare, I looked up and directly into Fumiko's eyes. She blinked at being caught and immediately turned away, saying something to Spraggel.

With Fumiko, it was hard to tell since she guarded her emotions so carefully. But I believe there had been an unexpected emotion in her gaze. Longing perhaps? I wasn't sure, but I prayed to the Creator that I was wrong.

So, we waited. All the servants except Yanmei retreated, and we were left to our own devices. We nibbled on food left for us, talked about what we had been through, and what we intended to do when we got back. Normal stuff. We even quizzed Yanmei on the empire about this and that, and the rumors we had heard. But the sun, easily visible from the garden window, traced toward the horizon with every moment that passed. And I grew increasingly impatient.

I asked Yanmei frequently when we would see the advisor and was told each time that he was busy and would call for us. I couldn't help feeling we were being purposely delayed. Subtly told, we were here at his pleasure, and he was not beholding to us for anything.

I tried to keep myself calm and not show my agitation. But I must not have been doing so well. At one point, Spraggel put a hand on my arm and asked if I would *please* stop my pacing.

Fumiko was as closed and guarded as a merchant's purse. She sat quietly to one side with a clear view of the room. I tried to engage her in conversation about the advisor, but she simply touched her ear and shook her head—indicating we were being listened to. Disappointed, I went back to look out the window.

And still, we waited. The sun sank below the horizon, and our host lighted several myst lanterns. What remained of the food was swapped out for a few platters of hot regional fare and steamed rice. It was tasty, but I was too agitated to eat.

And we waited some more! I was getting irritated. Spraggel went to sleep in his chair, and to keep me from pacing, Cabrina managed to persuade me to play some kind of strategy game. She beat me quite soundly.

It was late in the evening when a servant came and whispered in Yanmei's ear. She nodded and then turned to us. "Imperial Advisor Yonge has retired for the evening," she said. "There will be no further audiences, so I suggest you likewise retire."

I hung my head. I so badly wanted to have my Zofie back that I could barely resist the urge to kick and scream in frustration. Instead, I took my beloved's hand and pulled her up so we could make our preparations for bed.

After putting Zofie down for the night, I went back to the common room to check on the rest of my party. The lights had already been dimmed, and Yanmei had left, but I sincerely doubted we were unobserved. Both Spraggel and Cabrina were fast asleep in their beds. But when I checked on Fumiko, I found her bed undisturbed. I scratched my head, thinking she might be in the bath.

I jumped at the hand on my shoulder.

"Sorry I startled you," Fumiko whispered as she stepped in front of me. Her hand trailed down my arm and around to my chest. She paused to pull out the combs from her hair, and giving her head a shake, allowed her tresses to fall to her shoulders. She smiled at me seductively.

I stared at her wide-eyed and started to tell her I needed to get back to Zofie when she silenced me with a single finger to my lips. She leaned against me and slid her arms around my neck, pulling me close. She then stood on tiptoe to reach my ear.

"Follow along," she breathed. She took my hand and led me over to her bed, drawing back the blanket and pulling me underneath along with her. We lay down facing each other.

Shifting close, she threw her leg over mine and draped her arm around me. She settled with her face mere inches from mine. I couldn't help but notice how nice she smelled.

I fidgeted, not exactly sure what to do with my hands. For that matter, not exactly sure what to do with *me*. Fumiko's proximity made me extremely uncomfortable. I was a man after all, and she was an extremely beautiful woman.

And I was in bed with her.

She leaned close. I could feel her breath. "We can talk now," she whispered. "I've covered us with a tiny myst working, just enough to hide our voices. That's why we have to be so close."

"Wouldn't they notice?"

She nodded. "I'm sure they already have. They will assume I am secretly sleeping with you, and I am merely using the charm to hide the sounds of our passion from the others."

"I would never…" I stammered.

She gave me a sad smile and pushed my hair out of my eyes. "I know."

"Is this why you couldn't answer my questions on Yonge earlier today? Because they're listening?" My voice squeaked.

Fumiko nodded and settled in closer next to me. "They watch too. There are spy charms all around the rooms. Even in the bath. You wouldn't notice them unless you had…" She trailed off.

"Received special training?" I offered. "Fumiko, you don't need to be ashamed of what you were." I patted her arm. "I've accepted that part of your past. And I'm sure Zofie will too."

She relaxed even more against me. "Thank you."

"So, what haven't you told me about Yonge? Other than not to trust him."

I felt her stir uncomfortably beside me. "I think it best for you to see for yourself."

"You mean the memory thing again? Can't you just tell me?"

"Sharing the memory would be best." She paused and gazed at me a moment. "There is also one last thing you need to know about me. It's connected. Then everything will make sense."

I shook my head. "I don't know, Fumiko. That last one..." I trailed off, knowing I was a coward. Her memories were just too raw.

"It will take too long to explain." Her hand came up to gently stroke my cheek. "Please. If not for Zofie, would you do it for me? Sharing my past with you has been painful, but it's also been a relief. To finally unburden my soul a little."

I sighed. "All right."

Her hand slipped behind my neck. "Thank you."

And then she kissed me. It didn't last long, only a heartbeat or two. My eyes flew open in shock. "Fumiko..."

She put a hand on the side of my face and sighed contently. "Zofie is so lucky."

I felt her myst begin to gather. And with no fanfare, she sucked me into her memories.

CHAPTER TWENTY-TWO

The
Butterfly

*A*fter my tears had been cried, kneeling on that hard floor and cradling my first love, anger took over. Why had my masters ordered this man killed? He was a good lord. His people loved him, and he was fighting the darkness in the empire. Wasn't that what I was supposed to be doing? And why of all people had they sent Jiaying? Why had they forced me to kill my only friend?

I had to have answers.

I swapped out the ceremonial knife for Jiaying's sword and slipped out of Lord Luoyangei's manor, heading straight for Master Xiao's house. As expected, I didn't make it far. I was intercepted by others from the Emperor's Butterflies just outside his home. Three of them. I had expected as much. Master likely already knew.

They gave me no chance for explanation—no chance to persuade them to stop. Jiaying's borrowed blade had to do my speaking for me. We traded blows, back and forth. They were just as well trained as I, but they were not myst users. And like the dark creature I am, the shadows were my friend.

I left them wounded and confused, wondering how such a small person could wreak such havoc.

The sky was just lighting as I stormed into my master's house, easily defeating the few defenders I encountered and sending the servants fleeing.

I found him waiting for me. He sat on a cushion before a low table drinking tea.

"You dare to come here after failing in your mission!" he shouted.

And I nearly flinched in reflex at the stern voice that had disciplined me in my training. But my anger won out.

"Why was Lord Luoyangei ordered killed? What crime against the emperor did he commit!" I demanded.

I caught movement out of the corner of my eye. I leaned back and extended my myst, slowing the dagger that came speeding at me so that I could grab it out of the air. I sent it back, flying toward the attacker, who went down silently.

I stepped forward and slammed my foot down on the table, my blade stopping a mere finger's breadth from his throat. "Tell me! Why was he targeted?"

Master Xiao shrugged. "You'll have to ask the emperor."

"My father?" I asked in astonishment.

"He asked for you specifically."

"My father doesn't even care that I'm alive," I spat.

A new voice entered the conversation. "Quite the contrary, my dear. He's been following you very closely. Asks about you all the time."

That voice. Where had I heard it before? I wheeled toward it. Only I didn't see anyone. I glanced at my master—his expression was grim.

"Show yourself!" I commanded.

"I'm right here," said the voice. It came from the open window where a majestic butterfly rested on the window ledge. It took to the air and fluttered over to the table—its wings slowly opening and closing.

"Please excuse this form," it continued. "But it seemed the fastest way to stop your rampage."

"Who...?"

"I am Imperial Advisor Yonge."

My eyes went wide. The voice of the emperor. That's where I had heard his voice before. He was said to be the second most powerful person in the empire. And the person responsible for our group of assassins.

"Lord Luoyangei was targeted because he was disrupting the order of things." There was a brief pause. "And those that disrupt have to be put in their place."

"I saw a kind and just man..."

"You saw what he wanted you to see. He was going to stage a coup against the emperor. Such a threat had to be eliminated."

"And what was wrong with that? I've seen it myself. The empire is rotten. And it's the emperor that's allowed it to happen."

"I'm embarrassed to hear you speak of him that way. Although his eminence has been showing his age lately, he is a great man. A god almost."

"I'll kill him," I said through gritted teeth.

"Come then. He's resting in the palace garden at the moment. For someone of your abilities, it would be a simple task to get inside. I daresay you'll have little trouble getting past the palace soldiers and even his personal bodyguards." I could almost hear his smile. "But your mother would be dead long before you reached him."

I tried not to show any emotion. "So what do I care? I have no love for her."

There was a laugh from the butterfly. "Really? I think your relationship with your mother is a little stronger than you admit. Wasn't she the one that taught you how to use your myst? Even told you never to reveal you had it. And insisted that you disparage her at every opportunity so you would not be drawn into the politics of the court. Sounds more like a concerned parent than someone evil."

I shook my head in denial. How did he know so much?

He sighed dramatically. "Well, then come on to the palace. We'll be waiting." There was a pause like the advisor was pondering something. "I wonder if we have time to make this a public execution. That would bring great embarrassment to her, would it not? Perhaps have her mutilated body greet you at the door. That would get you all the more riled up."

"You wouldn't dare," I spat. "Her family will rise up in anger."

"Oh, really? Then I guess I'll need to dispatch some imperial soldiers to restrain them. Killing your grandfather would be a good start. He's been quietly plotting against us for a while now. In fact, we might need to execute the entire Zhangjunen family. Saying they were behind Luoyangei's assassination would be more than enough justification."

"But they had nothing to do with this," I protested.

"Oh, really? The report I received was that a young woman from the Zhang-junen family went into Lord Luoyangei's chambers alone. And later, when the staff checked on him, they found him dead with some type of ceremonial knife in his throat. And no sign of that young woman."

"But Jiaying's body..."

"There was no second body reported." I could hear the smile. "And we have no knowledge of this one called Jiaying."

With a sinking heart, realization struck me. I had been manipulated. Played right into his hands. I had not just lured Lord Luoyangei to his death, but I had given the emperor an excuse to execute all of the Zhangjunen family. Those lords aligned with my family were all that kept the emperor from moving against us. But with this overwhelming evidence, none of those lords would be able to raise a finger to help, lest they too fall under the sword.

I frowned, a growing pit of frustration in my stomach. I hated my father, but I also realized he could not have set this up. Someone else must have moved all the pieces on the board.

It had to be Yonge.

"So you see, my dear. You were supposed to be killed with Lord Luoyangei. A tragedy of the lord killing his attacker as he defended himself. When that failed, you were supposed to be killed on your way here by my humble servants. But you survived that too. Which brings us to now. There really is only one outcome." He paused. "You have to die. If you give up this madness, I will give you a quick and quiet death." He chuckled. "I warned your grandfather many years ago that he would pay for opposing us. And while it's been a struggle, I always *get my way."*

I stared at the butterfly and considered my options. Surrender quietly, or have my revenge and get the entire Zhangjunen family executed. Neither was much of a choice. I had been outmaneuvered. There was only one move left on the board.

The butterfly continued. *"Who knows, your family may still be able to salvage something from this. Your sister is of age, and with the right marriage, your family might be able to regain a little of their prestige. I hear the new Lord Longwei is looking for a bride."*

I frowned. I had killed the senior Longwei two years ago. He had been a cruel and despicable man. I had shed no tears for him. But his successor was by far much worse. He had tortured his last wife to death for spilling his tea.

"Of course," Yonge continued. "I might be able to recommend someone of higher status if you don't continue to dirty your family's name." He chuckled. "So you see, my dear. You have no choice but to surrender. Just give your sword to Master Xiao, and I'll let you walk to your very public execution where you will die in disgrace. I will even spare the rest of your family since the spectacle will make them lose credibility. None of the other lords will trust them again." He paused, the butterfly wings calmly going back and forth.

I was frozen in place. My heart pounded loud in my head. Yonge had arranged everything so carefully.

My hands tightened on my sword and began to shake. To die, or to cause the death of those I cared about. The choices were clear.

For some strange reason, I thought back to when Jiaying and I had fought at the sorting. It had been a similar choice. My friend or me. And just like then—

I chose neither.

Yonge continued. "So what say you..."

With one quick swing of my sword, I sliced the butterfly in two, its severed pieces flying across the room.

Master Xiao stared at me in horror. "What are you doing? Advisor Yonge always gets his way."

I stared at him. "Not this time, he doesn't."

I turned and walked away. My mind was already racing ahead. I couldn't beat Yonge. He was too strong a player, and he held all the pieces in this game against my family. But he forgot one vital thing.

I didn't have to play by his rules.

Concealing myself using the early morning shadows and making sure no one saw me, I ran to my grandfather's house. I slipped inside, finding him sitting on a back porch overlooking the small garden. I had not seen him in many years, and I was startled at how old he looked.

When I appeared in front of him, blood-spattered and dirty, he seemed surprised. He was drinking tea, but I smelled a more potent beverage from the empty mug beside him. He barked a command and dismissed all the servants. Eyeing my sword, they scurried out of sight.

Grandfather took a sip of his tea while looking off into the distance. "So are you here to kill me too? I've heard you've created quite the stir. You've no doubt been a helpless pawn, but your actions have doomed our family."

I knelt beside him and laid my sword at his feet. "No, Grandfather. I have come for a different reason. I bring salvation."

He looked at me skeptically. "And how so? I fear we are far beyond that."

I shook my head and began to speak. The words just poured out of me. I told him all about the Emperor's Butterflies, about Advisor Yonge's intentions, the location of Master Xiao's house, how to determine what really killed Lord Luoyangei, and where to find Jiaying's body. He listened carefully the whole time, unmoving, and digesting everything I said.

When I ran out of things to say, the sun had moved an hour's breadth toward the horizon. I felt drained—empty. All the aches from my recent fights began to pain me.

"And what, Granddaughter, should I do with this information? How will it save us?" I think he already knew, but he wanted to be sure of my intentions.

"Reveal the existence of the Emperor's Butterflies to the other lords. Show them the tattoo on Jiaying's body and the training grounds at Master Xiao's house. This will arouse the other lords, and Yonge will be revealed for what he is. Then show them how Lord Luoyangei really died. Point to the poison in his system and then lead them to Master Xiao's house, where you will find an ample supply of the same poison and several more marked with the same tattoo. They will all recognize the work of the emperor's tattooist. Once all is revealed, Yonge will lose the backing of the other lords. He may be all-powerful, but he is nothing should they decide not to follow. They will demand his butterflies be disbanded, robbing him of one of his primary tools. He will not dare make a move against you for fear of further angering the lords. He will have no choice but to vindicate our family."

Grandfather nodded. He called one of his servants over to him and issued quick instructions. The man's eyes widened as he listened, and he left at a run.

The elder looked at me sadly. "And what of you, granddaughter? Yonge will *not forget this betrayal. And I do not have the forces to protect you. You will be cleaned out with the rest of the assassins."*

I stood, my head down and my fists clenched. I honestly hadn't thought that far. My first impulse had been to protect my family... and my mother.

He leaned slowly out of his chair and picked up my sword. He inspected its dark blade and then held it out for me. "You could take the warrior's way," he offered.

Ritual suicide. It was the only path of honor. And it would be the easiest road.

I took the sword from him and looked at it. I had killed so many. I had even led my first love to his death and killed my only friend. My soul was so tainted it was black.

As I gazed at the sword, it seemed to talk to me in Jiaying's voice. "Death isn't good enough for you," it seemed to say.

I had to pay. I had to atone.

I slowly shook my head. "No," I said, my voice cracking. "I am not worthy."

He nodded. "Then you must leave at once. And you can never return. I'm sure Yonge will put a price on your head."

I nodded and turned away. I had not taken two steps when he spoke to my back. "I will make sure your mother is kept safe."

I blinked back a tear.

It's the best I could hope for. And I swore I would atone for my sins. Somewhere in this world, there had to be someone that I could do good for.

Someone that would give me a chance and wouldn't hate me.

I jerked as I came out of the memory. Fumiko had not moved away, but now she wore the expression of resignation like she was waiting for the ax to fall.

"What happened next?" I asked.

She blinked in surprise at my question. She had obviously expected me to say something else. "I... I left the empire. I had a few more encounters with Advisor Yonge's henchmen, but nothing I couldn't handle. Then from there, I traveled aimlessly, doing odd jobs here and there to earn a meal or perhaps a bed. I was in shock." She smiled warmly. "It was in the fall of that year, in a city far from here that I ran into Master Tormaigh. I had taken to disguising myself as a boy since it avoided unwanted advances. Not that they could beat me, but I got tired of the hassle. And he really was shouting at the top of his lungs for someone to help him. Unfortunately, it was in Ellish, and no one could understand him." She sighed, and I felt her breath caress my cheek. "When I revealed I could speak Ellish, he hired me on the spot." She thought for a moment. "Although I don't believe he ever paid me anything."

I chuckled. "Sounds like something Spraggel would do."

"It does." She brushed a strand of hair behind her ear and gazed at me. She seemed to be waiting for something. But I didn't know what to say. "Thank you for sharing your secrets with me," I finally said. "I feel better armed against Yonge now."

She looked puzzled. "Why don't you hate me? I expected you to draw away, or at least be uncomfortable around me, but you haven't. Why not?"

I chuckled. "Well, I can't say I approve of what you've done, but you've saved my life several times. That has to count for something." I took her hand and squeezed it. "Listen, I can't give you forgiveness for everything you've done. That's between you and the Creator. But I realize you were under duress when that happened. And you're definitely trying to be a better person. Regardless, I still count you as a friend."

Her lower lip began to tremble. She pulled me into a tight hug. "Thank you. I swear to you I will atone for what I have done. You have been so kind to me. You and Zofie both."

She continued to hold me, and when she didn't immediately let go, I became a little uncomfortable. "Ah, Fumiko."

She pulled back. "Sorry. I was being selfish."

We looked at each other a moment more. "I better get back to Zofie. Is it all right to leave?"

She smiled. "Yes, but we have an audience."

"Audience?"

Fumiko pointed over my shoulder. I turned to see a scowling Cabrina next to the bed. "You *are* cheating on her."

I shook my head. "Fumiko and I were just resting..."

Cabrina crossed her arms. "Uh-huh. Are you feeling rested now?" She sighed. "Well, don't let me stop you. Go ahead and kiss her."

"What?"

Cabrina rolled her eyes as only a young girl can. "Spraggel said that if I caught you again, I should remind you that you have to kiss them after having sex."

"But..."

Fumiko had her mouth covered and was trying her hardest not to laugh out loud.

I was going to have to have a talk with that man.

The next day was similar to the first. The servants brought us an excellent breakfast and bathed us again. Then after some conversation, they served us a splendid lunch. I asked if we could take a stroll in the garden, but was politely refused, saying there were security concerns. However, I suspected they didn't want us wandering.

So we napped, and Cabrina soundly beat me in two more games. I said it was because she had an Avenyts helping, but Spraggel disagreed. He said I was just that bad.

Evening rolled around, and they had brought in a delightful smelling dinner for us. We were just being served when a heavily armored guard stomped abruptly into the room. He stood in the center for a moment and then motioned us to follow.

Yanmei, her smile suddenly frozen on her face, immediately dropped what she was doing and bowed deeply to the guard before turning to us.

"Imperial Advisor Yonge will see you now," she said.

We had just been seated, so why now? It could be a simple timing thing, but based on what I had learned from Fumiko, it was more a reminder of who was in control.

We looked at one another. I shrugged, took Zofie's hand, and moved toward the door. But when Fumiko attempted to follow, the guard extended a restraining hand. "The young lady will remain here," he said in a booming voice. "She is a threat."

I froze on the spot. They were singling out Fumiko, and I was afraid of what they might do to her if they had her alone. That was something I couldn't afford to have happen. I glanced at Zofie standing beside me—her face expressionless as it had been for the last few days. I desperately wanted to see her smile again. Yonge knew it too and would take advantage of that to get what he wanted. I looked to the guard and then back to Zofie. What would she do in this situation? How would she deal with these types of games? I smiled.

I looked to the guard. "Fumiko is a trusted advisor and one of Princess Zophia's royal council. We require that she accompany us to ensure there are no misunderstandings. She is pledged to us now, and I guarantee she will not be a threat."

"No," he said flatly.

Fumiko leaned close and whispered. "This is not wise. You should not taunt him."

I gave her a confident smile and then addressed the guard. "We're not going without her. Please inform your master of our requirements."

The guard did not reply, and we all stood waiting with no one moving for several heartbeats. The awkward silence stretched on for a full minute. I became afraid I had overplayed my hand.

The guard abruptly turned and headed out the door. "Come," he said.

When we didn't immediately follow, he stopped just outside and motioned us forward. But he made no further attempt to exclude Fumiko.

We were led down a corridor, then outside under a covered walkway and into a massive building. Two more of the huge guards seemed to come out of nowhere and took their place as our rear guard. I couldn't help but notice that their strides were strangely in lockstep. I originally thought it must speak to the guard's discipline, but something in the back of my mind didn't agree.

We eventually arrived at a set of thick doors covered in ornate carvings and painted a brilliant white enamel. Two more of the identically armored guards opened the doors as we approached. Our escort led us forward without even breaking stride.

Inside we found an unusual room with a perfectly round raised floor of polished marble. On it was a couch, heavily cushioned and sitting much higher than I had ever seen before. The platform plus the couch had the effect of raising the couch's occupant to just above head height for those entering.

Reclining on it was a painfully thin man dressed in fine robes. An elegantly decorated blanket lay across his lap and legs. As we entered, he was facing a large window which took up the entire wall on our left and provided a clear view of the setting sun. I couldn't help but notice the window was covered in clear glass. While the wealthy would sometimes use glass instead of shutters, it was the window's size that caught my attention. Such a large and clear piece of glass must have been quite expensive and difficult to make. It just reinforced my opinion that the empire spared no expense.

To my surprise, the platform began to slowly rotate, bringing the reclining man around to face us. He raised two fingers on his right hand in greeting as it slowly stopped.

Although I shouldn't have been, I was surprised at his appearance. He had previously mentioned that his health prevented him from traveling, but I didn't expect it to be this bad. Healers could normally treat sickness and restore injuries, but even with myst healing, there were limits to what could be done.

"Welcome, my guests from the Kingdom of Brethnach. Princess Zophia Xernow, Sir Coren Hart, Scholar Spraggel van Deviante, and Cabrina Bryst, it is an honor to finally meet you in person. I am Imperial Advisor Tusita Yonge."

His voice sounded clear and strong. Considering his obviously weakened state, I briefly wondered how—his mouth barely moved. Then I saw the jewel at his throat and realized he had some type of myst amplification.

He had also not acknowledged Fumiko. In diplomatic circles, this would be considered a grave insult. I opened my mouth to correct him when Fumiko touched my hand. I glanced her way, and she subtly gave her head a quick shake. I frowned. She didn't want me to antagonize our host. Including her in our conversation had been risky, but to push it more would be rubbing his nose in it. And based on what I had seen, this could come back to haunt us.

I pasted on a smile. "It is an honor to finally meet you in person," I said. I bowed, and those with me followed my example—except Fumiko. I guess she felt she should at least return the slight.

Advisor Yonge chose not to notice. "Now you can see the reason I could not travel to you. This body of mine has an inherited wasting disease and requires significant maintenance to keep me alive. It is unfortunately close to its end." He managed a weak smile. "Without my myst tools, I would be completely at a loss."

"I understand," I said. I wondered about protocol, but I really wanted to get these bracelets off. I hope he didn't think I was rude. But he beat me to it.

"You are no doubt anxious to have me look at the items we've spoken about, so you can get your betrothed back to you. I can completely understand. First off, do you have the Griffin's Key?"

I held out my hand to Spraggel. He dug in his special pocket, and a moment later, laid the silver cylinder in my hand. "We do indeed."

Yonge's eyes locked on it the moment it came into view. The man smiled. The first time he had shown any expression since we had entered the room. "Will you, Sir Coren, Princess Zophia, and Mistress Bryst step up on my platform. Let's see what I can do about these nasty charms."

I gripped Zofie's hand more tightly. This was what we had come for. Doubts nagged at me. Would Zofie be all right? Would she return to normal after being exiled so long from her body? All sorts of worries nagged at me. I took a deep breath. There was nothing else to do but go forward. I glanced at Zofie's impassive face. I'm sure that's what she would want.

Beside me, Cabrina looked nervous, and for a moment, I was afraid she would balk. The Dark Avenyts inside her was about to lose all her leverage over Zofie and me. We could even kill her once the charms were off, and might likely try, if we could separate her from her host.

She looked over to me and held my gaze for a moment. To my surprise, she reached out and took my free hand. She held it tightly and gave me her signature grin. "Don't worry. I won't fight you. You have my word."

Together, we stepped forward, and Fumiko moved to go with us, but a heavy hand came down on her shoulder. One of the huge guards had silently maneuvered behind her.

"My dear Fumiko," said Yonge. "Surely you understand why I can't let you, of all people, close to me. You do have a history for revenge, and I don't plan on dying just yet."

Fumiko gave him an ice-cold stare and shook off the guard's hand, but did not try to follow.

We stepped up onto the platform and stood beside his couch.

"Place the key in my hand," he said.

I looked down at the silver cylinder, unable to shake off the feeling I was missing something. I was making a deal and didn't really understand everything's value. Plus, Fumiko said not to trust him.

But did I have a choice?

I put the key in his hand. His fingers slowly closed over it, and I thought I saw him give a tiny sigh of relief.

"Thank you," said Yonge. "Now, all of you hold out your bracelets."

We did as he requested.

"Hmmm. I can see the component that will kill you if they are removed." He studied them for a moment. "That's odd. I see that you and the princess have some type of connection through your curses. Most unexpected. I wouldn't have thought that was possible. That is likely interfering with the charms."

Rourke had suggested something similar when he had first examined them. I remembered he had emphasized that charms and curses don't mix well.

Advisor Yonge seemed perplexed. "Sir Coren, did you have any effects from the charm? It should have affected you the same as it did Princess Zophia."

I shook my head. "For me, the only thing it did was lock away Abhulengulus. It was like my curse took the hit for me."

Yonge frowned in contemplation. "Odd. I wouldn't have expected that." He gave a weak shrug. "It's not important. Now, I think I can release the worse parts of the charm, but I can't let you take them off just yet. The entrapment portion is entangled with your curses. I will need to study them some more before I can safely do that." He glanced up at me. "Will that be acceptable?"

I grinned. "Of course. I think we can live with that for a while longer. Anything to get Zofie back."

He seemed strangely amused. "Then let me work for a moment."

He closed his eyes, and I felt myst gathering. A violet glow enveloped the charms, gentle at first, but gradually growing in intensity. I felt my wrist begin to tingle. To my surprise, the tingling shifted to a burning hot, reminding me of the times Zofie and Abe had tried to warn me of some danger. Yonge frowned, but it quickly turned into a grin. The bracelets' glow intensified one last time and then extinguished.

Zofie shifted beside me. She straightened her shoulders and lifted her head like she was feeling out her body. Her face came alive, and she smiled. "I'm back."

A voice never sounded so good to me. I immediately took her in my arms, squeezing her tightly. She briefly hugged me back and then stepped away. She bowed to Yonge. "Thank you, Advisor. You have my deepest gratitude."

He gave a small smile. "My pleasure."

She leaned closer and took the key from Yonge's hand. "Now, with your permission Advisor, I would like to complete our end of the bargain. Then you can go ahead with your plans to move the Forever Nexus Shadow. I'm sure your guards can lead me there."

One of them immediately stepped forward.

Zofie patted me on the shoulder. "Coren, this won't take long. Why don't you and the others go back to our quarters and wait for me. Once I'm done, we can have a little party to celebrate my return. I'm sure the servants would be more than willing to help."

I was a little disappointed that she wasn't immediately coming with us. It seemed so out of character for her.

"Of course," I hesitantly agreed.

She smiled and turned to Fumiko. "My friend, would you accompany me? I don't want to have any misunderstandings while we do this. It's a very delicate procedure."

"Of course," Fumiko smiled. "I would love to."

As they stepped to the door, I couldn't shake the feeling that something wasn't right, but I couldn't put my finger on what it was. I called after her, "*A loved one's return is like fresh honey...*"

Zofie turned and smiled. "Why thank you, Coren. I'll join you in just a bit." She then followed the guard out of the room with Fumiko trailing. As I watched her leave, a tightness gripped my heart.

She hadn't completed my quote.

CHAPTER TWENTY-THREE

Deception

Spraggel, Cabrina, and I were escorted back to our rooms to wait for Zofie and Fumiko's return. Advisor Yonge had dismissed us with a single wave, and when we hesitated to leave, his guard wouldn't take no for an answer. I did manage to get in a question about restoring Abe, but all he said was that he would continue to work on it.

When we got back, we found our uneaten dinner had been cleared away and replaced with several kinds of dried fruits and nuts. Not that I minded—my stomach was in knots over Zofie. In my head, I kept going over the quote and why she hadn't completed it. I could easily rationalize that it wasn't anything bad. Perhaps she had been preoccupied and missed what I was trying to do. Or maybe I had chosen a passage just a little too obscure. But I quickly dismissed that. She *never* missed completing one of my quotes.

Never.

I asked Yanmei about having a party, and she said preparations had been made. The moment the princess returned, festive food and drink would be brought out. So there was nothing left to do but wait.

And wait.

Spraggel, nodding off in his chair, finally gave up and went to bed. He asked that I wake him when Zofie returned. Cabrina chose a different route and decided she wanted another bath. I could hear bits of conversation from inside as she and her Avenyts talked to each other. I couldn't help but wonder what our listeners thought of that.

And I waited some more. I stood watch at the window overlooking the dark garden. *Where were Zofie and Fumiko?* I began to worry that something had happened. I had asked Yanmei several times if she could take me to her but was politely declined each time. She explained that very few people were allowed close to the Crystal Vault, where the Forever Nexus Shadow was kept.

Just after midnight, Yanmei appeared and gave me a written note from Zofie. She then said she was retiring and left. A moment later, two of the huge guards took position outside the door. I suspected it was to prevent us from wandering during the night.

I frantically tore into the note. *"Coren,"* it read. *"We have run into a problem. Opening the vault is taking longer than I thought. Sorry, I'll join you as soon as I can—Zophia."*

I tossed the paper on the table in frustration and started to pace. *Where were they?*

I checked on Spraggel to find him snoring soundly, but Cabrina wasn't in her room. I guess she was still in the bath. I circled back around, jerked up the note, and stepped to my room.

Hoping it magically said something different, I paused beside the bed and read the note once again. It wasn't like her to ignore me. The signature at the bottom drew my eyes. She had signed it Zophia. She never signed her notes Zophia—it was always Zofie. Plain old Zofie. I wadded up the paper in my hand, convinced now more than ever something was wrong. And I needed to find her and get to the bottom of this. *But how?*

In my frustration, I blindly threw the wadded up paper toward the open door. Unfortunately, Cabrina chose that moment to step into it. The wad bounced harmlessly off her chest.

She frowned. "You could have just asked me to leave."

I smiled sheepishly. "I'm sorry. I didn't see you there." I bent down and picked up the paper. "Did you need something?"

She entered and sat down on the end of my bed. "With Zofie and Fumiko gone, this place is too quiet. Plus those big guards out there are creepy. I was hoping you would play a game with me to take my mind off them."

I frowned. I really needed to figure out how to contact Zofie. "I don't know..."

But I stopped when I noticed Cabrina frown and flick her eyes toward my bed. Did she want me to sit too?

"Please," she begged. "Just something simple. Mistress Fumiko and I were playing a staring game earlier. How about that? I bet you can't outstare me. She couldn't."

What was she up to? I sat on the bed a respectful distance away from her. "All right. But just for a little while."

She grinned. "First one to blink loses. On three. One... two... three!"

Suddenly, we were surrounded by a glowing blue myst barrier. She smiled smugly.

I pointed to the barrier around us. "What are you doing?"

"It's so we can talk in private," she stated matter of factly. She grinned and bounced over to the glowing blue wall. "Pretty good, huh? On the outside, it looks like we're quietly staring at each other." She put her hands behind her back and rocked on her heels. "Cabrina thought it up. She's getting better at using her myst." I detected a note of pride from No-name.

"Won't they know what you're doing?"

She shrugged. "They might, but it's the best we could come up with."

I nodded. "What did you want to talk about?"

"That advisor's myst working." She sighed. "While it may have looked impressive, it wasn't really. He only adjusted the princess's charm and didn't even touch yours."

"I suspected as much."

"But he did do something to mine."

I looked up at her in surprise, and she turned away.

"What did he do?"

She sighed deeply. "Sir Coren, please don't hate me," she looked up at me in apprehension. "But I lied to you."

My eyes went up in concern. Had I trusted her too much? While she looked and acted like a girl, she was still a Dark Avenyts. "In what way?"

She grimaced. "Cabrina knows what I'm about to tell you. It's what we were talking about a few moments ago. She's been saying we should tell you ever since you saved us from Mistress Fumiko's questioning. But I was afraid, and we held off." She looked up at me. "You see, the charms I placed on you and the princess are quite powerful and require a lot of myst to activate. So much that it would have completely depleted our myst." She gazed at me levelly. "After I activated the charms, *Cabrina and I were supposed to die.*"

My eyes widened. It explained a lot. "That's why you don't have any directives. You weren't going to need any."

She looked down and nodded. "The entrapment portion never included me. It was only for you and the princess. I lied about it because I was afraid you would kill Cabrina. And I couldn't allow that to happen. You could have cut mine off at any time, killed me even, and nothing would have happened." She licked her lips. "Only now, Advisor Yonge activated it. I can't take it off now."

Which meant Yonge was likely behind Zofie's strange behavior. But one more thing bothered me. "You said the charms were supposed to drain you. But they didn't. How did you survive?"

Cabrina took a deep breath. She stepped close and gazed at me for a moment before answering. "Someone saved us. It was in that fraction of a second that the spell was activating. All of Cabrina's myst was draining away, and we were dying. The pain was horrible. I remember telling her I was so sorry, but I had no choice. I could only do what I was made to do." She grabbed the front of my shirt and looked up at me with tears in her eyes. "And you know what she told me? She said she forgave me. I couldn't understand why, *still* can't understand. What I did was killing her. And yet she forgave me." She released my shirt. An expression of wonder came over her. "And then I felt a presence behind me. A big presence. It was nothing like I had ever felt before. And this deep booming voice spoke to me saying, *It's not yet your time, little one. You are everything I hoped for.*" Cabrina gazed into my eyes. "It was Abhulengulus. He did something. Opened some hidden gate, and myst flowed through us. A lot of it." She looked away. "That's when we passed out."

My mouth gaped open. I remembered the event. At the time, I had thought Abhulengulus was speaking to me. But it had been to Noname. He had not only acted to provide her myst, but had simultaneously deflected whatever harm the charm had intended for me, taking it on himself. I sighed. There was no doubt, Abe had saved us both. Not for the first time, I wondered at Abe's depth. He was much, much more than he appeared to be.

Which meant I had another reason to confront Yonge. I wanted Abe back.

"We need to find Zofie and Fumiko." I looked toward the door and the guards that were standing outside it. "But we have to get past them first. A direct assault won't work. We have no weapons, and their armor is likely myst shielded."

Cabrina shrugged. "Easy. Just be ready, and don't worry about me. I'll catch up to you later." She sat back down on the bed in the same spot she'd been in before erecting the barrier. She grinned. "Now play along." The blue glow suddenly vanished.

She rubbed her eyes. "I don't believe it, you beat me," resuming the ruse she had started. "Maybe we can have a rematch. But first, I need to visit the bath."

Cabrina rose and strode into the common room but paused in its center...

And gave a blood-curdling scream.

Both of the guards immediately stepped into the room, alert for any attackers. She ran to the nearest and put her arms around him. "I'm so afraid! I saw someone heading toward the myst light. He looked so creepy!" Suddenly a myst barrier surrounded them. I could hear Cabrina scream again. "He turned out the light! Don't let him get me!"

My eyes went wide. Why that little... genius. She had put up another myst barrier. Only this one was black inside. While I could see in, they couldn't see out. She waved at me and grinned.

I quickly ran out the door and down the hall, trying to remember the way we had come and the direction I had seen them go.

It was long past midnight and well on the way to early morning, so I didn't encounter anyone in the halls. I couldn't help but think this was just too easy. I had no doubt these corridors were filled with various myst devices to track movement. So it would only be a little more before I was discovered.

Which way?

I shook my head. Too bad Fumiko hadn't shared her knowledge of the palace along with her fighting skills. Even just knowing the buildings would have helped.

I suddenly noticed a flicker of motion in the corner of my vision. But when I turned toward it, I didn't detect anything. I shook my head. I must be seeing things. The corridors had been darkened for the night with only the occasional myst lantern producing illumination. The dim light provided ample opportunities to mistake something.

Then I noticed it again. I whipped around and stared at where I thought it had been. And I saw it. A tiny patch of shadow, no bigger than my hand and just slightly darker than the rest, was moving ever so slowly along the wall.

Looking at the patch reminded me of Fumiko for some reason. I took a step toward it, and it moved away the same amount. I took another step and another, but it maintained its distance. I moved faster, breaking into a trot and then into a run. It flowed from one corridor wall to another, going one way at an intersection and then the other.

It suddenly stopped on the floor in front of a set of stairs leading down, and when I caught up, the patch of shadow slid down the stairs disappearing into the dim light. I followed cautiously.

It got darker the farther I went, finally going completely black when I reached the bottom. I pulled out my faithful glowing amulet and was shocked to find one of the guards looming in front of me.

I jumped back, prepared to run, but he gave no reaction and stood there unmoving. I held my light up and waved my hand in front of him. Not even a blink.

That was certainly odd. I hesitantly touched the guard's throat and could feel his skin was warm, and he had a slow pulse. Sleeping maybe? It was certainly odd. I quickly moved to the door behind him and pulled it open enough to slip inside. A weak myst lantern illuminated another set of stairs leading farther down into the depths. A damp smell assaulted my nose, and I knew instantly what it was—their dungeon. They might call it something different, but this is where the prisoners were kept.

I went down the stairs and came to a narrow corridor with three small doors aligned on one side. I heard someone moan and the clank of chain against stone.

I stepped forward cautiously. Not the first one, nor the second, but at the third door, the occupant broke into a fit of coughing. I went back to the immobile guard, and taking the keys from his belt, I returned to the cell and unlocked it. The creak of the door sounded extraordinary loud as I opened it to find its lone occupant chained to the wall.

"You came," whispered Fumiko. Her voice was raspy as if she had been screaming. I ran forward, horrified at what I saw. Even in the feeble light of my amulet, I could tell she had been severely beaten—a trail of dried blood ran from her nose and lip. And her face was cut and battered with gradually darkening bruises. Her left eye had already started to swell shut. Her clothes were torn, and I could see splotches of dried blood on her arms and legs.

I knelt before her and started trying the keys on the ring, finally finding one that worked.

"You came," she said again as if not believing I was really there. "I cast a shadow. I was praying you would see it."

"What happened?"

Her manacles came free, and she collapsed into my arms. I gently lowered her to the floor. "I was ambushed. There were too many of them to fight. They beat me."

"What did they do with Zofie?"

She looked up at me with her good eye. "She led me right to them. And when they attacked, she just watched." Fumiko licked her lips. "It's not like her."

I frowned. "I noticed something odd about her too. I almost wonder if that is really Zofie in her body."

Fumiko looked down. "I have heard some things about Yonge. You saw how he used those bugs." She gazed at me levelly. "What if he can do that to people?"

"You mean like a Dark Avenyts? Is he one of them?"

She tried to sit up, and I helped get her upright.

Fumiko shook her head. "I don't think so. These rumors circulated even when I was still one of the emperor's butterflies. I warned you not to trust him. The man is evil." She muttered under her breath. "I should have listened to my own advice."

She grabbed my shoulder and tried to pull herself up. She stood slowly, favoring her right side. "They discovered my cracked ribs."

I helped her out of the cell, and we went up the stairs. Like me, Fumiko was puzzled by the guard seeming to be asleep. I put the keys back and helped myself to one of his knives.

Just as I turned away, I heard the guard's breathing change. I immediately turned to hide, but Fumiko reacted faster and covered us in shadow. We watched as the guard suddenly came alive and went into the dungeon. I quickly got Fumiko to climb on my back, and I carried her up the stairs to the empty corridor. I put her down, but she staggered and fell to her knees.

"This is not going to work," she mumbled while holding her side. She closed her eyes, and I felt myst gathering. She glowed briefly and then straightened. The pain on her face lessened, and her movements seemed smoother.

"What did you do?" I asked, puzzled.

"I used some of my myst to reinforce my body."

"You healed yourself?"

She shook her head. "No, I have no such power. I just made it so I no longer feel the pain of my injuries. But I have to be careful with it since they're still there."

I frowned. "That can't be good for you."

She gazed at me a moment and then turned away to point down the corridor. "That way," she said. "And quickly. He will know I escaped in only a few moments."

"Dammit, Fumiko. You're hurting yourself, aren't you. You can't do that."

She glared at me. "Coren, I love you dearly, but you are not my keeper. I do what I choose. So don't lecture me." She bounced her finger on my chest. "Yonge has killed or hurt everyone I cherished. And now he's done it to Zofie. I will not allow it to continue." She stood and held out her hand to me. "Now, are you going to follow me to the Forever Nexus Shadow, or do I leave you behind?"

I sighed and took her hand. "You've been taking lessons from Zofie."

One corner of her mouth curled up. "Maybe. We have been comparing notes."

She turned, and I followed her down the corridor.

I wasn't sure what time it was, but it had to be early morning. As Fumiko led us carefully through the corridors, we had to occasionally hide from a few yawning servants as they made their way to their stations. There was one peculiar one carrying quite the pile of dirty bed linens. We encountered her on three different occasions. I think she was lost. Fumiko successfully hid us in shadow each time.

Eventually, we passed into what appeared to be an older section of the palace. The walls and floor were of different color stone and looked more worn. Fumiko paused when our passage intersected with what looked like a broad corridor. She peeked around the corner and immediately drew back. She motioned me forward to have a look.

At the end of the broad corridor was a massive set of doors with two of the heavily armored guards in front of them. The doors were open, but the view inside was blocked by thick curtains just past the door.

We moved back down the corridor away from the intersection to a small alcove. We sat down to rest a moment.

"The vault is through those doors," Fumiko whispered. "I've never been inside, so I'm not sure what to expect beyond them."

"Think your shadow can get us inside?" I asked softly.

Fumiko frowned and shook her head. "The curtains are likely meant to detect entry. Even a shadow wouldn't prevent us from disturbing them."

I sighed. "Then what we need is a distraction. I guess I could..."

Fumiko held up a hand.

Farther down the corridor, a servant turned the corner heading straight toward us, carrying a pile of dirty bed linens. I frowned in puzzlement. It was the same servant we had passed several times before.

Fumiko ramped up her shadow to cover us, but just as the servant drew even, she paused. "Sir Coren?" she whispered. "Mistress Fumiko?"

I looked closer, and peeking out from the pile of linens, was none other than Cabrina dressed as a servant. Creator knows where she got the uniform.

"I've been looking for you. Do you know how many times I've traveled up and down this corridor? Thankfully no one questions a linen servant." She chuckled. "Something about dirty laundry makes people squeamish."

I blinked at her in surprise. It was definitely her, but now her hair was a much darker shade, perfectly straight, and her eyes had changed to match the shape of those from this region.

I pointed at her in puzzlement. "How?"

She brightened. "You mean my illusion? Pretty good, isn't it? We saw Mistress Fumiko do it once and thought we might be able to replicate it. It was easier than we thought. Cabrina's starting to get the hang of using her myst."

I smiled. "You're just in time. We need a distraction. Think you can handle it."

"Coren!" interrupted Fumiko. "She's a Dark Avenyts. We can't let her near the Forever Nexus Shadow."

The youth shrugged. "Then I won't go in the vault. I don't want to be where I'm not wanted. Now about your distraction..." She looked up at the ceiling. "What's that?" She was listening to her host.

Cabrina smiled. "That's an excellent idea. Do you want to lead?" She paused. "All right then. And don't worry, I'll be ready to help if you get stuck." She looked over at us, wearing the expression of a mother whose child had just learned to ride a horse. No-name really was trying to help Cabrina become more confident. Maybe there was hope for the young Avenyts.

The youth's expression subtly changed, and I knew the real Cabrina was in control. Her face was a mask of determination. "W-w-wish me luck," she said. Then she paused. "Mistress Fumiko, how do you say, 'I'm sorry' in your native language."

Fumiko said it to her, and Cabrina repeated it back perfectly—or least to my ears, it sounded that way.

Nodding once, Cabrina did an about-face and lurched down the corridor, seeming to struggle with her load. When she reached the intersection, she turned toward the guards. We quickly moved to the corner and listened.

One of the guards barked something in their native language.

"He's telling her to halt," Fumiko translated. "That servants are forbidden."

I looked around the corner. Cabrina immediately repeated the phrase she had just learned and tried to bow. Naturally, the pile of linens became unbalanced, and when she tried to catch them, managed to throw all of them up into the air. They seemed to go higher than I would have expected, so there was likely a little myst push involved.

They settled over the guards, who frantically began to pull them off, but had trouble due to their armor. Cabrina stepped up to them, continuously repeating, "I'm sorry." But in her supposed aid, managed to keep them entangled.

Fumiko and I took the chance and slipped past the struggling guards into the vault. Behind us, Cabrina kept right on apologizing.

I couldn't help but smile. Cabrina and No-name really made quite the team.

Fumiko and I carefully weaved our way through the layers of curtains. We finally came to the last of them and paused to take in the large room before us.

What we saw was totally unlike anything I had seen before. A colossal oval crystal floated in the center of the room. There were no strings or supports of any kind. It just hung there like it had forgotten to fall.

And it was huge. It had to be two or three times a person's height and had what seemed to be millions of facets carved into it. They caught the light in the room and reflected it back, making it a dazzling display of twinkling light. I remembered looking at similar jewels when I had been shopping with Zofie. While I was not an expert by any means, I fully believed it to be a giant, perfectly cut diamond. I had only ever seen tiny ones, with the largest I had ever heard about being no bigger than your fist. So one that size had to be a myst construct.

It appeared to be almost perfectly clear—all except for a single darker facet at its center. It was a light gray, and unlike the others, did not twinkle.

A platform of dark wood had been constructed next to the jewel within easy reach of the grayish facet. It had a series of ramps leading to the top.

But that was not the only surprise. Zofie stood at the base of the platform, her expression slack and staring off into the distance. And along with her was Advisor Yonge reclining in a chair with wheels. He was saying something to Zofie, but I couldn't make out the words.

Several of the huge guards were stationed strategically around the room. That was going to make getting closer difficult. The best I could think of was to sneak up on Yonge under Fumiko's shadow and then threaten him to release Zofie. The plan felt a little weak, but it was the best I could come up with.

I quickly explained my plan to Fumiko, and she agreed. We were just about ready to leap out when I caught movement on the floor next to me. Glancing down, I saw a cricket—it's antenna moving excitedly.

"Ah, Sir Coren and Fumiko," it said, using Yonge's voice. "Just the people I wanted to see."

"Now!" I yelled. Fumiko and I sprang forward.

A dagger suddenly appeared in Zofie's hand, and she held it to her throat. She grinned wickedly. It was so unlike her it gave me chills.

"I wouldn't do that if I were you," the cricket said. "One more step and she dies."

We froze in place. It only took moments for a guard to pluck the knife from my hand. We were roughly shoved toward Zofie and Yonge. Then with a hand on our shoulders, we were forced to our knees. Those guards were incredibly strong.

"You're the one," I shouted. "Why did you do it? I thought you were going to help us."

The cricket landed in front of me and spoke. "The answer should be obvious..."

Zofie took up the thought. "...Just look at my body..."

Yonge finished, "I'm dying."

Then all the guards, Zofie, the cricket, and Yonge himself all said in unison. "And I don't want to die."

CHAPTER TWENTY-FOUR

Opening
The Vault

The talking through several bodies was unnerving. Likely Yonge's intent. He was maintaining control over at least seven people inside the room, and Creator knew how many outside. If they wore one of his charms, then he could likely take over at any time and treat them merely as an extension of himself. I was amazed he could control so many at once. Or maybe not completely at once. I thought of the guard that had been in front of the dungeon's entrance. Maybe he switched back and forth between them and put the ones he wasn't actively controlling into a kind of sleep. And the switching wasn't completely instantaneous. I had noticed a very slight lag in the time it took to go from one body to another.

I cocked my jaw. I couldn't let his body-switching throw me off. "What's your dying got to do with us?"

Zofie lowered her knife and stepped over to Yonge. She patted him on the shoulder. "This body has a wasting disease. One the healers are unable to correct. I have now reached the point where I can barely move, and if it wasn't for some clever myst devices, I wouldn't even be alive now." She looked over her shoulder at the crystal. "But all that ends as soon as I open this vault. And for that, I needed the key."

It suddenly made sense. The charms Cabrina had put on us had been obtained from Yonge. I had been told several times how unusual it would be for the Dark Avenyts to use them.

But that didn't explain everything. It had definitely been a Dark Avenyts that had given them to Cabrina, so they were involved somehow. Also, I had to wonder what Lilith's role was in all this. It appeared she wanted to prevent Yonge from getting the key. And what would sealing away Zofie and Abe have to do with him dying? I seemed to still be missing some important pieces.

Zofie began to pace. "It might be because of her curse. I had thought she would have removed it by now. Or it might also be because of intent. Perhaps the vault knows the princess does not have her own mind." She nodded to herself. "It might even be that she doesn't have the ability to open it." She sighed. "I guess we'll have to...."

Zofie suddenly looked up and strode over to the kneeling Fumiko. She kicked her hard in the ribs. It was on the side she had injured.

Fumiko moaned before coughing up blood—splattering dark spots on the tiles before her.

My beautiful Zofie's face screwed up into an evil grin. "Don't even think about attacking me." She reached down and removed a small dagger from Fumiko's hand. "Ever resourceful, aren't we." She passed the weapon off to one of the guards.

Zofie stopped in front of me. She looked thoughtful. "And then we have Coren." The guard's pressure on my shoulder eased. "Stand up."

I did as instructed.

"Remove her curse."

My reply was immediate. "I can't. Abe is inactive due to your charm." I held up my wrist.

Her eyes widened, but it was the cricket that came forward. "So that's why you aren't under my control. Your curse is interfering."

One of the guards came forward and lifted Fumiko up by the throat. Her feet danced, seeking purchase as she slowly strangled.

"I'm going to release you," said Zofie, gazing at me levelly. "I want you to remove her curse. But don't even think about causing trouble, or your dear Fumiko will die. Oh, and you should probably hurry. Sounds like she's having a little trouble breathing."

Despite the guard's grip on her throat, Fumiko managed a tiny shake of her head.

"No," I said firmly. "Not until you release Zofie and put Fumiko down."

A chuckle came from Yonge's body. "Why should I? They're my insurance that you obey?"

I frowned. "Then I guess we're at a stalemate."

All of Yonge's bodies paused, like he was thinking.

"Hmmm. I guess I could," said the roach. "The charm may be interfering with opening the vault."

"Seems reasonable," said the guard behind me.

Yonge himself spoke, "I'm not sure I should though."

The guard holding Fumiko said, "I should just kill her now."

"She is a threat," said the guard behind Zofie.

I began to suspect that the years of controlling people had done something to Yonge. I didn't think he was completely sane.

I interrupted the back and forth. "Well? At least release Fumiko while you make up your mind."

Fumiko was released, and she collapsed in a gasping heap.

Yonge seemed insulted. "Make up my mind? I was merely stalling."

Just then, Cabrina walked into the room still wearing her servant's uniform. Her illusion was gone, and her face was emotionless. My eyes went wide. Yonge must have done something to her charm too.

Cabrina suddenly broke into a cruel smile. "Since Fumiko isn't providing enough incentive," said Yonge through the youth. "I guess I need to use this one too."

She held out her hand as she casually walked past my guard. Without missing a beat, he handed her a knife. She stepped up to me and took my wrist. "Fitting, isn't it, that the one who gave you the charms should take them off."

Cabrina deftly sliced off my charm and then did the same to Zofie.

Suddenly, Zofie's eyes changed. They grew wide in shock. There was no doubt in my mind this was the real Zofie.

"Coren!" she exclaimed and threw her arms around me. I hugged her to me tightly despite our situation.

But it only lasted a moment. We disengaged, and she turned toward Yonge. "I demand you release us this instant," she shouted, with the full tone of one in authority.

Now that, was my Zofie.

The cricket hopped forward. "Of course, Princess. Just as soon as Coren removes your curse."

I rubbed my wrist like a manacle had been removed. "And what about Cabrina."

"No," the youth said, pointing the knife to her own throat. "This one, I keep for insurance."

"I'm surprised you can control an Avenyts," I said.

Cabrina smiled. "I don't have to. I merely need the body."

"Now, remove her curse," demanded the roach.

I had no choice. "Abe?" I asked.

Hello Coren. It's been a while. Wish I could say it's good to be back. For someone with meat for brains, you certainly are a trouble magnet.

I couldn't help but smile. "I would definitely trade my brain for a little less trouble."

Your brain? No one would want it!

While I would never have admitted it just a short while ago, I had missed the old bastard.

I sighed. "I'm assuming you heard. I need to remove Zofie's curse." I stepped forward, but Zofie put a restraining hand on my chest. She looked concerned.

Well, about that. You really need to talk to the princess first.

"Why?" I asked. "Let's just do this." And without pause, I put a finger on her chest and said the words. "Your curse to my curse."

Nothing happened.

Uh... Coren. I can't remove her curse. Like I said, you really need to talk to the princess.

Zofie gave me a hesitant smile, no doubt listening in on our conversation.

I was puzzled.

"Abe, why can't you?"

Remember back on Mount Eternal when you asked me to remove that curse from the high priest, and I couldn't. It's one of the few restrictions with myst. I can't do something that creates a contradiction.

"I remember that. But what has that got to do..." I trailed off as it hit me. My mouth fell open as I looked into my beloved's eyes.

"I had planned to tell you at the picnic." She glanced irritated at the roach. "But things got in the way."

Then she smiled. "We're going to have a baby."

My mouth fell open as my less than ideal brain tried to process her words.

A baby.

A complex set of emotions when through my head. *I was going to be a father.* I felt woefully inadequate for the task.

Assuming we lived that long.

"I am unable to remove her curse," I announced.

Cabrina pressed the dagger point a little deeper into her throat—a thin trickle of blood oozed around it. "Remove it. You know I'll kill this girl. And then if you still won't, I'll kill each of your party one by one. I think I'll start with Spraggel."

I glanced at Zofie and then back to Yonge. "It's not that I don't want to. It's that I can't. It won't come off."

Cabrina lowered her knife. She looked to Zofie and squatted down in front of her—the youth's head level with Zofie's stomach. "Oh, I see," she said with an exasperated sigh. "And here I thought the princess wouldn't whore herself out to the first commoner she came across."

Cabrina stood, but it was the cricket that continued. "I will just have a healer expel the unborn one. I have no need of it."

Zofie jerked as if punched. She placed a protective hand on her stomach. "No! You mustn't."

Cabrina stood and gave Zofie a puzzled expression. "Then tell me how we're going to open the vault while you're still cursed."

She licked her lips. "Maybe it's not the curse. Maybe it's my *will* to open it. Since you were controlling me, my will was not being expressed. I'm sure the ancients thought of that."

The cricket leaped toward the giant jewel. "It could be."

Yonge himself mused. "Definitely possible."

The guards all answered in unison. "Then let's try it."

At the guard's direction, Zofie headed up the ramp to the platform. One of the guards took Yonge's wheeled chair, and I followed, with Fumiko and her guard bringing up the rear.

Zofie stepped up to the jewel. A guard approached and handed her the long silver cylinder that was the Griffin's Key. She looked at the darkened facet on the diamond's surface and then back to the cylinder in her hand. Her gaze did the circuit again, then she took a step back and looked up at the entire vault. I could tell she was thinking. She finally turned toward Yonge. "Something doesn't seem right. In the other artifacts, there was either a passphrase or multiple people were required to activate them. Is there any record of such a thing?"

Cabrina frowned. "A phrase? I am not aware of any such thing. There was no mention of it from my scholars."

The cricket jumped up to perch on the rail around the platform. "All we know is that if the Forever Nexus Shadow had to be moved, the Xernow heir would provide the key."

Zofie looked to me. "Was there anything in the key's chamber that might be a clue?"

I shook my head. "The guardian only said he was sorry to see me."

She looked back at the crystal. She stepped forward and placed her palm against the darkened facet. "I am Princess Zophia Olwenna Xernow, the current Xernow heir. I command you to open."

The crystal seemed to shudder and then gave out five beautiful, musical tones. I could feel the platform vibrate with each one. The sequence was strangely familiar. *Where had I heard it before?*

The cricket jumped up and down excitedly. "It didn't do that last time."

Cabrina looked at us in surprise. "But what do the tones mean?"

Then I knew where I had heard it. It was from Zofie. She would sometimes hum it to herself when she was stressed or anxious.

I noticed Zofie was tearing up. She glanced my way and gave me a half-smile. "It's the lullaby Father used to sing to me all the time when I was a young girl. He told me it had been in our family for generations." She put a hand on her middle. "And when I got older, I was to sing it to my child." She looked back to the crystal. "Now I know why."

She placed her hand on the facet again. The tones sounded once more, but this time she was ready and started to sing. The jewel took up the song with her, and together they sang.

I had never heard her sing before, and I was struck by its beauty. As I listened to her, I couldn't help but wonder how many more times I was going to fall in love with this woman.

As they sang, a line appeared on the huge jewel running from top to bottom. And when they finished the song, the gray facet turned a pale blue, and a small round slot appeared in it. Zofie took the Griffin's Key and inserted it in the hole, which fit the key perfectly. She then pushed it home.

A loud gong sounded three times, like a warning bell. Then the jewel slowly parted along the vertical line, and a puff of chill fog rose from it, carrying the scent of times long past. As the vault continued to open, it exposed a small chamber inside, brightly lit from the glow of its crystal walls. A round marble pedestal, identical to those we had encountered with the other ancient artifacts, rose from the floor. There was only enough space in the chamber to barely walk around the pedestal. On the stand rested a perfectly shaped pyramid about as big as my fist and made of some type of metal that was a deep cerulean blue. If you held it up to a clear sky, the color would have matched perfectly.

As I gazed at it, I thought I saw patterns flowing across its surface, like ripples over a pond. It hurt my eyes to look at it.

The guards pulled Zofie, Fumiko, and me away from the jewel, while a third reached in to take it.

As soon as the guard touched it, there was a thunderous crackle, and the guard instantly turned to dust.

Zofie gasped, and I flinched away. Fumiko just stared at it in stoic silence, a hand on her injured ribs.

Yonge himself cackled. "Ho, Ho! I wasn't expecting that. The ancients certainly meant business."

I looked down at the small pile of gray dust on the floor of the chamber. What power the ancients must have had to reduce someone instantly to ashes. How much had we forgotten? And then I had an odd thought. What if we hadn't forgotten so much as been forced to forget.

Zofie looked over to Yonge. "We've done what you've wanted. The vault is open. Now let us go."

The cricket, Cabrina, and the other guards all laughed. "I disagree Princess. While the vault is indeed open, I'm not able to touch what I need." The cricket suddenly jumped—arching through the air to land on the Forever Nexus Shadow. It too was instantly turned to ash.

Cabrina spoke up. "So even a bug can't get past the defense. What to do, what to do?"

Immediately, another guard stepped forward, drew his sword, and gently touched it with the tip. That guard was also instantly turned to ash.

I was struck by how closely this pedestal resembled the others we had encountered. And each one had followed a pattern. I couldn't tell from this angle, but could that be a small square at the back?

One of the guards roughly shoved Zofie forward. "Let's see if a Xernow heir can remove it."

"Wait!" I shouted.

All the guards looked at me.

"Let me try." I moved to enter the jewel.

"Coren, no!" Zofie yelled.

I looked back at her just before the chamber's threshold and smiled. "I think this one is for me."

I carefully stepped around the pedestal until I came to the side facing away from the others. As I thought, there was a small square of marble with the impression of a hand in it. I took a deep breath and gave a reassuring smile to Zofie. Then I pressed my own left one into it.

The marble felt warm and smooth. For a moment, nothing happened, and I wondered if perhaps I had been wrong. Then suddenly, I was sucked into the world of curses.

The world all around me was the gray on gray I had come to associate with the realm. It was like all color had been filtered out.

Before me stood a stick-figure person with the characteristic large round head. Only inside this one was the image of a pedestal. It seemed to be considering me. "What do you want?" it spat. "You're never supposed to bother my slumber."

I felt a presence at my back. Glancing over my shoulder, I saw that Abe stood with me, also in his stick figure form. He put a thin hand on my shoulder.

I turned back to the pedestal figure. "I am here to take the Forever Nexus Shadow."

"You can't have it!" it snapped.

"Why not? Have we not done everything we were supposed to in order to remove it."

"It's never supposed to be removed. Never!"

"Then why was a way built into it for the Thief of Curses to remove it?"

It shook its head in agitation. "I do not know." It looked up at me in worry. "But I do know that if you take it, all the defenses against the dark enemy will collapse. The world will be at their mercy. And just because you have Abhulengulus behind you doesn't mean it's right."

Abe surprised me by speaking. "Be it right or wrong, it is their decision. If you deny them, then aren't you doing exactly like the dark ones and making the decision for them. Our role is to help them, advise them, but never, ever decide for them."

The pedestal figure seemed to consider Abe. It then turned away and flicked a stick hand in dismissal. "Take it then. I am not responsible for what happens next. My watch is done."

And with that, I found myself back in front of the pedestal. A moment later, the illumination coming from inside the crystal went out, leaving the jewel dull and dark. I reached forward and plucked the Forever Nexus Shadow from its cradle.

And outside the vault, I heard Zofie gasp in alarm. "It's gone," she looked at me in horror. "I can't feel it anymore. The Grand Tapestry is just... gone."

And Yonge started laughing. I stared at him in shock. He'd known the barrier would come down once the nexus was removed. Yet he did it anyway. He just didn't care.

The guards took the nexus from me and indicated we should head down the ramp off the platform. Cabrina extracted the key from the now-dead crystal and followed just behind. Just as we were about to reach the bottom, several panicked officials ran into the room.

"Advisor!" their leader yelled. "The Grand Tapestry has disappeared! We're completely unprotected. What should we do?" They tried to come closer, but the guards held them back.

"Fools!" he shouted. "Prepare the troops. We've plans to handle this. Now don't bother me again."

They cringed at his anger, bowed, and immediately left.

As we reached the floor, I glanced toward the room's exit. We needed to get out of not just this room but the entire palace. Maybe even the whole empire. I had a feeling things were about to get really crazy.

The empire had been protected by The Grand Tapestry for a thousand years. And in that time, had built up quite a few grudges in the surrounding kingdoms. But now with the shield gone, those grudges were likely going to come home. And the empire had no idea how to protect themselves.

Zofie must have been thinking likewise. She turned to Yonge. "We've done as you asked. Now let us go."

Cabrina stepped forward. "I will free you," Yonge said through her. "But there is someone who requested you stay until he retrieves the nexus. He'll be here shortly."

"Who?" Zofie asked.

Suddenly, a long-range portal appeared in the chamber. I would have thought that the palace would have been protected against such intrusions. But they likely lost that protection with the removal of the nexus.

As it slowly materialized, the guards moved toward it, forming a line and saluting.

Even though I had no way to protect her, I moved closer to Zofie, placing myself between her and the portal. Fumiko must have felt the same and moved to stand with me. Something bad was going to happen. I could feel it.

A cold breeze drifted out of the portal, and a moment later, a lone man stepped through. He was young, still in his teens, with dark red hair the same shade as Zofie's.

My princess gasped, and I clenched my fists. I think Fumiko growled.

The young man—conniver, murderer, and destroyer of Brethnach's defenses—came to stand before us.

"Hello, sister," he said with a cruel smile on his face.

It was Wynn.

CHAPTER TWENTY-FIVE

Unlocking
The Forbidden

Zofie's brother, and murderer of their father, stood before us with his lips twisted into a half-smirk. Zofie was white with rage—her fists balled up tight. She visibly shook. A guard extended his sword in front of her to make sure she didn't do anything rash.

Wynn briefly glanced our way but otherwise ignored us and went to Yonge. He bowed. "I have come as we agreed, your excellency. Is everything ready?"

Cabrina clapped her hands. "The Forever Nexus Shadow is ready for you, and the Griffin's Key is right here." She waved it back and forth for emphasis. "And the last component is on his way here."

"Excellent!" said Wynn smiling. He rocked on his heels. "Let's do this quickly, so I don't hold you up. I believe you have an empire to save."

Zofie couldn't hold back her rage any longer. "You murderer!" she shouted.

He turned his smile in our direction. "Well, sister. I must say you're looking well. Especially for someone who continually eludes death. You have to be the luckiest person on the planet."

She spoke through clenched teeth. "I happen to have one excellent knight."

"Evidently." His lips pulled back into the perfect smile. But his eyes were dead cold. "But they do say that the third time's the charm."

Zofie wasn't fazed. "Just what evil are you up to now?"

He chuckled. "You'll see. After all, this is Advisor Yonge's show." He turned to me. "And hello to you, Sir Coren. Too bad you didn't join me when you had the chance. That offer is long past now but just think. You could be on the winning side now." He grinned.

I frowned, reminding myself that despite his youthful looks, he was evil.

"You're the last person I wanted to see."

Wynn's eyebrows went up. "Charming as always. You never know, I might be able to arrange it so that *I am* the last person you see."

He turned to Fumiko. "My dear, you no doubt remember me, but I don't believe we've formally met. Last we spoke, an Avenyts in my service was perfecting you. A pity Coren destroyed her. She was one of my favorites. I thought she made you kind of cute."

Fumiko's eyes were on fire, but she said nothing.

Wynn looked up. "Where's Master Spraggel? Coren never goes more than a few feet without him."

Yonge himself chuckled. "The old man is trying to get in to see the emperor. He doesn't realize that I've been controlling his excellency for years. Apparently, they worked together in their younger days."

I shook my head in disbelief. Is there anyone Spraggel didn't know?

Cabrina moved to Yonge's chair and pushed him forward. "Our agreement, Lord Wynn," he said. "I would have it now. Then you can do with the Forever Nexus Shadow as you see fit."

With his back to Yonge, Wynn frowned at the interruption and rolled his eyes. Then immediately pasted on a huge grin and turned to his host. "Why of course, your excellency." He moved to stand beside him.

Just then, a young man was escorted into the chamber. He wore loose-fitting pants and fine slippers, but no shirt. My eyes went large. He was a perfect specimen of manhood—tall, dark eyes, black hair, with arms and chest practically rippling with muscle. My tastes definitely ran toward the female gender, but I could see where this man might tempt some to change their preference.

Wynn smiled, his eyes going up in surprise. "I'm impressed Advisor Yonge. That is quite a nice body."

"Isn't it?" Cabrina smiled broadly. "I've been preparing for this for years. Carefully selecting candidates to pick just the right one."

I heard a whisper beside me. "Hao?"

I turned to Fumiko. Her eyes were wide, an expression of utter shock on her face.

Cabrina nodded. "I see you recognize your fellow butterfly."

"Why?" she whispered.

"Surely, you've not grown that stupid. This body of mine is dying, giving me no choice but to obtain a new one. So why not choose the best?"

Fumiko shook her head in denial. "It can't be."

Cabrina nodded emphatically. "I only wanted the best for my new body—a truly superb one. I didn't care if they were male or female. My only requirement was that they have some sort of royal lineage." She frowned. "But then number one messed herself up, and I had to settle for number two."

Fumiko looked at him in horror.

Yonge himself spoke. "That's right. He's taking your place. You were supposed to be the one."

Fumiko's eyes went wide in shock. "No."

"Did you really think the Emperor's Butterflies were just a bunch of well-trained assassins? If that were the case, then why have the eliminations? No, my dear, you were all nothing more than my insects, my beautiful butterflies. With each of you dancing for my pleasure." He smiled cruelly. "And if you stopped being beautiful, then I would simply pull off your wings."

"No!" Fumiko moved.

For a moment, my eyes saw two Fumikos running in different directions: one toward Yonge, the other toward Wynn. The guards reacted immediately—their blades coming out and slicing through the images, dispelling the illusions. I heard a meaty wallop and then a whimper as Fumiko's shadow dissolved. She appeared on the floor before Hao—the man's fist extended at where Fumiko would have been standing.

Cabrina gave a big sigh. "Fumiko, Fumiko. Did you think I couldn't see through your illusions? You're good dear, but nowhere near as good as I am."

Zofie and I knelt beside her. She looked up at us in utter despair as a new trickle of blood came from her nose.

Wynn looked at Yonge, rocking on his heels and clearly growing impatient. "Can we get on with this? I really must be moving on. My return portal will be opening shortly."

Cabrina smiled broadly. "Why, of course. How would you like to do this? You promised to show me the technique in case I need to repeat it."

Wynn gave a polite smile. "Of course." Wynn walked over to stand beside Yonge's wheeled chair, and Hao joined them.

Wynn cleared his throat. "Now each of you take one end of the key." Yonge feebly grasped one end while Hao took the other.

Wynn put a finger in the middle of the key. "For the next step, all you need to do is feed it just a smidgeon of myst to get things started." The metal bar began to glow a brilliant white, and Wynn snatched his finger away.

I whispered to Zofie. "What is he doing?"

She shook her head.

Cabrina walked over to stand by us. Her grin the one of a child getting the perfect Day of the New gift.

The glow grew brighter.

Coren! announced Abe in my head. *This is bad.*

I cocked my head to one side. "How?" I whispered, glancing at the guards around me.

Zofie cut her eyes in my direction, listening in to our conversation.

The Griffin's Key can unlock anything. Worse, it looks like Wynn has fig-ured out how to use it. It was never intended for this. And it is forbidden even by the Dark Avenyts themselves.

"But what is it?" I whispered.

You know that Dark Avenyts are curses so advanced they are intelligent?

I nodded my head, watching as Wynn took an additional step back from the pair.

Abe continued. *Well, guess how the original ones were made.*

"The originals?" I asked.

Come on, Coren. You can't be that dense.

"It's... it's talking to me," yelled Yonge excitedly, his wobbling head turned to Wynn in amazement. "What do I do?"

Wynn grinned. "Tell it what you want to unlock."

Yonge took a deep breath. "I want to move to a new body."

Wynn shook his head. "Not what you want to do. Tell it what to un-lock."

Yonge licked his lips. "I want to unlock... myself."

Both Yonge and Hao were instantly enveloped in a blue glow. He gasped. "It burns!"

Wynn nodded. "It always does."

The glow continued to grow brighter. Yonge groaned. He suddenly went limp. At the same time, all the guards collapsed, and Cabrina staggered, falling against me.

I wasn't sure what had just happened, but I knew we needed to get away quickly. I tugged on Zofie and nodded with my head toward the door. I passed a dazed Cabrina to her and helped Fumiko stand. We moved toward the door.

A myst barrier sprang up, blocking our path. "Now, now," said Wynn. "Can't have you wandering around by yourselves. No telling what mischief you'll get into. Besides, you'll not want to miss this."

The white glow gradually subsided. Yonge had collapsed in his chair and was unmoving. I wasn't sure he was breathing. Hao stag-gered back and looked at his hands, then felt along his face. "I'm in a new body," he whispered. He turned toward us. High on his chest, just above his heart, was a curse mark that hadn't been there before. Most curse marks were relatively small. No larger than a gold royal. But this one was larger—much larger. Almost the size of Abe's curse mark.

A chill ran down my spine as it all came together. The key had turned Yonge's personality. His soul... into a curse.

He was now an Avenyts.

Wynn grinned at us. "See, I told you, you wouldn't want to miss it."

Yonge raised his arms and flexed his muscles. "This is amazing."

Wynn nodded. "And with that..." He stepped toward the Forever Nexus Shadow and looked back at Yonge. "May I?"

Yonge waved him on. Wynn grasped the pyramid and tucked it into a leather pouch, which he slung over his shoulder. He gave it a pat. "Thank you..."

He broke off as a sudden commotion came from outside the room. In the distance, I could hear fighting.

Wynn gave a heavy sigh. "I really have to go now. I suspect she will be coming soon."

Yonge looked up. "Who?"

Wynn sighed wistfully. "She was supposed to be my partner but got a better offer from the Collectivity and decided to betray me instead." He waved a dismissive hand toward us. "Can't say I blame her. That group is pretty powerful." He shook his head. "I wish I'd just killed her when I had the chance."

He stepped to the center of the room.

Yonge looked up. A look of concern on his face. He pointed to his collapsed guards. "My charms aren't working. I thought you said I'd be able to use my myst."

Wynn sighed impatiently. "I did. But if you will remember, I said you would be able to use your body's myst." He grinned. "Your current one. Myst abilities are dependent on the body, not the soul. So none of your charms work now." He shrugged. "Sorry, just one of those things." He turned but then looked back for a moment. "Of course, you could always go back to your old one."

Yonge glanced nervously at his former unmoving body.

Wynn grinned. "I thought not."

A long-range portal opened in the center of the room. I couldn't help but wonder who was creating the portals. The wayfarer behind them must be extremely powerful to do two in one day.

Yonge went to squat beside a fallen guard and flipped him over. He began fiddling with the charm the unconscious man wore.

Wynn stepped toward the portal and glanced our way. "Sorry I can't stay longer, but I must be moving on." He patted his pouch. "I need to get this someplace safe. I have great plans for it."

Suddenly a myst barrier sprang up in front of Wynn. A really thick one. From its shape and color, I knew it was Cabrina's.

The young man turned to glare at the youth in annoyance. "Really? You dare attack someone of higher cothe? I was going to let you live, but no, you had to poke the bear. Your new directive..." He turned away. "...is to kill your host. *Now!*"

Cabrina sucked breath like she had been struck. "No!" she wailed, falling to her knees. The knife she had used to cut off our charms sprang into her hand and inched toward her throat.

Fumiko grabbed her hand and struggled to pull the knife away.

I sprinted after Wynn. He turned just as he was stepping inside. I reached in to grab him but missed, only managing to catch him by the pouch holding the nexus. He grabbed it and tried to pull it away from me. But I hauled on the strap as hard as I could, leaving him half out of the portal. He glared at me.

A harsh cold emanated from the portal, and its edges began to fluctuate. We only had a few moments before it closed. One didn't want to be caught in it when it did.

"Let go!" he screamed. He kicked at me.

Behind me, I heard Fumiko yelling. "Don't do this No-name!"

"I can't stop," the youth wailed. "I have no choice. I must do what I was made to do."

Zofie ran over and grabbed me about my middle and added her strength to pulling me out.

Wynn and I glared at each other. "Release her," I shouted.

He just snorted.

That really pissed me off.

But not as bad as it did to the woman at my back.

Zofie punched him.

His nose sprouted blood. "I'll kill you!" he screamed. "Both of you!"

She punched him again. "Not if I can help it." I made a mental note to never, ever piss her off.

Wynn's head rocked back.

The portal's fluctuations became more erratic, and I knew we only had seconds left. I felt his fingers slipping and thought he was going to let go—

Suddenly, a pair of female hands came out from the darkness of the portal behind him, and while I couldn't see her face, I could make out two dark eyes peering over his shoulder. They reached around his waist and grabbed my wrists. I was dragged forward with my arms just inside the gate's darkness.

The portal began to close, and I had time to wonder what life would be like without hands.

"Now!" Zofie screamed, and we both jerked back hard. At the same time, the woman holding my hands let go, and the purse's straps slipped through my fingers.

Zofie and I fell, landing on our backs. I felt one more puff of icy air, and the portal immediately closed. I cursed. Wynn had gotten away.

Zofie and I scrambled up and tried to help Fumiko with Cabrina. Fumiko was wrestling with her and nearly had her pinned. A sudden burst of myst flung Fumiko away, where she lay for a moment clearly stunned. Zofie and I immediately took her place.

"Please let go!" pleaded the youth. "I don't want to hurt you. But I must do what I was made to do."

Fumiko shook off her daze and joined us. I couldn't help but be struck by the irony. Only a few days ago, Fumiko would have gladly killed Cabrina. But now, she was trying to prevent her from dying.

"Abe," I yelled. "Is there anything I can do?"

Are you sure you want to? He said calmly. *She is on the path to becoming a Dark Avenyts. She is an enemy of humanity.*

"I don't believe that. She would choose light if she had a choice."

Then give her one.

I felt her myst building, and suddenly all of us were flung away. Fortunately, she lost the knife in the process but quickly scrambled to retrieve it. Zofie and Fumiko rushed to stop her.

I picked myself up. "How...?" I asked Abe. But I knew. "You can name her, can't you? You're a Creator blasted Avenyts."

I am, but I'm not. I'm something different. But for this, I am close enough to fill the role. Just be warned, if I name her, then we are taking responsibility for her not going dark. It will not be easy.

I didn't hesitate. "How do I do it?"

You can't.

I watched as Zofie and Fumiko struggled with Cabrina. "Then how..."

Abe paused and spoke in an unusually subdued tone. *To do it, you have to turn over control of your body to me. You're going to have to trust me.*

My eyes went wide. Evelend's bindings prevented him from doing something like that unless I was directly endangered. But to willingly give up control? Who knows what would happen.

He might not give it back.

Cabrina gave another burst of myst, throwing both Fumiko and Zofie off of her. This time Cabrina kept her knife.

Fumiko always said I was too trusting. She might be right. Then again...

What's a world without trust.

"Do it."

Suddenly, I felt as if I was shoved aside, and my body moved by itself. It reminded me of being in the audience of a play where everything was happening, but I could do nothing to affect the outcome.

My body rose to my full height, arms at my side, and fists clenched. I looked at Cabrina and spoke. It was my voice, but yet it wasn't. "Ye who has No-name! Attend me!" I yelled in an old dialect of Ellish.

Cabrina paused with the knife just in front of her throat. She jerkily turned to look at me. The conflicting directives making the knife quiver in her hands.

I pointed at her. "By the rights granted by the progenitors. Your seal, I do claim. Henceforth, no other may direct you, no other may shape you, and no other will be your master. From now until eternity, you will cease to be a No-name. You will instead be known as..." Abe paused.

"*Hope.*"

Myst flowed from me to Cabrina, and she was instantly surrounded by a deep purple glow, the same shade the clouds take on just as the sun is about to rise. She fell to her knees, and the knife clattered to the floor. She stared at me in disbelief.

It felt almost as if a door was opening between us. And through it, I could see a symbol taking shape—the lines twisting and turning as if they were having trouble deciding its form. Suddenly, the lines froze and then moved into position, forming the stylized image of a rising sun.

Then the door closed, but I could still feel the connection. I knew it would be there till I died.

The glow went out. Cabrina's eyes rolled up, and she fell to the side.

I staggered, and my body was suddenly back in my control. Zofie and Fumiko knelt beside Cabrina. They turned and gave me a questioning look.

Then Abe surprised the hell out of me by what he said next.

Thank you.

He then seemed to catch himself. *She will be out for a bit. We've adjusted her Avenyts, so she will need time to process. And monkey brains, when she does wake up, don't abuse her. I know your pervert mind is already thinking of ways to take advantage of her.*

"I won't abuse her."

Of course, you won't. I won't let you. She's my apprentice, after all.

I couldn't help but grin. But there was a question in the back of my mind. "Why did you name her Hope?"

That, my friend, is my secret. One day you'll know. I've always hated those long names anyway.

I couldn't help but smile. Creator, I can't believe I missed this foul-mouthed, good for nothing curse. But I had.

"Abe, it's good to have you back."

He paused in surprise. *Well... Don't be getting all sentimental on me. I...* He suddenly paused. *Damn. We've got company. And not the kind you want to have tea with.*

I heard swords clanging outside the entrance and turned to see a guard fall through the door with a hole in his chest. A moment later, the attacker strode into the room.

Lilith shook her sword in anger. "I missed him!"

CHAPTER TWENTY-SIX

Jiaying's Lesson

"**D**amn him!" shouted Lilith. She swung her sword through the air in a sudden diagonal slice. I could hear it sing as it cut the air and felt the splatter of a few drops. I looked down to see a thin line of red splotches across my robe.

"How did you get in here?" Yonge asked, his voice breaking. His new body possessed a higher-pitched voice and obviously wasn't trained to project authority.

"Did he get the Forever Nexus Shadow?" she demanded. "Did he leave with it?"

I gently lifted the unconscious Cabrina into my arms and then jerked my head toward the door. Zofie and Fumiko nodded. We then began to slowly back away. Lilith was too much of a wild card, and none of us were in a condition to fight someone of her level. But we didn't get two steps before a small group of men entered and moved to guard the door. They were Lilith's men, and among them was a particularly tall one—Wort.

Yonge dropped the man's wrist and stood to his full height. "Yes, Wynn did. Now answer the question. How did you get in here?"

Lilith smirked. She sheathed her sword and shrugged. "It was nothing really. This place is like a kicked anthill. Everyone's running around, but nobody seems to know what's going on. So I thought it a golden opportunity to bring the boot down."

Lilith glanced at the prone figure lying in his wheeled chair and then back to the body Yonge possessed. She smiled—only it was a deadly smile. "He showed you how, didn't he?"

She put her hands on her hips. "You're an illegal. An aberration. What he showed you was forbidden knowledge. Even the Collectivity is forbidden to use it."

She glanced at one of the fallen guards and gave an amused snort. "Let me guess. He offered you the knowledge in exchange for the For-ever Nexus Shadow. And he told you everything would be exactly the same except you got a new body. But you're finding that your charms don't work anymore."

Yonge took a step back toward his original body.

She cocked her head to one side and stepped toward him. "Be care-ful of offers that are too good to be true—because they are."

Yonge took another step toward his old self, but a knife suddenly appeared in Lilith's hand. She lunged forward and plunged it into the chest of Yonge's old body. "Whoops! I slipped. But it shouldn't be a problem since you didn't want that body anyway."

His eyes went wide in horror. She gave him a wicked smile and stepped closer. He backed up but was stopped by the edge of the vault.

"Take what you want and leave!" he yelled. "My guards will be here shortly, and you'll be dead."

Lilith shook her head. "I don't think so. They all ran when the tap-estry fell. I'm not sure you realize just how much panic you've caused. The few that haven't run have all gone to protect the emperor. So no one will be coming to your aid."

He tried to slide away and then bolted toward the door. Lilith easily caught him and threw him to the ground. "I'm sorry advisor person, but I can't let you live. You can blame Wynn for this. I'm always having to clean up after him." Lilith's dagger flashed, and she sliced his throat.

As he reached for his throat, she patted his shoulder. "Believe me. I'm doing you a favor. The Collectivity would do much worse."

She stood and wiped her blade on his clothes before lifting the Griffin's Key from his belt and tucking it into her own.

We made a dash for the door, but they easily caught us. Cabrina was too heavy for me to hold any longer, and they let me lay her on a bench nearby. I thanked the Creator that Spraggel wasn't with us. At least he would be spared.

"Now it's time to do the final sweeping up," Lilith grinned as she pulled her sword. "I'm feeling generous today. I'll make this quick."

Zofie raised her head. "Risten. Do you remember our conversation two years ago on the riverbank? The one in the spring where we saw that deer and her fawn."

Lilith looked puzzled. "Yes, it's in her memories. Speculation on which one of you would have children first."

Zofie smiled. "I won."

Lilith stared at her a moment, contemplating the information. "If you're expecting to get some kind of reaction from me, you're mistaken. The Risten inside is gone. She couldn't take it anymore and fled to the recesses of her mind. I'll occasionally hear thoughts of weeping, but nothing more. She's totally broken."

Zofie's expression turned grim. "That may be true, but I wanted Risten to know." The princess frowned. Her eyes hardened, and behind them I could see an anger—a controlled rage—the like I had never seen from her before. You could almost see it burning behind her eyes. "One day, you will regret ever *perfecting* her."

Lilith snorted. "I've enhanced hundreds of beings, both human and not. Rode them until they were a mere husk." She leaned closer. "And I don't regret a single one."

"You won't win," I said. "Humans have beaten your kind before, and we'll do it again."

Lilith's lips spread into a condescending smile. "Typical human.

Believing you're better than everyone. There is no way you can stop the invasion. Unlike your kind, we have learned from our mistakes. This time, we've prepared for the worst."

"Then why haven't you just taken over already. Seems we're a little more of a problem than you thought."

She shrugged. "Not for long. And I'm about to eliminate a few of those *problems*." Lilith considered us with wicked amusement. "Now which one to start with?" She looked over to the still unconscious Cabrina. "That one I'll take back with me. I see you've already sealed her, but that shouldn't be a problem. She'll make a fine addition to our army." Then her gaze turned back to me. "And I'll have to wait on you. The Collectivity is dying to get their hands on your curse."

She looked at Fumiko. "I guess I'll start with the eastern bitch."

Fumiko struggled, but the men holding her were too strong for her weakened state. They forced her to kneel while Lilith drew her sword.

"Please don't, Risten," pleaded Zofie.

Lilith stepped over to Zofie and backhanded her. "Will you shut up. You're getting on my nerves."

Zofie glared at her.

Lilith nodded. "Better."

She turned back to Fumiko.

Lilith shook her head. "I was so hoping I would get to fight you, but I can see you're just not up to it."

I raised my head, knowing what I had to do. *"Then fight me,"* I said.

Lilith looked up in surprise.

"No!" yelled Fumiko. "You're not ready."

Despite quaking in my boots, I turned my most confident smile on Lilith. "Unless you're afraid."

Her eyes drew down in anger. "No one says I'm afraid." She turned to her men. "Release him," she commanded. "And give him a sword. Don't any of you dare to interfere." She grinned. "I'll tell the Collectivity that I had to kill you in self-defense. Hopefully, they'll be happy with your corpse."

The men holding my arms released me, and I staggered forward a step. A moment later, a sword was presented, hilt first.

"Take it," Lilith commanded. "Fight me. And if you don't, I'll strike you down where you stand."

She pulled her weapon lightning-fast and lunged at me. I grabbed the presented sword and swung it up just in time. The force of the blow made our blades ring.

Lilith smiled. "You know you can't win. Risten taught you the few moves that you know, and I know a few hundred more. I have been fighting in both men and women's bodies long before your grandfather was even dreamt of."

She shifted her movement and came at me from another angle, which I barely parried. But she didn't stop, and the blows kept coming. She nicked me on the shoulder. Then on the leg. She would laugh at each one. All I could do was defend.

And grow more frustrated.

I couldn't access the skills Fumiko had given me. I didn't know what was wrong.

It had seemed so easy during my practices. But now, I couldn't find them. It was like the skills were lost. It was likely from the stress of the situation. Too many things to think about. Too much at risk. My brain went immediately to the old patterns while ignoring the new.

Lilith was going to win.

"Coren," I heard Fumiko behind me. Her voice was cool and calm. "Jiaying's lesson."

I parried another blow. Why was Fumiko calling that out to me? The skills wouldn't come. All I could think about was Risten kicking my butt every time I practiced with her. She was going to do it again.

Jiaying.

She had been the one that taught Fumiko the forms she had missed. My eyes went wide. Those forms were exactly what I needed.

Lilith paused, and I stepped back. I knew from my numerous practice sessions with Risten, this was what she did before launching her final attack. I only had one chance left to beat her.

I focused on the memory. I could see young Jiaying standing before me, her expression determined, her form excellent, and her stick held high.

It was like looking in a mirror.

A mirror.

Suddenly my body moved into the right form. My head tilted up a bit more, my feet slid apart ever so slightly, and my sword slowly came up into a vertical position. It felt so right.

I smiled.

Lilith gave me a puzzled look.

But this time, it was my turn.

I attacked.

Lilith was taken off guard. She danced back, but I followed, forcing her to counter and putting her on the defensive. I flowed flawlessly from one form to another. I paused, and she stepped back.

Lilith glanced down at her arm, where a single slice, a scratch really, was just starting to turn red. Lilith turned to me in shock. "How?"

I couldn't help but grin. "A very good friend taught me."

Lilith roared and charged. I parried but immediately returned to the offensive. The shock was evident on her face.

We continued to fight, but as we traded blows, I realized I was tiring. While I may have had the skills, my body was nowhere near as well trained. It was a war of attrition, which I was going to lose.

I needed another solution.

Lilith pulled back, and we circled each other.

"Abe," I barely whispered. "Can Zofie transform?"

Definitely not. Her pregnancy nullifies her curse. It's completely inactive.

"What about your ability to change luck?"

I dare not access it. The princess made me use it liberally to save your butt. She has unfortunately built up a deficit. If I'm not careful, something really bad will happen.

Lilith and I continued to circle, each looking for an opening. There had to be something else. "What about Lilith? Can I steal that curse?"

I heard a surprised gasp from Fumiko as I passed in front of her. She must have overheard me.

You're not asking for much. He paused for a moment before finally saying. *I'm not sure.*

Abe was obnoxious most of the time, but I'd never heard him be unsure.

I could see Zofie off to the side where the men still held her. Her eyes widened as she listened in on our conversation. She slowly shook her head.

Abe continued. *I wasn't made for taking a curse as complex as a Dark Avenyts. There could be unintended consequences.*

It might even break me.

Lilith lunged, and we traded a few more blows before separating once again. She was testing me. Looking for a weakness.

"Got any better ideas?" I asked Abe.

Ideas? I've got lots of ideas. Like how I should have never gotten involved with you. Or maybe I should have found a way to have the princess as my host instead. Even Fumiko would have been better. All you are is a monkey-brained trouble magnet. He gave a big sigh. *Creator no, you stupid piece of meat, I don't have a better idea. That's what I hate about this.*

"Can you do it?"

Lilith and I traded another quick set of blows before once more stepping back. I could tell she was about to do something.

He gave an almost human sigh. *I can try. But it will take longer than a normal curse. You'll need to touch her and hold on for at least ten seconds.*

"You're kidding me? That's an eternity."

I don't make this stuff up. Not only is she a massive curse, but she has locked herself tightly into her body. It will take time to get her out. Assuming I can do it at all.

Zofie looked over at the guard holding her, sizing him up. I hoped she wasn't going to try something.

I glanced over Lilith's shoulder, and for an instant, locked eyes with Fumiko. She gave a slight nod.

Lilith paused, and we glared at each other. The room was so quiet you could hear a pin drop. *Now or never.*

I took a deep breath. *This will be the longest ten seconds of my life.*

"Let's end this!" I shouted and raised my sword.

I charged.

I prayed to the Creator that I could do it.

While I tried to make an opening, we continued to circle and trade blows. Over Lilith's shoulder, Fumiko came into view. I could see her looking at me. Her body was tensing, subtly shifting her position. I got the feeling she was getting ready to move.

Zofie lunged forward and suddenly broke free, running right toward us. Simultaneously, the men holding Fumiko yelled. Out of the corner of my eye, I could see that Fumiko was no longer there.

Lilith didn't even pause. She ignored the approaching Zofie and instead stabbed at empty air. But the blade seemed to find flesh.

The image of Zofie vanished, and I saw that she had never freed herself. It had been an illusion. While beside me, a bit of shadow solidified into Fumiko. She had done it. Created the distraction I needed to get in close.

But the cost. I grimaced at the sight.

Lilith's blade had pierced Fumiko's chest and stuck out of my friend's back.

She grabbed Lilith around the waist and pulled her closer, causing the blade to slide deeper. Blood came from her mouth. "Hurry," she whispered.

A surprised Lilith tried to extract herself, but I grabbed her arm. "Your curse, to my curse," I shouted.

A blue glow enveloped my hand and gradually spread up her arm, reaching for her heart.

It's working! I thought.

Lilith's eyes narrowed in anger. "How dare you."

The blue glow creeping up her body slowed and then stopped.

Lilith's mouth curled up into a confident smirk. "You're not skilled enough to unseat me. I've had many years to perfect this." With a shrug of her shoulder, the glow began to reverse itself.

Inside my head, Abe howled in pain. *I can't hold her!* he shouted. *She's so strong!*

Lilith started to shove me away. But I fought to keep contact, refusing to let go.

Suddenly, I found myself in a world of all gray—the world of curses. To my left, I saw Risten in some kind of cage. She was lying on her side—naked and curled up into a tight ball. I could see dark bruises all over her body. I somehow knew these were not physical, but more a reflection of the mental abuse she had taken at Lilith's hand.

In front of me, two of the line figures were locked in a struggle. I recognized one of them as Abe. But the other was new to me. In its large round head was a cluster of lines emanating from a central point. Each of the lines was capped with an arrow pointing outwards. I instantly recognized the symbol.

It was for insanity.

It was Lilith's symbol.

The curse reached forward and grabbed Abe's arm. With a quick snap of her wrist, she broke it off and quickly stuffed it inside her head. It flowed into one of the existing lines.

Abe cried out in pain, and my mouth fell open in horror. She was slowly eating him.

Help me, he cried.

But I didn't know how. I ran toward them, but I couldn't get any closer no matter how much I ran. All I could hear was the sound of Lilith's laughing.

A new voice spoke to me. *Use the key*, it said.

I turned to see yet another stick figure kneeling on the ground. Inside its head was a symbol I had just seen. It was the rising sun.

On the ground in front of the curse was a sleeping Cabrina, her head resting on the curse's bent knees.

"Hope?" I asked.

She nodded. *Use the Griffin's Key. It's the only way.*

Instantly I was back in my body, struggling with Lilith. I felt along my attacker's side, and tucked inside her belt, my fingers brushed the Griffin's Key. I had time to wonder if I could do it.

Please, oh, please work.

I grasped it and said the word. "Unlock."

The key exploded with light and enveloped us both in a blinding white glow. I heard a voice inside my head. *What do you want to unlock?*

I didn't hesitate.

"Lilith."

The Dark Avenyts looked at me in horror. "No!"

The white light went out. I felt more than heard a vibration, which ran through both of us, becoming more and more intense. Abe's blue glow continued to recede, and I feared it hadn't worked.

Then the blue glow's movement gradually slowed and finally stopped. I heard Abe groan in the effort. The vibration turned into shaking, and I began to feel power grow, like a thunderstorm in the distance. It was coming, and it was powerful.

The blue glow on her arm began to advance upwards. Slowly at first, but gradually moving faster.

"No!" Lilith screamed. She struggled to get free.

The shaking turned into a low rumble, and I felt the ground moving. I began to fear that the building might fall on our heads. Abe groaned again, and then his glow accelerated, racing toward her heart.

"No!" Lilith cried, frantically trying to break free. "You can't!"

The blue light became brighter, and the power continued to grow. I could feel a myst working like none I had felt before—so much power. The floor began to heave, and I felt lightning in the air. Our hair came alive and stood up on its own—tiny sparks began to fly from us to the ground.

Finally, the blue glow reached her chest, and Lilith gave a death scream.

The pent-up power suddenly released. A giant bolt of lightning, from Creator knew where, struck all three of us, and we were flung apart. I sailed off the ground and landed hard on my back, hitting my head on the stone floor.

I lost consciousness.

CHAPTER TWENTY-SEVEN

Last Wish

I gradually became aware of the world around me. Fleeting thoughts ran through my head, but I couldn't seem to grasp them. I heard weeping, which seemed close and yet very far away. For a moment, I thought it was my mother. It sounded just like her crying when she first saw my father's body. I was only twelve at the time. I remembered watching this woman who was the model of a strong heart, the center of our home, the rock upon which we all stood, brought to her knees in racking sobs.

I forced my eyes open. My head was turned to the side, and not too far away, I could see someone's back. Between us, a sword lay discarded, its blade painted with blood.

Where was Lilith? Did we stop her?

I knew I should be feeling panic, but I couldn't seem to get my brain to connect with my body. I smelled something burnt, and I tasted soot in my mouth.

I heard voices. Feet stomping. And that awful sound of crying continued. I knew I had to move. I sat up, and the world spun. I felt every hurt I'd ever received across my body. I put a trembling hand to my head and tried to steady myself. I saw Lilith—or was it Risten now—laying sprawled out across from me, still unconscious. Her men were trapped inside a barrier, and I saw Cabrina standing beside it. Her expression was grim.

Who was crying?

"Abe?" I asked.

I did not receive an answer.

"Abe?" I asked more forcefully.

Still no response. Could curses be knocked unconscious?

Someone's crying.

I finally turned toward the sound. It came from the person with their back to me. I knew them. *Who were they?*

I noticed men and women standing around us. Guards. But they were in a different uniform. They looked sad.

Why wouldn't the crying stop?

Mother had cried for hours. I remember telling her I was sorry. That I didn't mean to fall in the river. That I didn't mean for him to come after me.

But she ignored me and continued to wail.

I managed to roll myself onto all fours and then crawled over to the person with their back to me. As I crawled, my bruised brain gradually noticed other details. The person was kneeling—leaning over someone lying on the floor before them. As I got closer, I could make out the face of the person on the floor.

"What do you mean there's no healers close by?" yelled someone in anger. I didn't recognize the voice. It was a man's voice and not someone I knew. I saw the kneeling person press their hands on the chest of the woman lying down. Her hands were covered in blood.

Through her tears, the person kneeling yelled. "Why won't the bleeding stop!"

I looked up at the person kneeling and realized who it was. I was both thankful and sorrowful at the same time. Zofie was unharmed.

The princess was kneeling, pressing down hard on the person's wound.

I turned to the one that had fallen, and as I stared at her, my bruised brain gave me her name.

Fumiko.

She lay unmoving, deathly pale, her chest soaked in blood.

Zofie noticed me beside her. She wiped her tears on her sleeve and tried to compose herself. "Quickly, Coren. Curse her. Transform her into something... anything."

"Abe?" I called again. But there was no reply.

Awareness of the situation began to return.

"I... I... can't," I said. "Abe's not answering. I don't know what's wrong."

"Try anyway," she demanded.

So I did, but nothing happened. I felt utterly helpless.

I could see Zofie's tears had resumed. They rolled down her cheek and then dripped onto Fumiko's chest, mixing with the blood.

Fumiko groaned. She opened her eyes and looked at us both. Her mouth moved, but no words came out.

"Don't talk. We're looking for a healer," said Zofie, never letting up the pressure on her friend's wound. She tried to project confidence, but the tears betrayed her. We all knew what was coming.

Fumiko tried to lift a hand, and I took it in my own, squeezing it tightly. Fumiko searched my eyes for a moment and then Zofie's. To my surprise, I felt myst gathering.

Zofie and I were instantly sucked into something like a memory, but yet it wasn't. It felt more immediate. Like she was sending her thoughts directly to us.

What I saw was Fumiko standing, dressed in a fine gown and her hair now long and pulled back in an elaborate style. She was smiling at us. Fumiko's eyes slowly flicked from Zofie and then to me. She gave us a deep bow.

"Thank you," she said, as she slowly righted herself. "While it was short, my time with you was the most enjoyable of my life. Never forget. I love you both." I felt the vision begin to get blurry, like she was losing focus. "And Coren, you *are* too trusting. But I thank the Creator that you are." She looked to the side, and I could see a bright light in the distance. "I have to go now. My love is waiting for me." She turned back to us and smiled. "As I'll be waiting for you."

I suddenly found myself back in my body. I watched helplessly as Fumiko seemed to look at something in the distance, give a gentle smile, and then take her last breath.

Zofie bent over her body and sobbed uncontrollably.

I looked at my hands, which were now tainted with Fumiko's blood. As the tears flowed on my own cheeks, I realized this blood would join my father's. I had caused someone else I cared for to die. I couldn't help but wonder when it would end.

A short while later, as Zofie's sobs softened and my own tears grew less, an older man entered the room. He appeared thin and frail, but at the same time, had a spark of intensity in his eyes. He wore several layers of fine robes and carried himself with authority. His escort was a dozen well-armed guards, and of course, Spraggel.

As we continued to kneel beside Fumiko, my master came to stand beside us and laid a hand on each of our shoulders. He said nothing because he knew there was nothing that could be said.

The unfamiliar man went to Fumiko's other side, and with the help of his guards, knelt beside her. He put his hands together and silently prayed for a few moments. Then he opened his eyes and looked down at her.

"I wish I had known her," he said softly. "I only got to meet her once, but she was only a child then. That was just before I came under the control of Yonge." His voice was deep and gravelly as one who had not spoken in a while. He looked up at us. "I am her father, Emperor Huang." He leaned forward. "What was she like?"

Zofie smiled gently. "She was smart and witty, a little too uptight, but always a good friend. She wanted to put her old life behind her and do something for others. She had volunteered to teach at our new school."

I wiped my eyes with the back of my hand. "She saved my life countless times. And she taught me how to fight."

The emperor nodded. "As I expected from this child." He brushed a strand of hair out of her face.

We all paused for a moment before he gave a large sigh and motioned to his guards. They helped him stand. Then taking off his outer robe, he laid it gently over her.

After regarding his child a moment longer, he turned toward us. "Please forgive me, but the empire calls. Many things have been neglected while I was under the control of that fiend." He turned to leave, but paused.

"I would like to give Fumiko a hero's funeral..."

"*No!*" Zofie cut him off.

The emperor looked shocked at the outburst.

She shut her eyes for a moment to focus herself, and then she spoke again, but with a softer tone. "I am sorry, Emperor. But I must decline in Fumiko's stead. This isn't her home any longer. I want to take her back with me. She would rest well with us."

The emperor regarded her for several heartbeats before nodding. "You are correct, Princess Xernow. Please do as you wish. Ask the servants for anything, and it will be granted."

Zofie nodded in thanks.

"Would you also let me know when the funeral will be held. If you are agreeable, I would like to attend."

She gave a sad smile. "I think Fumiko would like that."

He nodded once and then headed for the door. But just before leaving, he turned back. "Oh, and one more thing. Now is not the time, but later, I would like to discuss the affairs in your kingdom. I would like to consider you as a partner in the coming war."

Zofie gave a slight bow. "I would love to, your highness."

He nodded and then left.

Cabrina came over to us as the emperor's guards herded Lilith's men out of the room. "I just checked, and Lilith's curse mark is no longer on Risten. Apparently, Abe was able to remove her." She looked down. "But I can't feel Abhulengulus anymore."

"I can't get him to answer me either," I said.

She nodded distractedly. "I fear that my master has been injured. I hope it wasn't too bad."

Zofie and I looked at each other. Her face was a mirror of the mixed emotions I felt. We had accomplished our purpose—removing the charms and beginning an alliance the kingdom sorely needed. We had even gotten Lilith out of Risten. But the cost had been very high. Extremely high.

And Wynn had still escaped with his prize.

I glanced at Fumiko's body, then over to the unconscious Risten, before looking back to Zofie. Her eyes confirmed the same feeling.

That the worst was yet to come.

CHAPTER TWENTY-EIGHT

Back
Home

Two days later, we arrived back in Brethnach in a snowy field not far from Edlingreen Castle. Captain Milner and Master Rourke, as well as several of the staff, were waiting for us as we emerged from the long-range portal, courtesy of Emperor Huang. He had even sent messengers ahead of us to ensure there were no surprises. He had offered to let us rest in his palace, but we assured him we had to return. Zofie had a kingdom to feed.

Not to mention, the Dark Avenyts waited for no one.

While the air may have been chill, we were warmly greeted by the others, and quickly ushered inside to once again begin governing the kingdom. I was glad of the gentle warmth of the castle. We were all tired. I wasn't sure where Zofie got her energy. For me, it was an effort to just stand.

Spraggel surprisingly volunteered to stay behind, promising to work through the negotiations with the empire. My master never ceased to amaze me.

Cabrina was with us and came along quietly. She was no doubt wondering what her fate would be now that the charms were off. With the Avenyts inside her, it was hard to know how to treat her. She had started this whole adventure, and yet, she too had been a victim. For now, we confined her to a room in the castle while we discussed her fate.

Risten came with us on a stretcher. She had recovered consciousness a few hours after Lilith had been removed, but it wasn't much of a victory. All she would do was stare straight ahead, seemingly unaware of her surroundings. The healers assured us that she was physically fine. But the havoc Lilith had caused while possessing her must have been too much. I could only imagine the atrocities she had seen.

Of course, Fumiko was with us. Zofie had insisted on preparing her friend herself, dressing her in a fine gown almost identical to the one we had seen in her last vision. For the journey home, her coffin had been draped in flowers and carried by the emperor's finest honor guard through the portal.

While all the staff was sad and made expressions of condolences, Master Rourke was especially stricken at seeing the coffin. He volunteered, actually insisted, to oversee all the arrangements for her.

Zofie seemed to be taking the return very well. She greeted everyone with a smile, talked animatedly with her staff, and made plans for the following day. But when we entered Zofie's study, she paused gazing at the tiny desk to one side of her own—Fumiko's desk. She stepped slowly over to it and placed a gentle hand on it. She stood that way for several minutes and gazed out the window.

I turned to everyone and asked them to give us a few moments. They all reluctantly filed out, and I closed the door leaving Zofie and me alone. I took a deep breath, determined to keep my emotions under control.

I went to her and turned her to face me. Tears were on her cheeks as I wrapped her in my arms.

"I'm going to miss her," she said.

"Yes," I nodded as she buried her face in my shirt. "Yes, we will."

After a moment, she looked up at me. "I've decided something."

"And what is that?"

"The baby's name."

"Oh?"

She nodded. "Fumiko." She looked up at me. "Little Fumiko. Has a nice ring to it, don't you think? I want my daughter to have a strong name, and I can't think of any better."

"How do you know the baby will be a girl?" I teased.

She gave me one of those looks that questioned my intelligence. "She will be. I just know."

I pulled her tight. "Then, I think it would make Fumiko proud."

We stood that way for a moment, and my head suddenly bobbed. Zofie looked at me in surprise. "Are you all right? You don't seem yourself."

In fact, I hadn't been feeling well since the fight with Lilith. It was more than the grief over Fumiko's death, but I wasn't sure what it was. One of the empire's healers had checked me over but had not found anything.

And Abe still wasn't talking to me. I intended to see Rourke about it at the first opportunity.

"I'm just tired. This whole trip has been exhausting. I might even have picked up a case of the sniffles or some such. It is winter, after all."

She laid her head on my shoulder. "Promise me you'll have our healer look you over. And no excuses. I need my knight right now."

I pulled her tighter. "I will."

And so we stood until the troubles of the world couldn't wait any longer. And gently knocked on our door.

We separated, and Zofie dried her tears. She gave me a reassuring smile. "The kingdom waits for no one."

I nodded and opened the door, letting in those outside to resume taking care of the kingdom.

And so, life went on. A long-range portal mysteriously opened in the field where we had arrived. But when it closed, it left behind several giant piles of neatly stacked sacks. Rice, courtesy of the empire. This was quickly distributed to the people who were close to starvation. And the shipments continued until we had more than enough.

Zofie decided not to reveal her pregnancy yet. She thought it best to get through Fumiko's funeral. Preparations took several weeks as she and Rourke meticulously planned it out. And a stately funeral it was too. Zofie declared her a hero of the kingdom and made Fumiko's final resting place inside the royal tomb. She thought her parents would enjoy having her near.

For myself, I struggled to make it through the ceremony. The creeping tiredness continued to get worse. As Zofie had suggested, I had gone to the healer about it, but he could not find anything wrong. He diagnosed it as stress and suggested I rest more. I had simply rolled my eyes. Like that was going to happen.

And even after several weeks, Abe still refused to answer. I felt guilty about it. I couldn't help but wonder if his absence was my fault. He had warned me about the consequences of stealing Lilith's curse. But strangely, her curse mark had not appeared on my chest.

And just like Abe, Risten's condition did not change either. She had stayed in her catatonic state, which was far worse than what Zofie had experienced. I couldn't help but feel guilty about this too. Had I damaged her while trying to save her? Had I sentenced her to a life of unconsciousness?

About a week after Fumiko's funeral, I was sitting at my desk rubbing my eyes when Zofie came in with a basket on her arm. I had just given Rourke permission to try waking Risten. He had a new idea he wanted to try but was a little mysterious about what it actually was. I had told him to just do it.

"You're looking especially tired today," Zofie said.

"I am, but I'll get over it. I'm sure it's nothing some rest wouldn't fix." I glanced at the basket. "Are you going somewhere?"

She nodded. "If you feel like it, I thought we could all eat together." She gazed at me hopefully.

How could I resist?

"Any place special?" I asked.

She smiled—something she hadn't been doing a lot of lately. "I think it's time for us to announce our new addition."

I looked at her skeptically.

She took my hand. "Come on. You'll understand."

I followed her as we wound our way through the castle and then down into its depths. I suddenly had an inkling of where she was going.

She pulled out a myst lantern at the entrance to the royal crypt and led me deeper inside, until we came to the end of the tunnel. The same place our latest adventure had begun so many weeks ago.

She went to her parents' sarcophagi and paused in front of them. "Hello, Mother and Father. I hope you're doing well." She then stepped to the newest sarcophagus next to them. "And you too, Fumiko, I hope you are also well. I pray my parents haven't been giving you too much trouble."

She came over and took my arm, pulling me close. She smiled up at me before turning back to the stone coffins. "Father, Mother, Fumiko... I wanted you to be the first to know that Coren and I are expecting. I am very confident that the baby will be a girl, and I've already picked out a name. Winstella Fumiko Xernow. What do you think? I hope you don't mind me naming her after you two ladies."

"I think it's a fine name."

We jerked at the unexpected voice. We heard a scraping sound, followed by shuffling coming down the darkened corridor. I quickly stepped in front of Zofie and drew my sword.

"Who's there?" I called.

The shuffling continued toward us. My eyes went wide as I recognized the person before me. Zofie gasped and ran forward, quickly pulling the person into a deep hug, which was richly returned.

Risten looked at me and smiled. I could tell it was her and not the impostor that had been possessing her. She held out her other arm, and I also moved in for a hug.

"I'm back," she croaked. Tears were in her eyes. "I can't thank you enough for saving me. I'd given up."

"What woke you?" I asked.

Risten snorted. "It was Rourke along with that blasted brat and her Avenyts. He brought them to see me." She shook her head. "That Avenyts is something else. She visited me in my head, saying it was safe to come out." She smiled. "I didn't want to at first, but then she told me it was the only way I'd get to see my niece."

Zofie gave her another hug. "I'm glad you decided to return. I've missed you." She patted her abdomen. "And your niece is going to need her aunt."

Risten nodded and looked away. "I... I'm still not well." She licked her lips. "You would not believe the things she did to me. Or the things she made me do." She shivered.

I couldn't help but wonder how Cabrina and Hope had managed it. And then it hit me. "She possessed you, didn't she? She promised she wouldn't do that again."

Risten shrugged. "I told you, she's something else. And don't worry, Rourke was standing by in case something went wrong." Risten's eyes were drawn to the newest addition to the crypt. "Can you excuse me for a moment?"

She slowly stepped over to Fumiko's sarcophagus. She put a gentle hand on it. "Thank you. You kept me from committing a sin from which I would have never recovered. I can never repay the debt I owe you."

Zofie came up behind her and also put a hand on the sarcophagus as she patted Risten's back. They shared a moment of silence.

The princess turned away and drew Risten with her. "Now, let's eat. We'll have to share because I didn't know we were having guests." And Zofie began to set out the food.

I sighed, rubbing my eyes and giving a tired smile. The kingdom now had enough provisions and possessed a new alliance with the empire. Things were finally looking up. We might even gain the trust of the neighboring kingdoms. We would definitely need their cooperation if we had any hope of driving back the Dark Avenyts.

And then there was Wynn. Why did he want the Forever Nexus Shadow? It couldn't be anything good.

I leaned against the corridor's rock wall. I was so tired. I had never been this tired in my entire life.

It was at that moment that I felt a sudden chill go through me. It was like my spine had been replaced by a block of ice, and my limbs turned into solid lead weights. Then I felt something speaking inside my head from far away. It sounded like Abe, but the words were stretched out. *Cor—en... he—lp... I... bro—ken....*

The world around me swam. I opened my mouth to call out, but then the floor did the damnedest thing.

It rose up and smacked me in the face.

CHAPTER TWENTY-NINE

The Promise

From the personal journal of Princess Zophia Olwenna Xernow, included here at the command of her majesty.

Coren won't wake up.

My beloved has been unconscious for three weeks. His face relaxed and calm, like he should just open his eyes and bounce out of bed. From the flicks of his eyes beneath their lids, he seems to be dreaming. But I have no clue as to what those dreams might be.

I called healers and myst users to examine him from both within my kingdom and the neighboring ones. None of them could tell me anything. I called the Keepers, thinking something in their ancient library might be able to help him, but they could offer me no hope. I even begged the empire to send their best, which they did, but could find nothing wrong.

But still, my beloved won't wake up. And to add to the mystery, the curse mark on his wrist has been fading. The myst user from the empire proposed that his curse had somehow been damaged when he fought to free Risten. He thought it might have affected his mind as well. It's as good a guess as any.

But I swear on my parents' tomb that I will find an answer.

I will awaken him.

My child *will* know her father.

All I need is a miracle.

Even if I have to make one myself.

The story continues in
Book 4 of the
Chronicles of Coren Hart Series

MEMORIES

OF

CURSES

Acknowledgments

As the saying goes, it takes a village to raise a child. The same can be said with books. *Assassin of Curses* would not have happened had it not been for the help of many others. Thanks go out again to Jennifer for her help with proofing and copyediting. She makes me look better than I really am. I also need to thank Daniel and Kasey for their writing advice and many corrections. And of course, I need to thank my beta readers, Callista, Kelly, Jenna, Diana, and Tanya, who gave me some important feedback.

I owe the fantastic cover art to Daniel Eaker. His creativity and patience was exceptional as we worked through all the stages of its creation.

And once again, my wife deserves major kudos for putting up with all the time I spent glued to my keyboard. She also knew exactly when I needed a good dose of homemade lasagna.

About The Author

Jessie Eaker lives in central Virginia with his wife, son, their cats, and (her) parakeets. Originally a native of North Carolina, he's lived in Virginia so long, he's lost his southern accent (much to his wife's disappointment). When not writing, he watches anime, reads, and works on his ever-growing list of things to fix around the house.

Check out jessieeaker.com for his latest works and updates.

www.ingramcontent.com/pod-product-compliance
Lightning Source LLC
Chambersburg PA
CBHW021427240626
47153CB00001B/58